CW00566843

M.R. Mackenzie was born and li
at Glasgow University and has a
Studies.

In addition to writing, he works as a Blu-ray/DVD producer and has overseen releases of films by a number of acclaimed directors, among them Dario Argento, Joe Dante, Hideo Nakata and Jacques Tourneur. Writing as Michael Mackenzie, he has contributed chapters to books on cult cinema and regularly provides video essays and liner notes for new releases of celebrated films. He used to work in a library, before leaving to spend more time with books.

In 2019, his first novel, *In the Silence*, was shortlisted for the Bloody Scotland Scottish Crime Debut of the Year and longlisted for the McIlvanney Prize. His third novel, *The Library Murders*, was featured in Crime Time's Best of the Year 2020 list.

Praise for M.R. Mackenzie

'Brings a fresh new voice to the field of Tartan Noir.'
JAMES OSWALD

'Writes with precision and passion.' CARO RAMSAY

'Splendidly written stuff.' BARRY FORSHAW, *CRIME TIME*

'An immersive slow burn of a tale, peppered with disquieting fire-crackers of revelation.' MORGAN CRY

'Mackenzie has come up with something that defies easy definition and is truly original.'
PAUL BURKE, *NB MAGAZINE*

'Up there with the best contemporary authors working today.'
DAVID B. LYONS

Also by M.R. Mackenzie

* To get this free Anna Scavolini short story
and keep up to date with all the latest news,
subscribe to the M.R. Mackenzie Mailing List
at **mrmackenzieauthor.com/mailinglist**

M.R. MACKENZIE

CRUEL SUMMER

AN **ANNA SCAVOLINI** MYSTERY

MAD**HOUSE**

Cover design by
Tim Barber / Dissect Designs

Typeset in 11pt Minion Pro

First published in 2019 by Mad House

ISBN: 978-1-9160948-0-2

Version 2.0c

www.mrmackenzieauthor.com
facebook.com/MRMackenzieAuthor
@landofwhimsy

Notes on the Second Edition

Cruel Summer is the second Anna Scavolini mystery, but its protagonist is in fact one Zoe Callahan – a curious state of affairs to be sure, but one that, if you think about it, makes a certain amount of sense.

At the end of the first novel in the series, *In the Silence*, Anna came face to face with the serial killer who had been terrorising Glasgow – revealed as none other than her best pal Zoe's brother Victor, who ten years ago participated in the gang rape of a classmate and was now murdering his co-conspirators one by one, driven by a combination of guilt and rage. When I first began thinking about a sequel, it was immediately obvious to me that, harrowing though Anna's own experiences had been, her trauma paled in significance compared to that of Zoe, who until that point had lived a relatively charmed life but was now forced to confront the fact that her brother – shot dead by police marksmen during the climax – had been both a rapist and a multiple murderer. It therefore stood to reason that there was ample fertile ground to be mined from exploring Zoe's attempts to come to terms with both who her brother had been and her own precarious sense of self.

So Anna – who still appears, but in a supporting capacity – took a back seat and Zoe assumed centre stage. Admittedly, it took me some time to change gears and make the mental shift required to see the world through her eyes rather than Anna's. Though they have their similarities – not least their persistence and determination to right the many wrongs that exist in the world – they are, by design, polar opposites with radically different personalities and attitudes. Where Anna is logical and methodical, her worldview formed by rigorous academic study, Zoe tends to have more of a gut reaction to the situations in which she finds herself. She has very fixed views on right and wrong, but little awareness or understanding of the systemic nature of what she instinctively recognises as injustices. (As the novel itself puts it in the first chapter, 'Politics didn't interest her except in the most rudimentary sense: more money for hospitals good, more money for bombing brown people bad, and so on.') She's easily led and tends to respond without pausing to think through the ramifications – the perfect recipe for making a bad situation worse despite going in with the best intentions.

As I delved into Zoe's psyche and got to grips with the person behind the gregarious party-girl persona to which I'd introduced readers in *In the Silence*, I realised that, fundamentally, I was telling a story about a character trying to figure out both her own identity and how she fit into the world. Towards the end of the previous novel, I'd revealed that the 'mystery man' Zoe kept sneaking out to spend time with was in fact a woman – socially conscious bartender Carol. It dawned on me that Zoe's upended assumptions about her own sexuality and the nature of the world she inhabited were really two sides of the same coin, and that both provided fertile ground through which to explore her multiple uncertainties and insecurities. In doing so, I almost felt as if I was writing a treatise on millennial angst, distilling the uncertainty of a generation, and the precarious nature of their existence, into a single, red-haired package.

In many respects, I found writing Zoe to be a liberating experience. Her rage at the injustices she perceives is more knee-jerk, and therefore somehow more 'pure', than Anna's more informed, measured approach. In putting myself in Zoe's shoes, I was able to explore the part of myself that never feels suitably equipped to understand the great ideological battles of our time; that feels that no 'side' is talking to me or representing my views; that wishes life was simply a matter of doing what you like as long as you're not directly harming anyone else. The reality, of course, is vastly more complex than that, as Zoe soon learns when she gets sucked into the world of up-and-coming politician Dominic Ryland and the various forces utilising him for their own ends. Therefore, while I remain of the opinion that I have more in common, personality-wise, with Anna, it's Zoe for whom I feel the most empathy. She is, I suspect, the more immediately likeable of the two, and it's not hard to feel sympathetic towards her – both on account of all the hardships she endures and her yearning for a world that is more straightforward and morally clear-cut than the one we actually inhabit.

While very much a direct sequel to *In the Silence* and a continuation of the characters and storylines established in that novel, *Cruel Summer* is nonetheless a radically different beast than its predecessor, and not just in terms of its protagonist. It's more character-driven and less rigidly defined by the conventions of its genre, and – I think – all the better for it. While *In the Silence* was a murder-mystery in the most classical sense, with a whodunit to solve and fresh murders served up at regular intervals, the precise nature of *Cruel Summer*'s central mystery is revealed more gradually, incorporating elements as disparate as political conspiracy, courtroom drama and organised crime thriller. The inciting incident may be a brutal assault, but the first and only dead body doesn't show up until three-quarters of the way in, and it relates to a subplot rather than the main investigation. It may not be advisable to undertake such a radical gear-shift when writing the second instalment in a series, but the move was an organic one, driven by the needs of the characters and where they found themselves as a result of the events of the previous novel, and I'm quite proud of the fact that I didn't take the easy route and simply serve up 'more of the same'.

With this new edition, I've taken the opportunity to make some adjustments to the text to create additional clarity and improve its overall flow. Most of these changes consist of minor tweaks to the wording without affecting the overall meaning of the passages in question. Additionally, in three instances, I've taken what was originally a single chapter and split it into two where it seemed to me that a natural break occurred.

As with *In the Silence*, I've also reinstated a small amount of material that was removed from the previous release during the final editing pass, most notably some character-centric scenes which don't necessarily advance the 'A' plot but which flesh Zoe out more as a character and provide crucial insights into both her crumbling relationship with Carol and her growing feelings towards Fin. These include a discussion between Zoe and Carol about Jasmine's profession in Chapter 1 ('Zoe'); a phone call between the pair of them in Chapter 2 ('Spanish Night') which contributes to Zoe's fateful decision to go out drinking on Friday night; a couple of additional scenes focusing to Zoe's efforts to help Jasmine in Chapter 5 ('Safe'); a more steamy conclusion to Zoe and Fin's council of war in what is now Chapter 14 ('Bukkake Surprise'; Chapter 13 in the previous version); and an extended scene in Chapter 31 ('The Deal'; formerly Chapter 28) in which Cottrell's men make Zoe go to greater lengths to prove that she isn't wearing a wire. In addition, I've restored a couple of previously deleted scenes set during the second day of Gavin Price's trial. These scenes, which provide some additional follow-through to the events of *In the Silence*, are to be found in the new Chapter 19 ('Knowwhatimean?'), created from splitting the old Chapter 17 ('And Nothing but the Truth') into two.

Finally, I've done a light pass on Zoe's dialogue, keeping the overall wording the same as before but adjusting the various elisions and inflections to be more in line with how I represent her speech in *The Shadow Men*. In the process of rereading all three books in the series, I realised I'd been somewhat erratic in how I 'transcribed' speech that didn't conform to the narrow parameters of the Scottish Standard English spoken by the likes of the resolutely middle-class Anna. It will probably never be one hundred percent consistent – but that is, to some extent, by design. SSE and Scots exist on a continuum, with those who speak both languages shifting between them on a context-dependent basis. (You might notice that Zoe 'code-switches' a fair amount based on both her emotional state and who she's speaking to.) Furthermore, because Scots lacks a standardised orthography, I had to make some decisions about spelling and punctuation. For instance, should the Scots word for 'with' be transcribed as 'wae' or as 'wi' – and if the latter, should it be presented with or without an apostrophe? Similarly, should the word for 'haven't' be 'havnae' or 'havenae' . . . or perhaps even 'huvny'? (Or some other combination of the above?) You might disagree with the choices I've made, but I've done my best to be internally consistent and to convey the quirks and idiosyncrasies of the dialogue without rendering it unintelligible to non-native speakers.

(For the record, it's 'havnae'. 'Havenae' looks weird.)

M.R. Mackenzie
July 2021

I am a world of uncertainties disguised as a girl.

Nicole Lyons

Prologue

Hogmanay 2012

The summons came, as always, via a call to Ryland's private line. The appointed hour was 8.30 p.m., the place: Lombardini's on the top floor of Princes Square shopping centre. A reservation had been made in the usual name. On his arrival, the waitress informed him that they'd been expecting him and showed him to a table for two.

Alone at the small balcony table, Ryland gazed out at his surroundings. The square had first opened to the public in the late eighties, coinciding with Glasgow's great renewal as a City of Culture – a gaudy, glitzy affair, all designer shops and glass elevators, designed to inject some cosmopolitan glamour into the lives of the commonfolk. Multiple conversations mingled with snatches of half-recognised lyrics as neighbouring restaurants pumped out competing songs. He could see why the venue had been chosen. Anyone listening in would be hard pressed to hear anything over the din. Not that he was unduly worried about being eavesdropped on tonight. His wasn't a face you tended to see splashed across the front pages of the tabloids. Being a backbench MSP for the third-largest party – or third-smallest, depending on how you wanted to look at it – did have its advantages when one wished for anonymity.

His dining companion arrived over twenty minutes late and without even the grace to muster an apology. Huffing and puffing, he collapsed into the seat opposite, summoned a passing waiter with a florid wave and ordered himself a dry martini. As the waiter departed, he folded his pudgy hands across his round little belly and gave what was presumably meant to be a smile – though, given his rather unfortunate features, it looked more like a leering grimace. He was a short, bug-eyed little man with the jowly cheeks, grossly protruding bottom lip and non-existent chin that seemed to afflict so much of the political establishment. He had a name, of course, but Ryland had privately christened him the Poison Dwarf.

'So, laddie, how does life find one this fine evening?'

'Can't complain, all in all.'

Ryland was hoping they could skip the pleasantries and get straight to business. He could think of umpteen things he'd rather be doing on Hogmanay night than spending it in the company of the Party's vice-chairman and go-to hatchet man.

'Splendid, splendid. And the good lady wife? She fine and dandy? Been having rather a rum time this last year, by all accounts.'

'Doing much better since she started seeing that chap Hugo recommended.'

'New doc an improvement on the old one, hmm? Marvellous, just marvellous.' The Poison Dwarf gave another of his unfortunate smiles, then turned to his menu. 'What looks good?'

They continued in this vein for another quarter-hour – the bland, hollow enquiries as to the wellbeing of significant others, the trading of war stories about their respective Christmases. It wasn't until starters and main courses had been ordered, and they'd nearly finished the first round of drinks, that the Dwarf finally deigned to move beyond the banalities.

'You'll have heard the rumblings about the Farmer,' he said, nonchalantly picking a fleck of dandruff off the collar of his pin-striped three-piece.

The Farmer. Archibald Adam Croft, sixty-four-year-old leader of the Conservative Party in Scotland, so nicknamed not because he *was* one but because he represented the fiercely rural constituency of Selkirkshire North, coupled with his fondness for being photographed in rolling fields, decked out with flat cap, jodhpurs and hiking staff. The surname didn't hurt either.

'I've heard rumours,' said Ryland cautiously.

'Oh, they aren't just rumours, dear boy. It's all but official now. In the coming months, the dedicated but charisma-deprived leader of our little group in Holyrood will announce his retirement from the front line, ostensibly on health grounds. Not keeping too well these days, they say. Dicky ticker.'

'That's regrettable.'

'Not for us it's not.' The Dwarf tapped the side of his nose. 'Events, dear boy, events. Not to put too fine a point on it, but the Elders have been – shall we say ambivalent? – about the man's performance for some time now. The phrase "shoogly peg" springs increasingly to mind. Oh, they were content enough to put up with him for a spell – let him settle in, give him a couple of elections to find his feet. Right sort of chap, y'see.

'Anyway' – he paused, glancing left and right, as if concerned that the nearby creeping ivy might have sprouted ears – 'of late, the Elders have begun asking questions. The Party successfully turned around its fortunes down south a few years back, which begs the question: why is its northern chapter still firmly perched on the remedial step, placing third or even fourth in election after election? Well?'

Ryland said nothing. He suspected an answer would be forthcoming irrespective of his input.

'Image.' The Dwarf stabbed the table surface with a stout index finger. 'The prevailing wind is that a new approach is needed. Out with the tweedy landowners and in with . . . well, the sort of people that actually win elections. Some charismatic young go-getter who can inspire folk's imaginations and persuade the average voter that we're not just the party for octogenarians and the landed gentry. And if he can do a respectable job of not looking repulsed whenever someone thrusts a photogenic infant into his arms, so much the better.'

He was referring to a notorious incident during the last election campaign when an enterprising strategist had arranged for a local Party member to hand her newborn to Croft, anticipating a photo op of the sort that won votes from young mothers. Far from taking the stunt in his stride, Croft had immediately become stricken with horror, the expression on his face suggesting he would have been more at ease if someone had handed him a bundle of steaming manure. Not to be outdone, the baby had promptly begun to howl, and both child and party leader had had to be separated from one another before things got any worse. The Conservatives had gone on to lose the local seat, which they'd previously held since the Parliament's opening in 1999.

Ryland allowed himself a thin smile. 'What you're saying makes a measure of sense, but the difficulty surely lies in finding someone who fits the bill. Not to put too fine a point on it, but pickings aren't exactly rich among the current crop.'

'Oh, I can think of one or two names.'

'Such as . . . ?'

The Dwarf cocked his head slightly to one side and extended his oily smile.

Realisation dawned on Ryland. 'You cannot be serious.'

The Dwarf spread his arms. 'And why not? You can't deny you tick all the requisite boxes. Don't tell me you think you're not up to it.'

'It's not that. It's just . . . ' He paused to collect his thoughts, then took a measured breath and went on, 'Well, for starters, I'm a list MSP, and a backbencher at that.'

'Why, my dear fellow, so much the better. I doubt there's a single figure on the frontbench not mired in corruption and sleaze. You'll be a fresh face – no existing baggage attached. I'm telling you, laddie, it's all grist to the mill.'

'Aren't we getting ahead of ourselves here? Who out of the current mob would back me? I'd need—'

'One hundred nominations, yes.' The Dwarf was growing impatient. 'Hardly an insurmountable challenge. And the support of at least a handful of elected representatives, past or present. Again, that can be arranged.'

Another furtive glance in both directions of traffic, and another drop in volume, so that Ryland now found himself having to lean forward to make him out.

'Our mutual friend,' he said, 'very much wants to see this happen. He intends to make it abundantly clear to the relevant people that your successful application is to be little more than a box-ticking exercise, and that your bid will have the full weight of the Party machine behind it.'

The latest mouthful of G&T turned to oil in Ryland's mouth. *Our mutual friend.* Should have guessed *he* was behind this.

'It's the bright young things who'll secure our future, you know.' The Dwarf was in full flow now, savouring the sound of his own voice. 'Even the most dyed-in-the-wool of the old guard are coming round to accepting that. The face of the new, trendy, modern conservatism: more relatable, more in touch with the hoi polloi. Public school but not *too* public school. The Jockos will never elect an Old Etonian, that much we know. But a poor boy made good who's retained just enough of the local patois to pass muster as one of their own? Therein lie the seeds of our eventual rebirth, dear boy.'

Seeing that his previous efforts had fallen entirely on deaf ears, Ryland played his last card. 'Truth be told, Alice has been hankering for a move back down south for some time. Climate up here's never agreed with her, you see. Too much damp. Bad for her allergies. And just between us, last time we rubbed shoulders, the PM was making favourable noises about a seat down there becoming available in the not too distant future. And, well, that's a gift horse one can't exactly afford to look in the mouth.'

The Dwarf's smile faded, all trace of bonhomie leaving his features. 'Let's be toe-curlingly honest for a moment, dear boy. This isn't up for negotiation. Our mutual friend has made his feelings quite clear. Always remember, the Lord giveth, and the Lord taketh away.'

Ryland didn't reply. His mouth tasted like ash, and his glass had chosen this most inopportune of moments to be bone-dry. The hubbub of conversation around him continued unabated. On the speaker system in a nearby café, Mariah Carey was butchering *Auld Lang Syne*. Like oil and water, some things just weren't meant to go together.

The Dwarf continued to fix Ryland with his icy stare. '*He* put you where you are today, and *he* can and will see to it that everything you've acquired – the wealth, the status, that asinine column you write for the *Spectator* – goes up in smoke the moment you're no longer useful.' He paused to take a sip from his own, irritatingly full, glass. 'As for holding out in the hope that there's a better offer waiting in the wings – some safe seat in the Shires where the local bumpkins will elect a donkey provided it's wearing a blue rosette – forget it. The grandees of the Home Counties would never have it. Public school but not *too* public school, remember? And the accent you've gone to such pains to mask?' He tutted. 'No one's buying it. But put in the man-hours, do as you're "telt", and we might just let you manage our wee Scotch region more or less as you see fit.' He inclined his head to one side, smiling the smile of a man who knows he holds all the cards.

Not for the first time, Ryland reflected that those whom fate had deigned to make his political bedfellows were a truly remarkable bunch: the only people he'd ever met who were capable of both sneering and cringing at the same time. People who knew they were a breed apart, but who also knew their place in the hierarchy and relished their status in life's natural pecking order.

'You shit,' he said. 'You absolute shit.'

'The Elders expect Croft to announce his intention to stand down by March. April at the latest. And by *expect*, I naturally mean *insist*. That means a spring campaign, making the most of the brighter days and longer nights, followed by the election in July or August. Gives us ample time to build your profile: get you in the right papers, shake hands with the right community leaders. You know how the charade goes.'

'I do indeed,' said Ryland, his tone devoid of any emotion.

The Dwarf smiled. 'So pleased we understand one another. We'll meet again early in the New Year. Discuss strategies, personnel, begin sowing the seeds of our future triumph, all that rot. Breathe not a word to anyone in the meantime. Not even your better half.' He drained his glass. 'I, ah, shan't stay for dinner after all. A pleasant New Year when it comes. Give my regards to the good lady wife.'

He got up, threw on his coat with a flourish and strode out, giving Ryland a brisk pat on the shoulder as he passed.

Ryland was so deep in thought when the waiter brought his food that he barely noticed. He had much to ponder. They had him over a barrel; trussed up like the proverbial Christmas turkey. He was used to being treated like a piece on a board; to the feeling that others besides himself were in control of his life's trajectory. And yet, even as he sat there, silently cursing the Poison Dwarf and the

Elders and their mutual friend and the ground they all walked on, the words of a former leader of the party to which, for better or worse, his fate was intertwined, came to mind:

A pessimist sees the difficulty in every opportunity; an optimist sees the opportunity in every difficulty.

Stirring words, no doubt, but he'd always considered them just that: words on a page, to be trotted out as the climax to a rousing speech or as part of some generic appeal to the virtues of entrepreneurialism and self-sufficiency, in a *pull up your socks and stop moaning about your lot in life* sort of way. Now, though, he wondered if perhaps he should be taking them to heart himself. Though the situation he found himself in was neither of his making nor his choosing, it also presented him with an opportunity few men even dreamed of – provided he had the mettle to grab the bull by the horns.

Carpe diem and all that.

PART ONE

1

Zoe

Get a degree. Get a job. Get ahead.

It sounded so simple in theory, it was almost a surprise it hadn't worked out in practice.

Name? Zoe Joan Callahan. Age? Thirty-one years, six months and seven days. Place of birth, current residence and quite probably death as well? Glasgow. Occupation? Housekeeping operative at Neptune House overlooking the M8 motorway. At least that's what it had said on the application form. In reality, it amounted to twenty-one and a half hours a week hoovering floors and scrubbing toilets with nary a word of gratitude from the men in suits who occupied each of the building's five floors.

Ambition in life?

Er . . .

It could be worse, or so she told herself. At least she *had* a job – something not everyone in her circle could claim, particularly given the current economic climate. She also had a roof over her head. A somewhat undersized roof suffering from an acute onset of mildew – but again, it was more than some people had. And she was IN A RELATIONSHIP – one which, against all the odds, had

11

lasted the course and was still, if not exactly the hotbed of passion it had once been, a reassuring constant in her life for which it seemed churlish not to be grateful.

Still, it was hard not to look at her life and wonder what she had actually accomplished in the last thirty-one years, six months and seven days. 'What do you want to be when you grow up?' was a question she'd been asked by a succession of teachers and guidance counsellors during her six years of high school. She'd never had an answer back then but had always assumed one would come to her when it actually mattered. 'Never mind,' they'd said when she looked at them blankly. 'You don't have to make up your mind for a long time yet.' Now, having inhabited this earth for three decades and counting, she couldn't help but feel she should have figured it out by now.

Get a degree?

Check – a 2:1 in Media Studies from Glasgow Caledonian, class of 2002.

Get a job?

In a manner of speaking.

Get ahead?

Get tae fuck.

It had just gone quarter past four when she stepped out into the street, the interview over, her name no doubt struck off the list of prospective hires the moment her back was turned. By her reckoning, she'd been in there just over seven minutes. As such, she didn't hold out much hope for a call-back. Mind you, it would probably have helped her case considerably if she'd been able to remember, while she was sitting in the hot seat, just which particular job she was actually interviewing for. In the last few weeks, she'd been responding to postings willy-nilly, with the result that they all blended together in her mind like so much gravy.

By the time she'd completed the brief walk up the road to Central Station, she was already sweating into her Sunday best and cursing her ill fortune to have been born with the red-haired, pale-skinned complexion of an undiluted Celt and an aversion to the sun that bordered on pathological hatred. The forecasters had been warning of a heatwave to hit in the next couple of weeks that was to last till at least the middle of July, but it was already plenty hot by her reckoning and she wasn't sure she could survive another month of it. It was bad enough being forced to endure her own private torment. What made it far worse were the constant exaltations about how wonderful it was by all and sundry, even as they fanned themselves with newspapers or dabbed their moist necks with tissues. She was convinced that, deep down, most people hated the hot weather almost as much as she did and just pretended to like it because of social conditioning. She'd long ago concluded that it was easiest just to respond to the endless variations on 'Gorgeous weather, in't it?' with a smile and a bland 'Aye, in't it just', even as she silently wished them a slow, painful death. Or at least a moderate-to-severe case of sunburn.

As the train wound its way west, she rested her head on the window, headphones on, Amy Macdonald in her ears, and gazed out at the view of the riverside passing by before her. Past the Squinty Bridge, the Hydro and the Armadillo, towards the newly gentrified harbour area where the old granary building used to be. Rotting cranes on one side of the river, luxury flats on the other: it said something about the disparity in opportunities faced by the city and its residents. The cranes were no longer in use, of course, but they were kept around as a bit of eye-candy to be enjoyed ironically by the yuppies who'd moved in on what was once the beating heart of industrial Glasgow.

The train came to its juddering halt at Partick Station and she joined the exodus of passengers heading into the terminus, then down the stairs and out into the open air. The pavement was packed, the pedestrians kitted out in an array of summer dresses, shorts and tank tops, along with the odd bewildered-looking figure in a duffle coat or fleece, either caught unprepared for the uncharacteristically warm weather or steadfastly refusing to believe it wasn't just a mirage.

The flat that had been Zoe's home for the last three and a half years, give or take, was on the first floor of an old four-storey tenement a stone's throw from the station, bang in the middle of the studenty part of Partick and flanked on either side by salons, betting shops and takeaways. On the ground floor directly below the flat, A Taste of India was gearing up for another night on the trot. Heat belched from the open door, accompanied by the charcoal smell from the tandoori oven. It seemed perverse that anyone could have a hankering for spicy food in weather like this, but the sunshine appeared to have done nothing to dent their trade. Zoe wondered what was lined up for her dinner. Rabbit-food as usual, most likely.

A gust of hot air greeted her as she let herself into the flat. It was even warmer inside than out, thanks to the heat from the oven rising up through the floorboards. In winter it was a godsend when it came to the leccy bill, but the summer months were always unbearable.

'Zo? That you?'

The voice came from the living room, rising above the chatter of the TV. Zoe winced and considered making a run for the bathroom and locking herself in. Her indecision proved fatal, and before she had time to even rehearse the lies she was going to tell, Carol was coming towards her and Zoe was dutifully proffering her cheek for the customary peck.

'So? How was it?' Sounding for all the world like Zoe had just returned from a trip to Saturn rather than a crappy interview for a crappy job in a crappy office.

'Eh, hard tae say, really. Ye know what they things are like.'

She tugged her pants out of her bum-crack and eyed the bathroom door at the other end of the flat longingly. Carol's presence had created a traffic jam: the corridor was narrow even before you took into account Carol's bike, propped against the wall, and the various cardboard boxes and items of furniture piled high on the right-hand side – hangovers from Zoe's old family home that she'd refused to part with when she moved in.

'You answered all their questions? Made sure you covered all the competencies?'

'Aye.' Zoe found her eyes straying to the condensation stains on the ceiling behind Carol's head.

'Well then, you gave it your all. No one can ask for more than that. Now it's down to them.'

'They said they'd loads of interest in the job, so it's a bit of a long shot, really.'

Carol tutted. 'You always do that.'

'What?'

'Sell yourself short.' She reached out and touched Zoe's chin, lifting her head slightly. 'There's enough people in this world that are more than willing to put you down without you doing it yourself.'

Zoe forced a smile and thought what a duplicitous scumbag she was, standing here accepting Carol's praise as if she'd put her heart and soul into it.

Carol smiled. 'Come here, you.'

As she leaned in to kiss Zoe, the walls began to rattle as a train sailed by on the down line – a constant annoyance that all but cancelled out the convenience of living so close to the station.

Zoe took the opportunity afforded by this interruption to make good her escape.

'Just gonnae freshen up. I'm pure boggin.'

She pulled away from Carol and squeezed past her, heading for the bathroom.

When she emerged some twenty minutes later, Zoe could hear Carol bustling to and fro in the kitchen, while a droning voice she recognised as that of the presenter of the five o'clock local news emanated from the living room. She wandered through and flopped on the sofa facing the TV, disinterested eyes drinking in the sight of the sharp-boned woman seated in front of her giant window overlooking the Clyde, reciting the day's events in her usual blandly measured diction.

' . . . we afforded the Council the opportunity to tell their side of the story, but no one was available for comment.' She paused momentarily before launching into a fresh item. 'The race to become the next leader of the Conservative Party in Scotland continued apace today, with all three candidates attending a hustings in Glasgow. The event, held behind closed doors for party members, was one of several being held up and down the country ahead of the new leader being crowned in August.'

Zoe was zoning out already. Politics didn't interest her except in the most rudimentary sense: more money for hospitals good, more money for bombing brown people bad, and so on. She'd been vaguely aware that a leadership election of some sort was taking place but had paid no heed to the personalities involved. Coming of age in Scotland following the great rout of 1997, during which every single Conservative MP had lost their seat, the Tories were little more than a distant southern bogeyman, the punchline to any number of off-colour jokes – *yeah, he's a twat, but at least he's not a Tory twat.* She knew, as a born-and-bred Glaswegian – living in the heart of Red Clydeside, no less – that she was supposed to hate them, even though at times she was at a loss to remember why.

'Tomorrow we'll be hearing from Fergus Leach, who served as

the outgoing leader's depute and *had* been tipped by the pollsters as favourite to win. But today we hit the campaign trail with the backbencher who, in the past few weeks, has emerged to challenge the established narrative. So who *is* Dominic Ryland? Our political correspondent, Siobhan McCaffrey, spent the afternoon with him.'

The camera cut to an outdoor scene: a well-tended children's play-park somewhere in the West End, where a tall, sandy-haired man in his early forties, a gratuitously large blue rosette pinned to his lapel, was down on his hunkers in a sandpit, an amiable grin plastered across his features as he attempted to converse with a gaggle of toddlers who clearly couldn't care less about the oversized intruder. As the footage continued to play, a woman's voice began to intone in perky, overly accentuated tones.

'It may look like fun and games, but running for leadership is serious business, and no election this year is likely to be more hotly contested than this one. Dominic Ryland – born to humble beginnings in a Bridgeton tenement, now being called the charismatic new face of modern Scottish Conservatism.'

'Oh, great. Him.'

Zoe turned to find Carol standing in the doorway, arms folded. She neither looked nor sounded best pleased.

'How? Who is he?'

'Just this guy they're bigging up as the great white hope of the Tory party. Cos he . . . I dunno, cos he's under retirement age and does a passable imitation of not being a lizard or something.'

Zoe turned back to the screen. Ryland was schmoozing some yummy mummies, giving big, exaggerated hand gestures, making them all laugh. 'And if these Hillhead mums are anything to go by,' McCaffrey's voiceover continued, 'he certainly seems to have the common touch.'

The report cut to a fresh scene. Ryland was facing the camera, a microphone directed towards him by the off-screen McCaffrey.

'Dominic Ryland, you say you're standing on a platform of renewal and engagement, pledging to transform both the party's image and its approach to winning elections. What's wrong with the current model?'

'Well, Siobhan,' Ryland purred, 'quite simply, it hasn't been working. We've come back fighting down south, and yet up here we remain stuck in the doldrums. I don't believe there are fundamental differences between voters north and south of the border, and yet we're faced with a vast discrepancy in terms of electoral results. What I'm saying is that, until the party in Scotland is able to take a long, hard look at itself and make an honest assessment of what it's been getting wrong, it can't hope for a revival in fortunes.'

There was something oddly pleasant about his voice. He had one of those strange, unplaceable accents – kinda Scottish but kinda not really, like the ones you heard coming out of the mouths of journalists and pundits who'd spent too long living in London. They always sounded vaguely patronising to Zoe, but at the same time they spoke with such authority that you had to assume they knew what they were about.

'You were only elected in 2011,' said McCaffrey, 'and during your time as an MSP, you've never held a frontbench role. What makes you the person to spearhead that revival?'

Ryland gave a little self-deprecating laugh. 'I think you effectively answered yourself there, Siobhan. If you look at every Scottish Parliament election since 1999, it's the same crusty old faces appearing again and again. And no harm to them as individuals – some of them are personal friends. But as a great man once said, *The definition of insanity is doing the same thing over and over expecting different results.* It's time for fresh faces and fresh thinking.'

Carol snorted. 'Christ, he's like a wind-up toy. Lob him a softball question, stand back and watch him go.'

'Wheesht!' said Zoe, eyes not leaving the television. 'I wanna hear this.' In spite of her long-standing antipathy towards politicians of every hue, she found herself unaccountably enamoured by this man and his melodic voice.

Ryland was facing the camera now, McCaffrey all but forgotten as he addressed the viewers directly. 'And frankly, I think the electorate are just waiting to be given a reason to take a punt on something different. Folk are sick and tired of being let down by the other parties, whether it's the economic incompetence of the official opposition or the endless constitutional grievance-mongering of the current regime. They want political representatives who're willing to address the bread and butter issues – the issues that real, everyday people care about. Those are the values I stand for.'

'What values?' exclaimed Carol, gesticulating at the TV with her entire arm. 'Tell us what they are. Name a policy. Go on, name just one.'

'Look,' Ryland went on, 'let's not be coy. The general consensus is that our party is somewhat . . . distant. Out of touch with the concerns of the ordinary punter. But I'm not like that – far from it. I grew up not a million miles from here, in Bridgeton.' He even pronounced it 'Brigton', like a veritable local. 'My mother, a *formidable* woman, raised me single-handed in a council flat with no central heating, sharing a toilet with five other families. I know what it's like to grow up with nothing, to put in the hard work, to raise myself out of poverty, and I know the sort of problems ordinary, hard-working families are facing. They want someone who's willing to take responsibility – someone willing to step up to the plate and say, *This isn't good enough. Something needs to be done.*'

'Oh, come on!' Carol shouted. 'Jesus Christ, challenge him! Debate him! Do your bloody job, woman!'

Zoe stared at her, incredulous. 'Who shat in *your* ice cream sundae?'

'This guy.' Carol waved at the TV. 'He's a fucking hypocrite is what he is. Dines out on his roots and his single mum but he represents a party that's cutting unemployment benefit and child maintenance support to the bone. All these contradictions and no one ever calls him on 'em. What's the point of having a so-called free press if they're not actually going to hold the likes of him to account?'

Zoe had no answer to that. She didn't really understand the ins and outs of what Carol was saying, or whether it was even accurate. She turned back to face the TV screen, where McCaffrey was now bringing things to a close.

'Before we let you go, what's your pitch to the party members who'll be voting in this contest – particularly those who might have reservations about supporting an unknown?'

Ryland paused to think. When he spoke, he once again addressed the camera rather than McCaffrey. 'Look, I know how it goes. Many of you will be looking at me right now, thinking, *Who does this jumped-up upstart think he is, coming in and telling us we've been doing everything wrong for the last fifteen years?* And I get it. If I were in your shoes, I'd be wary of me too. No one likes change, especially when you've been doing things the same way for so long. But you know what? Sometimes it takes an outsider to say, *Wait a minute – maybe we need to take a step back and fundamentally reassess our way of doing things. And if we're not willing to change, to make the difficult decisions, maybe we need to think about turning to someone who* will.'

He paused and gave a conciliatory 'I'm a reasonable guy' sort of smile. 'I'm not asking you to recant your long-held political beliefs. I have the greatest respect for the Party, its values, and yes, its members. All I'm asking is for you to take a chance on a fresh face. The worst that could happen is that, three years from now, we find ourselves no better off than we are already. But if you elect me as your leader, I truly do believe we can turn things around, transforming ourselves from a party of perpetual opposition into a government-in-waiting.'

'Dominic Ryland, thank you very much.'

The screen went blank with a soft *foom* as Carol snatched up the remote and switched it off.

'And that was a party political broadcast on behalf of the Scottish Conservative and Unionist Party,' she deadpanned.

'I never heard of him before,' said Zoe. She felt slightly sheepish for admitting it and wondered if he'd been the talk of the tavern for ages now and she just hadn't noticed.

Carol turned to look at her. 'And what did you make of him?'

'He seems . . . ' She shrugged helplessly. 'I dunno. Kinda reasonable. He talks a good talk, anyway.'

Carol sighed sadly. 'Got it in one. He's got the gift of the gab. His gums flap but he says nothing. But that doesn't matter cos he's able to charm people with his smile and his smooth words, and no one stops to point out that actually, no, he's just a vacuous waste of oxygen who'd sell his own granny down the river in return for a sniff of power.'

Zoe shrugged. 'Pretty much like every politician, then.'

It was the wrong thing to say.

'That's just it, though – he isn't. He's not some toffee-nosed land baron who couldn't relate to the public if his life depended on it. He's a different breed altogether. He's plausible. Likeable, even. And these days, that's enough. Folks' imaginations don't get fired up by integrity or well-reasoned policies. They just go with their gut. *Oh, I like him. He seems like the kinda person I could have a beer with.* But we're not talking about some bloke you're gonna shoot the breeze with on a Friday night down at the pub. It's about the future of this country. And what worries me is that there's a very real chance of him winning this contest and that shower of reprobates riding into power on his coat-tails.'

She was getting herself so lathered up about it that Zoe desperately wanted to laugh, if only to defuse the tension in the air. But she knew that was positively the worst thing she could do under the circumstances. So instead she turned to Carol, tilting her head and smiling affectionately.

'Aw, lookit you, my fiery Amazon queen. Anyone ever tell you ye look dead sexy when you're about to have a coronary?'

And there it was: the familiar sag of the shoulders, the lowering of the head, the rueful half-smile, all of which indicated that the flare-up was at an end. 'Don't. I know you're making fun of me.' But she couldn't hide the inklings of a smile. 'I was agitpropping again, wasn't I?'

'Like a champ.'

'Sorry.'

She gave Zoe's shoulder a brief squeeze. It was a small gesture, but, in its own way, more loaded with unspoken meaning than a million I-love-yous.

Zoe gazed up at her, wrinkling her nose. 'Ach, it'll never happen. What right-thinking Scot's gonnae vote them lot into power?'

For a moment, Carol stood there in silent, sober contemplation. 'It's not the right-thinking ones I'm worried about,' she said eventually.

Zoe sat by the open window, forlornly searching for a non-existent breeze while, next door, Carol got ready for work. The street below was a hive of activity, the late afternoon sun's rays glistening on the roofs of the slow-moving cars and buses. At one point, Partick had been a burgh in its own right, but in 1912 had been annexed by the city of Glasgow, a move that some with particularly long memories still believed amounted to a hostile takeover. The true fundamentalists would have it that the area's boundaries were Partick Cross in the east and Crow Road in the west. For most, however, the question of where Partick ended and where the rest of the world began was a lot more nebulous. Dumbarton Road was its main thoroughfare, beginning at the western edge of Kelvingrove Park and snaking its way along the course of the River Clyde, in so doing incorporating everything from the cosmopolitan West End to the less prosperous locales further west, and everything in between. It was rarely quiet and never boring. No matter the time of day, there always seemed to be people coming and going. And, as Zoe watched, the stairwell door on the other side of the road – the one sandwiched between Cash Converters and the alluringly-named VapeStation – opened and a woman stepped out.

She was the sort of woman who couldn't fail to attract attention – and, judging by her getup, that was very much her intention. Tall, leggy, with long silky hair and a sequin dress which showed off just enough of her upper legs to hint at the gap between her thighs, she looked about as out of place on Dumbarton Road as a condom wrapper on the steps of the Vatican. She paused to look both ways, then turned and began making her way up the pavement, heading east towards the bright lights of the city centre.

'There she goes again,' Zoe said as Carol entered the room behind her. 'Every night at five-thirty, just like clockwork.'

Carol joined Zoe at the window, following her gaze. She'd changed into her work gear: dark jeans, black T-shirt with the 'Pulse' logo emblazoned on the breast pocket.

'S'all right for some – out partying in her glad rags every night, then slinking home in the wee hours to spend the rest of the day in bed.'

Carol arched an eyebrow. 'I'm not sure she'd describe what she gets up to as "partying". Though I suppose that's what it is . . . in a manner of speaking.'

'How? What does she do?'

'She's a good-time girl. A lady of negotiable affections.'

'Eh?'

Carol smiled thinly. 'She's a hooker.'

'No!' Zoe turned to stare after the departing woman, then back at Carol. At the sight of her face, Carol burst out laughing.

'I never . . . ' Zoe began, feeling her cheeks beginning to colour – though whether in response to the nature of the revelation or Carol's amusement, or both, she couldn't quite be sure. 'I mean, ye wouldnae think. No to look at her, anyway.' She shot Carol a suspicious glance. 'She's not *really* . . . is she?'

'Oh, she is.' Carol's lip curled in such a way that Zoe couldn't be sure whether it signified disapproval or mirth. 'You honestly had no idea?'

'Not a scooby.'

She wondered briefly whether, like the guy on the TV who was running for election, this was a piece of common knowledge she was somehow deficient for not being aware of. But then, Carol always had a far better idea of what was going on in the neighbourhood than she did. She noticed things Zoe didn't. Put two and two together. Talked to the neighbours and got wind of things almost before they happened. If she said it was so, it probably was.

Still, she couldn't quite believe it.

'Pure mad, in't it? I mean, ye don't exactly expect to find out ye've got someone like *that* for a neighbour.'

'Well, where are they supposed to live? In a reservation for fallen women?'

Zoe lowered her eyes, sensing that she'd said something objectionable. With Carol, it was so easy to say the wrong thing in jest. There were so many times when Zoe would find she'd inadvertently crossed a line by saying something that was regarded as culturally insensitive or insufficiently politically correct. She got the feeling this was one of them.

Carol stirred. 'I'd better head. Just so you know, I'll probably be late back. We've got this shit-hot local band playing live tonight and it's anyone's guess when I'll get off.' She gave Zoe a brisk peck on the cheek, then straightened up, brushing a strand of dirty blonde hair out of her eyes. 'I left something in the fridge for when you get hungry. Oh, and if you can mind and do the dishes, that'd be awesomesauce.'

This was the reality of their relationship these days – these brief moments of crossover in-between one of them coming home from their work and the other heading out to theirs. It had only gotten worse since Carol had got the assistant manager's job. She was forever staying late to cash up, or going in early to do the accounts, or some variation along those lines. It was a long time since their shifts had aligned sufficiently to actually do anything together – even something as rudimentary as sitting down to a shared meal. Parallel lives and all that.

Zoe remained by the window, watching as Carol emerged into the sunlight, wheeling her bike, then hopped on and pushed off up the pavement. She made it look so effortless, a lithe figure sailing past the dawdling pedestrians. As her gaze followed Carol up the road, Zoe inadvertently allowed her eyes to stray towards the university bell-tower, rising up in the distance beyond the rooftops and shimmering slightly in the late afternoon smog, as if it wasn't entirely corporeal. It was hardly the first time she'd done that – indeed, living within a mile of the place, it was difficult to avoid catching sight of it – but she nonetheless averted her eyes immediately, suppressing an involuntary shudder at the memories bubbling up inside her.

To take her mind off them, she headed through to the kitchen to see what was in the fridge for her. The answer, it turned out, was an orzo salad topped with spinach and feta, the prospect of eating it holding only marginally more appeal than wet cardboard. Nevertheless, she took her boring salad through to the living room and sat on the sofa watching a boring programme about a boring sub-urban couple who were trying to sell their boring flat and relocate to the boring countryside. Then she dutifully washed her dishes at the sink and left them drying on the drainer. She tried texting a few of her pals, but none of them were in the mood for a meet-up. Couldn't, they said. Work night. Going to a residents' association meeting. Taking care of the weans. She wondered when it was that they'd all grown up and become so dreary and sensible, and why it hadn't happened to her yet.

The sun sank lower in the sky, painting the sandstone buildings outside blood-orange. The roaring traffic grew quieter, giving way to the lively chatter of the passers-by – folk from all walks of life, with their own stories, their own hopes and aspirations. The evening wore on, punctuated at regular intervals by the familiar tremor in the walls and floorboards as another train passed through Partick. Eventually, darkness fell, and she gave up the ghost and went through to bed, where she spent a good hour tossing and turning in a tangle of sticky linen before throwing off the covers and lying spread-eagled atop the rumpled sheets. When that too failed to bring sleep, she got up and sloped through to the living room, where she sprawled on the sofa, half-watching the late-night snooker through half-closed eyes with the volume low.

The sun was low on the horizon when she heard feet pattering on the pavement outside. She made her way over to the window and peeked between the curtains. It was the woman Carol had outed as a prostitute, looking a little more dishevelled than before but other-wise none the worse for what had presumably been a successful night's business. She walked barefoot on the cooling pavement, stilettos tucked under her arm. Zoe watched as she let herself into her building, the door closing behind her with a soft click. Then, silence. The street was still and deserted once again. Every man and his dog had gone home to their bed.

Taking this as a sign that she should do the same, she killed the TV and dragged herself back through to the bedroom. She was on the verge of finally drifting off when she heard the familiar sound of the key turning in the lock. She was dimly aware of Carol padding about the bathroom, getting ready for bed, then of her coming in, getting undressed and sinking down next to her.

'Hey,' she said softly.

'Hey,' Zoe murmured.

She was about to ask how the gig had gone when the alarm clock on the nightstand began to rattle and wail – its incessant tone, which she hadn't the energy to silence, informing her that it was 5.30 a.m.

Time to get up and go to work.

2

Spanish Night

In the days that followed, things continued in much the same vein as they had for as long as Zoe could remember: working her weird and thoroughly antisocial shifts at Neptune House, whiling away the mid-morning to early afternoon downtime on her split shift days wandering around the shops on nearby Sauchiehall Street, ogling the clothes and DVDs and other things she couldn't afford. Her working pattern hardly seemed like the most efficient use of anyone's time, let alone hers, but presumably someone with a really big spreadsheet had calculated that it allowed the firm to save X amount on its national insurance contributions or whatever.

The call came at just after two o'clock on Friday afternoon while she was vacuuming the top-floor conference room. They weren't supposed to have their phones on them while they were on duty, but Zoe had seen the super using hers on the sly and had taken that as a green light to do likewise. She fished the humming device out of her pocket, frowning at the unfamiliar number on the screen.

'Hello?'

'Zoe Callahan?'

A man's voice. One she didn't recognise.

'Aye – who's this?'

'Zoe, it's Peter Martin from Azura Solutions. We met earlier this week. The interview for the clerical assistant's post?'

'Oh . . . oh *yeah*.' She tried to sound upbeat and relaxed, but it came out sounding as if she was over the moon to hear from a long-lost pal. 'How ya doin'?'

'I'm doing good, Zoe, yeah.' A pause. 'Listen, is this a good time to talk?'

'Ach, you know me, Pete. Just hingin aboot waiting for ya to call.'

'Heh heh, yeah, great stuff, great stuff. So Zoe, first of all, I'd just like to thank you for your interest in the post and for coming to see us on Monday.' He sounded nervous, and the fact that he kept repeating her name only made him seem doubly so. 'As you know, we received a high volume of applications, and the pool of candidates was unusually strong . . .'

If she'd been labouring under the forlorn hope that she might somehow, against all the odds, have landed the job, those words laid that notion to rest once and for all. Folk didn't tend to throw around a bunch of caveats about numbers of applicants and over-flowing talent pools if they were gearing up to tell you, *Congratulations, see you at 9 a.m. sharp.* They did it when they were trying to let you down gently.

And now she was no longer listening. She still heard his voice; heard its conciliatory tone, distantly registered the various stock phrases being trotted out. *Difficult decision. No reflection on you. Elected to go with a candidate more suited to the role.* But she'd stopped actively processing his words in any meaningful sense. There seemed little point. He wasn't telling her anything worthwhile. She knew she'd been shit. He knew she'd been shit. Why pretend otherwise? Might as well just rip the band-aid off and get it over with. She muttered a quick, insincere thank-you and hung up.

Truth was, she felt nothing. There was nothing special about today's call. It was only the latest in a long line of rejections, and she was way past the point of taking it personally or letting her hopes be dashed. They'd been obliterated long ago.

She rang Carol, more out of duty than because she had any desire to talk to her.

'Hey. It's me.'

'Zoe? You still at work?'

'Aye.' Beat. 'I didnae get it.'

'Sorry?'

'The job. They gave it to someone else.'

'Oh.'

She pictured Carol standing in the middle of the flat, phone to her ear, free hand on her hip, brow furrowed as she racked her brains, trying to work out which job they were talking about. Might as well have saved herself the effort.

'Oh, baby,' she said eventually, 'I'm sorry.'

'Aye, well.'

'What did they say?'

'You know. The usual. "Thanks but no thanks".'

'No, what I mean is, did they give you any feedback? Some pointers for doing better next time?'

'Didnae ask.'

A pause. She could practically smell Carol's disapproval coming down the phone line.

'Well, there'll be other opportunities.'

'That right?'

'Course there will.'

'Aye, and more rejections.'

'Zoe.'

She sighed. 'What?'

A moment's hesitation. When Carol spoke again, it was in her *I'm not angry with you, just disappointed* voice. 'You know, maybe firing off applications all over the place, shopping yourself to anyone who'll give you the time of day . . . maybe that isn't the best strategy. Maybe . . . ' A strained sigh. 'Maybe, if you identify what it is you actually want to do in life and focus on pursuing that, maybe you might start to have a bit more success.'

'Aye well,' Zoe muttered, 'it was you who pushed me to find another job in the first place.'

'Only cos you're always going on about how much you can't stand your current one!'

'Guess in future I'll keep ma mooth shut, then.'

Another long, disapproving pause, then: 'We'll talk more about this when you get home.'

'Cannae fucking wait,' said Zoe, and hung up.

She parked herself on the table and let out a sigh of utter despair. She was the one with the university degree. The one who kept going on about how shit it was having no money all the time. She wished she could take it all back – wished that, instead of getting arsey, she'd nodded and uh-huh'd at Carol's entreaties to better herself and said, *Yes, darling, in future I'll try harder*. She ought to call her back now and apologise, then spend the rest of her shift giving serious consideration to how she was going to make it up to her. But she couldn't face it. Couldn't face having to admit that she'd been the one in the wrong. Couldn't face the further blow to her self-esteem it would represent. Instead, she decided that, tonight, she was going to stay out very late and get very shit-faced indeed.

She finished up at work and set off, heading towards the city centre. After wandering around aimlessly for a while, she ended up at Casa Mona, a recently opened tapas place on West Nile Street with a big glass façade and an impressively well-stocked bar. It looked a little too urbane for her tastes, not to mention seriously out of her price range, but she was experiencing a strong compulsion to spend as much of the money she didn't have as possible, just to compound her misfortune. Besides, if she managed to get drunk enough she might cause a scene and give the chattering classes something to keep their tongues wagging for a while – the prospect of which appealed considerably to her baser urges.

She made for the bar and, settling into a chair, caught the attention of the goateed youth serving drinks.

'Get ya?'

'What's the most expensive drink yese do?'

'Elixir margarita,' he said, without having to think about it.

'Any good?'

'Between you and me, tastes like cat piss.'

'Make it a double, then.'

When it arrived, the drink did indeed have a taste that she could believe corresponded to that of feline urine, but she surmised that it would improve proportionally to the quantity consumed, so she downed it with abandon and ordered another.

She was well on her way to finishing her second when she became aware of a gaggle of people sitting at a nearby table. There were five in total – three men and two women, in the midst of a heated debate of some sort. Or, at any rate, two of the men were, their adamant voices vying with one another and with the tasteful accompaniment of flamenco music coming from the wall-mounted speakers.

'I'm not saying he doesn't put in the hours. Christ knows, he's always at his desk when I get in and most days he's still there when I leave—'

'Which, my dear Raymond, says all too little about his work ethic and all too much about yours.'

There was general laughter from the group, and Raymond, who was in Zoe's line of sight, appeared to take this with good humour. 'Yes, yes, all right. I'm not wedded to the job, and I make no apologies for that. But my point is, when our esteemed colleague was elevated to middle management, there was no indication that we mere mortals would be saddled with the classes he now considers it beneath his status to teach.'

Zoe allowed herself a knowing smile. She should have pegged them as a bunch of academics. Most of the ones she knew were more than capable of starting a fight about an Oxford comma at a Buddhist retreat. They all had that lethal combination of limited self-awareness and no internal filter which made confrontations like this hard to avoid whenever you got two or more of them in a room together.

'I don't think it's so much that he thinks he's above it,' said another voice – a woman's. 'You have to take on board how much his workload has increased.'

'I should hope so, at sixty-five K a year,' said Raymond.

'Now you're just being glib,' said the woman, and with a jolt of surprise Zoe realised she knew who that voice belonged to. 'He's effectively doing the work of two people.'

'Is he now? Well, hold on one minute while I get out my teeny-tiny violin.'

He pursed his lips and mimed playing said violin. But Zoe was no longer looking at him. Her attention was focused instead on the woman who'd spoken. She had her back to Zoe, but Zoe didn't need to see her face to know who she was. The short stature; the dark, shoulder-length hair; the rigid, straight-backed posture; and most of all that clear, tinkling Kelvinside enunciation – there was only one person they could belong to.

It had been three or four months since Zoe had last seen Anna Scavolini in the flesh, and these were hardly the circumstances she would have chosen for a reunion. For one thing, she was in no mood for putting on her happy mask and pretending everything was hunky-dory. For another, she still had enough self-respect to not want to be caught drinking alone at a bar like some saddo. But, by the same token, she was loath to just slap some money on the counter and slip away like she had something to be ashamed of.

By chance, Anna turned at that moment and, before Zoe had a chance to look the other way, their eyes locked. Anna's initial expression was one of surprise, perhaps even verging on alarm, but it quickly gave way to a smile. She rose slightly and gestured to Zoe to join her. With escape no longer an option, Zoe fortified herself by downing the remains of her glass of cat piss, hopped down from her stool and approached the table.

'Zoe!' Anna was out of her seat now, the smile plastered across her features a bit too overdone to wholly convince. 'This is mad! What are you doing here?'

'Och, y'know. Just eyeing up the local talent.'

Anna nodded, a trifle *too* enthusiastically, then appeared to suddenly remember her manners. 'Oh, um . . . everyone, this is Zoe.' She gestured to each of her companions in turn. 'This is Raymond, and Larraitz, and this is Xavier. And you already know Daniel.'

The man seated next to Anna, the only one of the four Zoe had met before, gave a benign smile and a nod. Zoe returned both, though they required some effort on her part. Anna and Daniel had been together for just over a year, and had been living together for a little more than half of that. He had dark curly hair, a neat little beard and little round glasses – as well as, by Zoe's reckoning, at least ten years on Anna and a pressing need to shed a few pounds. Zoe didn't like him. Not because he was unpleasant or obnoxious or anything like that. On the contrary, he was always the epitome of politeness; the sort of man you could picture giving up his place in the queue to little old ladies and spending his weekends volunteering to pick litter with the community council. It was just that he was so utterly, irredeemably vanilla. She couldn't fathom what Anna was actually doing with him. Anna, who'd been adamantly single all the time Zoe had known her and who'd once said that the day she started showing signs of looking to feather her nest was the day Zoe had permission to take her out back and shoot her, but who now seemed content to settle down and play house with a man who looked like he wore sleeveless wool cardigans and dunked his digestives in his tea.

'So what's the occasion?' Zoe asked brightly.

'Oh, um,' Anna gestured to the other woman in the group, 'Larraitz just had a paper she co-authored published in the International Journal of Criminology. We're having a little impromptu after-work celebration.'

'Come and join us,' said Larraitz.

Zoe felt herself beginning to back away. 'I dunno. Wouldnae wanna crash the party.'

'Nonsense,' said Xavier. 'The more the merrier.' He was already on his feet, offering her his seat. 'What's your poison?'

Zoe stole a glance at Anna, whom she got the distinct impression was a little uncomfortable with these two different sides of her life colliding like this.

'Aye, all right, then,' she said, sparing Anna the embarrassment of having to formally adopt a position. She slid into the chair vacated by Xavier, who went off in search of one from another table.

'So what is it you do, Zoe?' said Larraitz.

'Me? Oh, sort of a jack of all trades, me. A bit of this, a bit of that. Whatever pays the bills.'

'Zoe studied Media at Cali,' Anna said brightly, as if she thought this was a helpful contribution. Zoe felt like kicking her under the table. Given the choice, she'd rather this lot thought she was a bum with no qualifications instead of a bum who was sitting on a halfway respectable degree.

'Really?' Raymond both looked and sounded genuinely interested. 'So what's your take on the way the press are reporting this cash-for-access scandal at the City Chambers?'

To her deep discomfort, Zoe found the whole table gazing at her in anticipation of some profound insight. She shifted awkwardly, wishing she had the first clue what the guy was babbling about.

'To be honest,' she said eventually, 'I don't really follow the news. I mean, chances are they're gonnae be lying tae ye anyway, so, way I see it, might as well just live in a state of blissful ignorance.'

The others said nothing. They just stared at her in a mixture of confusion and discomfort. A ripple of awkward laughter spread round the table. Only Anna didn't join in.

'Quite right,' said Xavier, giving an approving nod.

'I'll drink to that,' said Larraitz, raising her glass.

'You know,' said Daniel, turning to Raymond, 'I did read a piece about a study which showed that people who watch Fox News are actually less informed about current affairs than those who don't consume *any* news programming . . . '

And so the conversation ran on, with Zoe already cold-shouldered, her contribution deemed nothing more than a launching-off point for a deep and philosophical discussion that, of course, went right over her head. Every now and then, one of them – usually Anna – tried to bring her into the talk, but the damage was done. The rest had pegged her as an idiot, the proverbial child sitting at the kiddies' table while the adults discussed matters of great importance. After a while, she got up, making the excuse that she was going in search of the loo. They were so busy debating the finer points of Chomsky's propaganda model that they barely even noticed her leaving the table.

It would be fair to say Zoe and Anna's friendship had survived a lot: six years of high school together, a decade with no contact whatsoever, and the elephant in the room that was the events of December 2009 – events which had cost Zoe's brother, Victor, his life, and had left her struggling to come to terms with the realisation that her only sibling had been both a rapist and a serial killer. A year later, when Anna had moved back to Glasgow, Zoe had instantly leapt on this as a chance to hit the reset button; to go back to a simpler, happier time before all the badness had come into her life. She'd been convinced they would immediately rekindle their old dynamic from their schooldays, making up for all the years Anna had spent out of the country and out of touch.

The reality had proved somewhat different. Despite once again living within a mile of one another, their paths seldom crossed, the gulf between their respective social circles an increasingly widening chasm and Anna's calendar always full, consisting of an endless series of conference trips and speaking engagements. Last year, she'd spent three months on secondment to the University of Vienna – a fact which Zoe had only discovered after she'd already been back for over a fortnight. Fair enough, Anna had obviously made a good name for herself, and Zoe couldn't begrudge her that. But at the same time, she could never shake the suspicion that Anna was going out of her way to not cross paths with her. And she could guess why. She wanted desperately to tell Anna that it was OK, that she didn't hold her responsible for what had happened three Christmases ago, that it didn't have to come between them. But she couldn't do it. The right circumstances never arose – and besides, the wounds were still too raw.

She'd been standing outside for about fifteen minutes when she sensed a presence behind her. She knew, even without turning, who it was.

'Come back inside, Zo.' Anna drew alongside her, arms wrapped round herself – even though, by Zoe's estimation, it was still plenty warm.

'I dunno. Mibby.' She turned to Anna with an apologetic grimace. 'Ach, look, you're better off wi'out me in there lowering the intellectual bar.'

'Is that how you think I see you?' Anna looked so genuinely shocked that Zoe immediately regretted saying anything.

She gave a wan smile. 'Nah, but . . . well, ye've got to admit, they're your people, no mine. I dunno anything about journals and propaganda models and what have ye.'

'Maybe.' Anna gave Zoe's shoulder an affectionate nudge. 'But I bet there was only one person at that table able to recite every line from *Showgirls* by heart.'

Zoe cackled, throwing her head back and snorting through her nose. 'And tae think they call theirselves intellectuals.'

Anna smiled and rubbed Zoe's arm. 'I *am* glad we ran into each other.'

'Aye, me too.'

They fell silent, content to stand in one another's company for a while. The sky above them was turning to a bruised purple.

It was Anna who broke the silence. 'Is everything OK, Zo?'

Zoe frowned. 'In what way?'

'Just . . . in general.' Anna hesitated. 'Only it looked to me like you were drinking on your own.'

'No law against that.'

For a moment, she said no more. Then, sensing Anna's gaze still firmly fixed on her and knowing there was no way she was going to just leave it at that, she let out a deep sigh.

'I got knocked back for a job earlier.'

'Oh. I'm sorry.' Anna made it sound like she'd just told her the world was ending in forty-eight hours. 'What kind of job was it?'

'Just a clerical thingy. No biggie. But ye know – would've been a foot on the ladder.'

'Well, for what it's worth, they clearly don't know a good thing when they see it,' said Anna.

Zoe said nothing. She felt sheepish and substandard and useless and a dozen and one other adjectives her brain was too pickled to dredge up. Of late, she'd become increasingly aware of her own inadequacies whenever hers and Anna's paths crossed. Once upon a time, their differences hadn't seemed to matter. If anything, they'd only made their friendship stronger. She'd always known that Anna was smarter than her, better off than her, had bigger boobs than her. But growing up, none of that had mattered. Neither of them had had anything to prove. At no point had there ever been any sense that they were in competition with one another, even when they were in the same classes, studying for the same exams. Now, however, each and every one of Anna's fresh successes simply made Zoe's own failures taste that much bitterer in her mouth.

'I thought . . . ' Anna paused again. 'I thought maybe it was because of the trial.'

Zoe just blinked at her. 'Trial?'

'Gavin Price's trial. It's . . . ' Anna trailed off as she looked into Zoe's eyes. 'You didn't know.'

A jolt ran up Zoe's spine. It seemed to lodge in her throat, causing her to have to force the words out. 'Know what? What's happened?'

'They . . . they've set a date,' Anna stammered, unable to wrest her eyes away from Zoe's. 'The thirteenth of July. I really thought you knew.'

'I came here straight fae work. I havnae had a chance to—'

'No, no, what I mean is, it was set weeks ago. The date. I rang as soon as I heard. You were at work, but Carol said she'd . . . ' She stopped short as the realisation that she'd just put her foot squarely in her mouth hit her.

Zoe's eyes narrowed. 'But what? What'd she say?'

Anna blinked rapidly, doing her wide-eyed I've-just-shat-myself thing. The implications of what she'd just revealed were lost on neither of them.

Zoe had known, from the snippets of information she'd been able to glean about the way things were progressing, that it was only a matter of time before there was a date for the trial, so the fact that there now was one wasn't exactly a total bombshell. It would have been nice not to have been hit with it out of the blue, but she was already over the shock. What remained was the sense of betrayal, of being kicked in the teeth, of having the wool pulled over her eyes by Carol. No question about it, it had been a deliberate omission. You didn't take a message about something as significant as that and simply forget to pass it on. And for what? What had she thought she was going to achieve? Was she trying to protect Zoe? To stop the old wounds being ripped open again? Showed how much *she* knew. The wounds had never healed. They still burned, each and every day. Some days the pain was less acute, some days more, but it was always there.

In Carol's absence, Zoe instead focused her ire on Anna. 'Ye could've got me on my mobile.'

'I know. I should have. Sorry.'

But then you'd have had to talk to me, wouldn't you? And you've been going out of your way to avoid that.

'It was in the papers too,' Anna added, as if this counted as mitigating circumstances.

'You know I don't read those.'

Anna winced, biting her lip. She reached out and gave Zoe's arm a gentle squeeze. 'Come back inside. It's getting cold.'

Zoe didn't look at her. 'You go. I'll come in a bit.'

Anna hesitated, and Zoe could picture the strained anxiety etched across her features. After a moment, she gave Zoe's arm one last squeeze, then turned and headed back inside.

Zoe didn't move. She stared up at the sky, watching the sun sink lower behind the rooftops. A light breeze drifted down from the top of the street, stirring her hair. Anna was right – there was a distinct nip in the air now. Behind her, the warm lights of Casa Mona beckoned. But she didn't go back in. Now, more than ever, she wanted to be on her own. There had to be somewhere in this city where she could get smashed in peace and quiet.

She switched off her phone, arched her shoulders and began to walk.

Glasgow Tribune

Thursday 16 May 2013

UNIVERSITY LECTURER RAPE
TRIAL GIVEN GO-AHEAD

BRAVE VICTIM BREAKS HER SILENCE

A date has been set for the long-awaited trial of a former Glasgow University lecturer. Gavin Price, 31, will stand trial in July for aiding and abetting the rape of his former girlfriend.

Price, it is alleged, pressured the victim to attend a raucous after-school party with him in December 1999. There, he failed to intervene while four other boys – all former pupils of the prestigious Willow Bank Academy – subjected her to a brutal and sustained group assault. The prosecution asserts Price knew in advance that the rape would take place, and that he and one of the other boys, his cousin Andrew Foley, even planned the incident together.

Four years ago, Price attained some notoriety as the sole survivor of the so-called Kelvingrove Park

Murders, which claimed the lives of four men as well as that of their killer, Victor Callahan. The *Tribune* understands Price's former girlfriend has named Callahan and three of his victims as her attackers.

Now, in a sensational development, we can reveal that the alleged victim has waived her right to anonymity. Jennifer Guilfoyle, 30, believes that, by going public, she will encourage other rape survivors to pursue their attackers in the courts.

'My daughter has suffered in silence for more than a decade,' her father, Mr Anthony Guilfoyle, a former detective superintendent, told the *Tribune*, 'and the fact that four of the individuals responsible died before facing proper justice has been a source of deep pain for us both. Though it has been incredibly difficult for her, my daughter believes that only by securing a conviction in a court of law can she achieve any measure of closure.'

Various provisions exist to protect vulnerable witnesses in court, including giving evidence via video link or behind a screen. But Ms Guilfoyle has declined all such measures, and has requested that the public gallery remain open for the duration of the trial, breaking with normal convention for sexual assault cases.

'I feel strongly that this trial should not be held behind closed doors,' she told us in a pre-written statement. 'I don't want him to be able to hide. I want the public to see him for what he is.

'I want to look him in the eyes. I want to show him that, though he caused me immeasurable pain and suffering, he didn't break me.'

Advocate Depute Hector Quaid QC will lead for the prosecution, while Price will be defended by Euan Streule QC. The trial will commence at the High Court on 13 July.

3

Smashed

She let her legs set the course, navigating the warren of lanes between the main streets of the city centre. As darkness settled, she found herself in the Merchant City – once home to Glasgow's tobacco barons, now the beating heart of modern yuppiedom. Here, the lights were brighter and the pavements cleaner, and as Zoe traipsed into the Madeira Bar and Guesthouse, she felt like she was committing an incendiary act, trespassing on land to which she held no claim.

As she sat propping up the bar, Vodka and Coke in hand and a refill on its way, she cast a disinterested eye over the clientele. Most were your typical Merchant City fare: city slickers in shirtsleeves and crumpled ties, kicking back after a gruelling week gambling the nation's finances on the stock markets, or whatever it was they actually did to earn a crust.

At the other end of the bar, a woman in her mid-twenties was sitting on her lonesome, swirling a tall glass of some colourful mixer in her hand. She had a beguiling sort of glamour about her – provocative and classy all at once. In any event, the short, sleeveless cocktail dress she had on was working for her. Zoe wondered if her date hadn't shown, though she couldn't for the life of her imagine any red-blooded male standing up someone who looked like that. Maybe she just came here because she liked the vibe. She seemed strangely familiar, and Zoe spent several minutes staring at her through the alcohol-induced haze that clouded her vision before she realised why. She was her neighbour from across the street – the one who went out every evening and didn't return till sunrise. At that moment, she glanced in Zoe's direction and caught her looking. Then, as if having complete strangers gawping at her was a perfectly normal state of affairs, she raised her glass to Zoe in silent toast and turned to face forward once again.

The bell above the front door jangled – an unnecessary touch, for the new arrivals were making their presence known all by themselves. There were three of them, all men. A little older than the rest of the crowd, perhaps, but kitted and garbed in much the same fashion. The leader of the pack was a fair-haired, good-look-ing guy in his forties, taller than his two companions and, again, vaguely familiar in a way Zoe couldn't place. She had a feeling she'd seen him on TV at some point, which wasn't beyond the realms of possibility: more than a few soap actors and other minor celebrities called the Merchant City home. The way the other two orbited around him, laughing at his jokes while simultaneously positioning themselves to shield him from any unwanted encroachments, certainly suggested he was some kind of big noise.

Zoe half-watched, slurping the remains of her Vodka-Coke through its straw, as one of the two groupies – the slightly pudgy one with the cropped black hair and close-set eyes – collared a passing waiter. Some words were exchanged, the waiter nodded profusely and gestured to the men to follow him. He ushered them through a door marked 'PRIVATE BAR' at the back of the room. A moment later, the woman in the cocktail dress, who might as well have had 'This Evening's Entertainment' stencilled on her well-formed arse, finished her drink, slipped off her stool and headed in the same direction.

Zoe turned back to her own drink. It was a surreal sort of night – the sort that started with drinks, then moved on to sexy dancing, then copping off in a toilet cubicle with some guy whose name you hadn't caught. And then, before you knew it, you were waking up in an unfamiliar bed with a dodgy tattoo you couldn't remember consenting to. Zoe actually *had* woken up with a dodgy tattoo once, following an all-night bender in her uni days – a gecko just above her right ankle, the significance of which was as much of a mystery to her as everyone else. She didn't do that sort of thing anymore, of course. That had been the old Zoe, before Carol had come along and domesticated her. Mind you, she could think of worse ways to end a day of soul-crushing disappointment. She knew, from the warm, slightly tingly sensation in her body and the way her sur-roundings kept slipping in and out of focus, that she was well past the point of being completely sozzled. Time was slipping by, and she was well aware that she should have been home hours ago. She thought about calling Carol, letting her know where she was, but swiftly concluded that, given the mood she was in, the only possible result would be a monumental screaming match.

In any event, she concluded that the solution to all her problems was more drink, and signalled to the bartender for another refill.

She awoke with a splitting headache and an acute sense of disloca-tion. She was lying face-down on something soft, which upon closer examination turned out to be a bed. Momentary panic set in, only to dissipate as she realised she was both alone and fully clothed. No unexpected tattoos either, at least not in any of the obvious places. That too was something.

As the fog cleared from her eyes, she eased herself upright and took stock of her surroundings. She was in one of those blandly tasteful guesthouse rooms – the sort with floral pattern wallpaper and pictures of generic rural landscapes hanging on the walls. An itemised receipt lay on the nightstand, consisting of a breakdown of the evening's drinking plus the cost of a night's stay. They might as well have just taken her wallet out of her arse pocket and helped themselves. Add to that the cash she'd frittered away at Casa Mona, and the night's frivolities had cost her half a month's wages. She was going to have a hell of a lot of explaining to do when she got home.

Her neighbours in the next room were having what might euphemistically be described as an intimate moment. Loud groans of both the male and female varieties mingled with the creaking of bedsprings, followed by a crash as something fragile hit the floor. *All right for some,* she thought. It had been nearly a month since she and Carol had last done the business, and of late their increasingly infrequent encounters between the sheets had developed a distinct air of going through the motions. At least these two, whoever they were, seemed to enjoy an element of spontaneity in their love life, even if it did involve wanton destruction of hotel property.

As she lay there listening to the continuing sounds of frenzied rutting, she became aware of a new and pressing need, growing in intensity with each passing second: the need to empty her bladder. She didn't want to move, but she knew she'd have to sooner or later. So, gingerly, she slid her feet onto the thick carpet and eased herself upright. Once the room stopped spinning, she had a quick look around. It wasn't en suite (of course not, that would have been too convenient), so she headed out into the corridor in search of the facilities.

The toilet on the first floor had a giant 'OUT OF ORDER' sign on its door. She made her way downstairs, clutching the handrail in case her feet chose to give way under her. A couple of drinkers were still propping up the bar – lonely, solitary types whose own problems no doubt gave hers a run for her money. Arriving outside the ladies', she found her way once again barred, this time by a yellow plastic 'CLEANING IN PROGRESS' sandwich board. The hum of a floor polisher emanating from within told her this wasn't simply a ruse to give her a UTI.

'Fuck it,' she said, and pushed open the neighbouring door.

The gents' was, thankfully, deserted, though she doubted anyone would have actually challenged her in any event. From past experience she knew that, if you acted like you belonged there, most people were too disconcerted to say anything. She chose the least disgusting-looking of the four cubicles, locked the door, dropped her drawers and alighted on the throne. As she sat there, doing an uncanny imitation of Niagara Falls, she eyed up the various messages scrawled on the walls and door by the resident graffiti artisans. Some wit had written the words 'ARTS DEGREES' above the bog-roll dispenser, with a little arrow helpfully pointing downwards for the slow-off-the-mark. It would've been funny if it didn't hit so close to home.

The well had run dry and she was just beginning to make a move when she heard the door opening, followed by feet on the vinyl flooring and men's voices. She froze, half off the seat, undies still around her ankles, and listened as they drew increasingly near. There were two of them, the tone of their voices indicating a familiarity bordering on chummy.

'So, a good time was had by all, I trust?'

'She knows what she's about, that one. And the bod on her!' A low, appreciative whistle. 'My eyes were out in stalks, let me tell you. Where the devil'd you find her?'

'A gift from our mutual friend, with his compliments.'

'Tell our mutual friend he has impeccable taste.'

Zoe thought she recognised the second voice – a curious blend of muted Scots and the strangulated vowels of a southerner.

The footsteps stopped directly in front of her cubicle. She heard the familiar sound of zips being undone, followed by piss splashing on porcelain as the two men blessed the urinals.

'Oh, I meant to say' – the first voice again, deeper and more obviously local than the second – 'I've arranged for you to have a sit-down with Greg Forsythe next week. Nothing too formal – exchange pleasantries, identify areas of common ground, that sort of thing.'

'Christ, really? That great clod? You've got more chance of meaningful conversation with a Border Collie.'

Carefully, Zoe took the door off the latch and eased it open a crack. Facing the urinals, their backs to her, were two men in dress shirts and slacks, pissing together in harmony. Men, she concluded, were weird: in so many respects afraid of showing intimacy to one another, yet perfectly relaxed about communal urination.

'Now, now. The community council plays a vital role in improving public accountability and fostering social cohesion.'

'A vital role in wasting taxpayer money, more like.' The man with the wonky accent sighed. 'All right, all right. I'll shake the fat slug's hand and tell him what a bang-up job he and his merry men are doing. Sound good?'

'I'll have Cheryl update your diary.'

Both their taps, it seemed, had now ceased dripping, and as Zoe watched through the crack, they headed for the sinks, disappearing from view. She strained to hear their voices over the sound of running water.

'Listen, Steve,' said the plummy one, 'about what we were discussing earlier . . . I'm afraid there's a bit of a mess to be cleared up in Room 108. You know how it is. In the heat of the moment, you lose control, things get a little out of hand . . . '

A brief, awkward pause. 'Well, I'm sure she knows better than to say anything.'

'That's what I'm counting on. Still, I feel we should impress upon her . . . '

'Say no more, Dom, say no more.'

Dom? That rang a bell too. Zoe was on her feet now, ear pressed against the laminate partition, trying her damnedest to make out what was being said over the roar of a blow-dryer.

'Knew I could count on you. And I trust you'll ensure the good lady is sufficiently compensated for her discretion? To be kept off the books, of course.'

'But of course.'

'A round of Dutch courage before we proceed, then? I gather the bar's still doing a trade.'

'Always a pleasure, never a chore.'

The door slammed shut. Two sets of footsteps receded.

Zoe knew now where she'd heard that voice before. Knew too where she'd seen the person to whom it belonged: the same sandy-haired bloke who'd come striding in with his posse and disappeared into the private bar.

Dominic Ryland, darling of the media and would-be leader of the Scottish Conservatives.

And the vigorous humping sounds from the next-door bedroom, so innocuous at the time, now took on a decidedly more unsavoury tone – the groans less those of a couple in the throes of passion than those of a powerful man bending a struggling woman to his will.

She was out of the cubicle before she even had her jeans buttoned. She bombed it up the stairs, not bothering with the handrail this time – the urgency of the situation seemed to have given her an agility that belied her recent alcohol intake. She pelted along the first-floor corridor, eyes skating over the numbers on the doors. 105, 106, 107 . . . She reached the door to Room 108 and wrenched it open.

Her neighbour the courtesan was crouched on the floor amid a sea of broken glass, spilt wine and tangled bedclothes, dabbing at her lip with a bloodstained paper tissue. One of the straps on her cocktail dress was torn, and her bare shoulder showed painful-looking red marks in the shape of fingerprints. She spun around, frozen in fear, staring up at Zoe with her one good eye. A rivulet of blood trickled from her nose. They faced one another, motionless, the only audible sounds the competing rasps of their harried breathing.

'We have to get out of here,' said Zoe.

The woman didn't move.

Taking matters into her own hands, Zoe grabbed her by the arm and hauled her to her feet. They took off, the woman following Zoe wordlessly as she strode down the corridor, heading in the opposite direction from the bar. Down a flight of concrete steps at the back, they found a fire escape. As Zoe shoved the panic bar, an alarm began to peal. It was still ringing in her ears as she burst out into the back lane, dragging her neighbour behind her, stiletto heels clacking on the cobblestones. There were no sounds of pursuit behind them, but as she ran, Zoe didn't dare look back for fear that, if she did, she would see Dominic Ryland or his accomplice standing in the doorway, silhouetted against the light, watching them go.

4

Jasmine

If Zoe had had any expectations as to how her evening was going to pan out, they certainly hadn't included ending up in the toilets at the Trongate branch of McDonald's at two in the morning, trying her best to clean up a hooker's battered face with paper towels and liquid soap. A hooker who, in an outrageous display of ingratitude, persisted in flinching and ducking and trying to bat Zoe away.

'Stand still! Jesus God, ye're worse than a wean!'

The woman relented and submitted herself to Zoe's clean-up operation, though it was clear from her whole demeanour that she thought she was the one doing Zoe a favour. Zoe made as quick and decent a fist of the task as possible, then rinsed the blood from her hands while her neighbour stood leaning against the sink, dabbing her split lip with a moist tissue.

'I've seen ye around.'

'Oh?'

'We're neighbours. You live across the street fae me.'

'Right.'

Evidently, this revelation was not going to result in them bonding over their shared status as residents of the former burgh of Partick. Nonetheless, she persevered.

'I'm Zoe.'

No response.

'Aaaand that's your cue to say who *you* are.'

The woman sighed. 'Jasmine.'

Zoe gave her an incredulous look. 'What, is that like yer porn name?'

'I don't do *porn*.'

She was English. Quite well-spoken, too. She'd obviously had An Education. Which of course begged the question as to why she was doing what she was doing. In any event, Zoe had clearly struck a nerve.

'What *do* ye do, then?'

'That's between myself and the client.'

'It aye ends in sex, though, right?'

Jasmine gave Zoe an acid look. 'And just where do you get off on judging me? I'd hazard a guess I make more in a single night than you make in an entire week.'

Zoe gestured to Jasmine's bruised fizzog. 'Aye, but when I hang up my togs at night my face disnae look like it's collided wi a flat-iron.'

'Believe me, this isn't normally part of the arrangement.'

'Arrangement?'

Jasmine sighed irritably. 'What I do, there are certain . . . conditions. I'm not just some random hussy you look up in the phone box and order a quick session of rumpy-pump. My clients include men from the highest echelons of society. Men who would be . . . shall we say, severely compromised should word of their after-sundown activities get out. They have certain standards and certain expectations. One of these is a fabulous night that fully justifies my fee. The other is my utmost discretion. In return, I enjoy the right to expect a certain level of courtesy from them. I set the ground rules, not them. I decide what is and isn't on the menu.'

'Take it he wasnae one of your regulars, then.'

'Look, I was told he was hot stuff. Tight with the big boss, know what I mean? I was to roll out the red carpet for him – really push the boat out, make it a night he'd never forget. If I'd known what he was into, I'd have told them to find someone else.'

'What *was* he intae?'

The good side of Jasmine's lip curled. 'You've got an imagination, haven't you? Use it. The point is, he asked for something I wasn't prepared to give him, and when I said no, he decided to take it anyway.'

Silence fell. Zoe scuffed the floor with her toe and kept her eyes down. A part of her wanted to know just what the sandy-haired prick had done, though she had a feeling she was better off not finding out.

At length, she spoke again. 'If you said no and he carried on anyway, that's rape.'

'A lot of people'd disagree with you there. It's not like me and him went up there to play cards.'

'Aye, but ye're no gonnae let him get away wi this.'

'Says who?'

'Says me. C'mon – there's a police station five minutes down the road.'

Jasmine said nothing.

'C'mon,' Zoe repeated, more urgently. 'The longer we wait, the longer he's got to get his story straight.'

Jasmine scoffed quietly to herself and shook her head. Zoe was about to ask what was so funny when there was a rap on the door.

'Are yese all right in there, laydeez?' called a voice. It belonged to the pimple-faced youth on night duty.

'We're fine, fuck off,' Zoe called back breezily. She waited till she heard retreating footsteps, then turned to Jasmine once more. 'Ye cannae just pretend this didnae happen.'

'Who's pretending? And what part of "utmost discretion" don't you get?'

'What part of "respect" don't *you*? You just told me—'

'Yeah, well, talk is cheap.'

Zoe couldn't believe it. How was it possible to be so resigned about having your own head kicked in? She tried to put herself in Jasmine's shoes, tried to imagine herself in a line of work that enjoyed an, at best, ambivalent relationship with law enforcement. But she couldn't. If it was her, she'd want the prick to swing. She was sure of it.

She tried a different approach. 'And what if he goes on and does this to some other poor cow? How'll ye feel then?'

Jasmine shrugged stiffly. 'That's her look-out. Hate to break it to you, darling, but I'm not big on the whole "together we are stronger" thing. Never did get round to taking out my membership with the International Union of Sex Workers.'

Zoe was silent for a moment, staggered by this stubborn refusal to respond either to common sense or emotional blackmail. It suddenly occurred to her that there was something else she could try – a last-ditch effort, a firing of the big guns. In a lot of ways, it felt like a betrayal of trust using this, but she'd exhausted all her other options.

'Look.' She moved closer to Jasmine, hemming her in and forcing her to give her her undivided attention. 'Years ago, a pal of mine went through something like what happened to you. No exactly the same, but close enough. She kept it to herself, didnae tell a soul, and believe you me, it ate her up fae the inside. It's too late for her now. The guy who done it's long gone. Probably married wi two kids and a dug now, driving a flash car and pure raking it in. And she regrets it. I know she does. Every day she has to live wi what she could've done but didnae.' She met Jasmine's eyes with renewed intensity. 'But see me and you, we can still nail this fucker, if we move now.'

'You and me?'

'Aye, me and you. I was there. I heard him in the bogs, pure boasting tae his lackey about what he done to you. And I seen the results. I'm a material witness.'

Jasmine looked singularly unimpressed, but Zoe thought she detected a change in her. It wasn't much, just a slight flicker behind the eyes, but somewhere deep down, her words had found their mark.

'You know what they'll say, don't you? "Hazard of the job".'

Zoe shook her head firmly, even as the nagging voice at the back of her head, emboldened by her own less than rosy experiences with the police, shouted at her to button it. 'Naw they willnae. It's no like it wis once. They've got specialists and everything now to deal wi this sorta thing.'

She laid a hand on Jasmine's arm. Jasmine flinched at her touch but didn't pull away.

'C'mon. Do the right thing.'

At 02:33 precisely, Detective Sergeant Rona Cauley finally hit the power button on her PC, shrugged on her suede biker jacket and switched off the light in the open-plan office of which she was the sole remaining occupant. As she tramped down the two flights of stairs to the ground floor, she fished in the jumbled hell that was her shoulder-bag and popped a Nicorette tab.

Forgive me, Father, for I have sinned. It has been eight days, seventeen hours and fifty-three minutes since my last cigarette. I am guilty of the following sins:

1. *Using excessive force while apprehending a little scrote on suspicion of smack-dealing because I hadn't had a cigarette first thing and was feeling even crabbier than usual.*

2. *Calling said scrote a whining little prickweasel during*

interrogation because he kept going on about his human rights while caring not a jot about those of the people fucked up by his dealing.

3. *Chaperoning said scrote on his legally-mandated comfort break and actually wishing I could trade places with him because he had a cigarette in his hand and I didn't.*

4. *Daydreaming about cigarettes instead of typing up my report on said scrote's snivelling confession, secured after six gruelling hours in the interview room.*

5. *Craving cigarettes every waking hour of every day and telling myself we're all going to die of something horrible sooner or later so why not just stick with the fags and make it quick?*

Her GP had ordered her to quit when a chest X-ray, taken after she'd presented to him complaining of persistent breathlessness, had revealed her to have the lungs of a geriatric coal-miner. *You're thirty-nine years old, Rona,* he'd said. *You're not over the hill but you're no spring chicken either. Time to start taking care of your body before the damage is irreversible.* With each passing day, her fervent wish that she'd just told him it was her fucking body and she'd wreck it any way she liked grew stronger. Only the fact that admitting defeat was not in her repertoire kept her going, though she had serious doubts as to how much more of the accompanying mood swings, restlessness and those awful, awful cramps she'd be able to hack.

The waiting room, which stood between her and the outside world, was swarming with life's no-hopers – the usual assortment of Friday night drunks and petty thieves, as well as a handful of unfortunates who were there not because of anything they'd done but because things had been done to *them*. She wasn't sure which group she despised more. There was, when all was said and done, something reassuringly straightforward about dealing with crims because at least the relationship she had with them wasn't blighted by icky feelings like pity or empathy.

She'd made it as far as the doormat when she heard the raised voice of the desk sergeant behind her.

'Rona.'

She stopped in her tracks, shoulders already tensed. She turned to see him beckoning to her from behind his plexiglass partition. With a sigh, she picked her way back through the throng of unfortunates and undesirables.

'This one's got your name written all over it. Rape with a side order of assault to injury.'

He pointed over her shoulder with his pinkie. She turned to see two women sitting in a corner in the waiting area. One, a redhead with a snub nose and a serious freckle epidemic, reminded her a bit of Sissy Spacek in her younger days. But it was her companion who really caught Cauley's eye – tall, glossy-haired, wearing a cocktail dress with a torn shoulder-strap. Under normal circumstances, she'd have been a proper head-turner, the like of which didn't walk into London Road Police Station every other Friday night. Right now, however, her face looked like it had recently made the acquaintance of a runaway freight train, with one eye swollen shut and her bottom lip bloated and already beginning to scab. No need to ask who was the victim.

She turned back to the desk sergeant. She knew what she should say. *Fuck off, Frank. I'm already four hours late getting out of here, and owing to the lack of nicotine in my system am in even less of a mood for hand-holding than usual. There must be someone else on active duty tonight in possession of two X chromosomes . . . because that's why you heard the word 'rape' and thought of me, isn't it?*

But she said none of those things. Because Frank, for all his faults, was a decent soul who didn't mean to be a sexist boor. Because she knew that, if she walked away now, then these two women, faced with the prospect of waiting hours to speak to someone else, would probably cut their losses and do likewise. And because she knew that saying no would, in its own way, be tantamount to giving up. And giving up wasn't in her repertoire.

She headed over to the two women.

'I'm DS Cauley. Shall we go somewhere more private?'

Zoe had been in police interview rooms before. Immediately following Victor's death – shot by police marksmen to prevent him from killing a man who really didn't deserve to live – Yorkhill Police Station had become something of a home away from home as detectives grilled her repeatedly, trying to ascertain what, if anything, she'd known about her brother's murder spree. But she'd never encountered anything quite like the suite she now found herself in. With its cushioned armchairs, pastel wallpaper and flat-screen TV, it put her in mind of the hospice where her granny had spent the last few months of her life, albeit without the Zimmer frames and cloying smell of antiseptic. She sat in uncomfortable silence as Cauley and a neat, bespectacled woman in a hijab whom Cauley had introduced as Farrah, the Sexual Offence Liaison Officer assigned to the case, took Jasmine through the evening's events. It was all very informal, very gentle, and Zoe couldn't help but wonder where this softly-softly approach had been three Christmases ago when she'd been trying to answer all manner of accusatory questions while simultaneously coming to terms with her brother's death.

They wrapped up Jasmine's interview, then Farrah went outside with her phone. A moment later, she poked her head back round the door and said that the Sexual Assault Referral Centre could see Jasmine first thing in the morning. At this, Jasmine became decidedly agitated, apologising over and over for wasting every-one's time, telling them to forget about it and saying she'd rather just go home. It took the combined reassurances of Zoe and the two other women to calm her down and get her to sit down again. Cauley took the phone from Farrah and, after a short, sharp exchange, ended the call and explained that there had been a change of plan: the duty Sexual Offence Examiner would instead be coming directly to the police station to conduct her examination there.

She arrived half an hour later – a tall, frizzy-haired woman with something of the air of a primary school teacher about her. She introduced herself as Dr Marion Chambers and explained to Jas-mine that her role was to examine her injuries and collect forensic evidence of the assault. Jasmine turned to Zoe as if to say, *Do I have to?*, and for a moment she reminded Zoe more of a wide-eyed child than a worldly-wise lady of the night. Zoe gave her a little nod, and that seemed to settle it. Jasmine got to her feet and went with Dr Chambers and the two policewomen.

They took her off to an adjoining room, leaving Zoe sitting on her tod. She could hear them getting down to business behind the door: the rattle of curtains being drawn, the snap of a latex glove, Dr Chambers asking Jasmine if she'd washed, brushed her teeth, eaten or drunk anything or urinated since the assault took place. It all made Zoe feel decidedly uncomfortable. She thought about chapping the door and asking them if they knew she could hear them out here, but she didn't like to interrupt, and the longer she held off, the more awkward she figured it'd be if she let on she'd been listening. So instead she took herself out to the corridor and sat on the floor, listening to the sounds of shouts and slamming doors emanating from the rest of the building.

Eventually, the door opened and Cauley came out, running a weary hand through her greasy shoulder-length hair. She drew alongside Zoe and looked down at her with a grimace, her back resting against the wall.

'Sucks, doesn't it? That feeling of not being able to do anything?'

Zoe wrinkled her nose in agreement. 'So what's next?'

'I've sent a forensics team to the Madeira. With any luck, what they find will back up the evidence taken from your friend by Dr Chambers.'

'She's no really my friend. I was just there is all.'

Cauley shrugged. 'Well, you cared enough to stick around. In this line of work, that's something we don't often see.'

'What d'ye reckon the odds are? Ye gonnae get the bugger?'

Cauley rolled her shoulders back, wincing as the bones creaked in complaint. 'We need to find him first, and that's half the battle. A million to one he'll have booked in under a false name. They always do. Which gives him time to well and truly cover his tracks while we trawl through CCTV footage and witness statements. Speaking of which, we could do with sitting you down to work up an e-fit.'

Zoe shook her head. 'Waste o' time. Just turn on the TV and odds are ye'll see him. He's never off it.'

Cauley turned to her in surprise. 'Why? Who is he?'

'That plummy politician bloke. Y'know, man of the people. Thingummy.' She snapped her fingers, trying to conjure up the name. It was on the tip of her tongue. 'The one who bangs on about how he grew up in the East End and slept in a drawer.'

'Are you talking about Dominic Ryland?'

There was a sudden quiet intensity to Cauley. She seemed awake in a way she hadn't done previously. She stared down at Zoe intently, the muscles in her scrawny neck stretched taut.

'Aye – sandy hair, fancy suits, talks like he's got a mouth fulla plums. That's him, right?'

Cauley didn't answer. Instead, she glanced over her shoulder, towards the room where Jasmine's forensic exam was still under-way. 'If the two of you could pick him out of an ID parade . . . ' she murmured to herself.

For a moment, she stood there in silent contemplation, lips clenched together, two fingers pressed to them as if she was smoking an invisible cigarette. At length, she stirred and turned back to Zoe.

'Wait there.'

Zoe mooched around the corridor for the next half-hour. Then, when her eyelids began to grow seriously heavy, she got up and went in search of a caffeine fix. She was feeding change into a vending machine in reception when she heard the mechanically-operated doors sliding open behind her. As she turned, four men came striding in. Dominic Ryland was at the head of the parade, exuding the same relaxed self-confidence he had at the Madeira, seemingly oblivious to the two burly officers flanking him on either side. A squat, older-looking man whose appearance and comport-ment both screamed 'legal counsel' brought up the rear, a briefcase in one hand and a leather document holder tucked under his other arm.

As the posse approached the desk, Cauley, who'd evidently been waiting in the wings for this moment, stepped into view. Spotting her, Ryland gave a little smirk and shook his head, as if privately finding something very funny indeed.

'Well, well! Hello, Sergeant. Still here? I'd have thought you'd have moved on to bigger and better things by now. Still, I suppose one must admire your loyalty to the old place.'

Cauley refused to rise to his bait. In fact, she barely even acknow-ledged his presence. She remained stock still, poker-faced, arms folded, as she addressed the desk sergeant. 'Book Mr Ryland in, will you, Frank? See to it that he's housed in our finest suite.'

Still smiling, Ryland made his way over to the desk. Producing a pen from his breast pocket with an exaggerated flourish, he began to peruse the form the desk sergeant had placed in front of him. 'I wish it to be noted for the record,' he said, 'that I am here voluntarily in my capacity as an upstanding citizen who is always glad to assist the police with their enquiries in any way possible.'

He looked around, as if to gauge the effect of this performance on his audience, and in doing so his gaze briefly fell in Zoe's direction. She shrank back instinctively, convinced he'd remembered seeing her at the Madeira. But his glance was only fleeting, and a moment later it came to rest on Cauley, who looked to be exerting immense effort to maintain her composure.

A moment later, the paperwork was all in order, and Ryland and his lawyer were escorted away, Cauley following hot on their heels.

Zoe headed back to the victim suite, where she found Jasmine, hair post-shower wet, now wearing a shapeless grey tracksuit that suited her about as well as a fur coat on a vegan. About ten minutes later, Farrah came to fetch them and they were each taken in turn to a room with nothing in it but a flickering TV screen which showed a row of five men: Ryland and four others who looked to Zoe like a bunch of neds dressed for an appearance in court, which probably wasn't too far off the mark. In any event, it took her less than a second to pick Ryland out of this motley line-up, despite Farrah's insistence that she take her time and look at each man at least twice.

When her turn was over, she headed out to reception instead of returning to the victim suite. She knew she wouldn't be able to thole it – not the sickly, artificial niceness of the décor and not Jasmine. She finally switched her phone back on, and for the next minute or so it blinged non-stop as a sea of texts came flooding in. The first was from Anna, asking where she'd gone and saying she hoped everything was OK, followed by about a million from Carol, each asking essentially the same question as Anna but with an escalating sense of urgency. Knowing she'd have to face her sooner or later, Zoe took a deep breath and rang her. Carol answered on the second ring, her angry remonstrations giving way to shock and concern as Zoe gave her an abridged version of what had happened. She said she was coming straight to get her and rang off before Zoe could tell her there was no need.

When Cauley strode into the small, windowless interview room, Ryland and his lawyer, seated on the far side of the Formica table, were engaged in earnest discussion. Their conversation came to an abrupt halt and both turned to face Cauley, their expressions impassive. Cauley stood before them for a moment, breathing the stale air in deeply through her nostrils as if it was scented with an ocean breeze, savouring the moment – those brief, precious seconds while doubt and uncertainty filled their minds, before they knew what she was going to say.

'Dominic Ryland, I am detaining you under Section Fourteen of the Criminal Procedure (Scotland) Act 1995, on the grounds that I suspect you of having committed an offence punishable by imprisonment, namely the rape and assault to injury of Jasmine Mooney at the Madeira Bar and Guesthouse between the night of June twenty-eighth and the morning of June twenty-ninth 2013. Do you understand?'

Ryland began to laugh. He shook his head mirthfully, glancing across at his lawyer, who remained poker-faced, as if inviting him to share in the joke. It took all Cauley's willpower to keep her cool.

Gradually his laughter subsided. He gazed up at her, wearing the self-satisfied smile of a man who believes himself to be beyond reproach. He gave a little sigh and shook his head, as if to say, *Fine, I'll play along with your little game.*

'Yes, yes,' he said, 'I understand.'

'You will be detained to enable further investigations to be carried out regarding the offence. You are not obliged to say anything, but anything you do say will be noted and may be used in evidence. Again, do you understand?'

His eyes bored into her. He was still smiling, but those eyes burned with an all-consuming contempt that would have caused a lesser woman to step back. But Rona Cauley stood firm.

'I said, do you—'

'Yes,' he said quietly. 'I understand, Sergeant. You've made yourself quite, quite clear.'

Zoe was sitting in the now-empty waiting area when Cauley materialised. The older woman headed over and sank wearily into the seat next to her. For a while they sat side by side, saying nothing, until Zoe finally broke the silence.

'What happens now?'

'Our friend in the expensive suit has been formally charged. Because he chose to commit his misdemeanour on a Friday night, we'll now have the pleasure of his company over the weekend. God willing, I'll have him in front of a judge first thing once the courts open on Monday.'

To Zoe, this all seemed to be happening incredibly fast. She didn't know a massive amount about the way this stuff worked, but given that the authorities had spent almost two and a half years faffing around before Gavin Price was finally charged, it seemed unfathomable that Ryland could be in the dock barely forty-eight hours from now. That had been a less cut-and-dried case, true, but still. For whatever reason, Cauley seemed to be intent on ramming this one through the system as quickly as possible, like she was in a hurry to get home for tea or something.

'And what happens then?'

Cauley sucked her teeth. 'The Procurator Fiscal will decide, based on the report I submit to them, whether there's sufficient evidence to prosecute, and whether it would be in the public interest. Fortunately, I'm on fairly good terms with one of the senior deputes at the National Sexual Crime Unit. If it ends up on her desk, we should get a sympathetic hearing. But that's a big "if".'

'What about in the meantime? Ye gonnae keep him locked up?'

Cauley gave a thin smile. 'I expect he'll be bailed immediately – with the usual terms and conditions. He's got no priors, and he's at low risk of absconding. He is, in every sense of the word, a thoroughly respectable citizen.' The contempt in her voice was unmistakable. She looked at Zoe with cool, unsmiling eyes. 'But we know better, don't we?'

'Aye.'

Zoe wondered what Cauley's back-story was with this guy. The way she'd come to life at the mention of him, as if someone had shoved a boomstick up her arse, put paid to any notion of her just having a general dislike of lanky, well-spoken poshos in overpriced suits. And when he'd arrived at the station, Ryland had greeted her like an old friend – or, more likely, sparring partner. *Hello, Sergeant. Still here?* Nah – she knew him and he knew her. One way or another, they'd done this dance before.

At length, Zoe got to her feet. 'Know where I can cadge a ciggy round here?' Cauley had the look of a smoker, she reckoned.

Cauley went for her jacket pocket, then stopped. She lowered her arm with a look of profound regret.

''Fraid I can't help you there.'

In the end, Zoe managed to get one off the desk sergeant, along with a loan of his lighter. She was standing on the step outside, the sun rising pale and watery behind a band of thin cloud, trying in vain to get the lighter to catch, when a taxi pulled up to the kerb.

Carol scrambled out, chucked some money at the driver and sped across the concourse towards Zoe. She snatched the fag out of her mouth and tossed it away.

'Hey!'

'You don't smoke.'

Zoe shrugged. 'Felt like starting.'

Carol had been a smoker herself until a year ago, and having given up the habit had developed something of a holier-than-thou complex about it. She looked at Zoe, shaking her head.

'Oh, Zo, what've you been doing?'

And then, before Zoe had a chance to respond, Carol enveloped her in her arms, holding her tight, pressing Zoe's face into the fabric of her denim jacket, all but smothering her in the process.

'It's OK,' she murmured. 'It's all over now.'

She continued to hold Zoe, stroking the back of her head with a signet-ringed thumb. And yet, try as she might, Zoe couldn't relax. She remained stiff in Carol's arms, her back arched and her own arms rigid by her sides. Because she knew, whatever Carol might think, that it wasn't over – not by a long shot.

5

Safe

The three of them shared a cab back to Dumbarton Road. The journey unfolded in silence, Jasmine making it abundantly clear that she wasn't in the mood for any chat. It was after six when they pulled up outside A Taste of India, and while the rest of Partick was still tucked up in bed, the sun was already riding high in the sky, promising another fine summer's day.

'D'you want us to come up with you?' Carol asked, as Jasmine prepared to cross the road to her flat.

'I'm fine,' Jasmine muttered, shaking her head. She was still clutching the flyer Farrah had given her – the one that covered such disparate matters as her rights, emergency contact details, and info about STIs and emergency contraception.

'Have you got everything you need? How are you fixed for supplies? Food and whatnot?'

Jee-ZUS, woman! Zoe thought. *Leave her be. Can ye no see she just wants her own space?*

'I'm good. I mean, if I think of anything . . . '

They stood there in uneasy silence for a moment, no one looking at anyone else. Then Jasmine gave an awkward shrug.

'Well, that was fun. We should do it again sometime.'

And with that, she turned and crossed the road, quickening her pace to avoid the oncoming traffic.

For the remainder of the weekend, Zoe lived the quiet life, spending nearly all of Saturday and most of Sunday alternating between sleeping and mooching about feeling sorry for herself. She was still experiencing the after-effects of her Friday night bender nearly forty-eight hours later, though she said nothing about it to Carol and Carol, in turn, said nothing about it to her. They seemed to have reached some tacit understanding that neither of them was going to mention the way she'd behaved on Friday. As a result, it – and Carol's duplicity about the Gavin Price trial, about which Zoe still hadn't let on that she knew – continued to fester away below the surface like a termite slowly eating away at them.

She was woken on Tuesday morning by a furious pounding on the door. She reached for her phone, lying charging on the nightstand, and angled the screen towards her. 09:42. The pounding continued relentlessly. Next to her, Carol, who'd only got in a few short hours ago from another night on the trot, gave a semi-conscious groan and pulled the sheet over her head. Leaving her to her lie-in, Zoe crawled out of bed, pulled on some clothes and stumbled out into the hall.

She opened the door to find Jasmine standing on the mat. Without saying so much as a howdy-do, she wordlessly thrust a newspaper in Zoe's face.

It was a local tabloid, one that as a rule only covered politics when some washed-up former MP or other was going to the jungle to eat bugs. Today, however, it bore a large colour photograph of Dominic Ryland, captured at some party rally or other. Above it, the headline screamed in bold, black type:

TOP TORY IN SEX SCANDAL!

Zoe shrugged. 'So?'

Jasmine grabbed the paper back from her and jabbed an insistent finger at a paragraph halfway down the page. 'It says he was bailed yesterday. They let him out. They fucking let him out.'

Zoe glanced back towards the bedroom. If Carol hadn't been woken by the banging, she almost certainly would have been by all this shouting. She slipped out of the flat, shutting the door behind her.

'All right, keep yer heid on. It'll be OK.'

'How the hell can it be OK? I get the man arrested, I accuse him of rape and battery, I ruin his reputation, and you think . . . what? That he's just going to leave it be? That I'm somehow going to be safe? I got a call from that policewoman this morning. She said the guestroom was wiped clean. Nothing to suggest anything untoward had taken place there. And the staff said the room was vacant. No one booked in. So, somehow, *they've* been got at.'

For the first time, Zoe properly took in Jasmine's face. The swelling was starting to go down, but in its place was emerging a cornucopia of bruising that made her actually look worse than she had on the night of the attack. But all that was as nothing compared to the wide, white fear in her eyes.

'You know what else she told me?' Jasmine continued. 'She told me it could be a year before he goes to trial. A *year*. I have to spend a year looking over my shoulder, always wondering if the next set of footsteps I hear behind me is him coming to finish the job.'

'He's no gonnae come after ye,' said Zoe, managing to sound considerably more certain about this than she actually felt. 'He's no that daft. He knows the moment he sets foot within a mile of you, they'll throw him straight in the clink.'

Jasmine shook her head and smirked. The overall effect, coupled with the bruising and swelling, was profoundly ugly. 'God, you're naïve. You think the law's there to protect people like you and me? It's not. It's there to protect people like him.'

Zoe stared at Jasmine helplessly, unable to come up with any sort of insightful counter to this proclamation of despair. 'But you're not on yer own,' she said helplessly.

Jasmine looked at Zoe for a long moment. 'I am, though. In the end, when it comes down to it, we're all of us on our own.'

Nothing Zoe said would console Jasmine, and she departed in as much of a state as she'd arrived. She left behind the paper, which Zoe took to the kitchen table to read. It said Ryland had appeared in the Sheriff Court on Monday and made no plea or declaration. Later, however, his campaign manager, Steve Michener – whom Zoe surmised was the dark-haired, pudgy one who'd been with him in the gents' on Friday night – issued a statement on his behalf, quoted verbatim in the article. In it, Ryland claimed he and his campaign team had gone to the Madeira to celebrate the latest round of internal polling, which had given him a hair's lead over his closest rival in the leadership race. He denied booking a room there and claimed never to have seen Jasmine in his life, let alone done to her what he stood accused of. Jasmine herself was not, of course, named, referred to instead as 'a high class escort whose clients are believed to include footballers and a former Lord Provost'. Zoe briefly wondered how the paper had got wind of Jasmine's profession, then realised Ryland's camp had probably leaked it to discredit her. Ryland insisted it was all an unfortunate case of mistaken identity, adding for good measure that he unreservedly condemned the buying and selling of sex and, if elected as leader, would immediately table a motion in Parliament calling for the criminalisation of both. An unnamed spokesman insisted the Party had 'complete confidence' in him.

The evening news that day was all but given over to Ryland's arrest, with expert after self-appointed expert called in front of the cameras to offer explanations – that is to say speculate unfoundedly – as to what this meant for the coming leadership contest, the Conservative Party and indeed Scottish Politics As We Know It. Carol, who was attuned to these matters of great import, eagerly lapped up all the coverage, but Zoe was already beginning to lose patience with all the ill-informed pontificating. It seemed to her that, in the rush to dissect what this all meant for Ryland and his mob, the small fact that a woman had been beaten and raped had passed everyone by.

The following day – Wednesday – the morning headlines continued to be dominated by Ryland's spot of bother with the law, though by midday the big news story was the guilty verdict and lengthy jail sentence handed down after a long-running trial at the High Court to a notorious gangster, Francis 'Freddo' Brady, whose offences included gun-running, money-laundering and attempting to kill a rival hood with a power drill. Zoe, who'd never before heard of a gangster named after a chocolate bar, couldn't help noting that the ridiculousness of criminals' nicknames always seemed to be inversely proportional to their savagery. An axe-murderer would probably be called 'Tinkerbell' or something.

She continued to keep an eye on the street from the living room window, but she no longer saw Jasmine coming out glammed up in the evenings. In fact, she didn't see her at all. Her curtains remained drawn even during the daytime. As the afternoon drew in, her anxiety continued to mount. That evening, while Carol was out picking up some messages, Zoe's concern finally got the better of her, so she headed across the road and chapped the door of Jasmine's second-storey flat. After almost a full minute, Jasmine opened it a crack, keeping it on its chain.

'What?'

'Open the door, Jas. It's me.'

'I know it's you. What do you want?'

'Just open it.'

Jasmine sighed, but she nonetheless unhooked the chain and opened the door fully. The cuts on her face were healing, but the bruises remained – a livid array of blacks, yellows and everything in between.

'What?'

'Just came to check ye were all right. Havnae seen ye about lately.'

'Yeah, well. Don't want to frighten the horses, now, do we?' She gestured vaguely to her battered features.

'Folk've seen worse. So how've you been? Been getting any grief off the press?'

Jasmine scoffed slightly. 'They haven't managed to identify me yet, though not for lack of trying. The latest theory is that I work out of a top-secret brothel in a mansion house in Mount Florida.'

Zoe wondered whether she was kidding. So much of what came out of Jasmine's mouth was laden with sarcasm it was hard to tell.

'How ye doing for money?'

Jasmine gave a thin, sneering smile. 'Well, I'm not plying my usual trade, if that's what you're getting at. I refer you back to the aforementioned horses.'

Zoe was about to ask her how soon she expected to be back to work, then realised that perhaps she oughtn't to be encouraging a swift return to her chosen profession.

Jasmine curled one leg round the other awkwardly, eyes rigid on the floor. 'Um, look . . . you couldn't run to the shops and pick up some things for us, could you? Milk and toiletries and some other bits and pieces. I'll pay you,' she added quickly, as if anticipating a refusal.

'Sure. Just tell me what ye need.'

'I mean, I would myself, only I've got this phone call I need to wait for and—'

'It's fine,' Zoe assured her. She knew full well that this wasn't about any phone call or even vanity concerning the state of her face. Jasmine was afraid to leave the flat.

'You're a sweetie. Here.'

Jasmine produced a handful of crumpled notes from her pocket and tried to press them into Zoe's hand.

'Nah, ye're all right.'

Jasmine's eyes flared angrily. 'I'm not a charity case,' she snapped. 'Take it.'

And so Zoe was dispatched to the corner shop, armed with instructions to buy milk, bread, fruit and bog-roll. She brought the shopping bags up to the second floor and, sensing that Jasmine's pride wouldn't stretch to receiving them in person, left them at the door.

She crossed back over to her side of the road, ruminating on Jasmine's situation. This was no life to be living, holed up behind a locked door and dependent on the benevolence of your neighbours to get by. It just wasn't feasible long-term, especially if the proceedings against Ryland were likely to drag on for a year. There had to be something practical she could do that didn't involve becoming Jasmine's personal shopper.

By the time she got back to the flat, an idea had begun to take shape. She got out the laptop and sat with it on the sofa, exploring the practicalities. She was so consumed by the task that she didn't hear the front door opening and Carol coming into the room behind her.

'Whatcha doing?'

Instinctively, Zoe snapped the lid shut. 'Nuttin.'

'Didn't look like nothing. C'mon, let's see.'

As Carol sat down next to her on the sofa, Zoe reluctantly opened the lid. Carol angled the screen towards herself.

'Self-defence classes? What's brought this on?'

'Well, I mean . . . ' Zoe shrugged self-consciously. 'You're always on at me to get a hobby and get outta the house more. I just figured it looked kinda . . . y'know, interesting.'

'Mm-hm. This wouldn't happen to have anything to do with a certain someone who lives across the street from us, would it?'

'Might do.' A moment passed, then Zoe turned to Carol imploringly. 'Aw, Caz, ye havnae seen her. She's shit-scared of her own shadow. I just thought – I dunno, mibby gie her a wee bit of confidence back.'

Carol smiled and brushed a stray strand of hair from Zoe's eyes. 'Who needs the Samaritans when they've got you, eh?' She hesitated, then, almost as if she was reluctant to say anything, added, 'But I'm wondering . . . are self-defence lessons really the solution? Is it not a bit like shutting the stable door after the horse's bolted?'

'I s'pose, kinda. But I'm thinking, if she knows how to take care of herself, if there's a next time . . . ' She trailed off, aware that it didn't seem like an entirely coherent argument.

For several moments, Carol sat, arms folded, chin tucked in, doing her *I know you don't want to hear this, but I'm going to say it anyway* thing.

'I just can't help thinking,' she said eventually, 'that it's all a bit victim-blamey. It's like you're saying it's our responsibility to make sure something like this doesn't happen to us. It's erasing the role of the men that are actually to blame.'

OUR responsibility. Happen to US. She might have known Carol would find a way to make this into a Woman Thing, boiling it down to some abstract issue, as if you could shoehorn everyone into a predetermined, right-on ideological framework. As if individual circumstances and personalities didn't come into it.

'I mean,' she went on, 'how does her learning a few karate chops help us stop men like that scumbag thinking they have a right of access to women's bodies?'

'It doesn't,' said Zoe. 'But I'm figuring it'll help *her*.'

*   *   *

Carol's intransigence only made Zoe more determined, and the next morning, she rolled up bright and early at Jasmine's door with a bunch of print-outs and a grand plan. There was a women's self-defence group that met every Friday evening in the gym hall at the local community centre, and a quick phone call to the woman who ran it had established that she had a few empty spaces going. Zoe had enrolled them both then and there, and paid the deposit for good measure. At first, Jasmine was singularly unreceptive to the idea, going as far as to try to shut the door in Zoe's face. But, bit by bit, Zoe succeeded in chipping away at her resolve, until she eventually sighed and said that all right, she'd come along for one session just to see what it was like.

And so, that Friday at 5.30, they found themselves standing in the gym hall with a dozen or so other women of various ages, shapes and sizes, being given an introductory pep-talk to the Safer Streets Self-Defence Initiative. The instructor, the improbably-named Donatella Vigorelli, was one of those short, compact little women about whom everything is rock-hard: her features, her abs, and most of all her resolve. This was a woman who, in spite of her size, you got the impression no one fucked with – or at least lived to tell the tale. Zoe hadn't set foot in a gym since her first week at uni when, carried on a wave of good intent, she'd taken out a semester's membership and promptly allowed it to lapse, and had, until now, had serious concerns about how much physical exertion would be involved. One look at her classmates quickly allayed her fears: a number were severely overweight, and a couple looked to be of pensionable age. She even began to suspect that the sports bra and lycra bottoms she'd borrowed from Carol – well, half-inched without asking – might have been overkill. Jasmine, wearing the same peat-grey trackie top and bottoms she'd been given at the police station, had had the right idea.

'I see one or two new faces today,' Donatella said, standing on tiptoe with her neck extended as she sized up the crowd gathered before her. She had one of those broad, faintly patronising smiles that extends from ear to ear but never quite reaches the eyes. 'So I'll start by saying a few words about what this class is and isn't about. First and foremost – and I appreciate this might come as a disappointment to some of you – you won't be learning how to kill a man with one finger.'

A few strained smiles and polite laughs. Zoe got the impression the other women had heard this speech before.

'Safer Streets is not in the business of advocating violence. Rather, we seek to provide you with a skillset to help you get out of potentially violent situations. All the techniques you'll learn are designed around a single, straightforward principle: do what you need to do in order to escape, and then get out of there as quickly as possible.

'In Scotland, one woman experiences domestic violence every ten minutes. In the last year, over seven thousand sexual offences were recorded, and incidences of rape rose to over twelve hundred – a thirteen percent increase on the previous year. And those are just the ones we know about. The real figures will be much higher. It could happen to any of us. For some of you, it probably already has.'

Zoe was conscious of a number of furtive glances in Jasmine's direction. It couldn't be helped – the results of her recent ordeal were still etched on her face.

'Certain individuals and organisations are fond of saying that it shouldn't be a woman's responsibility to take precautions against physical and sexual assault. And I agree, it shouldn't. But it is. It is because that's the world we live in, and ideals are worth nothing if they mean cutting off your nose to spite your face. I've yet to meet a single woman who's told me, "Yes, I was raped, but I made the right choice in not learning self-defence because it shouldn't be my responsibility".'

Ha! Put that *in your peace-pipe and smoke it, Carol.*

'Now, we'll get onto specific techniques to employ if you find yourself in a situation where a physical response is the only way of getting yourself out of danger, but at least half the battle is up here.' She tapped her forehead. 'That means employing common sense, practising safe habits. For instance, getting your keys out before you reach your door, travelling with friends whenever possible. And I can't stress this enough: always be aware of your surroundings, so lose those earbuds and get your nose out of your smartphone. And for the love of God, don't be tempted to carry a knife. You may think you're protecting yourself, but all you're doing is increasing the risk of ending up on the wrong end of it yourself, or in jail. With all that said—'

At that moment, Donatella's sermon was interrupted by the door at the back of the hall opening. Like a herd of sheep, they all turned in unison.

A young woman stood in the doorway with her hands resting on a metal-studded belt. She was in her mid-twenties and dressed in Caterpillar boots, combat trousers and a men's white tank top which showed off her impressively muscular biceps. Her short black hair was gelled into thick spikes, giving her a look that wasn't quite punk but wasn't quite rock 'n' roll either. She surveyed the sea of faces before her with a superior smirk.

'Howdy-ho, girlies. What's shakin'?'

Zoe was familiar with the phrase 'own the room', but until now she'd never seen it manifest itself in such a perfect illustration. The entire dynamic in the hall had changed. The new arrival was now everyone's focus, and as she sauntered in, looking from face to face as she sized up each of the women in turn, the impression was very much given that this was her place and the rest of them were only there by her grace.

'Fin. I wasn't sure whether you'd be joining us.' It was plain from the strained note in Donatella's voice that she'd been fervently hoping she wouldn't. 'Unfortunately I'm not sure we've room for another body. We'll be pairing up for group exercises shortly, and we need an even number—'

'Oh, I can do my own thing,' said Fin airily. 'Don't be putting yerself out on my account.'

She had a deep, raspy voice and an Irish accent, so strong that Zoe had to seriously concentrate to make out what she was saying.

'Well, all right,' said Donatella, looking more than a little uncertain. 'Just as long as—'

'That's grand, sure.'

Fin strode over and took up a position at an empty spot next to Zoe. She flashed her a grin and a wink, then immediately launched into a series of limbering-up exercises without any heed to the rest of the class.

They got underway again, but it took a while for Donatella to regain her natural flow. The balance of power had clearly shifted, and it seemed to Zoe that a number of the women were unhappy about Fin's presence. Fin, for her part, clearly didn't give two figs, and carried on doing her thing while Donatella got the others to do a variety of physical exercises, including deflecting an assailant, breaking a wrist hold, and Zoe's favourite: the good old-fashioned knee-to-scrotum manoeuvre. She paired up with Jasmine, who, to her delight, genuinely seemed to get into the spirit of things, laughing as she and Zoe took turns playing the victim and the aggressor and, at the end of the hour, joining in a rousing chorus of 'BACK OFF!' with as much gusto as anyone else.

Afterwards, Donatella reminded them that next week's class would be on Wednesday rather than Friday night, due to the small matter of the hall being requisitioned by the Jehovah's Witnesses Reading Society. Then, she and a couple of the other women set up trestle tables and began to lay out biscuits, cups and a tea-urn. Barring Fin, who'd swaggered off the moment class was over, everyone else seemed to be sticking around for refreshments, but Jasmine was making it quite clear from her body language and not-so-subtle overtures to Zoe that she wanted to leave, and so the pair of them made their excuses and walked back to Dumbarton Road together. As they came to a halt at the traffic lights, Zoe was fully prepared for Jasmine to declare her half of the bargain fulfilled and that she wouldn't be coming to the next session. To her surprise, however, Jasmine turned to her with an awkward, slightly sheepish smile.

'I sort of enjoyed that,' she admitted. 'I didn't think I would, but it was actually all right. So, um . . . thanks, I guess.'

Zoe said nothing for fear that a retraction would be forthcoming, but as she stood at the crossing, waiting for the man to turn green, she allowed herself a little victory jig. Perhaps, just perhaps, it was possible to affect some small but meaningful change for the better in this world.

6

Fin

Over the weekend and into the next week, the temperature climbed steadily, though, in the interests of preserving the peace, Zoe kept her displeasure to herself. The news continued its steady diet of murder, football and kittens, with a particular emphasis on the former. There was more gang violence in Glasgow, with a notorious hood – whose parents had evidently hated enough to actually name Jimmy Stewart – under armed guard in intensive care after being knifed in the spleen in a Morrisons car park in Cardonald. The wider world didn't seem to be faring much better. There was growing youth unemployment, a federal judge was urging the American president to halt the force-feeding of detainees in Guantanamo Bay, and a runaway train carrying crude oil had derailed and blown up in Québec, killing forty-seven people. Zoe wondered if the whole world was going to shit or if it had always been like this and she'd only just started noticing.

Gavin Price's trial, due to start the following Monday, loomed on the horizon like a cloud of noxious gas. She continued to make no mention of it to Carol. In fact, she was doing her best not to think about it at all. She wanted it to happen, because then at least the waiting would be over and some sort of line could be drawn under it, regardless of the outcome. But at the same time she also wanted it postponed for as long as possible, and a part of her kept hoping for that phone call to say it had been delayed for some reason. Because if it all went tits-up, if Gavin got off, then she knew she'd look back on this period of purgatory, this 'before', with fond memories.

It hasn't happened yet, she told herself. *I still have another week.* But a week became six days, and six became five, and with each day that passed, the knot in the pit of her stomach tightened.

At 5.30 on Wednesday evening, she stood outside the community centre, checking her phone over and over. Jasmine hadn't been in her flat when she'd called round for her; she'd banged on the door for ages but had got no reply. At first, she'd assumed Jasmine had gone on ahead by herself. But there was no sign of her, and she wasn't answering her phone. Perhaps she'd forgotten about the change of day? Having left it as late as she felt she reasonably could, Zoe cut her losses and headed on in.

The class got underway, and still Jasmine failed to materialise. Zoe found herself paired with Mona, a dumpy woman in her forties with non-existent physical coordination and an aversion to eye contact. After a thoroughly frustrating hour, she was all set to head round to Jasmine's place and demand an explanation, but the trestle tables and refreshments were coming out again and Zoe, concluding that this was the done thing after class, reluctantly stuck around for tea and biscuits and small talk. She was deliberating over whether to have another chocolate digestive when she sensed a presence by her side.

'Mm, they all look so yummy, don't they?'

She turned to see Fin standing next to her, wearing the wry smirk which Zoe was quickly coming to realise was the young woman's default expression.

'Yer pal with the bruises not with ya today?'

'Who?'

'One in the grey trackies who looked like she'd just gone six rounds with Ricky Hatton.'

'She, um, couldnae make it.'

'Such a shame. And yet you're still here.'

Zoe shrugged and turned back to the table.

'Don't tell me, you came for the cuisine.' Fin made a play of eyeing up the array of discount snacks and smacked her lips. 'Mm-mm! Nothing like a spread of Farmfoods' finest to get yer juices flowing.' She turned towards Zoe again, hand outstretched. 'Name's Fin.'

'I know. Uh . . . Zoe.' She accepted Fin's firm, decidedly masculine handshake.

'Pleasure's all mine. Listen – I dunno 'bout you, but today I'm jonesing for something to drink that doesn't taste like reheated pond-water. Whaddaya say? My treat?'

They ended up in an American-style diner at the bottom of Byres Road. Fin, augmenting her combat bottoms and vest combo with a leather jacket despite the heat, chose a booth at the window in the full glare of the sun. A jumpy waitress in a retro fifties outfit came and took their order, repeatedly saying 'y'all' despite her accent being as Glaswegian as they came. Fin flirted shamelessly, licking her lips suggestively at her and telling her she had a grand arse. As the poor girl fled for cover, Fin looked around and gave an approving nod.

'I like this place,' she declared. 'It's cornball, but a good kinda cornball. You know what you're getting so you're never disappointed.'

'Like a Roland Emmerich film,' said Zoe.

Fin gave her a look as if to say, *What are you on about, you mad rocket?* and Zoe instantly regretted saying anything.

She decided the best course of action was to change the subject. 'So, um, what d'ye get up to when ye aren't gate-crashing self-defence classes? What is it ye do for work?'

'Oh, I keep my hand in.' Fin made a vague gesture. 'You?'

'Cleaning lady.' She felt more than a little sheepish admitting it.

'Hey, fair play to ya. World'd grind to a halt pretty sharpish without a healthy supply of cleaning ladies. So tell me, that something ya always wanted to do or did ya just . . . '

'Well, it's no exactly a vocation.' She hesitated, unsure whether to divulge any more, then decided she might as well go for it. 'Turns out there isnae that big a market for media studies degrees.'

'Why'd ya do one, then?'

Zoe was a little taken aback by the directness of the question. Still, it was a fair one.

'To be honest,' she said, 'back then I hadnae really figured out what I wanted tae do with my life. But all my pals were going to uni, and I figured, "One degree's as good as another, so might as well pick one that sounds halfway interesting".' She shrugged. 'There's worse ways of spending three years than watching films and TV programmes.'

'And now?'

'What?'

'You figured out what ya wanna do with yer life?'

For several moments, Zoe said nothing, her mind a blank slate. How did you even begin to answer a question like that?

'Um . . . guess ye could say I'm a work in progress?' She gave a hesitant smile.

It was abundantly clear from Fin's expression that she wasn't impressed by this answer. Fortunately, at that moment Zoe was spared any further embarrassment by a waiter – a male one, this time – arriving with their drinks. As he departed, Fin raised her glass.

'*Sláinte.*'

They clinked glasses, Zoe's JD dwarfed by Fin's almighty tankard of Red Oak. Fin drank deeply, then leaned back with a contented sigh.

'So what's the verdict on Donatella's wee enterprise? Satisfying the itch for ya?'

'How d'ye mean?'

'Well, it's plain as a pikestaff you're not some lily-livered little wifey who lives in mortal fear of having her handbag snatched by the bad men. So c'mon, spill the beans, Bright Eyes. What made ya sign up?'

Zoe shrugged, tracing the rim of her glass with her finger. 'It's no for me. I figured it'd do Jasmine some good. She . . . well, she had a bit of a scare.'

'Oh aye?' Fin raised her high-arched brows. 'A scare, was it? What'd she do? Catch sight of her own reflection?'

Zoe ignored this quip. 'Anyways, I figured mibby it'd help her get back on her feet.'

Fin looked around as if she expected to find Jasmine hiding out inside the diner. 'Woulda helped if she'd turned up.'

'Well, like I said, she couldnae make it,' said Zoe shortly. She was rapidly running out of patience for Fin's 'observations', each of which seemed to carry with it an implicit if ambiguous criticism. 'Could ask you the same. Nae offence, but ye look like ye already know how to take care of yersel.'

Fin shrugged, unconcerned. 'None taken. To be sure it's boredom, mostly. Keeps me outta mischief, stops me crawling up the walls. Plus it's a chance to inflict mayhem in a sanctioned environment.' She paused to swig from her tankard. 'A lotta these women come looking for some sorta reassurance, or cos it makes 'em feel like they're part of a community. Not me. I'm just there for the fuckin' violence.'

Zoe wondered just how seriously she should be taking this statement.

'So what exactly happened to her – yer pal Jasmine? Don't tell me – it involved walking into a door.'

A part of Zoe was strongly tempted to tell her it was none of her business and to take a running jump. She was tiring of Fin's glibness, and wondered if this odd, spiky-haired woman took anything remotely seriously. But something stopped her. She'd been carrying what had happened at the Madeira around with her for nearly two weeks without properly processing any of it, and as she sat there, toying with her glass of JD, she realised she desperately wanted to unburden herself of the thoughts inside her head – to talk them through with someone. And Fin was clearly a someone.

So she gave the York Notes version of what had happened at the Madeira and their subsequent trip to the police station. Fin listened to the whole account without giving any indication as to what she was thinking.

'It's with the police now,' Zoe said when she'd finished her story. 'So I guess it's just a case of waiting for 'em tae do their thing.'

'Heh, yeah. Well, you'll be in for a grand old wait.'

'Aye, they said it could take up to a year. The wheels of justice turn slowly an' aw that.'

'Or not at all.' Fin sighed, extending her limbs in a full body stretch. 'Putting it in ye olde English, it'll go in a file somewhere, they'll say they're "working on it", and the whole thing'll drag on and on till either one of two things happens: either she gets fed up and tells 'em to park it or the whole thing collapses due to lack of evidence. 'Twas aye thus.'

'He's been *charged*,' said Zoe, conscious, even as she said it, of how feeble it sounded.

Fin rolled her eyes. 'Big whoop. You mark my words: a million to one says it's the good guys who suffer while fuckers like yer man get off scot-free. I tell ya, the only way to deal with these creeps is to retaliate in kind. If someone hits ya, you've gotta hit 'em back, only a whole lot fucking harder. Cos until you do, "victim" is all you'll ever be.'

'I hear they prefer "survivor" these days,' replied Zoe.

She knew she was being flippant, and worse still that it was the sort of linguistic pedantry Carol would have indulged in had she been here. But it was all she could come up with in the face of such relentless cynicism.

'Survivor? That's just the more politically correct word for victim. Dreamt up by the third wave pity party, even though they're the ones forever dining out on their own victimhood. End o' the day, you're still talking about something that was done *to* ya. You were a *victim* of rape. You *survived* having the stuffing knocked outta ya. Well, I'm not a survivor. I'm a fuckin' warrior.'

She said it with such utter conviction and the low evening sun was creating such a beatific glow around her that Zoe half-expected to hear a heavenly chorus ringing out. But instead, all she heard was 'Tequila' continuing to blast out of the speaker system.

'Ever looked up "victim" in the dictionary?'

'Cannae say I have.'

'Well, do it sometime. See what sorta words ya find. "Dupe", "patsy", "loser", "easy prey". Ya gotta wonder what sorta sucker would willingly choose to associate themselves with any o' that.'

Zoe was fast reaching the point of having heard enough. If she wanted to listen to a lecture, albeit of a different political hue, she just needed to go home to Carol and casually drop one of the usual trigger-words into a conversation.

And now Fin was looking at her curiously, tilting her head this way and that as if she'd just noticed something about Zoe that wasn't sitting well with her.

Zoe gave a belligerent shrug. 'What?'

'Ah, nothing. Just, now I think about it . . . I'm sure I've seen ya someplace before.'

'Guess I've just got one of they faces.'

'No, that's not it. I'm thinking . . . ' She gave a dry little laugh. 'Sounds weird, but have you ever been on the telly?'

Zoe shook her head firmly, shutting that particular avenue of thought down before it could develop legs. 'Nope. Definitely not.' Then, forestalling any further awkward questions, she slid out of the booth.

Fin glanced up. 'Off somewhere?'

'Need to take a leak.'

'Have fun!' Fin called after her.

Pausing in front of the bathroom mirror, Zoe wondered what she was doing here on a weekday night, listening to a mad Irish woman delivering her manifesto for change. Was she really so starved for human company that this was the best she could do?

She returned to the booth to find Fin lounging with her arms spread out across the back of the red leatherette seat. She slipped back into her own side of the booth with a nod.

'Who's Carol?'

Zoe jerked her head up sharply. 'Huh?'

'"Hope class was good. Back late. Remember and pick up milk."' Fin nodded in the direction of Zoe's phone, lying on the table-top. 'Text came in while ya were in the jacks.'

Zoe snatched up her phone and pocketed it, silently cursing herself for not taking it with her. Not that she'd thought she needed to – though clearly she'd reckoned without louche, hair-gelled busybodies being unable to resist sticking their noses in.

'So who is she?'

Ideally, Zoe would have liked nothing better than to tell Fin to

89

go hang, but she sensed she wouldn't get a moment's peace till she gave her an answer.

'My girlfriend.'

'Well, well.' Fin smiled lasciviously, flashing a row of large, slightly off-colour teeth.

'Well, well, what?'

'Seems there's more to you than meets the eye.'

Zoe gave a small, awkward laugh, aware that her cheeks were colouring. 'Um, no, don't think so. What you see is what you get.'

Fin scoffed. 'Pfff! What you see is never what you get.' She shrugged disarmingly. 'At any rate, I hadn't figured ya for a dyke.'

The word was like a slap in the face to Zoe. It had such an ugly, cruel sound to it that she struggled with the idea of any woman willingly using it to describe herself. Of course, she'd never been in any doubt that Fin was gay herself. If the hair, swagger, choice of clothes and shameless flirtation with the waitress hadn't tipped her off, the two interlocking Venus symbols tattooed on the left side of her neck certainly had. Her sexuality had to be seriously important to her for her to want everyone to know like that.

'I'm not . . . ' Zoe began, then stopped herself. This was an argument she had absolutely no desire to get into.

'What, prefer something a bit more PC?'

'No, I just . . . Look, I better get going.' She was already on her feet again. 'Thanks for the drink.'

Fin, not moving, gazed up at her, unimpressed. 'Home before sundown, huh? She's got you *whipped*.'

'It's no like that.'

'Course it's not.'

'And what would you know about it?' Zoe shot Fin a black look and turned to go.

'All right, all right. Just hold yer horses.'

Reluctantly, Zoe came to a halt and turned to face Fin once again.

'I'm sorry, yeah? Sure I didn't mean to hit a nerve. I was gonna say, if ya like we can hook up some night you've got nothing on and I'll show ya round the local scene. Introduce you to the seamier side of the city's nightlife. My treat. Whaddaya reckon?'

Nae chance. 'I dunno. We'll see.'

'Well, any time ya fancy, just bell me. I took the liberty of adding my number.'

Zoe's hand instinctively strayed to her pocket, where her poor, violated phone rested.

'Aye, mibby,' she said, and walked out without another word.

7

Dirty Work

Zoe waited till she was out of sight of the diner before stopping to check her phone – not least to make sure Fin hadn't interfered with it in any other way while she was reading her private messages and adding her name to her contacts uninvited like some weird presumptive stalker. Carol's message was indeed sitting in her inbox, word for word what Fin had recited, along with one from Anna, expressing regret that they hadn't managed more of a catch-up the other week and imploring her to call her. And just like that, Gavin Price's impending trial was once again squarely at the front of her mind.

What you see is what you get . . . It was a good line, but it wasn't really true. People, she knew, tended to take her at face value and assume there was nothing going on below the surface, and she was as much to blame for that misconception as anyone else, having never made much of an effort to persuade them otherwise. It still stung, though. It wasn't that they thought she was an idiot – at least, she hoped not. But she still couldn't shake the feeling that the Zoe Callahan they thought they knew was an artificial construct – a cartoon character rather than a fully three-dimensional human being.

She headed back towards the flat, pausing outside to gaze up at

Jasmine's window. It was shut and the curtains were drawn, even though it must be like a sauna inside.

Her resolve tightened. It seemed to her that Jasmine was responsible, either directly or indirectly, for everything that had gone wrong this evening: having to pair up with mopey Mona, Fin's probing questions and non-consensual probing of her phone, the veiled innuendos about her relationship with Carol. If Jasmine had just turned up like she'd said she would . . . Actually, no, scratch that. If Jasmine had never entered into her life, she'd never have become involved in any of this, and right now she'd be sat at home in front of the TV waiting for *Futurama* to start. The least she deserved was an explanation.

Heading into Jasmine's building, she bounded up the stairs and hammered on the door. As before, there was no response.

'Jasmine? Open up. It's Zoe.'

She tried the handle. The door swung open.

The moment it did, she knew something was badly wrong. The floor inside gleamed with fragments from a shattered wall mirror. Further up the narrow hallway, more evidence of destruction was evident: a broken vase, a trail of trampled soil running into an adjacent room.

The real devastation, however, was at the end of the trail – in the living room. The technical term, Zoe believed, was 'done over': chairs upturned, books and DVDs flung off shelves, a sofa slashed and spewing its foam guts, a TV lying on the floor with its screen kicked in. And at the centre of it all, trembling hands clutching a steak-knife, face streaked with tears, was Jasmine, cross-legged on the floor with her back against an overturned dining table.

'They were here,' was all she would say when Zoe demanded to know what had happened.

'Who? Who was here?'

'You said he wouldn't come after me and he did.'

'Ryland? He did this?'

Jasmine gave a contemptuous snort. 'Please. Men like him get others to do their dirty work.'

Zoe had a brief mental image of men in balaclavas, brandishing guns or baseball bats, forcing their way into the flat. Of Jasmine staggering backwards, pleading with them for her life.

'Did they hurt you? Did they touch you?'

Jasmine shook her head. 'Didn't need to. Powers of persuasion and all that. Told me this' – she gestured to the carnage around her – 'was a taste of what would happen to me if I didn't start singing from a different hymn-sheet sharpish.'

Zoe's stomach pitched. 'Aw Christ, tell me ye didnae . . . '

But she already knew the answer, and Jasmine's refusal to say it out loud, or meet her eye, all but confirmed it.

'So that's it? You're just gonnae let him get away wi it?'

Jasmine laughed contemptuously. 'Oh, wise up, darling. Him and his ilk have been getting away with it since records began. What's one more battered whore in the grand scheme of things?'

There was nothing Zoe could offer up by way of a response. She couldn't think of anything insightful to contribute, and in any event it was all too plain that whatever she came up with wasn't going to have the desired effect.

She lurched to her feet and left the flat.

She reached the police station on London Road at dusk. She'd timed her arrival well: as she stood scanning the car park she spotted Rona Cauley, a bowed figure fumbling with her keys outside a rickety-looking old Montego. Zoe made a beeline for her.

'I need tae talk tae ye.'

Cauley lifted her head momentarily, registered who Zoe was and turned away again, thrusting the car door open. 'I'm not on duty. Whatever it is, take it up with the desk sergeant.'

Zoe was taken aback. Where was the concern, the diligence, the compassion Cauley had shown her and Jasmine on the morning of the twenty-ninth?

'It's about Jasmine.'

Cauley paused momentarily, one foot already inside the car. 'Then I'm *definitely* not on duty.'

She got in and slammed the door shut. Zoe hammered on the window till Cauley lowered it with a scowl.

'Well?'

'Forget it. It's over. Finito. It's all fucked.' Cauley sighed at Zoe's expectant look. 'Your pal withdrew her statement earlier this evening. Said she'd got confused, that it wasn't Ryland who assaulted her after all. In fact, she made a specific point of saying it was all down to you putting ideas in her head – that you were the one who convinced her the bloke who attacked her was the guy off the TV.'

'That's . . . that's horseshit!'

Cauley smiled thinly. 'Aye, well, when you've got the right connections, you'll find there are only too many people willing to buy fertiliser off you. Anyway, it's all academic. Without Jasmine's statement, I've got zilch. Nada.'

She rolled up her window and was about to put her key in the ignition when Zoe wrenched the door open again.

'There must be something ye kin dae. What about my statement? I heard—'

'You heard someone who may or may not have been Dominic Ryland in the john, making remarks which may or may not have been in reference to a hooker who may or may not have been Jasmine Mooney. Don't take this the wrong way, but your recollections aren't worth the paper they're printed on.'

That stung. That *really* stung. Which is why what Zoe said next was designed to fatally wound rather than to advance any sort of coherent argument.

'She put her trust in you. You should've protected her. *You* did this to her.'

Cauley looked at her long and hard, her pinched features contorted into a scowl. 'You think I enjoy it, having every rape, every indecent assault, every domestic that comes through these doors chucked my way? "Give it to Cauley," they say. "She's a woman. She's got ovaries. She'll be able to empathise." Well, I'm sick to the back teeth of being empathetic, and I'm sick of taking on lost causes. I can't help people who won't help themselves.'

With that, she slammed her door shut, practically ripping Zoe's arm out of its socket, turned the key in the ignition and roared out of the car park, leaving a cloud of foul-smelling exhaust smoke behind her.

Zoe's mind was still racing when she stamped up the steps to her flat. It was only when she put her key in the door that she remembered Carol's message about the milk. She considered just saying she'd forgotten about it, but decided the recriminations would be more hassle than they were worth. So she doubled back and, across the road at the newsagents', picked up a two-litre bottle of skimmed. On impulse, she also chucked in a half-bottle of Smirnoff, to drown her sorrows. At the checkout, she found herself stuck behind an elderly man who seemed to think of something else he needed every time the cashier went to ring up his purchases. As she stood behind him trying to stave off the boredom, her eyes were drawn to the small TV on the shelf behind the counter.

It was showing some sort of current affairs discussion show. There were three people festooned on the sofas: the host – a chubby, ruddy-faced man in braces – and two guests – one female and one male. As Zoe tuned out the gabble between the cashier and customer and into the voices on the TV, she realised they were discussing the Ryland case. The woman – identified on-screen as Dr Sophie

Hennessy, a professional feminist permanently outraged on behalf of every woman everywhere – was railing against the iniquity of it all, stopping just short of saying they should lock him up anyway and to hell with due process. Her opponent – *Tribune* journalist Maurice Glaspie, a guy in his mid-thirties with hipster glasses and a positively shocking knitwear pullover – was treating the occasion as an excuse to indulge in the whataboutery that was his profession's stock-in-trade.

'Oh, I *certainly* think it's time for us to revisit the convention of publishing the identity of the accused,' he was saying, as Hennessy shook her head vigorously. 'If the past week's events have taught us anything, it's that a false accusation, for a crime as vile as the one we're discussing, has potentially devastating ramifications for the accused's reputation. Ramifications which he may never shake off, even after an acquittal. He'll always be pursued by those lingering murmurs of, "Well, there's no smoke without fire".'

'Devastating?' Hennessy's tone was incredulous. 'How about the devastation brought about by the trauma of being raped? I want— No, I want to make this point,' she insisted, raising a warning finger as Glaspie leaned forward, a retort on the tip of his tongue. 'This is about rather more than a politician inconvenienced by a public scandal, and I for one don't want to see any change to the law that would further inhibit women coming forward, or their attackers being convicted, as any move to give rapists the protection of anonymity is sure to do.'

'Isn't there a fundamental imbalance here?' mused the host. 'The purported victim has a right to anonymity, even in the event that a jury deems her to have been lying – or she retracts her original testimony, as is the case here.'

'A *tremendous* imbalance,' agreed the *Tribune*'s pontificator-in-chief, nodding so emphatically his head looked ready to come off his shoulders. 'The woman in question, whoever she is, can move on with her life despite having made an accusation she no longer wishes to stand by. But Dominic Ryland will forever be the MSP who was accused of rape. Just imagine,' he went on, holding up a dismissive hand as Hennessy opened her mouth to object, 'if this had actually reached a courtroom. Does anyone seriously believe he would have been afforded a fair trial after the media circus surrounding him? Now look, I really must stress that my concern is, first and foremost, with the victims.'

Hennessy rolled her eyes. 'And I'm sure the victims are incredibly grateful to you.'

'If you'd allow me to finish? As I was going to say, we mustn't forget that, in high-profile cases such as these, pressure is brought to bear not just on the accused but also on the accuser. We've seen, with the Ryland case, all sorts of efforts to identify the woman in question, which I can't imagine having been pleasant for her.' He shot Hennessy a chastising look over the tops of his glasses. 'You don't have a monopoly on compassion, you know, Sophie.'

Hennessy clearly had every intention of letting rip, but at that moment the host stepped in with good-natured but firm insistence. 'I'm sure we could spend all night discussing this matter and still be no closer to a consensus, but unfortunately we've run out of time. Maurice Glaspie, Sophie Hennessy, thank you very much.'

The two guests gave strained nods as the lights on them faded and the camera zoomed in on the rotund host. 'Whew!' He made a show of mopping his brow. 'I don't know about you at home, viewers, but I certainly felt the temperature going up several notches in here. Well, Dominic Ryland's recent brush with controversy seems not to have dented his chances of electoral success. A poll released today by Ipsos MORI, conducted since he was charged, puts him at the forefront of the race, giving him a clear, eight-point advantage over rival Fergus Leach. Earlier this evening, Mr Ryland had this to say . . . '

The scene cut from the studio to some pre-recorded footage. Ryland stood in the late afternoon sun on the doorstep of a Georgian-style manor, surrounded by a swarm of cameras and out-thrust microphones. An elegant, glacially attractive woman stood by his side, one arm looped through his, gazing at him with a level of devotion akin to beatification as he addressed the assembled throng.

'This has been,' he declared, in that plummy, silver-tongued voice of his, 'a tremendously stressful time for both myself and my wife, and I thank the press for covering the matter in their usual appropriate and measured manner.'

Zoe wasn't sure whether he was being sarcastic or not. With a voice like his, every utterance had the same smug, vaguely mocking tone to it.

'Of course, I was never in any doubt that common sense would prevail and the charges would be dropped. But I wish to stress that the real unfortunate in all of this is not me but the young lady who made the accusation in the first place. I've no idea what could have motivated her to concoct such an absurd story, beyond an ill-judged attempt to discredit me personally, and I trust that she will now receive the help and support she so clearly needs.'

Flashbulbs went off. A flurry of questions began, but Ryland raised his hands, appealing for calm.

'I wish to take the opportunity to reiterate my unequivocal support for our law enforcement agencies, as well as my commitment to law and order and to the safeguarding of family values . . . '

But Zoe wasn't listening. She'd had enough dishonesty and hypocrisy to fill several lifetimes. Taking matters into her own hands, she barged past the old man, still rabbiting on about the difficulty in getting hold of square sausage on Corfu, slammed her money on the counter and stormed out.

* * *

Back at the flat, she put the milk away, pausing briefly to read the post-it on the fridge door from Carol, reminding her that the plumber was coming at five tomorrow to fix the leak under the sink and to be home sharp to let him in. She poured herself a generous measure of Smirnoff and plonked herself on the sofa. A part of her was furious with Jasmine for her capitulation, but she knew the real blame lay with the system that had failed her and left her with no choice. And now, as things stood, Ryland was redeemed, resplendent in his triumph, and both sides of the gender debate seemed determined to use the whole sorry affair for political football, reducing Jasmine herself to a footnote.

She suddenly realised just how alone she felt. Carol wouldn't be back for hours yet. Not that Zoe particularly felt like talking to her about the evening's events. She had a pretty good idea what she'd say. Sophie Hennessy had covered most of that ground already: a whole lot of self-righteous gum-flapping and bugger all action.

She got out her phone and scrolled through her list of contacts. None of them were people she especially felt like seeing at this particular moment in time, and in any event she knew from bitter experience that trying to arrange a meet-up at this time on a weekday night was doomed to failure anyway. *School night. On an early the morra. Can't get a babysitter/dogsitter/boyfriendsitter at such short notice.*

It was then that she came to the number which Fin, in her boldness, had added earlier. Something told Zoe *she* wouldn't be burdened by such concerns as arranging childcare or getting a good night's kip before the next work-day, and that chin-stroking and empty platitudes wouldn't exactly figure high on her agenda either.

She let her thumb hover over the number for a few seconds, then dialled and put the phone to her ear.

8

The Pact

'Aye, well,' Fin said, 'what'd I tell ya? No sense crying over spilt jizz. It's how the world works. Chip?'

She angled the bag she'd been steadily munching her way through in Zoe's direction. Zoe took one and stuck it in her mouth, mainly to disguise the fact that she had nothing to say.

They were standing on the bridge just south of Finnieston, elbows on the handrail, gazing out at the expanse of the River Clyde below. Its proper name, thanks to its distinctive curved arch, was the Clyde Arc, but that sounded far too grandiose for the people of Glasgow, so everyone just called it the Squinty Bridge. At night, the arch was lit up in a pinky-purple glow, while the lights from the nearby Pacific Quay, home of the city's media hub, glistened in the still waters below. Beyond them, Zoe could see the Armadillo, the tourist cranes and the shimmering, all-glass façade of the Plaza Hotel. It was hard to believe her grubby wee flat in Partick was just a stone's throw away from all this opulence.

'It's like I said, Bright Eyes. The law doesn't exist to dispense justice. It exists to look after the interests of the Dominic Rylands of this world. Doesn't matter what sick shit they get up to, the likes of him'll never see the inside of a jail cell.'

She set her chips down on the rail so that she had full use of both hands for all the ardent gesticulation she clearly planned on doing.

'The trouble,' she said, 'is that the world ain't built to look out for the little guy. Every part of it, every line of every law, is designed with one simple goal in mind, and that's making sure the existing power structures get maintained. It's like the fella said: if voting changed anything, they'da made it illegal. Thing is, yer toffs, yer judges, yer prime ministers, they live in absolute naked terror of the masses noticing just how scummy the system is and rising up in revolt. So they settled on a compromise. Give 'em just enough of what they want: a welfare system that just about functions, a wage that gives 'em just about enough to get by, access to *Big Brother* and *River City* on tap, all the while drip-feeding 'em propaganda that tells 'em it's not the bankers and the politicians that're responsible for the state of the world – it's the miners, the immigrants, benefits claimants, take yer pick.

'And trouble is, it works. Everyone's ground down, apathetic. The one percent shits on us on a daily basis and ninety-nine percent of the other ninety-nine percent don't even notice. No one's asking the big questions. No one's saying, "Now wait just a minute. There's more of us than there are of them. If we all banded together and said we weren't gonna take this crap anymore, we could stop 'em getting away with murder". Literally. But tell 'em they might not get to watch *Strictly Come Bake-off* on a Saturday night if we upset the apple cart and all of a sudden everyone's kekking it. I tell ya, they could be rounding everyone up and putting us into camps and those lemons'd still be going, "Oh, but we mustn't rock the boat. It could be worse".'

And, with a brief 'there you go' shrug, she popped another chip in her mouth and fell silent.

'Jesus,' said Zoe. 'That was a bit full-on.'

Fin shrugged, mouth full. 'Can't handle the truth?'

'No, but it's just . . . I mean, it can't really be that bad . . . can it?'

'Face it, my friend. Your Mr Ryland's only the tip of the iceberg. He's just the one ya know about. It's the ones you've never heard of that ya really have to watch.'

Zoe spent a moment trying to figure out how she was supposed to watch people she'd never heard of, but Fin's mind had already moved on to fresh territory. She scrunched up her now empty chip bag and tossed it over her shoulder into the water, then turned to Zoe with a look of expectation.

'So what now?'

'Now?'

'Aye. You gonna just say "to hell with it", get absolutely stoatered and move on . . . ' She paused. 'Or ya wanna actually nail this fecker?'

'Nail him? Nail him how?'

'Bring him down. Do what it takes to make sure he never gets to treat another woman like he treated yer pal Jasmine. Make sure he never gets so much as another sniff of power as long as he lives.'

For a while, Zoe didn't say anything. Above all else, what got to her was the sense of powerlessness, of uselessness, of being sat on the sidelines watching events unfolding over which she had no control. She felt it in the Gavin Price business, she felt it in her day-to-day existence, and she sure as hell felt it in the way the Ryland case had been abruptly parked. Here today, gone tomorrow. Now, Fin was offering her . . . what? What exactly was she offering? A chance to make a difference? A chance to do something useful for once in her life? Ryland thought he could get away with doing whatever he liked just because he was rich, had connections and had had elocution lessons. Well, someone needed to show him that he couldn't, and given that no one else seemed willing to step up to the plate, why the hell shouldn't that someone be her? Jasmine might have pulled out of the fight, but that didn't mean *she* had to pack up and go home.

There was only one problem.

'How?' she said. 'I mean, where do I even start?'

Fin thought about it for a moment. 'OK, look, what do we know about yer man?' She began to count off on her fingers. 'One: he's a top politico with a lot riding on him, so he's not the only one who'd've had plenty to lose if this'd made it to the courts. Two: he's not above using hired muscle to shut people up, so I dunno 'bout you, but I'd *really* love to get a look at his Rolodex. Three: from what you've said, sounds like this Cauley's tried to nail him before and failed. Ergo, this wouldn't be the first time he's done something like this. So maybes it's never gone this far before, but I betcha a dollar to a dime he's been working his way up to this. You know how serial killers start out frying insects 'fore they graduate to humans? Same deal here, only think ex-girlfriends, one-night stands, other hookers, that wife of his. He'll have history.

'So here's what I'd do.' She had her back to the handrail, leaning on it with her arms outspread like the Cristo de la Concordia. 'I'd look into his past. Dig up all the dirt on him I could find. Leave no stone unturned. If we can't get him for Jasmine, let's get him for someone else.'

'We?'

Fin smiled. 'Nice girl like you's gonna need someone who knows the score watching her back. Stir up a hornets' nest and ya gotta be ready to get stung.' She straightened up, moving away from the handrail. 'You focus on the research. I'll start asking some questions.'

'Asking who?'

'Just some people I know.'

'What people?'

'People who know stuff. Guy like our Mr Family Values is bound to have made a few enemies for himself.'

* * *

As they walked back to the station at Finnieston, Zoe was already running through a plan of action in her head as to the shape her enquiries would take. As they made their way down to the open-air platform, Fin broke the silence.

'Lemme ask ya a question. What's in it for you?'

'How d'ye mean?'

'Ryland, Jasmine, all that jazz. What do you get out of this? Most people would've said "fuck it" and walked away.'

Zoe shrugged. 'Mibby I've just got a good heart?'

Fin sucked her teeth noisily. 'I don't buy that. We humans are pretty straightforward when it comes down to it. Ninety-nine times out of a hundred, if we do something it's cos we want something in return – even if it's just the satisfaction of being able to pat ourselves on the back and tell ourselves what good people we are.'

Zoe stared at her, half-laughing and half-appalled. 'My God, you're a total fucking cynic.'

'Total fucking realist, more like.' Fin picked at a stray bit of food stuck between her teeth with a blunt thumbnail.

Zoe folded her arms. 'All right, then, Miss Total Fucking Realist – what motivates you?'

'Motivates *me*?'

'Yeah – why're ye helping me? Ye don't have to. No one's holding a gun tae yer head, and I don't see what you get out of it.'

Fin gave an amused smile. 'Perhaps I've just got a thing for redheads with cute dimples and itty-bitty titties.'

'Thanks, I think.'

Is she hitting on me? Surely not. The two of them were like salt and sand, and in this particular case Zoe couldn't see opposites attracting. She had an idea of the sort of women Fin would be drawn to, and it sure as hell wasn't the ones like herself who wore nail-polish and shaved her pubes and didn't own a single pair of Doc Martens.

Her train was coming in – the last westbound service of the night on the Argyle Line. She turned back to Fin.

'Uh . . . this is me. You headed my way?'

Fin shook her head. 'Nah, you're all right. Gonna stay out for a bit. This town doesn't start to get *really* interesting till about three in the morning.'

The train came to a juddering, screeching halt behind them. Zoe was about to head aboard when Fin wordlessly extended her hand. For a moment, Zoe didn't move. She stared at the outstretched hand, reluctant, for reasons she couldn't quite grasp, to accept it. It seemed to represent something definitive – a pact that, once sealed, would be impossible to back out of.

Eventually, the whole thing became seriously awkward and she took Fin's hand and shook it, then quickly boarded the train just as the doors began to shut. She chose a seat on the opposite side from the platform and sank down low, a part of her already beginning to wonder if she'd made a mistake.

Oh well, she thought, as the train began to pull away. It could've been worse.

She could have insisted on drawing blood.

PART TWO

9

Research Mode

The following morning Zoe was, for once, early for work. She'd only slept for a couple of hours, but despite this, she felt as fresh as a daisy and more than ready to get stuck into her mission. But first there was the small matter of the morning shift at Neptune House to be endured. So, for the next three and a half hours, she gritted her teeth and got stuck into the task of cleaning up after the clattiest bunch of office drones in the Northern Hemisphere. As she hoovered, she listened to her colleagues blethering away about some woman who'd got back with her ex after aborting his baby only to discover that he was having an affair with her sister. It took her ages to cotton on that they were talking about a character in a soap opera rather than a real person. What empty lives they must lead, she thought.

At ten o'clock, she headed into the toilets, took off her hated nylon uniform and changed into a flimsy summer dress. The day was gearing up to be an absolute scorcher with a cloudless sky, and she knew it was going to be roasting where she was headed. Then, armed with an A4 notepad and a two-litre bottle of cherryade, both bought from the newsagent's round the corner, she headed up the road to the Mitchell Library, a resplendent Edwardian building with a distinctive green-domed roof, atop which a statue to Minerva, goddess of wisdom, kept a watchful eye on the roaring traffic of the M8 below. She circled round to the back entrance on Granville Street that was home to the lending library and internet café. There, she booked herself onto a computer, plonked her bottle on the desk beside her, opened her notepad and got to work.

By midday, she'd drunk most of the cherryade and had amassed several pages' worth of notes. In a lot of respects, it was like being back at uni, swotting for an essay on some film or other – only this time the subject of her research wasn't montage theory as applied to the crop-dusting scene in *North by Northwest* but a politician who got his end away through beating up sex workers. The principles were much the same: go in with an open mind, read a wide range of materials by different authors with differing perspectives, all the while taking copious notes – and, perhaps most importantly, don't try to force an angle. Do the research, and the shape of the narrative will reveal itself to you naturally. She was a little rusty at first, but she soon got back into the swing of things and began to positively relish her task.

As she continued to probe the nether regions of the World Wide Web, she began to build up a picture of her subject and where he'd come from. Dominic Michael Ryland was born in Bridgeton on 12 February 1971 to Jane Ryland, a school dinner lady, and a father whose name failed to crop up anywhere. Opinion was divided as to whether he'd died young or simply never been part of the picture, with Ryland having given vague and contradictory statements on the matter. Concrete details about his childhood were sparse, though there was no shortage of glorying in the fact that it had been characterised by deprivation and squalor; the 'sharing a toilet with five other families' anecdote was trotted out more than once. In spite of these difficulties, he managed to excel in the classroom and, in 1983, moved into secondary education at the prestigious – and expensive – Glenavon College.

'*How?*' Zoe wrote. '*Lottery win? Kindly benefactor? Disadvantaged kids scheme?*'

From then on, Ryland's trajectory was on the up and up. In the mid-eighties, his mother died suddenly after a brief illness, but that failed to put a dint in his studies and he left school with straight A's. His stint at Glenavon was followed by three years at Oxford, where he studied the holy trinity of Philosophy, Politics and Economics so beloved by the political classes. Here, it seemed, his attachment to the Conservative Party was born, and the student papers of the day were replete with tales of him wiping the floor with his opponents every Thursday night at the Oxford Union. There was even a grainy black-and-white photograph of him, a gangly youth in a penguin outfit, shaking hands with Mrs Thatcher – the widespread circulation of which, Zoe suspected, would do more damage to his fortunes with the Scottish electorate than a whole *string* of sexual assault allegations.

After Oxford came a series of research and SPAD jobs for various figures in the Party, including a brief spell as junior political secretary to the Home Secretary during the dying days of the Major regime. It was during this stint at the Home Office that he met and began a relationship with Alice Woolverton, a party researcher three years his senior, and twelve months later they were married. The wedding took place in Alice's home village in Kent, and the local paper covered the event in a fawning, double-page spread, complete with a photograph of the happy couple on the church steps.

After the Conservatives were ejected from power in 1997, Ryland dropped out of the political scene for a time, though Zoe managed to track his career with little difficulty. Like so many of his kind, he worked his way through a string of impressive-sounding positions – non-executive director, honorary board member, public relations consultant – for organisations as disparate as human rights charities and a supplier of munitions to the British Army. Then, in the mid-2000s, the Rylands came north, settling in the South Lanarkshire village of Thorntonhall, from where Ryland continued to manage his various interests, including investments in a number of what sounded suspiciously like holding companies, as well as his weekly column in the *Spectator* – a gig which, at last count, was netting him north of £100,000 a year. A brief perusal of some back issues told Zoe that his writing consisted of regurgitating the same half-dozen polemics about morality and social justice with slightly different wording.

Throughout the next decade, there were a handful of seemingly half-hearted forays into the political arena. In 2006 he stood as a councillor in a by-election in the East Kilbride West ward but lost to the SNP. The following year he stood again, this time on the regional list for Central Scotland in the 2007 Scottish Parliamentary election, but as the Tories' fourth-placed candidate would have needed a minor miracle to get himself elected. He tried his luck again in the 2009 EU Parliament elections, only to once more end up an also-ran. His breakthrough, if you could call it that, came in the 2011 Scottish Parliament election, when he once again made an appearance on the regional ballot. Third on the list, the path to Holyrood looked set to be denied to him yet again – until the candidate placed second was forced to resign a week after the election amid accusations of financial impropriety, meaning that the seat automatically went to the next name on the list. So Ryland was in, less by his own guile than by virtue of a fluke in an arcane electoral system – and the rest, as they say, was history.

Zoe leaned back, stretched her arms above her head, rubbed her stiff, sweat-soaked neck and looked up at the wall clock. It was three minutes to one.

Somehow, in the space of those three minutes, she managed to high-tail it back up the road to Neptune House, dive into a toilet cubicle, struggle back into her uniform and bomb it to the sign-in book, under the disapproving eye of her supervisor, Valerie Shaw-cross – a woman with the temperament one would expect of someone who'd given the best years of her life to cleaning up other people's effluent.

'Cutting it a little fine, aren't we, Ms Callahan?' she said as Zoe added her autograph.

'Ye know me, Val. Livin' life on the edge.'

She was quite pleased with that. It kept a smile on her face for all of the next five minutes, until reality set in and she remembered she still had another two hours and fifty-five to contend with.

Somehow, she got through the afternoon shift, though time dragged like a Basset Hound's nut-sack. Come four o'clock, she once again headed for the web café at the Mitchell, only to find that the place had filled up in her absence and all the terminals were occupied. Contenting herself with the knowledge that she could pick things up again tomorrow morning, she took herself to Charing Cross Station and, in the relative cool afforded by its stone walls and semi-subterranean design, sat with her notes in her lap, assembling them into some semblance of order. She thought she had the overall sequence of events figured out. It was filling in the numerous gaps that still existed in the timeline that was proving to be a headache.

She was so preoccupied that, the next time she looked up, it was after five and she'd allowed several westbound trains to come and go without even registering them. As a result, it was a quarter to six by the time she finally arrived back at Dumbarton Road and tramped up the stairs to the flat. She was still in high spirits, and even the fact that she'd spent the duration of the journey with her face smashed into a fellow commuter's sweaty armpit couldn't put a damper on her sense of achievement. For the first time in ages – since she'd left uni, in fact – she actually felt like she was doing something worthwhile. She was motivated, driven, and she had a reason to get up in the morning beyond the knowledge that, if she didn't, she'd soon find herself picking up her P45. And nothing was going to detract from that.

Or so she thought.

She got in to find Carol standing in the hallway in her work outfit, balled fists pressed into her sides, and the first words out of her mouth when Zoe stepped over the threshold weren't *nice to see you* or *hard day at the office, dear?* or *come in and put your feet up* but rather—

'What the hell time d'you call this?'

It was so out of kilter with Zoe's buoyant mood that for a moment she just stared back, face frozen in a goofy grin.

'The plumber. Five o'clock. Ring any bells?'

The smile left Zoe's face. She shut her eyes and winced. From the darkest recesses of her mind, she recalled the post-it on the fridge door – and the various other times Carol had mentioned it in person before that. At least twice, if not more.

'Shit,' she muttered.

'I had to call work and tell them I was waiting in for him. It's open mic night tonight. They had to get set up without me.'

Say nothing, Zoe. You done bad. Just take your telling-off like a good girl.

She rolled her eyes. 'What, they need ye tae supervise 'em plugging in a microphone and putting out some chairs?'

'That's not the point!' Carol all but shouted. 'Where were you?'

'The trains were off, awright? I got home as soon as I could.' The lie was out of her mouth before she was even conscious of coming up with it.

'Uh-huh? And what if I told you I checked the website and every single train for the last two hours has been bang on time?'

'So you're keeping tabs on me now?' Somehow, despite being caught in a lie, in Zoe's mind this revelation nonetheless gave her the moral high ground.

'I'd love it if I didn't have to! So where were you?'

Zoe glowered at her feet. 'I'm no gonnae answer that.'

'Why not?'

'Cos I don't answer tae you. Just cos I share a bed wi ye disnae mean I have tae share everything else.'

They stood there, facing one another, Zoe defiant, Carol consumed by a silent, seething anger. A part of Zoe wanted to just come clean about where she'd been – explain that she'd been off doing A Good Thing. And God knows, Carol spent enough time banging on about being the change you wished to see. She could hardly object. But that was just it. Zoe knew she could, and would.

Eventually, Carol stirred. 'You know,' she said pointedly, 'one of the essential components of a relationship is a willingness to be honest with one another.'

Zoe became very still. She suddenly felt quite calm. 'That a fact?'

Carol gave a little half-frown. She obviously sensed from Zoe's tone that this was going somewhere, even if she hadn't a clue where. 'I like to think so, yes.'

A moment of dead silence passed between them.

'Cos obviously *you* tell *me* absolutely everything.'

'Well—'

'Like, let's say, for instance, you took a phone call fae Anna Scavolini way back in May saying Gavin Price's trial was getting the go-ahead, obviously you'd've told me about that immediately, wouldn't ye?'

She saw the colour drain from Carol's face. *Oooh, jackpot, baby.*

Carol swallowed heavily, her Adam's apple bobbing like a tennis ball. 'How long have you known?'

At least she hadn't tried to deny it.

'Long enough.'

For several moments, neither of them spoke. Zoe was glad she'd kept quiet about the fact that she knew until now. If she'd confronted Carol at the time, she wouldn't have had the opportunity to deploy it now, at so perfect a time. And now Carol was speechless, unable to dredge up any sort of a response that could justify her behaviour.

'Were ye *ever* gonnae tell me?' said Zoe, finally filling the silence. 'Or were ye just gonnae wait till I heard about it on the STV news when they read out the verdict?'

Silence from Carol.

'Cos lemme tell ye,' Zoe went on, 'I'm going tae that trial, come hell or high water, and if you think ye can stop me, *boy* are you in for a shock.'

'We'll talk about this when I get home,' Carol muttered. Then she grabbed her bike, propped up against the wall, and headed for the door, squeezing past Zoe.

'Will we?' Zoe shouted after her. 'Or will we just say nothing like we always do?'

Carol ignored her, her footsteps and the wheels of her bike clattering down the stairwell as she made her escape.

Zoe remained where she was, still seething, stoking her sense of grievance. On one level, she was absolutely delighted with herself for having had the presence of mind to throw the trial back in Carol's face. But it felt like a hollow victory. This was what their life had become: her getting told off like a naughty child for being late home, and hitting back in turn with some riposte designed to do little other than wound and shut down any hope of them having an actual conversation that got to the root of the issue. It wasn't healthy and it sure as hell wasn't the basis for a balanced relationship. At some point, she realised, they'd stopped being a couple and become something more akin to parent and child.

And, when you put it that way, it was possibly just as well they hardly ever had sex anymore.

10

Day Out

The following morning, Zoe left the flat with a sour taste in her mouth, the previous day's optimism having all but evaporated. Things only got worse upon arriving at the library, where, in a fairly short space of time, her research hit a brick wall. The gaps in her timeline stubbornly refused to fill themselves, and the answers to the various questions she'd tasked herself with answering – like who put Ryland through private school if his mother was so impoverished? – continued to elude her. Most importantly, there was no sign of the smoking gun she'd been hoping to find – something that would prove he already had form for what he'd done to Jasmine. She wasn't sure what she'd hoped to find, beyond a vague sense that she'd know it when she saw it. Now, she began to wonder if he really was as squeaky-clean as his public persona suggested. Certainly there was no evidence of any previous brushes with the law, which presumably meant that whatever had drawn him to Cauley's attention before hadn't resulted in an actual charge. She briefly toyed with straight up asking Cauley, then realised Cauley would want to know why *she* wanted to know and dismissed the idea as fanciful nonsense.

Once again, she couldn't help but compare the situation in which she found herself to her uni days. Just like with her essays, she'd done a whole lot of research but was now left with next to no idea as to what she was going to do with all the data. The research stage was the part she'd always enjoyed the most – watching the films, reading the articles, making bullet points, convincing herself she was home and dry because she'd amassed pages and pages of references. But actually doing something with all that material, actually fashioning it into a coherent argument that didn't simply regurgitate what others had already said – that had always been the real challenge.

On top of all that, the sun was shining directly on the screen, making it hard to read the words on it. And the mouse, its innards clogged with Christ-knows-what, wasn't doing what she told it to. Even the heat, a minor irritant yesterday, seemed altogether more oppressive now. By late morning, she'd all but abandoned her original reason for being there and was scrolling through Facebook, watching silly YouTube videos and generally doing things that would have given Tim Berners-Lee an aneurysm.

The only possible lead which she supposed might bear fruit came in the form of a couple of references to an old girlfriend from Ryland's Oxford days: one Carmel Seabold, an irritatingly pert Sloaney type seen dangling on his arm in a photo accompanying an article about an address given to the student union by some hot-shot American politician. A few months later, an unrelated article mentioned in passing that Ryland had recently broken up with his girlfriend of seven months, the same Carmel Seabold. Five minutes on LinkedIn allowed Zoe to trace the woman to a London-based PR firm whose specialty was 'bespoke solutions in strategic risk management', whatever the hell that meant. Surmising that fortune favours the bold, Zoe took herself to a secluded corner of the library and dialled the number on the website.

'Carmel Seabold's office,' came the chirpy, Estuary-accented voice at the other end of the line.

'Uh . . . is that Carmel Seabold?'

'No, this is her secretary,' said the voice, in a tone that left Zoe feeling vaguely foolish. 'Have you an appointment with Ms Seabold?'

'No . . . but she's expecting my call. Is she available?'

She was using her best telephone voice – a forced but passable imitation of the sort of people she'd rubbed shoulders with during her days at Willow Bank Academy. There was more than a bit of Anna in there.

'Who shall I say is calling?'

Zoe's eyes darted to the display of books in front of her. *Fifty Great Novels by Women to Read Before You Die*. 'Angela Carter,' she said, then instantly regretted not picking something more obscure.

'Just one moment. I'll see if she's available.'

For the next fifteen seconds or so, Zoe was treated to a sped-up, techno-infused version of Beethoven's Fifth Symphony. Then, before she even had time to formulate a plan of attack, the music was replaced by a dial tone, followed by a click and a sharp, officious 'Yes?'

'Um . . . hi. Carmel Seabold?'

'Do I know you?'

'You don't, no. Uh, my name's Angela Carter and I'm with the, uh, the *Oxford Standard*. Um . . . we're doing a series of articles on former Oxford University alumni, and I was wondering if I could have just a few moments of your time to answer a couple of quick questions.'

Nicely played, Zoe. Her brief and altogether miserable stint a few years ago in a call centre was actually paying off.

'I really don't,' came the reply. 'How did you get this number? I've never heard of you or your paper.'

'I found it on the company website. Look, I'll level with you.' She was talking faster, her voice becoming increasingly hushed and breathless. 'I'm hanging by a *thread* here. My editor's just *looking* for an excuse to let me go, and our response rate so far's been just *dire*. If I have to go back to him empty-handed . . . '

For a moment, Carmel was silent, and Zoe was afraid she'd hung up. Then she heard an irritable sigh. 'All right, then. Ask your questions. But I swear to you, if we're not done in five minutes, I'm putting the phone down.'

And so Zoe asked her questions, lying with a fluency and dexterity that left her thoroughly impressed with herself. It was all suitably generic stuff – What have you done since you graduated? How many of your classmates do you keep in touch with? How would you rate your university experience out of ten? – and she kept it short and sweet, conscious all the time of Carmel's growing impatience.

'Oh, just one more thing you might be able to help me with. I've a few names on my list I've not managed to track down. Mibby you might know where I can find 'em?'

She could practically hear Carmel's eye-roll. 'All right, go on.'

She picked another name at random from the display. 'Elizabeth Bowen.'

'Doesn't ring any bells.'

'Sarah Waters.'

'No.'

'Dominic Ryland.'

Dead silence. She couldn't even hear Carmel breathing.

'You still there?'

When Carmel finally spoke again, her voice was just about cracking as she struggled to control it. 'What do you want?'

'I'm just trying to—'

'No, you're not. You're not *just* anything. I don't know who you are, I don't know what your game is, but I'm hanging up now, and if you ever call this number again, I shall be contacting the police and filing a charge of harassment.'

With a firm click, the line went dead.

Zoe wondered what to make of this. No question about it, name-dropping Ryland had got her a response, but it was hardly the bombshell evidence she'd been hoping for. What exactly did it prove? *His ex put the phone down when I mentioned his name. That* shows *he's a bastard.* Maybe it did, but all she'd succeeded in doing was to shore up her own already-formed impressions of the man. And she wasn't the one she had to convince.

She dialled Fin's number.

'Hey, Bright Eyes. What's the score?'

'So I've been doing what you said – looking into Ryland's past.'

'And?'

'And I've got fuck-all. Couldnae even find a parking ticket wi his name on it. And the one ex I found wouldnae speak to me.'

'Colour me shocked. Cover their tracks well, don't they?'

Zoe had been hoping for something slightly more constructive. She could hear music in the background, punctuated periodically by what sounded like the whack of a pool-cue. She had a sudden mental image of Fin sitting in a bar somewhere with her feet up, a tall glass of Guinness by her side.

'What about you?' she said pointedly. 'You manage to come up wi anything?'

'Nah, not a dickie-bird. Early days, though.'

Just as she'd expected.

'Nothing at all? What about they people ye said ye knew? The ones ye were gonnae ask.'

'It's in hand. Don't sweat it. You'll get frown-lines.'

'Who are they, anyway? These contacts of yours.' She was beginning to wonder whether Fin's 'people' were even real, or if it had just been something she'd said to sound impressive.

When Fin next replied, there was a note of tetchiness in her voice, almost as if she'd sensed Zoe's doubt. 'The kind ya don't wanna rush.

Not if ya know what's good for ya. The moment I hear something, I'll bell ya. Till then, play it cool, else I'll start thinking you've got separation anxiety.'

And, with a throaty cackle, she too hung up.

Zoe retreated to the nearest Burger King, her mood despondent. All the enthusiasm and optimism of the previous day had evaporated like so much hot air. She felt like an idiot. She'd been fooling herself, kidding on she was like Hardy Drew and the Nancy Boys or any number of other amateur sleuths whose books she'd lapped up when she was younger. She wasn't. She was just a daft lassie with too much time on her hands and a pressing need to do something to stave off her own feelings of inadequacy.

She sat at the window, chewing glumly on her Bacon Double Cheeseburger. Each time she came here, she told herself this was positively the last one. And yet she couldn't help herself, despite knowing they were bad for her, despite knowing what Carol would say if she knew this was where she was spending her lunchtime. She'd read all the articles – about what it did to your heart, about the miserable lives the animals lived before ending up as a piece of processed meat in a little cardboard box – but there was just something comfortably predictable about it. When the chips were down, she could always rely on it to make her feel better for all of ten minutes, before all the familiar sensations of inadequacy and purposelessness returned.

Today, as she sat there working her jaw mechanically, the act of chewing got her mind going. It occurred to her that there was one thing she *could* do that she hadn't attempted already. Thorntonhall wasn't a big place, and in any event the law required anyone standing for election to declare their home address. So she wolfed down the remains of her burger and hurried back across the road to the Mitchell, still sucking salt and grease off her fingers. She jumped onto a computer and, after a mere five minutes, had found Ryland's address on the Electoral Commission website and pinpointed its location on Google Maps. A visit to the ScotRail website told her that a train left Central Station on the East Kilbride line for Thorntonhall every hour. If she hurried, she'd make the next one. She made the decision then and there to dinghy her afternoon shift at Neptune House and head out there right now.

As she hurried up the steps to the station, she rang Valerie on her mobile and said she'd come down with something. Valerie made a lot of noise about short notice, but she accepted Zoe's account and told her she'd do her return-to-work first thing on Monday. Zoe rang off with a perverse feeling of satisfaction at having pulled the wool over the old cow's eyes, bought a return ticket at the kiosk and boarded the train with moments to spare.

Some twenty-five minutes later, the train rolled into a picturesque little station consisting of a single platform and a couple of squat huts. Zoe was the only passenger to disembark, already feeling like she was trespassing somewhere where she wasn't welcome. The feeling only increased as she made her way up the little path and followed the deserted main road as it led north into the village. Thorntonhall was only about six miles south of Glasgow, but it might as well have been deep in the heart of the English shires. Well-tended hedges and leafy evergreens shielded stately homes from the prying eyes of nosy neighbours. She could see why Ryland had made this his base of operations: the population might be tiny, but she bet a penny to a pound she knew which way every last one of them voted.

Ryland's home was on the outskirts of the eastern edge of the village, just off a small country lane that wound its way north before eventually joining the Westerfield Road leading back to Glasgow. As the house came into view, Zoe once again began to feel decidedly foolish. What was she expecting to happen? The chambermaid to come running out screaming, blouse torn open and Ryland's hand-print on her exposed breast?

She came to a stop in front of two electronically-operated gates. A stone wall encircled the garden. It was low enough to be able to see the sprawling bungalow beyond it, but the thought of climbing over it seemed to her a step too far. If anyone saw her, they'd be well within their rights to get straight on the blower to the police.

She followed the wall as it curved round the well-tended lawn. At the side of the house, there was a bolt-on conservatory – a modern wood-and-glass monstrosity that clashed horrendously with the rest of the building. As Zoe continued to follow the course of the wall, she saw movement inside and immediately dropped to a crouch. Slowly raising her head, she peered over the wall and watched as Ryland crossed from one side of the conservatory to the other, a legal pad tucked under his arm. He was wearing a wool pullover and an open-necked shirt – the universal 'casual' uniform favoured by male politicians of every stripe. As she continued to watch, he settled into a wicker armchair, folded one leg over the other, opened his pad, produced a pen and began to write.

Bent over virtually double, Zoe continued to follow the wall's course. At the back of the house, it bordered an expansive field of uncut wheat, which she concluded would offer her more cover than squatting on her hunkers out in the open. When standing, the wheat reached up to her midriff, and when she lay down on her front, it covered her completely while still giving her a clear view of the conservatory and of Ryland. There wouldn't be another train back to Glasgow for a while yet, so there seemed no reason not to stay put for now. She wasn't going to stay there all day – just watch him for a bit and have a think about what to do next.

Or so she thought. Perhaps it was down to boredom, or several restless nights in a row, or the warmth of the sun on her back and shoulders, or a combination of all three, but within fifteen minutes she was sound asleep.

She came to with a start, disoriented and aching all over. She blinked her bleary eyes, forcing them into focus. The air was markedly cooler now. The sun had moved west and partially disappeared behind a patch of cloud. She looked at her phone. Just gone four. She'd slept for nearly three hours.

Her eyes darted to the conservatory. There was no sign of Ryland. The legal pad lay abandoned on the chair. She lurched to her feet, her gaze whipping from one end of the house to the other with no rhyme or reason as she desperately tried to locate him.

As she stood there, trying to will her fluttering heart back to its normal rhythm, she became aware of a sound, incongruous against the backdrop of all this pastoral tranquillity: the roar of a car engine being gunned at full tilt. It was drawing nearer – coming, she judged, down the Westerfield Road. She hurried to the edge of the field in time to see a black Mercedes pulling to a halt outside the electronic gates. And then the gates were opening, the Merc was cruising in, gravel crunching under its tyres, and there was Ryland, striding out of the house to meet it with what, even from a distance, was clearly hostile intent.

As Zoe continued to watch, the driver's door opened and a man got out. He was dressed in what looked to be an expensive suit that went well with the flash motor. That was the only part of him that did, however. He was small and ratty-looking, with close-cropped hair and a scraggy beard. A tattoo of a snake coiled around his left ear and ran down the side of his neck, disappearing into his shirt collar. He spread both arms and grinned at Ryland – a gesture which wasn't returned. Zoe could see Ryland gesticulating angrily at his guest, and she could imagine what he was saying even if she couldn't hear him: *What the hell are you doing here?* The tattooed man merely continued to grin, jaw moving up and down as he did that gum-chewing thing which so many hard men think makes them look harder still. Words continued to be exchanged, but there was no way Zoe was in a position to hear them – not without getting closer.

Keeping low, she followed the wall back towards the road. She stopped about halfway to the gate, and, perched on her knees, raised her head as high as she dared, watching the two men from the cover of the wall. She still couldn't make out what was being said, but she heard Ryland's aggrieved protestations and the mocking retorts of his visitor. The tattooed man reached out and patted Ryland on the arm. As he did so, Zoe saw – or thought she saw – him slipping something into Ryland's pocket. Something small and easily missed. A sachet of something, perhaps. But then, she could have been mistaken. Perhaps she'd only seen what she *wanted* to see.

She suddenly remembered she was supposed to be on a fact-finding mission, searching for evidence of wrongdoing on Ryland's part. She wasn't sure if that was what this was, but there was no denying that everything about the setup looked dodgy as anything. She raised her phone above the wall and snapped a bunch of pictures. She didn't look through the viewfinder – to do so would have wasted time and risked being seen. All she could do was to take as many snaps as she could and hope that at least one of them would turn out OK.

The men's voices fell silent. Footsteps tramped across the gravel. Zoe lowered her phone and risked another peep over the wall. The one with the tattoos was getting back into his car while Ryland looked on, arms folded defiantly. The Merc performed a one-eighty-degree turn, kicking up a cloud of dust and gravel, then roared through the gates.

Moving as fast as she could while still keeping out of Ryland's view, Zoe hurried out into the lane in time to see the car roaring off into the distance, heading north towards Glasgow at full speed. She raised her phone, hoping to get a snap of its licence plate, but it was already too late for that. She was left standing in the middle of the little road, watching helplessly as it vanished into the distance.

11

G-Spot

Zoe got back to the flat just after six. Carol was long gone – the Friday night rush would be well underway by now. She flopped down on the sofa, got out her phone and went through her snaps of Ryland and his tattooed visitor again. She'd already examined them on the train ride back, but she wanted to take another look in case she'd missed anything important. Most of the pics were blurry and would be of no use to anyone, but one had come out relatively clear. Clear enough, at least, for the visitor's features to be reasonably visible, snake tattoo included, though Ryland himself was cropped out of the shot. She stared at it intently, unable to shake the feeling that she'd alighted on something significant, even if she didn't yet know what.

She decided to call Fin.

'It's me,' she said, when Fin picked up.

'Hello, Me.' Fin's voice boomed through loud and clear. 'I was just thinking about ya. To what do I owe, et cetera?'

'Think I mighta found something. Could be nothing, but I could do with running it by somebody. Can we hook up?'

'Oh, *honey*. I thought you'd never ask.'

Zoe rolled her eyes. 'Shut it. Ye know what I meant. So can we meet?'

'That all depends. Can you find the G-Spot?'

''*Scuse* me?' Zoe all but spluttered.

'Simple enough question, I'da thought. So d'ya know where it is or not?'

Zoe tried to think what to say. She wondered if she'd genuinely misheard, but it didn't seem likely. There weren't exactly a whole lot of words the one she thought she'd heard could be mistaken for. She ought to have responded with a polite 'fuck off', but it was too late for that now. Fin had heard her outburst – and, presumably, had got the response she'd been looking for.

'Well, I like to think so,' she muttered.

'Grand,' said Fin. 'See ya there at eight.' And hung up.

The G-Spot – as Google reliably informed her, and much to her acute sheepishness – was in fact a lesbian bar, located on West Regent Street near the city centre. She almost didn't dare show her face given what a prize tit she'd just made of herself – but that would mean dropping the thread of her investigation, and she couldn't bring herself to do that. So she wolfed down a quick dinner of instant Pot Noodle, then set about getting ready.

After spending the afternoon tramping around Thorntonhall and lying in wheat fields, she was feeling decidedly grubby, so before heading out she hopped in the shower, then set about the painstaking tasks of shaving her legs and other assorted bits and pieces, plucking her eyebrows into perfect arches and applying enough makeup to stock a king-size counter at The Body Shop and still have some left over for when supplies ran out. For good measure, she put on her skimpiest thong and girliest party-dress as well, and completed the picture with a pair of stilettos with heels long and sharp enough to take your eye out. She told herself it had nothing to do with impressing anyone, or doing everything she could to differentiate herself from the crowd of butch barflies she was expecting to encounter where she was headed. Nothing at all. She'd have followed the same routine regardless of where she was going or who she was meeting.

Honest.

She arrived at the G-Spot just after eight and stood outside, staring up at the flickering neon sign, fully convinced that Fin had chosen this place to ensure maximum discomfort on her part. She paced a bit to calm her nerves, wishing she had a cigarette to smoke – for some reason, she figured it would help – then took a deep breath and headed in.

Inside wasn't at all what she'd been expecting. In her mind, she'd pictured a scene straight out of *Bound*: air thick with smoke; Johnny Cash droning on the loudspeaker; brawny, middle-aged bulls in biker vests eyeing her menacingly, pool-cues in hand. Actually, the place looked pretty much like every other quasi-trendy nightclub she'd ever been in, and a lot of the customers were dressed and made up in much the same manner as herself. Chances were their depilatory regimes, too, were as exhaustive as her own. Only a few of the clientele came close to fitting the stereotype she'd had in her head. In fact, if she'd just wandered in randomly off the street, her only clue that this wasn't Just Another Nightclub would have been the fact that there wasn't a man in sight.

None of this, of course, made her feel like any less of an interloper, and she half-expected to feel a firm hand on her shoulder at any moment, prefacing a challenge to provide proof of her lesbian credentials.

Fin was waiting for her at a table in an alcove near the bar, a bottle of Pils already uncorked in front of her. She raised an arm above her head in greeting and beckoned her over.

'Made it, then? Find the place easy enough?'

'Seems so.' Zoe took her seat, phone already in her hand. 'So here's what—'

'Hold yer horses. Whatcha drinkin'?'

Zoe settled on a mojito and waited while Fin waved a waitress over. Once her order had been taken, she filled Fin in on her trip to Thorntonhall and the encounter between Ryland and the tattooed man.

'Hmph.' Fin held Zoe's phone in both hands, scrutinising the picture. 'I don't know him from Adam, but I'll tell ya one thing: he's got "hood" written all over him.'

Zoe reached for her phone back.

'Hold on a tick.'

Fin's thumbs danced over the screen as she tapped in some commands. A second or so later, Zoe heard Fin's own phone tinkling in her jacket pocket.

'There.' Fin handed Zoe back her phone. 'I'll show it around, see if anyone knows him.'

'Lemme guess – yer contacts. The ones who don't like being rushed?'

Fin pulled a face that was somewhere between a sneer and a smirk. 'You're catching on. Anyway, don't be getting all hot under the collar. Odds are someone's gonna recognise him. S'not exactly a face you'd forget.'

She leaned back in her seat, folding her arms behind her head. She had on one of those loose drop arm vests, which offered a clear view not only of the band of her bra but also a plethora of underarm hair, black and slick with sweat. There was something oddly exciting to Zoe about this display – a brazenness which bordered on the erotic.

The waitress returned with Zoe's mojito. She took a lengthy draw from the straw, then looked up to find Fin leaning sideways, eyeing up her bare leg.

'That a tat?'

'Oh, um . . .' Zoe self-consciously tucked her leg under her chair. 'Yeah. It's just . . .'

'Oooh, check *you*, ya rebel! C'mon, let's see it.'

With some reluctance, Zoe brought her leg out from under the table and angled the tattoo in Fin's direction. That wasn't enough for Fin, though, who grabbed hold of the leg and laid it in her own lap to inspect it.

'A chameleon. Sweet.'

'A what?'

'Chameleon. Type of reptile from sub-Saharan Africa. They're shape-shifters. Change colour to match their environment.'

'I thought it was a gecko,' said Zoe, feeling inexplicably sheepish.

'Oh,' said Fin. 'And there was me thinking it was some kinda personal statement.'

As she spoke, she stroked the area of skin in question with her pinkie, sending a bolt of nervous energy shooting up Zoe's leg to her gut. Zoe laughed, partly to cover up her own embarrassment and partly at the absurdity of reading so much into a meaningless tat she'd got when she was too minced to know what was happening.

'It's just a funny-looking lizard,' she protested, retrieving her leg and stowing it safely under the table. 'Disnae mean anything. Now that' – she gestured to the two Venus symbols on Fin's neck – 'is a statement.'

Fin shrugged. 'Well, see, that's the thing about me, Bright Eyes. I'm perfectly cognisant of the fact that, whatever advances might've been made the last couple o' decades, there's still a big chunk of society that'd prefer it if loud, rude dykes like me shut up and crawled back into the shadows, outta sight, outta mind. Well, I'm not gonna do that. And this' – she tapped her tattoo with a pair of fingers – 'this is my way of saying, "See me, this is who I am. And if you don't like it, get the fuck outta my way, cos I ain't moving for *you*".'

She leaned back and swigged deeply on her beer, eyes sharp on Zoe as if challenging her to disagree. Zoe wouldn't have dared, not least because she didn't think she'd survive to tell the tale if she did. She'd long since come to the realisation that there was nothing on this earth that Fin didn't have views on, and that none of them could remotely be described as moderate. Nor was she at all shy about letting people know precisely where she stood.

Still, as the evening progressed, and with it the refills, Zoe relaxed somewhat. Fin proved to be entertaining company, with a rare turn of phrase and a seemingly never-ending array of anecdotes up her sleeve. She also seemed to know who everyone in the bar was, staff and patrons alike, telling Zoe their names, stories and all their intimate secrets. Zoe couldn't help but note, though, that not one of them came over to say hello. In fact, much like at the self-defence class, she was left with the impression that people were giving her a wide berth. Fin, for her part, seemed singularly unperturbed about her status as a black sheep. She waxed lyrical about this subject and that, giving Zoe her expert analysis of a variety of hot topics, from the American global war complex to the sorry state of modern feminism.

'It's such a fucking sad middle-class circle-jerk,' she said of the latter. 'It's all safe spaces and trigger warnings and micro-aggressions. Women's studies wonks writing in the bloody *Guardian*, or brain-dead kiddies on Tumblr who've never cracked a copy of Germaine Greer but think they know everything there is to know about the Struggle. Fucking chin-strokers who reckon getting a few extra women into boardrooms represents some glorious advancement for the Sisterhood. Cos let's face it, if you're a woman living in a mud-hut somewhere in Africa or wherever or working some shit zero-hours job to put food in yer kids' mouths, then fifty-fifty representation for the one percent ain't a solution, it's a kick in the fucking teeth. I tell ya, this country doesn't need more gender studies graduates and women politicians. What it needs is a fucking revolution.

'These people,' she gestured vaguely around her, 'these . . . sheep. They're not like you 'n' me. Not switched on.' She tapped the side of her head for emphasis – the universal gesture for both deep intellect and batshit insanity.

Zoe nodded slowly, wondering what she could possibly have done to convey to Fin that they were of like minds. As it happened, she did actually agree with a fair amount of what Fin had been saying – or at least with her overall treatise that the world was a fucked-up and unfair place – though she couldn't help but find Fin's vision of how things *should* be a whole lot scarier than the present reality. Mind you, on a certain level she had to respect that. Strictly speaking, she'd never really thought of herself as much of a feminist. She believed in equality of the sexes, sure, but she'd never been altogether comfortable with the label, tending to associate it with people who were a bit sanctimonious, a bit overly prescriptive, and – worst of all – seriously lacking in the humour department. Case in point: Carol, who had a tendency to succumb to these traits whenever she got going about an issue that was important to her. But Fin's feminism – if that was even the right word for it – wasn't like that. There was something primal about it, something dangerously exciting. She didn't simply want to swap one set of rigidly defined rules for another set that was more to her liking. She wanted to tear up the rulebook, piss on it, pour petrol on it, set it on fire and obliterate the ashes with a targeted nuclear strike.

She looked at her phone and was surprised to see that it was nearly eleven. They'd been blabbing – or rather, Fin had been blabbing and Zoe had been listening – for almost three hours.

Fin glanced up, catching her in the act. 'Got somewhere ya need to be?'

'No,' said Zoe, turning her phone face-down to avoid the temptation of looking again. 'No, I'm good.'

'Right.' There were the inklings of a snide smile on Fin's lips.

'Thought maybe you needed to get home to *Carol*.' She said the word in a mocking, singsong sort of voice that immediately put Zoe on the defensive. 'So tell me, she cool with all this?'

'All what?'

'This.' Fin spread her arms. 'You out on yer own on a Friday night, all these fine eligible vadgitarians at yer disposal? She not worried ya might fall into enemy hands?'

Zoe shrugged noncommittally, studiously examining her mojito.

Fin's smile deepened. 'Ah. She doesn't know.'

'Well, so what?' Zoe shot back, hackles rising. 'She's no my keeper. I can dae what I like.'

'Glad to hear it. Nothing more pathetic in this world than a kept woman. Still, gotta say, I'm surprised.'

Zoe eyed her suspiciously. 'How?'

'Oh, you know – sounded to me like you two had quite the cosy little domestic going on. Nice little shared mortgage together, taking it in turns doing the dishes, curling up on the sofa on a Friday night to watch *Masterchef* together . . . I mean, no harm to ya if that's yer thing, but you do know it's all an illusion, right?'

It was a gross caricature of their relationship, and wide off the mark in many respects, but it cut just close enough to the bone to hurt.

'Oh right.' Zoe tried to sound unperturbed. 'How d'ye figure that?'

'Human race wasn't built to be monogamous. It's not in our DNA. Goes against the natural order of things. Marriage, co-habitation, civil partnership – put whatever gloss on it ya like, it's just an institution created by men to keep the ladies in line. Makes us into property, reinforces emotional dependency. And it's bad enough when it's a woman tying herself to a man, but when ya got two lesbians playing husband and wife like a pair of repressed hetties – well, that's just perverse.'

'Yeah, but I'm not a lesbian,' said Zoe, before she had the presence of mind to stop herself.

Fin's eyes narrowed. She looked at Zoe, incredulous. 'Is this one of those "bi-curious" deals? Cos if it is, lemme tell ya—'

'No, I'm straight . . . I think,' said Zoe, wishing to fuck she hadn't said anything. 'I'm just . . . '

'In a sexual relationship with a woman.'

Zoe stared studiously into her glass. 'Something like that, aye.'

Fin looked at her long and hard, then shrugged. 'Well, whatever butters yer biscuit,' she said, and took a swig from her bottle.

Zoe drank deep from her own glass to avoid having to say anything. She was relieved that, for the time being, Fin seemed to have no interest in pressing the matter, though she somehow knew there was no way she was going to let the matter rest for good.

It was after midnight – closer to one, really – when they finally made a move, though it was clear from the teeming mass of customers still there that the G-Spot would be doing a roaring trade for hours yet. Outside, West Regent Street was deserted apart from a pair of men walking up the pavement on the other side of the road. As Zoe and Fin set off in the opposite direction, one of them gave a shout.

'Ho!'

Zoe ignored the shout and carried on walking. Probably just your run-of-the-mill Friday night drunk who thinks everyone he sees is his long-lost bestest buddy.

'Zoe? Zoe Callahan?'

This time Zoe glanced in his direction for long enough to confirm that she had no idea who he was, then began to walk faster.

'Know him?' asked Fin, quickening her pace to keep up.

Zoe shook her head. 'Just keep walking.'

But she could tell from the sound of footsteps behind her that the man was giving chase. He and his friend hurried across the road. And then, before Zoe had time to process what was happening, a flash went off and she saw the DSLR camera in the hands of the silent one, while the one who'd called her name brandished a Dictaphone in front of him.

'Zoe? It is Zoe, isn't it? The Kelvingrove Killer's sister?'

Oh, *fuck*.

'I wondered if I could get a few words from you about your thoughts on the Gavin Price trial starting on Monday. Are you expecting a conviction? Are you disappointed your brother isn't around to stand trial alongside him?'

Zoe simply stared at him, unable to move or form a coherent thought beyond *Please, not this. Not now.*

Fin was staring at the gabbling man, a middle-aged and slightly portly fellow in an ill-fitting denim jacket, with an expression of utter incredulity. 'Who the flaming fuck are you?' she said.

Until now, neither man had paid Fin any attention. Now, however, the cameraman angled his lens at her and snapped another picture, while the knobhead with the Dictaphone once again addressed Zoe.

'And who's this? Is she your lesbian lover?' He gave Fin a leering grin. 'What do they call you, sweetie-pie?'

'If you don't get that thing the fuck outta my face, you're gonna find out,' said Fin, and made a grab for it.

The cameraman pulled back, clutching his precious cargo to his chest. Dictaphone Guy, however, seemed unperturbed, his smile widening.

'Now, now, don't be like that. We're only being friendly. Listen' – he was addressing Zoe again, having evidently concluded that she was the more reasonable of the two – 'why don't we go somewhere and get a couple of drinks? On me. You decide how much or how little you want to tell me, and if there's a story in it, then we all stand to make a tidy packet out of it.'

'I've got a better idea,' said Fin, this time placing herself directly between the man and Zoe, forcing him to give her his undivided attention. 'Why don't you and yer gimp buddy fuck off *tout suite* before I cram those expensive toys of yours up both yer jacksies?'

'Then I'll do you for assault,' said Dictaphone Guy, though much of his earlier cockiness had evaporated.

'Water off a duck's arse, pal. I've done time before and I'll happily do it again just to wipe that smirk off yer face.'

The man gave a little scoff, but his heart was no longer in it. As Fin feigned a lunge towards him, teeth bared in a snarl, he and his pal both took off, glancing furtively over their shoulders.

Fin stood, hands on her hips, threw back her head and laughed riotously. 'Ahahahaha! That's right, run home to yer mammies!'

The men quickened their pace, their pattering footsteps ringing in the otherwise silent air.

Fin turned to Zoe. 'That sorta thing happen to you a lot?'

'No for a while now,' said Zoe, somehow managing to muster a response.

'Least now I know why ya seemed so familiar. How come ya never said ya were the Kelvingrove Killer's sister?'

'How come you never said you were in prison?'

'Musta slipped my mind.'

'What'd ye do?'

'Nothing I regret.' Fin shoved her hands in her pockets. 'So. You've got secrets and I've got secrets.'

'Seems so, aye,' said Zoe, with little enthusiasm.

Zoe headed back to Dumbarton Road, having turned down Fin's invite to head along with her to the next bar in search of further drinking opportunities. She wanted time to herself. Time to think.

The encounter with the paparazzo had shaken her. It was a curious dichotomy, and one on which she'd reflected at the time, that, though the death of her brother was an intensely personal thing, every man and his dog had staked a claim to it. Everyone had an opinion about what Victor had done and what had motivated him, and the more ignorant they were of the facts, the more vociferous they were in their insistence of being right. She'd become used to the lack of privacy, to hearing her brother being described by people who'd never met him as a monster, to the total lack of disregard for her feelings. Now, all those familiar emotions were coming to the fore again.

The aftermath of the Kelvingrove Park Murders – so called despite only one murder having actually taken place in the park itself – had been a frantic, fucked-up time. The murders were on the front page of every paper, the main headline on every radio and TV news programme. The media dined out on it for weeks, dredging up every lurid scrap of detail they could find. Except, it seemed, the one piece of information that, in Zoe's estimation, should have been prized above all else: the motive. What could have possessed a chronically shy, self-effacing young man who'd never been in trouble with the law in his life to suddenly embark on a murder spree? There was an exclusive there just waiting to be written by some enterprising journalist. The story behind the story. The event that created the Kelvingrove Killer. And yet nobody seemed to care.

There had been five boys involved in the rape of Jenny Guilfoyle, but only one of them had had his name paraded through the press, tarred as a monster, a raving loony, a cold-blooded serial killer. In the weeks and months following Victor's death, the papers had done a number on him, painting him as a deranged psychopath who, from an early age, had been clearly identifiable as a wrong yin, based on a seemingly never-ending parade of quotes attributed to unnamed 'close friends'. They'd doorstepped Zoe relentlessly, pursuing her like a pack of wolves whenever she set foot outside, and when she refused to speak to them had done what their profession did best: made things up to suit themselves. She wondered whether the narrative surrounding Victor would have played out differently if she'd cooperated with the vultures. At least then she might have had some control of it. But it was too late for that.

And now, it seemed, it was all beginning again.

Back at the flat, she took off her dress, folded it and put it away carefully, keen to hide any signs that she'd been out on the razzle-dazzle, then cleaned the makeup off her face and trudged through to the bedroom. It was too hot in there even for a sheet, not even with the windows open and the rattly portable fan going full blast, so she flopped face-down on top of the covers and lay there naked, waiting for sleep to come – a futile exercise at the best of times, made all the worse by her mind refusing to power down.

She was still awake – if you could call it that – when Carol came in just after four. Zoe lay there, motionless, listening as she moved about the room, getting ready for bed. She felt the mattress sag as Carol nestled down beside her, then Carol's lips on the nape of her neck.

'You still awake?'

Zoe grunted an affirmative.

'I didn't wake you?'

'Naw.'

Another kiss. 'How was your evening?'

'Awright. Uneventful.'

'Sorry I was such a cow yesterday.' Kiss. 'I don't mean to be such a moany old bag, honest.'

She seemed to have conveniently airbrushed the revelation about the trial from yesterday's bust-up, but Zoe was too worn out for another rammy, and if acting like it hadn't happened helped them reach some sort of truce, she wasn't going to dredge it up again now. And in any event, now Carol was moving south, her kisses continuing down Zoe's back to the base of her spine and the cleft between her buttocks. Moaning softly, Zoe rolled over onto her back and spread her legs apart, offering herself up to Carol. Carol wrapped an arm round each of Zoe's thighs, lowered her head and began an altogether more intimate form of kissing.

And then, for a time, all conscious thought of fighting – or anything else, for that matter – was placed firmly on the back-burner. As Carol's lips and tongue continued their work, Zoe felt the familiar sensation of waves building, accompanied by that glorious loss of control of her limbs, the tightening of her muscles, the throbbing of her cunt, the feeling of weightlessness, of hurtling through space and being powerless to stop. The waves grew in strength and frequency. They were building, building, building until the pressure became unbearable and it took all her willpower not to scream out for release. And then, in the brief instant before they crashed over her, she opened her eyes and for a split second saw, quite clearly, Fin's dark, spiky head bowed in concentration between her thighs. She gasped *Shit!* and sank beneath the waves. And then she was floating to the surface, and her vision was coming back, and Carol was wrapping herself around her, enveloping her like a second skin, kissing her face, whispering *Shh, sweet girl* over and over, and Zoe felt the tears rolling down her own cheeks and realised she was crying.

Afterwards, she lay awake, listening to Carol's soft, regular breathing by her side. The wonderfully dizzy, helpless afterglow hadn't lasted long, and now her mind was once again abuzz. The brief moment of – what had it been? Hallucination? Trick of the light? Her sub-conscious playing wish fulfilment games with her? – had left her wracked by guilt and seriously confused. Admittedly, it wasn't exactly the first time her mind had gone to another place while Carol was going down on her, or vice versa. There'd been times in the past – more than she cared to count, in fact – when, to help herself along, she'd shut her eyes and imagined someone else had their lips around her nub. Thing was, before now, it had always been a conscious choice on her part.

And it had always been a guy.

She wasn't stupid. That there was a major and really obvious difference between Carol and every other lover she'd ever been with wasn't lost on her. It just wasn't something she'd ever actively tried to unpick. *Lesbian, bisexual* – these had always been labels she'd thought of as applying to other people. And truth be told, she still did. It wasn't as if getting with Carol had changed who she was. She was still Zoe Callahan, and Zoe Callahan wasn't someone who attached labels to herself or thought too deeply about why she felt a certain way about something. Or indeed some*one*. After a while, she'd stopped thinking about it at all.

But now Fin had come careening into her life, and it was like everything had changed. All of a sudden, she found herself completely reassessing what she thought she knew about herself. After all, you didn't involuntarily hallucinate about another person during sexytime unless you really had the horn for them – right?

Truth be told, there had been times when she'd wondered whether the only reason she was compatible with Carol on a physical level was because Carol so closely resembled a boy anyway – from the head down and the waist up, at any rate. Fin, though, was a different kettle of fish entirely. While at the decidedly macho end of the spectrum as far as personality and dress sense went, she was clearly very much a woman, with breasts and hips and all that. And that complicated matters. It complicated them something fierce.

Yeah, but I'm not a lesbian.

You sure about that, Zoe?

Are you?

Really?

12

Quality Time

Zoe awoke the next morning to the sounds of clinking crockery. She sat up, blinking sleep from her eyes, as Carol set a laden breakfast tray across her knees and stood back, smiling beatifically.

Zoe eyed the spread before her with undisguised suspicion. 'What's the occasion?'

Carol shrugged. 'Does there need to be one? Felt you deserved a treat is all.' She perched on the end of the bed, her eyes not once leaving Zoe.

Zoe wasn't buying it. Carol was a practical sort. Sweeping romantic gestures weren't exactly in her repertoire, and she was one of those people who thought Valentine's Day was a scam dreamed up by greedy capitalists to extort the gullible. And yet, looking into her eyes, Zoe could see no trace of an ulterior motive. She just continued to watch her expectantly, willing her to eat. Eventually, more because of how awkward the stand-off was becoming than anything else, Zoe relented and dug in. Carol continued to watch till she'd polished the whole lot off. Then, as Zoe was licking jam from her fingers, Carol declared that, since they hardly ever got a Saturday off together anymore, it was beholden upon them to make the most of this one.

Zoe, still suffering from a serious flare-up of guilt over last night's inappropriate sexual hallucinations, felt obligated to agree. So, for the next couple of hours, she played the dutiful girlfriend, trailing round the local open-air market in nearby Mansfield Park with her arm looped through Carol's, not offering up so much as a word of complaint as Carol inspected one organic vegetable after another, taking an inordinate amount of time before settling on the few that met with her approval. While she was engaged in an earnest discussion with a local seller about his rhubarbs, Zoe stole a look at her phone. There was nothing from Fin. A part of her was disappointed, but she figured it was probably for the best if she didn't have any contact with the subject of the previous night's nocturnal mind-wandering for a bit.

After a far-too-late lunch, Carol proposed a trip to Victoria Park to make the most of the good weather. Given that the heatwave was now well into its second week and showing no sign of going anywhere, Zoe couldn't see what the urgency was. But she'd promised herself she was Carol's for the day, so she bit her tongue and the pair of them set off towards Whiteinch. The park, when they arrived, was full of people who'd evidently had the same idea: a motley assortment of walkers, picnickers and sunbathers, all acting like they'd never seen the sun before.

They set up camp near a large oak tree – shade for Zoe, sun for Carol. A trio of lanky shirtless youths were playing Frisbee nearby, exhibiting a degree of energy and carefreeness that Zoe was convinced was designed specifically to test her patience. Carol slathered on the sun-cream, put on her shades and relaxed with her book, signalling that she was in for the long haul. But sitting still wasn't in Zoe's repertoire, and she shifted positions constantly, checking her phone every five minutes in the hope of a distraction – or, failing that, a message from Fin, which she would now have positively relished. Neither materialised, and, after an hour or so, she'd had enough.

'Are we spending the whole afternoon here?' she asked Carol, who'd abandoned her book and was now lying with her eyes shut, arms folded behind her head.

'It's not even three,' said Carol, as if that answered her question.

'Aye, but there's nothing tae do.'

'You should've brought a book, then.'

Zoe decided to try a different tack. 'I'm *hot*,' she said plaintively.

Carol sighed. 'Then go for a paddle in the fountain or something. Just give it a rest, Zoe.'

'Yeah, *Zooo-eeeee*,' cooed one of the youths. 'Give it a rest.'

Zoe turned and made the universal hand gesture for self-pleasure, but the boys just laughed and carried on with their game. She turned over and lay on her side, seething at this public humiliation. *Jesus, trading petty insults with teenagers. This is my life.*

It was after five before Carol finally deigned to make a move. They ate out on the way back into Partick, at one of those organic restaurants Carol seemed to think were the dog's danglies, after which she insisted on them going to the local comedy club to catch an open-mic performance from some friend of a friend of a friend. It turned out to be a politically-motivated one-woman play with, as the sign outside the door promised, 'a queer twist'. Zoe was bored rigid, but the rest of the audience lapped it up, whooping and clapping at every punchline and treating the artist to a standing ovation when she finally brought her act to a close.

Not for the first time, Zoe was left with a pronounced sense that Carol was doing her level best to change her, to make her into something she wasn't, and she didn't like it one bit. Trying to get her to eat healthy, dragging her to watch films with subtitles at the GFT, nagging her to read this and that feminist tract . . . And this whole 'not letting you out of my sight' business was so transparent it was a wonder Carol wasn't embarrassed by it. She wondered what was behind it. The only plausible explanation she could think of was that Carol had got some inkling about her Ryland investigation and was trying to put the kibosh on it, tying her up as much as possible so she couldn't sneak off. If so, she should come out and say so instead of hiding behind this 'quality time' charade.

And it wasn't over yet. Carol stuck around for ages after the lights had been put back up and the stage vacated, chatting with her pals from the Byres Road coffeehouse revolutionary brigades – the sort of folk who had po-faced conversations about cisgendering and intersectionality, and not even in an ironic way. Zoe couldn't stand them, and the feeling was nothing if not mutual. On one occasion early in their relationship, one of them, Marcella, had drawn Zoe aside and whispered in her ear that they all knew this was just a phase for her – the sort of experiment most people get out of their systems in their first year at uni. Zoe's own pals, in contrast, had been far more accepting of the new normal, at least to her face. There'd been no I-don't-know-about-this asides, no questions about what had made her 'turn', but Marcella and the rest of that crowd had never been able to hide their incredulity. That she and Carol were still together nearly four years later only seemed to enrage Marcella all the more, which gave Zoe a perverse sense of satisfaction, even if she was starting to wonder if the only reason she'd lasted the course was because it meant she was delivering the naysayers a giant F-you.

Now, sitting in the corner listening to them rabbiting on about whether they should consider starting a women-only party to contest elections locally, Zoe realised that, until now, she'd never fully taken on board just what an airy-fairy, talking-shop business Carol's purported radicalism actually was. Placed in sharp relief to Fin's far earthier, 'smash the system' variant, she looked every inch like one of those champagne socialists who'd marched under trade union banners in the eighties but, when the honours list came a-calling, couldn't kiss the Queen's ringpiece fast enough. For all her strong words, Carol's world was an incredibly square one, and Zoe was finding it harder and harder to see a place for herself in it.

It was almost dark by the time they finally got home. She went to bed early, even though she knew trying to sleep would be futile. Carol joined her shortly afterwards and, for the second night in a row, tried to initiate sex. But Zoe wasn't feeling it, and, truth be told, didn't trust herself to let herself go in case there was a repeat occurrence of what had happened the previous night. So she rolled onto her side and said she was tired and, if it was all the same, could they not?

And so they lay there side by side saying nothing, listening to the ratchety hum of the fan at the foot of the bed, doing little more than redistributing the same hot air to other parts of the room. Gradually, Carol's breathing from the other side of the bed grew steadier as sleep claimed her. But Zoe remained wide awake, stoking her sense of grievance long into the night.

The following morning, while Carol was in the shower, Zoe sat on the sofa in front of the TV, flicking through the channels. The main item on the national news was about a cargo lorry carrying electronic equipment that had arrived in Rosyth via the ferry from Zeebrugge in the early hours and had been held up in a country lane en route to Cumbernauld by armed men in motorcycle helmets. They'd stripped the driver naked and made him run north through the fields, not stopping till he reached the nearest town five miles away. The lorry was found incinerated in a lay-by several hours later, some thirty miles further south, all its contents gone. A police spokesman said that enquiries were ongoing – which, in layman's terms, meant they hadn't a clue.

It soon became clear that the day would be conducted in much the same fashion as the previous one, with Carol expressing a desire to visit the new transport museum down at the harbour. 'It's crazy,' she declared, 'having all that knowledge and history so close by and not taking advantage of it.' So off they went, Zoe feeling more and more like a wayward child being force-fed cultural enrichment by a well-meaning but tone-deaf adult. At least it was air-conditioned inside the museum, though that benefit was more than offset by how skull-crushingly boring it all was.

Once more, they spent most of the day on the trot, with Carol constantly coming up with new excuses to avoid going home. Zoe gritted her teeth and said nothing, but her sense of injustice was steadily growing. She was more convinced than ever now that Carol knew something about the Ryland business. It was after six when they finally headed for home, and by now, Zoe was beyond fed up. Her feet were killing her, and her lack of tolerance for the hot weather had reached fever pitch. Even in shorts and a loose spaghetti-strap cami, she was boiling. She was tired of being damp and sweaty all the time, tired of feeling like she was trudging through treacle, tired of her skin feeling tingly and itchy, tired of her forehead aching from screwing up her face at the sun.

Carol set about preparing what, to Zoe, seemed a pointlessly elaborate evening meal with multiple dishes and ingredients. What was wrong with a good old-fashioned microwave lasagne? She was peeling onions at the sink for Carol – partly out of obligation and partly to speed things along – when there was a knock at the door. Carol headed out to answer it, and a moment later, Zoe heard voices in the hallway: Carol's and another's. She recognised the latter immediately and was so taken aback she almost sliced her own thumb off.

'Look who's come to dinner,' said Carol brightly, presenting Anna to her from the doorway like a long-lost pet who'd turned up out of nowhere.

'Hey, Zoe,' said Anna, big beaming smile at the ready. 'How's things?'

* * *

The meal was a tense and awkward affair. Anna and Carol gabbled away to each other across the kitchen table with such insistent cheerfulness that Zoe wasn't buying it for one second. Nor was she buying the notion that Anna had just turned up at their door by chance. On the contrary, the whole visit had clearly been pre-planned between her and Carol – though its purpose, and their reasons for trying to pull the wool over her eyes, remained a mystery. They must have picked up on the fact that she knew something was afoot, since they compensated by dialling up the jollity even more, to the point that Zoe began to wonder if her glass was the only one that hadn't had happy pills slipped into it.

After a while, she excused herself and headed for the loo, partly to get away from all that overbearing fakery and partly so she could check her phone. Her heart leapt when she saw she had a missed call from Fin.

She immediately hit callback. The phone rang and rang. Then, just when she was on the verge of giving up, Fin finally picked up.

'Howya, Bright Eyes. You been forgetting to charge yer phone or something? Listen, think I might have something for ya on the subject of our tattooed friend.'

Zoe's pulse quickened. 'Oh – and, uh, and what would that be?' she said, trying to affect an air of casual indifference. Best not to sound *too* keen.

'Uh-uh. This sorta thing's not for the dog and bone. Let's meet up.'

Zoe glanced uneasily at the door. 'Thing is, I'm kinda in the middle of something.'

'Well, can't you make yer excuses?' There was a note of incredulity in Fin's voice.

'Not easily.'

'Oh, *right*. I see how it is.'

A surge of anger coursed through Zoe as she pictured Fin's know-it-all smirk. 'I'll see what I can do. I'm no making any promises, but.'

'Hey, no sweat. Away 'n' ask yer good lady wife if ya can come out and play. I'll be waiting.'

Not trusting herself to respond, Zoe killed the call with a violent flick of her thumb, took a deep breath and headed back out.

As she approached the kitchen, she could hear Anna and Carol talking. They'd abandoned their gregarious patter and were now conferring urgently in low voices, almost whispering. She halted in the corridor and listened. She couldn't make out everything that was being said, though she distinctly heard her own name and the words *for her own good* being spoken by Anna.

She felt a stab of resentment. Anna was meant to be *her* pal, not Carol's, and yet here the two of them were, plotting together behind her back, like they were getting ready to stage an intervention or something. Well, she wasn't going to let them get away with it. She clomped down the corridor as noisily as possible, giving them ample warning of her impending return, and resumed her seat.

For the remainder of the meal, she gave as good as she got, matching – and even exceeding – Carol and Anna in the 'enthusiastically talking shite' stakes, determined to make sure they had no opportunity for their laying on of hands or whatever it was they had in mind. In fact, she did such a good job of making out she was deep in the middle of a manic episode that neither of them seemed to quite know how to handle her, and she could see the uneasy looks Carol was shooting Anna's way, silently imploring her to do something.

'Zoe,' said Anna, in the sort of tone door-to-door Jehovah's Witnesses use right before they ask you to open your heart to God, 'is everything all right?'

'All right? Everything's fan-flippin'-tastic. I mean, what could be better than being sat down to tea on a sunny day with my girlfriend *and* my best pal? S'like two for the price o' wan. Anyone for fruit salad?' She offered the bowl to the other two.

'Zoe,' Anna began again, folding her hands on the table in a very business-like way, 'before we say anything else, we want you to know that we both love you very much and only want the best for you. You know that, right?'

'Aye?' said Zoe dubiously. It came out sounding like a question, as if she was no longer quite sure herself.

'So you'll believe me when I say that we both stand in complete solidarity with you.'

Zoe said nothing, which only caused Anna to grow more uncomfortable.

'See, the fact is, we're . . . well, we're worried about you, Zo.'

'Worried?'

'Not worried,' Carol put in hastily. 'Concerned.'

'That's right. Concerned.' Anna nodded forcefully, as if there was a vast and meaningful difference between the two words. 'We're not looking to judge you or tell you how to act or anything, but we . . . well, we feel that this particular path isn't good for you.'

Christ, so it *was* about her Ryland investigation? And now Carol had dragged Anna into the recriminations as well – which, given Anna's own actions just a few short years back, would be laughable if it wasn't so completely hypocritical.

'Guys,' she began, trying her best to come over all reasonable, like she was taking their concerns on board and giving them due consideration, 'it's fine, really. This "path"' – she did the air-quotes thing – 'it's . . . well, it's just something I have tae do. Cos let's face it, no one else is gonnae bother their—'

'We just don't want to see you get hurt,' said Anna.

'Absolutely,' said Carol.

'Any more than you already have been.'

Carol nodded vigorously.

'Which is why we don't think you should be going to the trial.'

Zoe opened her mouth to deliver some cutting retort, then stopped mid-breath. 'Wait, what?'

'God knows, this was always going to be a difficult time for you.' Anna was finding her stride at last. 'For all of us, really – but especially for you. It'll only dredge up bad memories. And frankly, a lot of the time you'll be bored. It's not like it is on the TV. But mostly, we're worried about what it'll do to you, emotionally speaking. We—'

'*You're* going, aren't ye?'

'Well—'

'Look me in the eyes and tell me ye're no planning on being there first thing on Monday morning, looking for a ringside seat.'

'That's—' Anna began, then stopped herself. 'It's beside the point,' she went on, more levelly. 'We're not talking about me. We're talking about you, and what it'll do to you if you insist on putting yourself through—'

'You think he's gonnae get off, don't ye?'

Anna blinked rapidly several times and said nothing.

'That's what yese think, in't it? Naeb'dy wants tae say it but that's how it is. So why don't we all just quit pretending? Yese think he's gonnae get off and I'll be pure gutted and want tae slit my wrists or something.'

'It's not about that!' A note of desperation now entered Anna's voice. 'It doesn't matter whether he's found guilty or innocent. Don't try and turn this into a proxy for something it's not.'

At some point, all three of them had ended up on their feet. Zoe had a feeling she'd been first and that the others had only done likewise in response. But however it had happened, here they all were, standing facing one another, Zoe versus the others, the table between them like the demilitarised zone between two warring states.

'I have to be there,' she said. Her words sounded shrill and plaintive in her own ears. 'For Victor.'

Anna shook her head sadly. 'It isn't Victor who's on trial.'

'Aye. Didnae even get that, did he?'

'This won't bring him back,' said Anna softly.

She moved forward, reaching out to touch Zoe's arm, that way she always did when she was trying to console her or calm her down. But Zoe anticipated her and took a step back. Anna stood there helplessly, hand hanging in mid-air, looking like she was trying to catch flies with it.

'Know what?' said Zoe. 'I reckon the pair of yese must think I'm a complete mug.'

'We don't—'

'Ye think I don't know yese planned this . . . this *ambush*? I'm no some dug yese can keep on a leash and walk tae heel. And I'm no a wean either, so stop kidding on yese can tell me whit tae dae.'

She was circling around them now, moving towards the door. Their wide, uncomprehending eyes followed her every step of the way.

'We're just trying to—' Anna began.

'What? Ye're gonnae tell me it's for ma ain good?'

'Zo . . . ' Anna raised her shoulders in a confused, helpless shrug.

Zoe glowered at Anna and Carol for a long, hard moment. They just stood staring at her as if they didn't have the faintest clue what her grievance was. Well, it didn't wash with her. Not for a moment.

'Fuck the pair o' yese,' she said. 'I'm gonnae be there the morra, bright 'n' early, and there's nothing yese can dae tae stop me.'

She looked at the table, at the bowl of fruit salad Carol had lovingly prepared.

'Enjoy yer dessert,' she said, and stormed out.

13

On a Warm Summer's Night

She stomped along Dumbarton Road, her anger already less raw but her sense of grievance at the injustice of it all continuing unabated. She knew what Anna had said was true. In their own feckless way, she and Carol *were* just trying to help her. Really, she should be grateful that they cared, however tone-deaf their intervention had been. She knew she bore all the hallmarks of a deeply self-destructive personality: lashing out at the people she loved, throwing their kindness back in their faces, goading them into fighting with her. And all to stoke her raging sense of being hard-done-to, of the whole world being against her. She wondered how Carol had put up with her for so long. In the just under four years they'd been together, Carol had been nothing but supportive, showing a level of patience for her moods and other assorted shortcomings that surely qualified her for at least a sainthood. And she knew what she should do right now: go to Carol on bended knee, make a grovelling apology, tell her she didn't deserve her and that in future she'd try not to be quite such a sorry excuse for a partner and human being.

And of course, because she knew that was precisely what she should do, she made up her mind to do the exact opposite.

As she boarded an eastbound train, she rang Fin. No answer.

She kept ringing and ringing all the way into town, finally getting a response not long after she'd stepped out of Queen Street Station.

'I managed tae get away for a bit,' she said, pausing at the mouth of Dundas Lane to wedge her phone in the crook of her shoulder. 'Can we meet?'

'Oh, I dunno.' Fin's laconic drawl wafted into her ear. 'What if I don't feel like sharing anymore?'

Zoe sighed inwardly. She wasn't going to grovel. She wasn't in the mood. 'Och, d'ye know what? You've either got something or ye havnae, so why don't we just cut the shite and get tae the point?'

'Hey! Relax the jacks, all right? I'm just screwing with ya. Where are ya right now?'

'Top of Buchanan Street.'

'Know the Bier Halle on Gordon Street? Next to TGI Friday's?'

'I'll be there in ten.'

'Make it five and the first round's on me.'

Seven minutes later, Zoe arrived on Gordon Street, overheated and a trifle breathless from the brisk walk downhill. Several of the tables in the outdoor biergarten were occupied by groups and couples enjoying the evening sunshine with their authentic Bavarian beer. The whole scene had a pleasingly continental quality to it, as if Zoe had stepped out of Glasgow and ended up in some side street in Munich or the French Riviera. Fin was there waiting for her at a table, a couple of tall flagons already within reach. She had on her leather jacket, plus the same Cats, combat trousers and vest combo she'd worn the day Zoe had first encountered her at the self-defence class. She was leaning back in her seat, legs spread in a wide, inverse V, head tilted up towards the evening sun.

She stirred as Zoe drew alongside her, and opened a solitary eye. '*Guten Abend, meine Liebling.* I took the liberty of procuring you *ein Bier.'* She opened the other eye and grinned. ''Fraid that's the extent of my Germanic.'

Zoe wasn't much of a beer drinker, but she wasn't about to look a gift horse in the mouth – not when it was still so hot and stuffy. She sat down, squinting against the glare of the sun, and took a long glug. Even her unrefined palate could tell it was good stuff.

'So what's this info about Snake Guy you couldnae tell me over the phone?'

Fin drummed the table with her knuckles for effect, then flashed a triumphant smile. 'Found out who he is.'

'Well?' Zoe tried to play it cool, but she couldn't stop herself leaning forward in anticipation.

'Name's Gordon Tannahill.'

'And? Who is he?'

'Only one of Jim Cottrell's enforcers.'

Zoe looked at her blankly. 'That name supposed tae mean something to me?'

Fin raised an eyebrow. 'Fuck me, you really *are* green. OK, quick history lesson, early eighties to present day.' She pushed their glasses off to one side. 'Right, so in the world of organised crime, you've got two major forces in play who've carved up the city between 'em.' Using her arm, she divided the table horizontally in two. 'South of the river is pretty much all in the hands of the McGills. They put the "family" in "crime family". This lot go back generations, and the men of the clan have something of a reputation for, shall we say, sowing their seed a little too enthusiastically – result being they've got more hangers-on than the Windsors.

'But the man we're interested in, one James McNair Cottrell, his territory's mainly the North and East. Cottrell's old guard – yer classic self-made man, been around forever, worked his way up the ladder from nothing. Got fingers in every pie: casinos, dealing, prostitution, gun-running, you name it. And he's old-school –

M.R. MACKENZIE

ruthless to a fucking fault, but there's a code of honour there, if ya
look hard enough for it. He doesn't crack skulls just for the hell of
it. He plays the long game; everything he does, he does for a reason.

'Naturally, both lots hate each other's guts. Each wants what the
other has, and the grand prize is control of the entire city. But as
long as both sides are evenly matched, which they basically are,
you've got yerself a stalemate. Course, every now 'n' then ya get the
odd skirmish. One of the McGills, or one of their gofers, torches a
casino belonging to Cottrell; he responds by breaking a few knee-
caps and everything's peachy again. But by 'n' large they keep to
their own turf – cos, end o' the day, no prick wants to be the one
who brings down the whole house o' cards.'

For several moments, Zoe said nothing. The happy chatter of her
fellow diners seemed a million miles away.

'I thought all this razor gang stuff got left behind in the eighties,'
she said, a tad feebly.

'Ya mean when the politicos got fed up with the place being
synonymous with glassings and drive-by shootings and decided to
rebrand it as a City of Culture?' Fin smirked dismissively. 'A garden
festival and a coat of paint'll only take ya so far.'

'And you know all this how?'

Fin shrugged. 'I keep my ear to the ground. Listen to what's being
said. 'Sides, most of it's common knowledge really. Every fucker's
heard of Cottrell and the McGills.'

'Well, I hadnae,' said Zoe, a little irked. 'Anyway, I don't get it. If
everyone knows who these people are, how come the cops don't lift
'em?'

Fin laughed. 'Awfy cosy view of life you've got. Think this is all
cops 'n' robbers? It suits the filth to have someone like Cottrell
calling the shots, keeping the small fry on the straight 'n' narrow.
He's a known quantity. He's manageable. You take him outta the
equation and you're looking at a bloodbath: every petty crook and

lordling the city ever shat out scrapping for a piece of the pie.' She paused to take a sip from her flagon, and gazed out at the quiet street with its bars and outdoor cafés. 'But I reckon change is coming anyway.'

'How?'

'The McGills. Scuttlebutt is they've got their eyes on the grand prize. Cottrell's no spring chicken. He won't be around forever. Rumour has it he's not in good shape. And unlike the McGills, his ain't a family concern. No Cottrell Junior to hand over the family business to.'

'What about this Tannahill?'

Fin shook her head. 'He's a big noise but not *that* big. Cottrell lets him have his wee corner of the East End: a few pubs, a couple o' brothels. But no way's he gonna trust him with the keys to the kingdom. You heard of Freddo Brady?'

Zoe nodded. 'The guy on the news. The one who got sent down.'

'Bingo. Time was, he'd've been the obvious candidate to take the reins when Cottrell called it a day. But he got stupid. Got fingered for some stuff no amount of witness intimidation was gonna cover up. Now he's outta the picture and old man Cottrell's tryna hold sway over a crumbling empire all on his lonesome. That heist outside Scumbernauld? Cops are saying they were after the official cargo, but no way d'ya take the trouble to hold up a van at gunpoint just so's ya can make off with a few tellies. And that business with the driver, making him strip down to his birthday suit and run like hell? Classic McGill behaviour. My guess is Cottrell had some kinda delivery coming in from the mainland – drugs, weapons, you name it – and they decided to help themselves.'

Zoe nodded eagerly. She'd remembered something. 'A guy got knifed earlier this week on his way fae getting his messages. I seen it on the news. Cary Grant?'

'Jimmy Stewart, but you get the picture. He's one of the McGills' mob. Prob'ly a spotta blowback for some other minor wickedness from the other side.' She paused to wipe some froth from her upper lip. 'That lot've been at each other's throats so long, odds are none of 'em can remember whether Han or Greedo shot first. Or cares.'

She fell silent. Zoe sipped her beer gingerly, her mind all a-go-go. None of it seemed quite real, like the plot elements from a Hollywood movie unceremoniously transplanted onto her wee corner of the world. And yet, it all had a ring of truth about it. Glasgow wasn't called 'No Mean City' for nothing, and she had enough of an awareness of its reputation as the domain of hard-drinking, hard-hitting gangsters and their wannabe counterparts for it not to sound completely implausible.

'OK,' she said slowly, 'but where does this Tannahill guy meeting Ryland fit in?'

Fin put down her glass with a grin. 'Thought you'd never ask. That's what we're gonna find out.'

Mystified, Zoe followed Fin round the corner, where a sturdy black and silver moped was attached to a bollard. As Zoe watched, Fin unlocked the chain securing it in place.

'Is this yours?' Zoe stared at the bike in awe.

'Ain't she a beaut?' Fin lifted the seat and pulled out a helmet. 'Here, catch.'

She tossed the helmet to Zoe, who fumbled but managed to grab it. Fin produced a matching helmet and put it on.

'Well, c'mon. Ain't got all evening.'

'We're going on *that*?' Zoe pointed uncertainly towards the moped.

'Either that or sprout wings and fly.' Fin grinned as she pulled on a pair of riding gloves. 'Don't worry. I'll not make ya do the driving.'

She clambered onto the bike, gripping the handlebars, ready for take-off. With considerable reluctance, Zoe put on her helmet and perched gingerly behind Fin, fingers digging into the leather pillion.

Fin glanced over her shoulder. 'Been on one of these before?'

'First time.'

'Well, don't worry. I'll be gentle with ya. Here – arms round me, 'less ya wanna come off at the first bend.'

Zoe did as she was told, looping her arms round Fin's waist. The whole setup made her uncomfortable. Her legs were spread wide, her crotch nestled against Fin's backside in a way that felt entirely inappropriate. Even more alarming than that was the knowledge that all that stood between her and a potentially fatal tumble were her own hands. It felt all wrong. Wasn't she supposed to have a seatbelt or something?

But before she could raise any objection, Fin kicked away the stand, revved the engine and took off, roaring off down Mitchell Street like a greyhound with a rocket up its arse.

At first, it was all Zoe could do to hang on for dear life, to lean in sync with the bike as it ducked and weaved between traffic and round bends rather than trying to correct for it. Gradually, though, she became more attuned to the bike's movements and allowed herself to relax a little, though she didn't dare loosen her grip. As she became less rigid, she allowed herself to rest more of her weight against Fin, their bodies becoming as one as they sliced through the concrete jungle.

Initially, she had no idea where they were going, other than that they were heading in a southerly direction. They crossed the river and continued on through the Gorbals, then Toryglen and Cathcart, past Linn Park and onwards down the B766 through Castlemilk. It wasn't until they were passing Carmunnock that she got an inkling of their ultimate destination.

They arrived on the outskirts of Thorntonhall shortly after ten.

The sun was low, but it was still relatively light and the birds were cheeping in the trees above. They came at the village from the north, following the same route Zoe had seen Tannahill's Merc taking two days earlier. About a quarter of a mile from Ryland's house, Fin pulled over into the overgrown verge, bringing the moped to a juddering standstill. Zoe scrambled off unsteadily. Her arse and thighs were numb, and she'd spent so long with her legs bowed outward that it took several moments of shuffling back and forth like an anally-violated crab before their normal function returned.

Fin collected their helmets and stowed them under the seat. She shouldered a small rucksack, then did a passable job of concealing the bike beneath the untended shrubbery. Anyone actively looking for it would find it instantly, but chances were someone driving by at speed would fail to spot it.

'What are we doing?' Zoe demanded as they set off towards the village, her whisper shrill in the still air.

Fin winked. 'Came across an item in the paper today. Old man Ryland and the missus are scheduled to appear as guests of honour at a charity shindig at the City Chambers tonight. They'll be gone till well into the wee hours. An opportunity that's positively gagging to be exploited.'

The gates to Ryland's garden were locked, but that proved no impediment to Fin, who promptly scaled the wall and beckoned Zoe to follow her. They hurried across the grass towards the house, Zoe imitating Fin's low crouch. At the back of the building, they found one of the awning windows lying slightly open.

'Thank the Lord for hot summer nights,' said Fin. 'C'mon, gimme a boost.'

It was at that point that Zoe noticed Fin still had her gloves on. For the first time, the magnitude of what they were doing fully hit her. She didn't say anything, but Fin clearly caught her reticence, for she turned to Zoe and took hold of her by the chin – not force-fully, but in such a way that Zoe had no choice but to meet her eyes.

'Hey. Now's not the time for cold feet. If we look this gift-horse in the mouth, there's no telling when another's gonna come canter-ing along. Ya wanna get this prick or not?'

'Aye.'

'Well, then. You stay here. Put those bright eyes to good use.'

She turned towards the open window, a hand on either side of the frame, one foot up on the sill. With Zoe's help, she managed to get her head and shoulders through the opening and, with some effort, wriggled through. She wasn't a large woman, but she was solidly-built and the gap was small. There was a soft thud as she hit the floor inside, then silence.

Zoe sank to a low crouch, her back against the wall, straining to listen for any sudden noises. *Well, Zoe, you wanted adventure. Now you've certainly got it.* She tried not to dwell on what she was doing. If she didn't think about it, it wasn't happening, she told herself.

A car roared by somewhere not too far off and she started, a warning cry caught in her throat, but it was travelling in the opposite direction and after a moment she relaxed once more. She re-membered that sound travelled for miles out here in the country. For all she knew, the car she'd heard might have been in a neigh-bouring village.

It grew steadily darker. The sky was clear and, this far from civili-sation, unpolluted by too many streetlights. The stars shone brightly – all those planets and constellations whose names she didn't know. She had a vague memory of her dad trying to teach her them once when she was a wee girl, but it was so long ago and she couldn't even remember his face now, let alone the names of a bunch of gas balls billions of miles away.

She shifted her position. She was beginning to get a raging cramp in both legs, but she didn't dare stand up. She had an image stuck inside her head of a spotlight falling on her the moment she did and a siren starting to peal, like in one of those old POW movies, followed by the inevitable hail of bullets as she made a break for it. So instead she contented herself with flexing one leg out in front of her and then the other, all the while wondering where the hell Fin had got to.

She didn't register the approaching car until its headlights were actually glinting off the gates. Then, before she had a chance to consider her options, the gates were opening and a silver Jaguar came crawling into the grounds, grinding the gravel beneath its tyres.

'Fin!' she hissed. *'Fin!'*

But there was no answer from inside, and now the car had come to a stop and she heard its doors slamming, and she knew she couldn't risk calling out again. She heard footsteps on the gravel coming towards the house, and voices: a man's and a woman's.

'Do you want anything?' It was Ryland speaking – of that she was certain. 'A Valium or something?'

'No.' A woman speaking now. 'I think I'll just lie down.'

A jangling of keys. A door opening and closing. Zoe didn't dare to breathe. She flattened herself against the wall. *Scream!* the voice in her head implored her. *Warn her, then get out of here and save yourself!* But she couldn't scream. She couldn't move. She was rooted to the spot in silent terror.

A shape suddenly landed on the ground directly beside her. It was too dark and she was too surprised to register what it was, but then she heard Fin's voice yelling 'LEG IT!' and before she knew it she was racing across the garden, hot on Fin's heels, blood pounding in her ears, barely even looking where she was going. She scrambled over the wall and took off down the road, plimsolls slapping on the tarmac as she ran blindly through the darkness, following the sound of Fin's own pounding feet as best she could.

They covered the quarter-mile back to the bike in a couple of minutes. Her eyes now adjusting to the gloom, Zoe watched, lungs burning, as Fin dragged it out from the shrubs.

'What did ye—'

'Later.'

Fin leapt on the bike. Zoe clambered on behind her and wrapped her arms round her. Fin revved the engine, spun them round a hundred and eighty degrees and floored it, roaring north towards the lights of the city.

14

Bukkake Surprise

They were back in the West End within half an hour. Fin left the main roads and wound through a series of backstreets, finally bringing the moped to a standstill beyond the bollards on White Street. They were just a couple of hundred yards from Byres Road, flanked on either side by sandstone tenements carved up into multiple flats.

Zoe waited while Fin chained the bike to the railings outside the house at the end of the block, then followed her inside and up the graffitied stone stairwell to the top floor. She unlocked the door to one of the flats and ushered Zoe into a communal living area with a sofa, recliner, TV and a whole load of old drinks cans. Zoe wondered how one person could create such a mess.

'I shack up with a buncha students,' Fin explained, as if sensing what Zoe was thinking. 'They're a clatty lot but we have a good laugh. They're all off on their summer jollies now, so no one'll bother us.' She caught Zoe's look. 'What?'

'Nothing. Just . . . dunno, kinda figured ye'd live in some weird lesbian commune or something.'

Fin laughed uproariously and gave her a hearty slap on the shoulder. 'Ah, you're a one-off. Make yerself at home. Ya drinking?'

'Aye, go on.'

As Fin clattered about in the kitchen, Zoe wandered over to the living room window, thrust it open and leaned out, trying to cool off. It felt almost as hot in here as in her own flat, though part of that might be the lingering excitement of the chase. As she flapped the collar of her cami, trying to get some air onto her skin, her mind returned to the fight she'd had earlier with Carol and Anna. She got out her phone and checked it for messages. She'd half-expected something nagging – or else grovelling – from Carol, but there was nothing, and she wasn't sure how she felt about that. On balance she supposed she'd have liked there to have been *something*, even just a string of profanities, because at least then she'd know her words earlier had actually made an impact.

At that moment, Fin returned, now stripped down to her vest, an open bottle of beer in each hand and her rucksack hanging from one shoulder. She dumped it on the ground with a clunk. Whatever was inside was clearly heavy. Zoe eyed it hungrily, eager for its contents to be divulged. But Fin, as always, evidently intended to take things at her own pace. She handed a bottle to Zoe, flopped down on the sofa and took a long, hearty slug from her own.

'You gonnae tell me what the hell happened back there?' said Zoe.

For a few maddening seconds, Fin continued to drink as if she hadn't heard. Then, at last, she put down her bottle.

'OK, so I came in through the living room. Nothing worth writing home about in there, 'part from a TV big enough to display yer man's ego at actual size, plus a bookcase fulla DVDs. Spy films, war movies, military history . . . Ya might describe the man as having a bit of an obsession. Nothing incriminating in the dining room either – though there *was* a very nice selection of single malts on the sideboard. I resisted the temptation to sample the goods.'

She paused to take another sip from her bottle. 'Next door I tried was locked, and I was like, "Bingo!" So I treated it to a wee bit of elbow-grease, and next thing I know, I'm in our friend's private study.'

'And? What did ye find?'

'Pretty much what you'd expect. Desk, laptop and books, books and more books. I swear, how he finds time to read 'em all beats me.'

'I don't think folk like him buy books to actually read,' said Zoe.

'Well, that's fucking stupid. Anyhoo, I figured the real juicy stuff would be on his computer, but first I wanted to see what he was stashing in those drawers of his. So I had a root around to see if I could find anything.'

'And did you?'

Fin held up a hand for patience. 'As it just so happens . . . '

She unzipped her rucksack and rummaged around inside it. What she eventually produced was so small Zoe had to lean in closer to get a better look. It was a small, see-through sachet. Its contents closely resembled flour, but Zoe would have put money on it being something else altogether.

'That what I think it is?'

'Aye. Turns out our friend the MSP for Central Scotland has been quite the naughty boy.' Fin tossed the package onto the coffee table in front of them. 'But just as I'm stood there wondering where a straight-up, salt-o'-the-earth chap like that gets his hands on a bag of pure-grade nose-candy, who should come cruising into the grounds but the man himself? So I knew it was time to get the hell outta Dodge. Gave the place as good a doing-over as I could in thirty seconds – y'know, make it seem like a break-in – then legged it back to you. And here we are.'

Zoe felt herself deflating. 'So apart fae the coke, ye didnae find anything.'

'Oh, ye of little faith . . . '

Fin reached for the rucksack again and slowly drew out a top-of-the-line Samsung laptop. As she looked up at Zoe, her lips slowly spread into a triumphant smile, as if this was the moment she'd been building up to all along.

It took Zoe a moment to realise she too was smiling. 'Ya beauty,' she breathed.

She joined Fin on the sofa, beer in hand, as Fin set the laptop on the table, lid open, and hit the power button. The Windows logo and spinning wheel appeared. A few seconds later, they were staring at the login screen, cursor blinking expectantly for a password.

Fin turned to Zoe. 'Any theories?'

'Try "password"?'

Fin shot her a withering look, but she dutifully obliged. The machine let out a resentful beep. *The username or password is incorrect. Try again.*

'How about "1234"?'

Fin tapped the numbers in. Same message.

Fin smiled grimly. 'Not like in the films, is it?'

'Try . . . I dunno, "bukkake surprise".'

Fin threw back her head and laughed uproariously. 'Oh, you slay me, Bright Eyes.' Still chortling, she typed it in, one key at a time, and hit Enter.

To the astonishment of neither of them, it wasn't that either. And, over the next ten minutes or so, they tried everything they could think of: Ryland's birthday; his middle name; his wife's name; his wife's maiden name; the name of the village they got married in; his place of birth; his favourite whisky, gleaned from his Wikipedia entry . . . They even tried 'Maggie', but by that time they were running out of clichés.

'Reckon we have to face it,' said Fin. 'Our boy's just a tad more security-conscious than yer average straight-to-video techno-thriller movie villain.'

Zoe nodded morosely. It was maddening having this potential wealth of information at their fingertips and yet inaccessible. She thought about asking one of her more tech-savvy pals, but she knew exactly what they'd say. *Whose computer is it? How did you get it? Why are you trying to open it?*

She was just about to throw up her hands and admit defeat when a thought suddenly occurred to her.

'Hang on – how'd ye spell his birthplace?'

'Usual way. "Bridge" as in the thing ya walk over, "ton" as in "weighs a".'

'Try B-R-I-G.'

She watched as Fin tapped out the word, then hit Enter. They both stared at the screen with bated breath as the little wheel spun for a bit, then was replaced by a full-screen picture of a Spitfire. Icon after icon appeared down the left-hand side, along with the taskbar, Start button and all the familiar accoutrements of the Windows desktop.

'Get it right up ya!' Fin murmured to herself in triumph.

They sat together on the sofa, bunched up close so they could both see the screen, one bare shoulder touching the other as they trawled through the contents of the laptop's hard drive. Their progress was slow: there was a lot to go through, and it seemed to have been organised in such a way as to sow confusion at every turn. Folders were nested within folders within folders, the names of which often bore no resemblance to their contents. Ryland was an obsessive cataloguer. He had receipts for *everything*, from nights in five-star hotels all the way down to dental floss – no doubt so it could all be charged to the taxpayer. Several monthly bank balance sheets were also present, confirming what they both knew already: that Ryland was loaded in every sense of the word. Scanned copies of letters from his accountant alluded to an additional bank account in Panama and one in the Bahamas – on neither of which, it was safe to assume, was any tax being paid.

All of which made it decidedly strange that he had a separate

ZIP archive, buried deep within the Program Files folder, labelled 'Accounts'. Fin dragged the cursor over it, double-clicked and watched as the screen filled with file after file in a seemingly endless list.

'Well, lookie here,' she said, leaning closer to the screen as she scrolled down. 'Seems yer man has quite the motion picture collection. *Slapped up sluts, Bound and begging for mercy, Submitting to her master's will* . . . Here, looks like you weren't kidding about the bukkake.'

For good measure, she played a handful of the videos. Zoe had encountered her fair share of porn in her time, much of it for her own personal gratification. She liked to think of herself as reasonably streetwise when it came to her own kinks and those of others. But the contents of Ryland's 'Accounts' folder were like nothing she'd encountered before. If there was a consistent theme – beyond the mandatory grunting, grinding and groaning – it was ritual subjugation and humiliation, and not just in the 'all porn is violence against women' sense. There was a good chance most of it was simulated, but the fact that she couldn't tell left her with a nasty churning feeling in the pit of her stomach.

'Jaysus,' said Fin. 'What's wrong with a good old-fashioned "rogered by the delivery guy" flick?'

Zoe found her voice. 'This proves it, then. He's a fucking sicko creep.'

'Aye, quite possibly.'

'It all fits. He gets off on watching women being tortured, and surprise surprise, turns out he's that way in real life.'

Fin raised a sceptical eyebrow. 'Well now, hold yer horses. Do you act out everything *you* fantasise about?'

Zoe opened her mouth to respond, then stopped short. After Friday night, that question felt just a shade too close to home.

'Thought not. I dunno 'bout you, but me, I go to some pretty dark places in my head. Like, stuff you'd never actually do, but sometimes ya get an itch yer normal vanilla PC-brigade-approved wank-matter just ain't gonna satisfy. Right?'

'I guess,' said Zoe, a tad doubtfully. She wondered what Fin's 'dark places' consisted of, and whether she truly wanted to know.

'Point is, you 'n' me both know what this guy's capable of, but the fact he's got an admittedly sizeable set of circumspect vids doesn't *prove* it. Not definitively. Looks iffy as fuck, sure. But Christ, if we judged everyone on their porno collection, I'm willing to bet you'd have to lock up half the population.'

'It's not just the rape porn, though, is it? It's everything else.'

Fin made a contemptuous noise at the back of her throat. 'What? Cos folk're gonna be totally shocked by a politico who has accounts in the Bahamas and enjoys powdering his nose? Big whoop. 'Sides, whatcha plannin' on doing? Going up to the nearest policeman and saying, "Hey, mister, last night I did a spot of breaking and entering, and while I was at it I happened to find evidence of criminal activity"?'

Zoe opened her mouth to reply, then stopped short. In all the excitement, she'd managed to overlook the small detail of just how they'd come into possession of the information they were now sitting on.

'Well, what if we dropped it off anonymously? Or . . . or we could hand it over to one of the papers.' She was warming to this idea the more she thought about it. 'They wouldnae turn down a scoop like that. And I'll tell ye something: after the rape business, his party's no gonnae be too crazy 'bout him being scandal of the week all over again. It'll be like, what's next? What else is still tae come out? No way they'll let him be leader after that.'

'That the limit of yer ambitions?' Fin said scornfully. 'Make him squirm over a few embarrassing headlines?' She shrugged. 'Maybe you're right. Maybe he'll have to pull outta the race. Doesn't stop him getting another bite at the cherry in a couple o' years once everyone's forgotten. And meantime he's free to go on fucking up the Jasmines of the world with no repercussions. Anyway, aren't ya forgetting something?'

'What?'

'Tannahill. We still don't know what his part is in all this. There's something going on there, and I guarantee it's bigger than him being personal dealer to Mr Family Values. Mark me – that's the main story here. Not the crack, or the funny money, or the dodgy porn.'

'So what do you think we should do?'

'I'm saying play it cool,' said Fin. 'I'm saying we bide our time. We hang onto the stuff we've got and keep it safe, and we don't make any rash moves – not till we figure out exactly where we wanna go with it.

'Listen,' she went on, getting to her feet, 'I dunno 'bout you, but I'm about ready to pass out from heatstroke. Ya mind if I lose this?' She indicated to her vest, soaked through with sweat and clinging to her.

Zoe managed an indifferent shrug, and half-watched as Fin peeled it off and tossed it aside. She didn't stop there, though. Before Zoe had time to look the other way, Fin had unhooked her bra and was standing before her, arms behind her head, inhaling and stretching luxuriantly.

'Aaahh! Now I can *breeeeeathe*.' She waggled her empty bottle. ''Nother?'

'Please,' said Zoe, eyes like saucers as she stared resolutely at the floor.

'Comin' right up.'

As Fin headed for the kitchen, Zoe remained on the sofa, willing herself to stop thinking about Fin and her free-swinging tits and instead focus on taking stock of her current situation. The reality of how deep in she was had begun to hit home. Before tonight, her investigation into Ryland's life had essentially been an intellectual exercise, amassing information without actively *doing* anything. Now, that had all changed. She was, at the very least, an accessory to burglary. Worse still, she now had concrete proof of Ryland's involvement in illegal activities but could do nothing about it without tying a noose around her own neck in the process. And, now that she thought about it, she realised she'd never really stopped to consider what bringing Ryland down actually meant. She'd been so preoccupied with finding proof of his villainy that what came next hadn't entered into the equation. She supposed she'd always imagined the police would be the final arbiters of justice. That was the way it was supposed to be, after all. But tonight's events made it abundantly clear that Fin was working to a very different agenda.

She wondered if she'd have been better off not knowing. Probably. If she'd never met Jasmine, never heard the name 'Ryland', she'd have been able to just carry on with her boring, unfulfilling, uncomplicated existence, none the wiser about any of it.

Mind you, in that case she'd never have met Fin . . .

She flapped the collar of her top again. *Jesus*, she was hot. The thought of an ice-cold shower had never held so much appeal. She glanced at Fin's vest and bra, lying discarded on the floor, and felt a stab of envy. Oh, to be so unencumbered, so uninhibited!

'Fuck it,' she said to herself, and pulled her cami over her head.

For all of fifteen seconds, sitting there on the sofa with the air prickling her bare skin felt like the most natural thing in the world. But then, as the seconds continued to tick by, she began to feel more and more awkward, the conviction that this was a mistake growing stronger by the second. She'd never been particularly shy about flaunting her wares, but there was a time and place for getting nekkid, and this sure as shit didn't feel like it. She had no reason to believe Fin's decision to strip off was motivated by anything more than a desire to cool off, but she worried that, by joining in on the act, she was inadvertently signalling that she'd read something more into it.

She'd just made the decision to knock this act of spontaneous exhibitionism on the head and was reaching for her top when Fin came sauntering in with a couple of fresh beers.

'Whew! I tell ya, all this code-cracking's thirsty work.' She gave Zoe the briefest of glances. 'You cool?'

'How d'ye mean?' said Zoe, an involuntary note of defensiveness in her voice.

'Looking a little constipated there.'

Well, at least it wasn't *nice mosquito bites*.

'I'm fine. I was just thinking.'

'And? Any flashes of inspiration?'

Zoe thought about it before responding. 'We sit tight for now. You're right – we don't need to do anything in a hurry.'

Fin grinned. 'That's the spirit! World'll still be the same hellhole in the morning as it was last night. Here, get this down ya.'

She handed Zoe her beer and sank into the recliner with a contented sigh, one leg draped over the armrest. As she set her own bottle aside and proceeded to unbutton her trousers, it briefly occurred to Zoe that she might be intending to disrobe completely – in which case she'd have a real dilemma on her hands as to whether to once again follow suit. But no, it turned out Fin was just making herself more comfortable and wasn't – for now, at any rate – planning to expose any more of herself.

Her indifference gave Zoe reassurance. She told herself there was nothing weird or inappropriate about this. Nothing at all. She thought of the Frisbee-playing youths in Victoria Park the previous day, indulging in an act of indecency no different from the one she and Fin were now committing – and in a public space at that. If they were a couple of blokes, it would be a non-issue.

She popped the cap of her beer, swallowed a mouthful and decided she wasn't going to worry about her state of semi-undress, or about Ryland, anymore. At any rate, not till tomorrow. She told herself that, however she ultimately decided to take the anti-Ryland initiative forward, it was a bridge she'd cross when she came to it. It was deferred, put on hold till such a time as she was forced to commit to a particular course of action. It was the philosophy she applied to everything else in her life, so why not this as well?

As the hours ticked by, Zoe and Fin engaged in nothing more controversial than talking and passing the time in one another's company. They were going to set the world to rights, the pair of them, rebuilding the social order according to Fin's views of how things should work – views which, the more time passed and the more beer she got down her, increasingly not only made sense to Zoe but seemed so obvious that she couldn't fathom why she hadn't come to the same conclusions herself long ago. At the same time, a part of her couldn't help but imagine what Carol would say if she could see them now, lounging around with their norks out after a housebreaking jaunt, a packet of cocaine and a laptop full of seriously iffy smut lying on the table between them.

Fuck her, she thought. Carol was too suspicious for her own damn good. She might as well be doing something to actually *earn* that suspicion for once.

The night wore on, and the sun began to rise above the rooftops to the east, and still their conversation continued.

15

Home Movies

Steve Michener stood facing the dining room wall, gazing at the giant cartoon phallus spray-painted on the once-pristine flock wallpaper, complete with the obligatory jet of horizontal dashes extending from the urethral opening. Cocks, he thought. Why did they always draw cocks? No one ever drew a nice fanny or a pair of tits.

He became aware of a presence behind him and turned to see Ryland standing in the doorway in his shirtsleeves, a single malt in his hand. He was very quiet and very still. Michener couldn't tell whether this meant he was angry or rattled. Or both.

'How's Alice?'

'Sleeping. I made her take a couple of Valium.'

Without another word, Ryland turned and left the room.

Deciding he'd better follow, Michener took off after him. He caught up with Ryland in the living room, standing in front of the wall-mounted TV, remote in hand. Some fuzzy monochrome footage flickered on the screen. The resolution was so poor that it took Michener's eyes a few moments to lock onto what they were seeing. When they finally did, he realised he was looking at a recording of Ryland's study, taken from an angle high above the desk. A spiky-haired young woman in a leather jacket and gloves was rooting through the desk drawers with a systematic efficiency that suggested she'd done this sort of thing before. With the poor quality, lack of sound and jerky, staccato movement, the footage had an eerie quality to it, reminiscent of that Japanese ghost movie where the girl with black hair comes out of the TV screen.

'Who's the dyke?' Michener asked, feeling compelled to add something to the uneasy silence.

'If I knew that I wouldn't be wasting my time showing you home movies of her,' Ryland snapped.

As they watched, the woman straightened up, holding something small and weightless in her hand, like one of those little packets of salt you get in cheap restaurants. Michener stole a glance at Ryland, who stood there, jaw tight, breathing slowly through flared nostrils. He had a feeling it wasn't salt in the bag.

'I want to know who the hell she is,' Ryland said, 'and what she was doing in here.'

The image on the screen was suddenly blown out by an explosion of light. It took a few seconds for the camera's sensor to adjust, stabilising the levels to reveal the burglar standing stock still, facing the window – reacting, Michener surmised, to Ryland's Jag pulling up outside. The girl hesitated for a moment, then took off the rucksack hanging from her shoulders, grabbed the laptop off the desk and shoved it in. She began to make her way around the room, overturning chairs, pulling books off shelves, grabbing a vase and smashing it on the floor. Within half a minute, the girl was gone and the study resembled Ground Zero.

Michener stole another glance at Ryland. Normally, when he got angry, Ryland shouted and screamed and generally threw his weight around. Once or twice, he also threw the odd ornament for good measure. The fact that he was now so still, so quiet, unnerved

Michener in a way that no amount of bellowing or foot-stamping could have done.

'Find her,' Ryland whispered, the ice jangling in his glass as his hand trembled. 'Fucking find her.'

16

The Whole Truth

Zoe came to with the sun's rays kissing the backs of her shoulders. She was lying on the sofa, face-down, wearing her pants and nothing else. She sat bolt upright and cast around wildly. The rest of her clothes – her cami, her shorts, her plimsolls – lay in a bundle at the foot of the sofa.

They hadn't – had they?

No, of course not. She'd remember if they had.

Wouldn't she?

Feeling as rough as a badger's grundle, she pulled on her clothes and shuffled to the bathroom. Sitting on the toilet, attempting to tune out the throbbing in her head, she tried to reconstruct what had happened the previous night. She knew, in the most general sense, that she and Fin had continued drinking and blethering into the early hours, with a vague memory of them calling it quits shortly after sunrise. She checked her phone. It was just after twenty past nine, which meant she'd probably slept for about four hours, if that. That, plus all the beer she'd knocked back, and it was no wonder she felt like reheated shite.

As she emerged from the bathroom, she noticed that the door across the hallway was slightly ajar. Curiosity getting the better of her, she padded over and nudged it open.

Fin lay on the bed before her, fast asleep. She was stark naked, stretched flat out on her back, one arm flung behind her head. Her right leg was straight, the left one bent outward at the knee, providing Zoe with a front row view of everything she hadn't seen the previous night.

She wasn't sure how long she stood there. It could have been seconds. It was probably longer. But for however much time passed, she was transfixed, drinking in Fin's intoxicating brazenness like it was going out of fashion. Then Fin opened a solitary eye and Zoe immediately turned tail and ran from the flat as fast as her legs would carry her, not even stopping when she missed her footing on the stairs and narrowly avoided spraining her ankle.

As she power-walked down Dumbarton Road, attempting the impossible task of covering as much ground as possible while simultaneously trying to quell the fire that burned on every inch of her skin, she remembered – the trial.

Jesus fuck, the trial.

She did the fastest about-turn known to man and set off east like the clappers, dialling the number for a local taxi firm as she went. A cab collected her a few minutes later just beyond the Kelvin Hall, and she spent a frantic half-hour being bounced around in the back of it, seeming to hit every roadworks and red light in the city, before they finally pulled up outside the courthouse a few minutes before ten.

The High Court of Justiciary was situated on the north bank of the River Clyde, across the road from Glasgow Green – where, once upon a time, they used to hang those convicted of the gravest offences. Zoe flung some cash at the driver and hurried towards the round, faux-Greek gatehouse that served as the public entrance. In front of it, a lantern-jawed man she recognised from the TV news was addressing a camera, oversized microphone in hand.

She scurried past him before she had a chance to pick up whether he was talking about the Price case or not, pushed through the revolving doors and stepped into the lobby with its gleaming marble floor. The place was heaving with bodies, some hurrying this way and that on what was no doubt important business; others, like her, stood about, looking lost.

She passed through security, depositing her phone and other odds and ends in a little plastic tray and stepping through the body scanner, just as if she was at the airport, going off on her summer jollies. The guard who handed her items back told her in no uncertain terms that her phone was to remain switched off for the duration of her visit. As she half-listened to him explaining the house rules, she looked around, hoping to spot Anna, but there was no sign of her. Of course there wasn't. Why would there be? She'd have already gone through this whole rigmarole ages ago. This was the woman who showed up early for her dentist's appointments, for God's sake, just in case by some miracle they were running ahead of schedule.

At that moment, the intercom crackled to life overheard to announce that the case of HMA vs. Price was about to start in court six. A crowd of people all started moving in the same direction, which she took to mean that they were headed where she was headed. After trailing behind them along a long corridor and through a set of double doors, she found herself in the courtroom.

The public gallery was on a slope at the back of the room, and Zoe's first impression upon entering was that it was nothing like what she'd expected. Raised on a diet of overblown movies and television, she'd imagined a huge, ornate place festooned with leather upholstery and monarchical regalia, a bit like the English Houses of Parliament. Instead, the room was small and understated, with wood-panelled walls and cheap functional seating. There were flatscreens mounted on the walls and 'no photography' signs everywhere. In the corner, red lights flashed on a comms box with a veritable spaghetti junction of wires coming out of the back of it, like something out of a server room. The only concession to pomp and ceremony was the Coat of Arms on the wall at the front. It was all a bit of an anti-climax.

Her second impression was how tiny everyone looked down at the front of the room. The various representatives of the defence and prosecution, dressed in their black gowns like old-fashioned teachers, were on opposite sides of a half-oval table, conferring as they shuffled stacks of papers and hooked up their laptops.

Zoe slipped into a seat near the back (the ones at the front had all been taken by people with better timekeeping than herself) and sized up the folk around her – again trying, unsuccessfully, to catch sight of Anna. They were a motley assortment, ranging from a couple of young women in trouser-suits whispering to one another to an old man in a duffle coat who sat with a little notebook on his knee, pencil poised even though there was no sign of things getting underway anytime soon. One man in his sixties with a belly like a space-hopper was perusing the day's edition of the *Press and Journal*. His outfit, a loud fluorescent T-shirt and a pair of shorts held up by braces, was utterly at odds with the solemnity of the place – though Zoe had to concede that she was hardly dressed for the occasion herself. At any rate, he hardly looked any more ridiculous than the lawyers in their capes and penguin suits.

She wondered what all these folk were doing here. Did they have a particular interest in the case or just nothing better to do on a Monday morning than sit in on a rape trial? Then she remembered that some of them would probably be friends and relatives of either Gavin or Jenny, in which case they had far more justification for being here than her. She was surprised not to see more of a press presence – though, now that it occurred to her, it was always possible the old yin with the notebook was a journo. But she'd been struck by the lack of cameras and news vans outside the courthouse on her way in. In her head, she'd built this up as the trial of the century, but she now realised the reality was that the media and the public at large probably didn't give a toss.

In the middle of the room, beyond the public benches but before the lawyers' table, there was a single bench, fenced off from the rest of the room by low half-wall. Now, Zoe watched as a big man in a G4S uniform appeared inside it, having seemingly emerged from a hole in the ground. As he made his way along the bench and sat down at one end, another man stepped up, then another. The third, who sat down at the other end, wore the same uniform and was of a similarly imposing build. The second, sandwiched between them, was almost as tall as they were, but considerably slighter. He wore a nicely-cut charcoal suit. His blond hair was cropped close to the skull. He turned to say something to one of the two guards, and Zoe caught sight of the small dark mole, almost a beauty spot, that adorned his upper lip.

Zoe hadn't seen Gavin Price in person since December three and a half years ago, and her stomach tightened involuntarily at the sight of him. On so many occasions before now, she'd thought about how she'd respond to him if she found herself in the same room as him. What she'd say to him. What she'd *do*. But there was no opportunity to either say or do anything now, and, before she had a chance to gather her thoughts, a sudden cry of *Court!* went up, and she realised everyone was getting to their feet – both the public and the professionals. She did likewise, and watched as a woman in a black cloak entered, carrying some sort of rod. Behind her, walking at a stoop, came an elderly man in flowing red and white robes and what looked like a dead sheep on his head. The woman escorted the little man to his seat at the head of the courtroom, below the Coat of Arms. The legal beagles all gave little bows. The whole thing was so farcical that Zoe had to stifle a nervous laugh. Then the man in the sheep wig sat down, everyone else followed his example, and the rod was installed in a little holder on the wall. It seemed things were finally ready to get underway.

Except they weren't. It turned out there was a whole bunch more business still to be played out. First, an officious-looking man stationed at a desk below the judge's seat got to his feet and asked the defendant to confirm that he was indeed Gavin James Price, which left Zoe wondering what they'd have done if he'd said no, he wasn't. But he said he was, and then his lawyer, a short man with a combover, wearing a purple waistcoat under his robes, rose to inform the judge that his client would be entering a Not Guilty plea. Again, Zoe was left wondering how this could possibly be news to anyone. Then came the selection and swearing in, using a variety of oaths and affirmations, of the fifteen jurors – a motley assortment whose faces betrayed a range of emotions, from fear and confusion to barely-concealed euphoria. That emptied the public gallery somewhat; it turned out the prospective jurors were all sitting in among the day-trippers and pleasure-seekers. There was a lot of muttering and shuffling, and the man with the braces, having evidently concluded that this wasn't going to be half as interesting as he'd hoped, got up and left, his paper tucked under his arm.

It was nearly eleven by the time everything was settled. The judge, who'd looked at times like he was going to nod off, leaned forward and addressed the jury in a firm but quavering tone:

'Ladies and gentlemen, the charge against the accused is that, on the twenty-second of December 1999, he participated in the abduction and rape of one Ms Jennifer Guilfoyle. At the time, Mr Price was eighteen years of age and Ms Guilfoyle was seventeen. Mr Price has chosen not to give evidence at this trial, as is his right, and I would remind you to infer nothing from this decision.

'Before we begin hearing from the witnesses, I would like to make some points about the unusual nature of this case. Unlike in a typical rape trial, the accused here is not the perpetrator. He is being tried under the Scots Law principle of Art and Part, which holds that a person involved in aiding and abetting a crime shares equal culpability with those responsible for carrying it out. Secondly, and again in contrast to the normal procedure for trials of this sort, the defence is not disputing that a crime has taken place. No one on these benches seeks to disprove that Jennifer Guilfoyle was raped. What the Crown *does* seek to prove, and the defence to disprove, is the foreknowledge of Mr Price and his presence, or lack thereof, during the perpetration of the aforementioned assault.

'A final point, and this applies as much to those seated in the public gallery as to the jurors. Normally, every rape trial in Scotland is held in a closed court. Today I have allowed the public gallery to remain open at the behest of Ms Guilfoyle and her family. I entreat you all to consider the sensitivity of this case, and to afford it the utmost dignity and respect.'

He allowed his words to hang in the air for effect. Then, satisfied that his point had been made, he turned to the left-hand side of the table. 'I will now invite the Advocate Depute to call his first witness. Mr Quaid?'

The Advocate Depute, a distinguished-looking man with snowy hair and a scholarly air about him, rose to his feet, one hand tucked into his waistcoat like Napoleon.

'Thank you, My Lord. The first witness for the Crown is Mr Anthony Guilfoyle.'

Jenny Guilfoyle's father was a big man in every way – broad-chested, with massive great hands and a lumbering gait. But from Zoe's vantage point he looked much diminished as he entered from a door to the left, crossed the floor and clambered up into the witness box. He raised his right hand and, in his gruff baritone voice, repeated the oath read out to him by the judge, swearing by Almighty God to tell the truth, the whole truth and nothing but the truth. Zoe wasn't sure what God had to do with it, but she figured they could use all the help they could get.

Clutching a bulging ring-binder, Quaid installed himself behind a lectern on the opposite side of the room to Guilfoyle. He paused to place a pair of small wire spectacles on his nose, stroked his chin thoughtfully, then lifted his head towards Jenny's father.

'Are you Anthony Guilfoyle?'

'Yes.'

'And are you the father of Jennifer Guilfoyle?'

'Yes.'

'And at the time that Jennifer was in fifth year at school, did she have a boyfriend called Gavin Price?'

'Yes.'

'And would you recognise Gavin Price if you saw him again?'

'Yes.'

'And do you see him in court today?'

'Yes.'

'Could you identify him, please?'

His expression remaining impassive, Guilfoyle raised his right arm and pointed a meaty finger towards the defendant's bench.

Zoe watched this whole rigmarole dumbfounded. *This* was what went on in courtrooms? Where were the bombastic opening statements by the lawyers, the strident *I objects*? Anna hadn't been kidding when she'd said it wasn't like it was on the telly. She wondered if these chancers got paid by the minute and that was why they wasted so much time talking dead slowly and asking questions everyone already knew the answers to. And now the lawyer was asking about Jenny and Gavin's relationship: how long they'd been going out, when Guilfoyle had first become aware they were an item, what they were like together and so on. Zoe felt a burning urge to get to her feet and shout out, *He let his pals rape her! What's it matter what they were like together?* But she managed to restrain herself, and as the plodding, monotonous questions droned on and the sun rose higher in the sky, she found herself beginning to zone out. To keep the tendrils of sleep at bay, she resorted to pinching her inner thigh with increasing forcefulness.

Quaid eventually steered Guilfoyle towards the day of December the twenty-second 1999. Was it the last day of school? Yes, it was. And at what time did school finish on that day? At midday. And what—

'I don't wish to cut you off in your prime, Mr Quaid,' said the judge, raising a trembling hand, 'but I fancy the attention spans of the jury would be better served by full stomachs than by empty ones. It's twelve thirty-seven. We will resume at one-thirty sharp.'

Zoe got to her feet and joined the exodus out of the courtroom. She hung about in the lobby, listening to the multiple conversations going on around her and wondering what the hell she was doing here. She thought about not going back after lunch, then decided against it. There was nothing else for her to do, besides go home and face the inevitable bollocking from Carol. She wasn't ready for that just yet.

And then there was Victor. He needed a witness. Someone to represent him.

She looked around. A little way off, near the reception desk, a well-to-do man and woman in their sixties or thereabouts were engaged in an earnest discussion with Gavin's lawyer, the little man in the purple waistcoat. Zoe recognised them from the public gallery, and it now occurred to her that they were probably Gavin's parents. Not trusting herself not to go off on one about their scumbag of a son, she gave them a wide berth and hurried outside.

She was standing in the shadow of the gatehouse – the coolest place she could find – when someone tapped her on the shoulder.

She turned to find Anna facing her. She was wearing a smart trouser-suit, as if she was attending . . . well, court . . . but she looked drawn and tired. Zoe suspected she'd probably got about as much sleep as *she* had, albeit for different reasons.

'I waited for you in the foyer before the start,' said Anna. 'I thought maybe you'd decided not to come.'

'Got stuck in traffic,' said Zoe, resisting the urge for a snide *sorry to disappoint you.*

'Well, I'm glad you made it.' It genuinely sounded like she meant it. 'You eaten yet? There's a canteen in there somewhere . . . ' She glanced over her shoulder. 'But I'd rather not run into any of the Price contingent if I can help it.'

'I already seen 'em – his folks. Back inside, talking to his lawyer.'

Anna thought about it. 'Come on. Let's get out of here.'

17

Red Top

The staff at Kinning Park Library had been warned to be on their best behaviour for the duration of their distinguished guest's visit, but their collective expressions of grim resentment as they watched from the confines of the enquiry desk said it all. They could be forgiven for their hostility towards the visitor: the odds were high that, if they hadn't read his *Spectator* article calling for underperforming public libraries to be sold off as housing stock, then they'd at least have heard about it.

The head librarian was taking Dominic Ryland, Conservative MSP for Central Scotland, on a guided tour of the facilities – one of the many local community appointments his minders had organised for him as his leadership campaign entered its final stages.

'. . . and over here we have our drop-in centre for welfare and benefits advice. In today's rapidly changing world, it's essential that libraries adapt from being mere book repositories to meet the evolving needs of the local populace.'

Ryland nodded and offered a slight smile of acknowledgement. A neutral observer might have concluded that he was somewhat reserved, perhaps even a little socially awkward. Those who knew him better would have been well-placed to recognise the tell-tale signs of anxiety and distraction. Ryland's mind was on other matters.

They were heading over to inspect the Man Booker display when Michener arrived, panting and crimson-faced, a newspaper tucked under his arm.

'I need a word.'

Ryland, looking a tad ruffled by the intrusion, excused himself and joined Michener behind a nearby bookshelf.

'Well?'

Michener responded by unfolding the paper. It was a local red top – one of the ones favourable to Ryland's party, though its tenor was so low-brow that its support was privately considered an embarrassment. He turned to one of the inside pages.

KELVINGROVE KILLER'S SISTER PARTIED WITH LESBIAN LOVER BEFORE PRICE TRIAL!

Below this strident headline was a slightly off-angle picture of two women walking side by side, heads turning towards the camera.

Michener jabbed a finger at the one in front. 'Our mystery intruder.'

Ryland said nothing. It took Michener a moment to realise that he wasn't actually looking at the girl he'd pointed at – the one with the short, spiky hair and leather jacket – but rather at her companion – a few years older, much more conventionally feminine, sporting a short, strappy dress and waist-length auburn hair.

'Her.' Ryland tapped the paper. 'I know her. I've seen her before.'

'She's the sister of the Kelvingrove Killer. You know – that loon who ran around castrating people a few Christmases ago. You probably saw her in the papers at the time.'

Ryland shook his head irritably. 'That's not it.'

For a moment, he stood massaging his jaw agitatedly, then gripped Michener's arm in a sudden pique of excitement.

'The police station! The night I was dragged in by that bitch Cauley. She was there, in the waiting area. I remember now.'

Michener studied the photo again, as if it contained some hidden detail that would explain this puzzle. He could see why Ryland was getting hot under the collar about this: it looked far too much like a coincidence to actually be one.

'So what's our next move?'

'Nothing,' said Ryland, after a moment. 'Hold fire for now.'

'*Nothing?*' Michener wondered whether he'd heard correctly.

'That's right.'

Ryland patted Michener's shoulder as if to say *don't worry*, then took the paper from him, tucked it under his arm and walked back towards the desk, where the head librarian was waiting for him.

Michener stared after him. The two of them went back a considerable way. He wouldn't exactly describe them as friends per se, but he felt he knew Ryland pretty well and had seen him at both his best and worst. But he'd never seen him like this before, and he couldn't make head nor tail of it at all. He seemed to have retreated into himself, refusing to acknowledge the problem rather than – as was his usual way – confronting it head-on.

One thing was for sure, though. He was rattled. Very rattled indeed.

18

And Nothing but the Truth

Zoe and Anna headed up to Saltmarket and, at Zoe's choosing, went into the local branch of Subway. Anna insisted on paying for both of them despite Zoe's protestations. 'Honestly, it's no bother,' she said – a statement which Zoe was sure was meant well but which only succeeded in further rubbing her face in their differing fortunes. They took their food to the bar at the window and, perched on stools eating with their fingers, it felt almost like they were teenagers again, grabbing a bite from one of the fast food joints on Great Western Road during lunch break. Almost.

'It's all dead bitty,' said Zoe, referring to the trial. 'I thought there'd be speeches at the start and whatnot – y'know, to set the stage.'

'Not in Scotland.'

'Right enough, aye,' said Zoe, feeling deeply inadequate for not having known that. 'And I wasnae expecting all they people in the public benches,' she went on. 'I thought it'd be mostly press and what have ye. 'Stead it's like a buncha day-trippers out on a jolly.'

Anna paused to finish chewing a mouthful. 'The whole thing's a circus. I don't know what Guilfoyle's thinking, putting his daughter through it.'

'Mibby it's what she wants?'

Anna shook her head. 'I sincerely doubt Jenny knows what she wants. She's not exactly *compos mentis.*'

'When d'ye reckon they'll call her? I'd've thought they'd've started with her.'

'They usually do. Start with the victim, I mean. But I guess they felt her dad would give a more coherent account to set the scene. I reckon they'll keep her for the big finish – hook the audience and reel them in gradually, building up to the star witness. So probably Wednesday or Thursday, depending on how long things run on.'

'Well, they're no hooking me. If I'da known it'd be this boring, I'da brought my copy of *War and Peace.*'

Anna laughed drily. 'Bit different from *Judge Judy*, isn't it?'

Zoe snorted back a laugh of her own. 'Aye, she'd've sorted 'em out.' She mimed banging a gavel. 'Judgement for the plaintiff!'

Anna grinned, a trickle of Southwest sauce escaping from the corner of her mouth. For a brief moment, she looked shockingly like her teenage self, and Zoe felt a sudden pang of longing for everything they'd both lost in the intervening years. She shook the feeling off and slipped her Funny Zoe mask back on again.

'Lookit you, can't take ye anywhere.' She reached out to wipe the sauce away. 'There. Cannae have ye looking like a scruff.'

Anna smiled. 'Thanks, pal. What would I do without you, huh?'

For a while, they sat side by side, chewing in silent solidarity. At length, Zoe piped up again.

'Listen, doll, I wanted to say sorry. Y'know, for yesterday. For being a twat.'

'It's OK. Emotions are running high for everyone. You're entitled to be a twat under the circumstances.'

'Aye, I know, but still, disnae excuse it.'

They were silent again for a while. Next to her, Zoe could sense Anna working up to saying something. After a moment, she spoke up.

'Listen, Zoe, don't take this the wrong way, but I've got some deodorant in my bag if you need to borrow it.'

They headed back to the courtroom and managed to get seats together, Zoe freshly desmellified but feeling decidedly self-conscious all the same. She kept her arms glued to her sides, hoping that would prevent her from stinking the place up too much. She was acutely aware that she was wearing the same clothes from the previous day – clothes she'd been running around and sweating profusely into for the better part of thirty-six hours.

The afternoon session got underway. The Advocate Depute resumed his questioning of Guilfoyle from where he'd left off, after first promising not to keep him any longer than necessary – a promise which, given how things had gone during the morning session, Zoe suspected was unlikely to be kept. She listened as Guilfoyle recounted his return home from work to find his daughter locked in her room – and, in the days and weeks that followed, her withdrawal from him and the world at large. She knew the story well, having heard it all from Anna before, but hearing Guilfoyle's gravelly voice cracking with emotion as he described finding his daughter's bloodstained knickers made it all the more raw.

Not for the first time, she wondered how Victor could possibly have gone along with it. Over the last few years, she'd gone over his involvement in her head countless times, considering the different permutations. On occasions, she'd recast his role as that of an unwilling participant, forced by the other boys to take part under pain of death. But it never worked for long. When it came down to it, there was no way of downplaying what he'd done, and she burned with anger at him even as she mourned him and raged against the injustices done to him by the press. And it wasn't just the rape itself. It was what had come after it: the lives he'd taken, and the lives he'd ruined in the process. She tried to put herself in his shoes, to imagine herself doing the same things he'd done, and she just couldn't. It was beyond her moral ken. What was more, the Victor she knew could never have done it either. Which left only one possible conclusion: that she hadn't really known him at all.

In the last few years, she'd returned repeatedly to an incident on the twenty-second of December 1999, which she now knew was the day *it* had happened. She'd got home late to find the house in darkness. Their granny had been out at the bingo, as she always was on a Wednesday night. She assumed, from the lack of lights, that Victor must be out too. It wasn't until she'd let herself in and gone upstairs to change that she heard sounds of soft snivelling coming from the bathroom. Opening the door, she was confronted by a sight that remained etched into her mind to this day: Victor, stark naked, his clothes in a pile at his feet, weeping, his little willy jiggling with each sob that racked his body. He lifted his head and gazed back at her through tear-brimmed eyes, not even trying to cover himself up. She continued to stare back at him for several moments, gobsmacked, then shut the door and fled to her room.

Everything about what Victor had done horrified and revolted her to her core. His actions were unforgivable, and if there was such a thing as a Hell, she didn't doubt that he was roasting in it right now. And yet, in Gavin standing trial, she'd always imagined that there was a chance for the imbalance to finally be redressed. A chance for the story behind the story to finally get an airing. It wouldn't even begin to wipe out Victor's misdeeds, but at least it would be a chance to show the world that he'd had a reason for doing what he did. That the people he'd killed were not just the poor, helpless, innocent victims the newspapers had made out. That maybe, just maybe, they'd deserved it. Now, though, with the trial actually unfolding before her eyes, that hope receded. Anna had been right: this wasn't about Victor. He wasn't the one on trial.

196

She and Victor had never spoken about the incident in the bathroom. It was as if some silent, mutual agreement had been reached never to mention it. But now, some thirteen and a half years later, she cursed herself for not having shown more compassion, for not having asked him what was wrong, for not having *guessed*. In truth, she'd been plain embarrassed – by his tears, by his nakedness, by her own sense of inadequacy. She was the big sister. It was her job to protect him, but when push came to shove she'd done nothing. If she'd persevered and got to the bottom of what had upset him so much, things might have played out very differently, and she might not be here now, watching the rape trial of the sole survivor of her brother's murderous rage.

The defence was clearly rattled by Guilfoyle's testimony, for when it came time for Gavin's lawyer to ask his questions, he treated him with a degree of tact and deference that Zoe hadn't expected. It didn't seem to her like a cross-examination at all. There were no attempts to trip the witness up, to infer that he was a liar and what have you. Just a lot of uh-huhs and I-sees and when-did-shes, accompanied by a lot of strained, understanding smiles, as if everyone involved was commiserating about what a rotten business this all was. Zoe kept glancing at Anna, trying to read how things were going from her expression, but her face remained tight and impassive.

The afternoon wore on, and once more Zoe found her mind beginning to wander. At one point, it looked like there might be a bit of drama in the offing when the Advocate Depute for the prosecution raised an objection about a particular question. The judge ordered the jury out and then he and the two lawyers had a very intense conversation about all sorts of legal fiddle-faddle. But eventually the issue was resolved and the jury was brought back in. They continued for a bit longer, but by that time it was after four and the judge, who'd been looking for a while like he'd been on the verge of falling asleep, decided that was enough for one day. He ordered the jury to be back tomorrow at 9.30 sharp and not to discuss the case with anyone. *Aye, that'll be right.* Gavin was escorted down into the basement by his two handlers, no doubt to disappear out the back of the courthouse with a sheet over his head. As the gallery began to clear, Zoe and Anna got to their feet and joined the crush to get out.

'What'd ye think?' Zoe asked as they stepped out into the sunlight.

'You never can tell with these things,' said Anna. 'It's early days yet.'

Zoe knew Anna too well for that non-answer to cut any mustard. She could read her as well as a book. 'There's a "but" in there, in't there?'

For a while, Anna was silent, lips pursed and chin tucked in tight. 'I don't like the way the defence is choosing to play this,' she said at length. 'They're being canny. I thought they'd do the usual thing of going hard at it, picking holes in everything. But this meekness, this softly-softly approach – somehow it feels worse.'

'How come?'

'An aggressive defence can sometimes swing things in the prosecution's favour. The jury sees a snooty lawyer laying into a witness and they think, "What an arsehole, giving them the third degree like that", and they go for a conviction, as much to hit back at the defence as the defendant himself. But this lot are coming over as reasonable. I don't know for sure what their game is, but best I can figure, they're going to just sit back and let the flimsiness of the case speak for itself.'

'It's no that flimsy, though, is it?'

Anna thought deeply about it before responding. 'I'd say it's all going to rest on how Jenny does on the stand.'

'But there's a chance, right? I mean, the case wouldnae've got this far if they weren't at least hopeful?'

Anna sighed. 'The test for the Crown Office isn't "will the jury convict?" It's "*could* they?" Even if they're not certain of a positive outcome, they'll still go to trial if the case is viable. And there's so much more in play than just the evidence and how well the lawyers do their jobs. There's the jury too. You don't know what their individual life experiences are; what prejudices they're bringing in with them. The cards might be stacked in our favour, but they might just as well be stacked against us.'

A thought occurred to Zoe. 'Ye don't think . . . ' she began, then stopped herself. 'Ye don't think there's any chance he didnae do it?'

Anna gave Zoe a long, hard look. For a brief moment, her eyes came alive with a steely resolve that had so far been absent.

'No,' she said adamantly, 'he did it. The only question is whether that's what the jury will conclude.'

They headed up to High Street and caught a train back to Partick. Anna told Zoe her understanding was that tomorrow, after they'd finished with Guilfoyle, the prosecution would move on to calling various other witnesses to strengthen their case – people who were present at the party at the house on Park Terrace where it had all gone down, others who knew Jenny and Gavin from school and could provide more background on their relationship and so on. She was going to be lecturing all day and doubted she'd be able to put in an appearance, but said she'd definitely be there for when Jenny took the stand, whenever that proved to be. It sounded to Zoe like she'd already given up. If she'd felt there was any point in being there tomorrow, she'd surely have found a way.

It was a shame Anna wasn't taking the stand herself, Zoe thought. She knew that, early on, the prosecution had made noises about calling her as a witness. She'd been present in the bell-tower when Victor had made Gavin spell out, in minute detail, just what had been done to Jenny and by whom, making her ideally placed to corroborate the 'conspiracy' narrative. But Gavin's legal team had predictably cried foul, citing the unreliable nature of second-hand testimony of a confession extracted at knifepoint, and the prosecution, keen to reach some degree of compromise in other key areas, had duly backed down.

At Partick, they went their separate ways, Anna going to collect her car and Zoe heading back to the flat. As she walked up Dumbarton Road, she switched on her phone for the first time since going through security. She expected to find herself faced with a barrage of texts from Carol, but to her surprise there was nothing. Nothing, that is, apart from a terse answerphone message from Valerie, demanding to know why (the hell) she hadn't turned up for her shift today. She thought about calling back and making up some excuse, but then she realised she couldn't be arsed. The way she was feeling at the moment, they could fire her for all she cared.

Carol had already left for work, and to Zoe's surprise – if not exactly disappointment – hadn't left anything for dinner. She took a shower, washing off the accumulated grime of the past two days, then made herself a Pot Noodle and put on the evening news, partly because there was nothing better to watch and partly out of morbid curiosity to see how they reported on the trial. There was a brief item on it towards the end, buried between a piece on a footballer who'd visited a terminally ill fan in hospital and one on supermarket chickens being recalled due to contamination fears. And that, it seemed, was the sum total of the media's interest in the case.

As she sat half-watching *Kitchen Nightmares*, her phone began to vibrate. It was Fin.

'Hi.' Zoe tried for casual but only succeeded in hitting breathless.

Fin tutted. 'Well now, what's a girl supposed to think when ya sneak off at the crack o' dawn without even a goodbye kiss? Do me a favour: next time, wake me up before ya go-go.'

Zoe winced. 'Aye, sorry. I, uh, had someplace I needed tae be. Didnae wanna disturb ye.'

'So I gathered. Least ya got a good eyeful before you left. Like what you saw?'

A wave of white-hot mortification engulfed Zoe. 'I–I just . . . sorry, I was looking for the bathroom and took a wrong—'

Fin gave a throaty cackle. 'Hey, ya don't need to bullshit me. I say if the view's good, make the most of it. Maybe someday you can return the favour.'

Zoe opted not to respond to that.

'So. Whatcha doing tonight?'

No, no. Bad idea. Bad, bad *idea.*

'I've made plans.'

'Oh. OK.' Fin sounded unperturbed. 'Well, if ya have a change of heart, just hit me up.'

'I'll bear that in mind.' Zoe went to end the call, then thought of something. 'Look, fae now on, gonnae just wait for *me* to get in touch wi *you*? It's easier that way.'

Fin was silent just long enough to make things uncomfortable. 'Fair dues,' she said, the shrug audible in her voice. 'Guess I'll see ya when I see ya.'

And with that, she hung up.

Zoe put down the phone. Her Pot Noodle had gone cold and she sat chewing morosely. Fin's call had brought to the front of her mind the other major ongoing concern of the moment: Ryland. The euphoria of last night's discoveries had faded away, leaving her filled with doubt about the wisdom of her present course of action. She wondered just how safe Ryland's laptop really was in Fin's keeping, and for how long they could realistically defer committing to a course of action. Fin was bad for her in all sorts of ways. That much was head-slappingly obvious, and she was rapidly coming round to the idea that it would be better all round if they didn't see each other again. Mind you, it would have been good if she'd figured that out before she'd, y'know, helped Fin break into someone's house.

She went to bed alone and despondent. When Carol came in just after three, she pretended to be asleep. Carol made no attempt to wake her or even say a word to her, and Zoe, surmising that she was still in a strop about Sunday night, decided to let her stew. At length, Carol got into her side of the bed and lay down with her back to her. And, though the heat inside the room remained well into the high twenties, the bed felt unaccountably cooler that night.

19

Knowwhatimean?

The following day, Zoe didn't come to until well after ten: despite fully intending to attend day two of the trial, she hadn't had the presence of mind to set an alarm for herself the previous night. Concluding that the morning session would be well and truly underway by now and that there was therefore no point in rushing things, she took her time getting ready, not leaving the flat until nearly an hour later. As she made her way into town, having left Carol still out for the count, she realised that, even without having made a conscious decision about it, she was taking the scenic route – changing trains at every station, taking unnecessary detours, delaying her arrival as much as possible.

It was nearly midday when she finally reached the court, slipping in as surreptitiously as possible and taking an empty seat in the back row. Down in the main body of the courtroom, Quaid was interrogating a man Zoe recognised as Richie Deans, a contemporary of Gavin's who had an unfortunate habit of looking shifty no matter what. He was doing his level best to downplay his relationship with the accused, humming and hawing and insisting that, while they knew each other, they didn't *know* each other, knowwhatimean? Quaid said he didn't, and Zoe sensed that he was getting pretty fed up with Richie – a common reaction from grown-up types, as she remembered.

'Let's turn to the matter of Mr Price's relationship with Ms Guilfoyle. Were you aware at the time that they were boyfriend and girlfriend?'

Richie was on surer footing here. 'Oh yeah, they were mad into each other. Like, they kept it pretty hush-hush, but pretty much everyone knew, knowwhatimean? They thought they weren't being obvious about it, but . . . well, you know.'

This time it seemed Quaid *did* know. 'And his cousin Andrew Foley,' he went on, 'how would you describe *their* relationship?'

'Oh,' said Richie, as if that was water off a duck's back, 'they weren't trying to hide *their* relationship.'

That got a few titters from both the public gallery and the jury bench, and the judge's head darted this way and that as he tried to identify the culprits. Quaid waited for the dust to settle, then regarded Richie with a withering look. The lopsided smile promptly left Richie's face.

'Er . . . what I mean is, they were close. Like, really close, knowwhatimean? Most of us, if we had younger brothers or cousins or whatever, we took nothing to do with them at school. Like, it would damage our street cred to be seen with them or something. But not Foley. Him and Gav – sorry, Mr Price – they were thick as thieves. Probably spent more time together than apart.'

'I see. And did Mr Price look up to Mr Foley?'

'Oh *yeah.*' Richie nodded vigorously. 'I mean, it wasn't exactly what you'd call a partnership if equals. Foley was definitely the alpha, knowwhatimean?'

Quaid nodded sagely, seemingly intrigued. 'How so?'

'Well, if Foley said "jump", chances were Gav would ask "how high?"'

The questioning continued in this vein for a while, with Quaid probing Richie further about the nature of the relationship between the two cousins. After that, the advocate for the defence, Streule, had his turn, asking the usual bitty questions and indulging in all manner of pedantry. Richie was followed by Keith Traynor, a somewhat gormless-looking man in his mid-twenties whose great claim to fame was having run into Gavin near the café on the southern edge of Kelvingrove Park on the evening the rape took place. Traynor had just come from the house on Park Terrace and, as he recalled, Gavin had been keen to know whether the party was still going strong. The inference was that Gavin had been trying to gauge the lie of the land before returning to the scene of the crime, but the defence wasn't having it, and to Zoe's disbelief the jury was once again made to troop out while Streule implored the judge to rule elements of Keith's testimony inadmissible. Eventually it was all resolved and the jury was brought back in, but by that time the judge was feeling peckish and ordered them to break for lunch.

With no Anna to talk to and little interest in eating another meal so soon after breakfast, Zoe wandered around for a bit before heading back to the public gallery, thinking she might find a quiet corner and try to catch forty winks. She was the first in, and as she made her way to her seat, she noticed Streule and Quaid down at the front, engaged in conversation as they nibbled sandwiches which some dutiful assistant had no doubt fetched for them. Zoe was taken aback. The manner of these supposed adversaries was relaxed – even friendly. Making as little noise as possible, she moved closer, straining to hear what was being said.

'Oh, Lachlan's dreadful at the moment, just dreadful,' Streule was saying. 'Driving us both up the wall night and day.' He affected a theatrical whisper. 'The terrible twos.'

'Ah.' Quaid nodded sagely. 'Just wait till he's in his teens. Then you'll truly know the meaning of dread.' He took a sip from his bottle of mineral water. 'My regards to Amanda, by the way. It's been . . . how long's it been?'

'Far too long. We really must organise a get-together before long – a "husbands and wives" sort of affair.'

'Indeed, indeed. I shall have to consult my diary.' He paused to bundle his crusts back into their plastic container. 'So what d'you make of it so far?'

Streule gave a little shrug. 'Eh. So far, so predictable. The father gave a good account of himself yesterday. His was the only testimony I thought was halfway compelling, even if you *are* going for the heartstrings with him rather than the cold hard facts.'

'Well, thing is, old boy, cold hard facts are in rather short supply with this one.'

''Twas ever thus. You have my sympathies.'

'Gratefully received.'

Zoe couldn't believe what she was hearing. Was it all a game to these people? Did they not care that lives were at stake? It was like when politicians with radically opposing views tore strips off each other for the cameras, then turned out to be bosom buddies in real life. If Quaid really believed in the case he was prosecuting, how could he exchange pleasantries – and plan double dates, for fuck's sake – with a man whose job it was to defend a rape enabler from going to jail?

She decided she wasn't going to stick around to watch any more of this freak-show. She got to her feet and left.

She'd missed work again that morning and saw little point now in heading along to her afternoon shift, so instead she stayed in the city centre, hanging about in the gloriously air-conditioned shopping centre at the top of Buchanan Street and then going to see a movie – one of those over-the-top summer blockbusters full of CGI, explosions and people flying about getting shot at. Normally she loved that sort of thing, but today she wasn't even feeling the 'so bad it's good' vibe.

She returned to the flat to find Carol getting ready for work. Once more, she was fully prepared for an almighty brouhaha, but once more it proved unforthcoming, with Carol's demeanour curt and oddly indifferent. Was this how it was going to be between them from now on, she wondered? Had Carol made it her mission to affect a bearing of bland indifference towards everything Zoe did, like a parent who'd given up trying to educate their child about the dangers of playing with rattlesnakes or whatever and had concluded they'd just have to learn the hard way?

It wasn't until Zoe had got changed herself and was channel-cycling on the living room sofa that Carol, looming in the doorway, finally deigned to make an utterance.

'Your boss phoned this afternoon. Wanted to know why you weren't at work.'

'Kinda got other things on my mind right now.'

She waited for the inevitable rebuke. *You should have booked time off in advance. You have a responsibility to your employer and to the International Collective of Workers.* But none was forthcoming. Carol merely shrugged and moved into the other room.

'Aren't ye gonnae ask me how it went in court?' Zoe shouted after her.

Silence for a moment, then: 'Fine. How did it go?'

'Well, since ye asked, there's a good chance he's gonnae get off, so on balance, it was fan-TAS-tic.'

She was goading Carol, trying to provoke a response. *Any* response.

Carol appeared in the doorway again. She looked at Zoe for a long moment, but her face held no emotion – not anger, not sympathy, just bland indifference. Then she disappeared from view again and resumed getting ready.

Zoe was playing *Candy Crush* on her phone when Carol next materialised.

'I'm off.'

'OK.'

Pause. 'You planning on going out again tonight?'

Shrug. 'Mibby.'

'Well, mibby send me a text when you know what your plans are.'

'Aye, mibby.'

She sensed Carol continuing to linger in the doorway behind her.

'There's something in the oven for you for when you get hungry.'

Thank you. The words you're looking for are 'thank you'.

Another pause. An intake of breath as if Carol was on the verge of saying something profound or heartfelt. Then, instead, the sound of her retreating footsteps, the slam of the front door, and she was gone.

Zoe lowered her phone. She'd lost the level some time ago but had continued mashing buttons to avoid having to face Carol. She listened to her footsteps and the wheels of her bike bouncing on the stairs; to the ground floor door opening and closing. Then there was nothing – just the hum of traffic seeping through the open window.

Zoe went through to the kitchen to inspect the contents of the oven. A casserole. More veggie crap. On a rational level, she knew she ought to appreciate the effort Carol put into these things, but she wondered how many more hints she had to drop that she had no interest in adopting a herbivore lifestyle before she got the message. Faced with a choice between forcing it down and leaving it uneaten for Carol to find, she instead settled for option three: scraping it into a carrier bag and depositing it in one of the bins out in the street.

Which, at the end of the day, was as potent a metaphor for the state of their relationship as it was possible to get.

20

Enemy Territory

Wednesday rolled around, and, though the thought of sitting in that stuffy room listening to plummy lawyers raking over irrelevant minutia still held about as much appeal as an anal probe, Zoe nonetheless concluded that she'd rather be there than at work. On some level, she realised this was a false choice – that, strictly speaking, she didn't have to do either – but, by going to court, she'd be able to justify not going to Neptune House to herself, or vice versa. And court won out. Just.

When she arrived at the courthouse at getting on for 1 p.m., she immediately sensed that something was different. There was a larger than usual press presence outside the building, including a couple of vans emblazoned with the insignias of the main news networks. She wondered whether some major criminal mastermind was being sent down.

She approached a nearby cameraman, who seemed to be in the process of shooting video of his own feet, and tapped him on the shoulder.

'Here, pal, what's going on?'

He looked up, tucking his camera under his arm. 'Have ye no been watching the news?' he said, as if it was an offence punishable by public humiliation. 'It's the grand finale. The Guilfoyle girl's giving her evidence after lunch.'

All sense of apathy promptly vanished. She rang Anna, letting her know what was what, then hurried inside and secured herself a seat at the front of the gallery. The stalls began to fill up. It was noticeably busier than on Monday and Tuesday, and the air crackled with a palpable sense of excitement. Over her shoulder, she saw Tony Guilfoyle slipping in and taking a seat on the back pew. Poor fucker looked like he'd been up all night sniffing glue. A couple of minutes before they were due to get underway, Anna came hurrying in, breathless and harried-looking. She slid into the seat Zoe had been saving for her and sat catching her breath.

A hush fell as the various dignitaries took their places. Gavin was brought up from the basement and settled in his usual spot between his two babysitters. The judge ascended his throne and everyone gave their little curtsies. Then Quaid got to his feet.

'My Lord, the final witness for the Crown is Ms Jennifer Guilfoyle.'

Jenny Guilfoyle had a disposition that might charitably be described as retiring. The reality was that what Gavin, Victor and the other boys had done to her thirteen years ago had fucked her up beyond all measure – to the point that, for the greater part of those thirteen years, she'd been completely mute, locked in a state of childhood regression, though her condition had never officially been diagnosed. The Kelvingrove Park Murders had provoked some sort of crisis in her, and she'd disappeared from her home the same morning Victor took Gavin hostage in the university bell-tower, only to turn up later in the afternoon at Yorkhill Police Station – where, in an uncharacteristic burst of lucidity, she'd made up for ten years of silence by telling the cops everything in an uninterrupted, hour-long info-dump. After that, she'd more or less reverted to type, but had, Zoe was assured, been making steady progress of late under the guidance of an array of psychologists and therapists, to the point that she was now deemed fit to give evidence. She'd better be, because the whole case was resting on her.

Dead silence resounded as the door leading to the witness waiting rooms opened and Jenny was led in. She was wearing a crisp duck-egg-blue blouse and a navy skirt that reached down to below the knees. Whoever had picked it out for her had done a good job: it was demure, but not to the point of ridiculousness. Halfway to the witness stand, she froze as if suddenly entertaining second thoughts, and the court officer had to take her by the arm and guide her the rest of the way.

The judge rose from his chair. 'Please raise your right hand and repeat the words after me: *I swear by Almighty God that I will tell the truth, the whole truth, and nothing but the truth.*'

Jenny repeated the oath haltingly, one clause at a time, her voice barely audible. At the end, the judge motioned to the court officer, who scurried over to the stand and fiddled with the microphone. Adjustments made, the judge resumed his seat and faced Jenny with a benevolent smile.

'Thank you for being here today, Ms Guilfoyle. I appreciate that this is an unfamiliar and perhaps even frightening experience for you. I wish to assure you that we will be as attentive to your needs as possible, and that you can ask to stop for a break if at any point it becomes too much for you.'

'Thank you.' Jenny's soft voice, amplified by the microphone, boomed out unnaturally loud through the speaker system.

The judge turned to Quaid. 'Advocate Depute?'

Quaid installed himself behind the lectern, binder spread open before him. 'Is your name Jennifer Rachael Guilfoyle?'

'Yes.'

'And were you, between June and December of 1999, in a relationship with Gavin James Price?'

'Yes.'

'And is he here in the courtroom today?'

'Yes.'

'Can you point to him for us?'

Jenny's arm shot out, index finger extending towards the dock. She didn't turn or even look where she was pointing – just kept her eyes fixed on the microphone in front of her.

Quaid gave a little nod of gratitude, murmured a 'thank you', and Jenny lowered her arm.

'Now, the twenty-second of December 1999 was the last day of school before the Christmas holidays, wasn't it?'

'Yes.'

'And on that day, did Gavin ask you to go with him to a party . . . ?'

And so it continued. Bit by bit, Quaid guided Jenny through the events of that day, asking her a series of closed questions that essentially amounted to him telling the story himself and getting a 'yes' or 'no' confirmation after each key point. It was the ideal way to handle Jenny, playing to her limited communication skills and keeping things clinical, detached and matter-of-fact. Zoe looked over her shoulder at Guilfoyle and saw that he was sitting hunched forward in his seat, watching his daughter intently. You could probably have socked him in the face and he'd have gone on staring without so much as blinking.

As Zoe turned to face front once again, a shiver ran up her spine – an involuntary response to something half-glimpsed as she'd turned her head. She counted to ten, not daring to move, then risked another glance over her shoulder and got the confirmation she'd been dreading.

Dominic Ryland was standing at the door, looking directly at her.

She faced front, spine rigid, hands slick with sweat as they clutched her thighs. Quaid's voice droned on, but she was no longer listening. She tried desperately to clear her mind. To think. The odds of Ryland having walked in off the street because he fancied sitting in on a random trial were slim to non-existent. There could be only one reason for him being here.

Her. He was here for her.

At first, she was scared out of her mind, imagining what he might do: everything from calling the cops on her then and there for breaking into his house to having his goons – the same ones who'd smashed up Jasmine's place – take her out back for a doing. But as the seconds ticked by, the fear gradually subsided, replaced by a low-boiling rage. How dare he come here, trying to intimidate her like this? She found herself experiencing an overwhelming desire to leap to her feet, march straight up to him and tear him a new urethra.

She heard movement behind her. Casting another furtive glance over her shoulder, she saw that Ryland had disappeared. The door at the back was still swinging.

She wasn't having this. No way. To hell with it – she was going to do it. She was going to confront the fucker. Muttering an incoherent apology to a deeply confused Anna, she got to her feet and headed after him.

She made it as far as the lobby before sighting Ryland again, passing through the revolving doors and out of the building. She quickened her pace and arrived outside in time to see him climbing into the back of a black cab. As she gave chase, it took off up Saltmarket towards the Merchant City. Owing to some fortuitously-timed traffic lights, she was able to keep it in her sights by running like the clappers, and succeeded in flagging down a taxi of her own before the traffic got moving again.

'Follow that car,' she ordered the driver as she collapsed into the back seat. 'Don't lose it.'

The driver laughed. 'Bit early in the day for a high-speed chase, in't it?' He caught her glare in the rear-view mirror. 'Aye, all right then, hen. It's your money.'

As they drove, keeping the tail-lights of Ryland's cab in sight, the driver repeatedly tried to engage Zoe as to what this was all about, but she proved stubbornly unreceptive, and eventually he gave up. Her desire to actually confront Ryland had waned, but she was determined to find out where he was going. Wherever it was, it was clear from the direction that it wasn't home to Thornton-hall.

At the top of Saltmarket, under the shadow of the Tolbooth Steeple, they turned onto the Gallowgate, joining the easterly flow of traffic, before turning down onto London Road about a quarter of a mile later. They drove through the East End, passing the police station, then turning off the main road and winding through a succession of backstreets and lanes. They were now deep in the heart of Bridgeton, Ryland's birthplace. Up ahead, Ryland's cab pulled up outside a small, distinctly seedy-looking pub identified by the faded letters painted on the façade as the Royal Arms. As Zoe watched, Ryland got out and headed inside.

'Keep going,' she said, as her driver looked to her for instructions. 'Round the next corner, then let me out.'

He did as he was told, pulling over in a side street a few hundred yards further on. She paid him, tipping him generously – too generously, given the state of her bank balance – for his troubles, then made for the pub on foot.

As soon as she stepped inside, she knew she was in enemy territory. This was the epitome of a hard man's pub, complete with loyalist flags hanging from the walls. She'd ended up in places like this before, usually by accident during a pub crawl, and had always wound up beating a hasty retreat. These were the only times she ever felt conscious of her own – or rather her parents' – Catholicism. Now, as she crossed the floor, she felt the stares of a dozen pairs of suspicious eyes, as if they'd smelt the Fenian blood in her the moment she set foot in the place. Her eyes skimmed over the various patrons, trying not to catch anyone's gaze. Ryland wasn't among them – of that she was certain. He'd have stuck out like a sore thumb among this lot.

She headed for the bar, fingers closed round her phone in her pocket, ready to whip it out and call for help the second it looked like she needed it. The sole bartender was a strung-out, middle-aged woman with a seemingly permanent sneer and a Red Hand of Ulster tattoo on her shoulder.

'What d'yese want?' It was more of a snarl than a question.

'Something to drink'd be nice,' Zoe said, managing to sound considerably more assertive than she felt.

'Aye? Well, I'd try the Duchess doon the road if I was you. You'll find it more tae yer liking.'

'I said I'd meet a friend here.'

The woman gave Zoe a long, hard look, then appeared to relent. 'What're ye having?'

'Rum and Coke?'

The woman held her gaze for a fraction too long, then turned away and began to prepare the drink. Zoe perched on a stool.

'Havnae seen ye round here before. You local?'

'Uh, no,' Zoe said, thinking on the hop. 'I'm fae, uh, Springburn.'

There was a door behind the bar marked 'PRIVATE'. It lay half-open, and Zoe surreptitiously leaned to one side, trying to peer in. Someone was standing just inside. He had his back to her, but unless there were two people in this place wearing the same poncy suit, there was only one person it could be.

'So . . . ' She leaned an elbow casually on the bar-top. 'This place been open long?'

'A while,' the bartender grunted, not turning.

'Well, looks like yous do a good trade. S'no often you see a pub this busy on a Wednesday afternoon.'

'That right, aye?'

'So is this, like, a family business?'

The figure in the back room was talking to someone – that much was clear from his gestures. Zoe craned her neck, but she wasn't going to get a better view without getting up and moving.

She was about to do just that when a shadow fell on her. She turned to find one of the patrons towering over her – a colossal shaven-headed man, white polo shirt stretched across his broad chest, belly protruding over his overly tight jeans. The reek of beer, cigarettes and BO oozed from his every pore, filling her nostrils and making her want to gag.

'You ask a lot of questions.' He moved even closer, forcing her off the stool. "Specially for someone who's got nae business being here. What is it you're after?'

Zoe backed off as he continued his advance, forcing her further along the bar. Her nerve had gone. She knew she wouldn't be able to handle herself if things got ugly, and equally well she had no desire to cause a scene and alert the wrong people to her presence.

'I was just looking for a friend,' she said, glancing sideways as she sized up possible escape routes. 'But I think mibby I'm in the wrong place.'

'Aye, I think mibby you are,' said the patron. 'Time for you to jog on.'

The bartender hovered uncertainly, Rum and Coke in hand. 'What about her drink?'

'She's no thirsty anymore,' said the man, not taking his eyes off Zoe.

Zoe reversed towards the door, hoping for dear life that she wouldn't trip over something and go sprawling on her arse. She made it to the exit unmolested, but every eye in the place was fixed on her, and the stares continued as she fumbled behind her for the door handle and stumbled out into the street.

With the sun and fresh air on her face once more, she allowed herself to breathe again. Her heart was racing. Someone rich and famous once said you should do one thing a day that scared you, but this was just taking the piss. But no matter. She'd got the information she'd been after. As the hairless orangutan had forced her to back away, she'd managed to snatch a better look at the inside of the back room.

The man in the suit had indeed been Ryland, and the person he'd been talking to, seated behind a desk and looking very much like he belonged there, had been none other than Gordon Tannahill.

21

Game Over

She arrived back at the courthouse to find that all hell had broken loose. Anna and Quaid were in the foyer with Guilfoyle, taking it in turns to try and reason with him, but their efforts were falling on deaf ears as he shook his head adamantly and batted their interventions away with a wave of his massive hand. Whatever had happened, he was in a raging mood.

As Zoe hovered uncertainly by the entrance, Anna caught sight of her and, leaving Quaid persevering with Guilfoyle, made her way over.

'What's going on?'

'Nice of you to show up,' Anna snapped, with a vehemence that took Zoe aback. 'It all went to shit while you were gone.'

'How?'

'Jenny broke down under cross-examination. She got through the Crown's questions fine, but when Streule started to drill into her, she just went to pieces.'

'You mean he was an arse to her?' Zoe couldn't picture that going down well with any jury.

'No. Not directly, anyway. He was oh-so-reasonable. Made a big deal about how concerned he was about her state of mind – even as he picked all manner of holes in her story. Inconsistency,

inconsistency, inconsistency. They even went through her bloody medical records. The memory lapses, the hallucinations – he as good as said she'd imagined the whole thing, or Gavin's part in it at any rate.'

She glanced in Guilfoyle's direction as he shouted an angry 'No!' and shook Quaid's hand off his arm, then turned back to Zoe.

'Quaid wants another go with her. He thinks if he gets her on the stand again, he can undo some of the damage. But her dad's not having it, and frankly I can't blame him. You didn't see her. You didn't see what it did to her.'

There was a hint of accusation in Anna's voice which Zoe found a bit rich. *Oh, so now you* want *me here?* She told herself Anna was just lashing out in frustration at the nearest target and tried not to take it personally.

Looking past Anna's shoulder, she saw Quaid once again trying to reason with Guilfoyle. She couldn't make out what he said, but she heard Guilfoyle's words as clear as day:

'I'm her legal guardian. I take full responsibility.'

And with that, he turned and, fists clenched by his sides, stomped off down the corridor. Quaid turned in Anna and Zoe's direction and gave a sad little shrug. Game over.

There wasn't much more to add after that. They returned to the courtroom, where the judge informed the jury that the star witness was indisposed and, as a result – and because no witnesses were being called by the defence – the trial would now move into the summing-up phase. Both lawyers gave brief speeches, with Quaid, to Zoe's ears, sounding tired and despondent. Speaking for the defence, Streule was on better form, stressing to the jury that the prosecution had sought to tug at their heartstrings with lurid details of what was done to 'this poor, unfortunate girl'.

'No one in this room,' he insisted, 'seeks to deny that Jennifer

Guilfoyle was the victim of an appalling ordeal. The question the jury must decide' – and here he pivoted to face the fifteen earnest faces staring at him from the stalls – 'is whether Gavin Price arranged for his beloved girlfriend to be at number eight Park Terrace with the explicit understanding of what was to take place there, and subsequently watched and did nothing as his cousin and three school-friends took it in turns to carry out a sustained assault so shocking in its brutality as to be beyond the comprehension of any civilised person.

'*Watched and did nothing.* That is the Crown's claim, based on a combination of conjecture, hearsay and the testimony of a woman whose own recollection of the events is confused and inconsistent. We, the defence, say: the facts don't add up. As you retire to deliberate, I ask you to remember that it is your duty to determine whether it can be proved beyond reasonable doubt that Gavin Price did what he stands accused of. Not mibbies aye, mibbies naw. Not even on the balance of probability. *Beyond reasonable doubt.* Well, the defence says no! The case has not been proven, and I therefore implore you to find Gavin Price NOT GUILTY.'

Streule gathered his papers and resumed his seat. The judge came to for long enough to instruct the jury to reflect carefully on what had been said, then dispatched them to hash it out behind closed doors. They filed out, then Gavin was escorted out, and around Zoe the public gallery began to clear. Anna remained seated until only a few people were still there, and Zoe knew it was so she wouldn't have to risk an encounter with Gavin's folks – or, worse still, Gavin himself.

'So when will we know?' Zoe asked, as they made their way down to the lobby.

'Depends how long the jury takes. They might decide it's an open-and-shut case and reach a decision tomorrow. But it could just as easily be Friday or even next week before we hear anything.'

'What d'ye think they'll decide?'

Anna turned to her with a weary shrug. 'We have to trust the system. That's all there is to it. If you don't, you'll only drive yourself mad.'

It sounded unbelievably hollow, and Zoe didn't buy it for one minute. She knew Anna's thoughts on trial by jury in rape cases, or thought she did. Once upon a time, Anna had been very much of the opinion that the absolute worst thing you could do to a rape victim was force them to relive their ordeal in a courtroom, then ask a gaggle of randos to decide whether she was telling the truth. And Zoe could see her point. Not one of these people was remotely qualified to make that decision, and yet they were being entrusted with what was as close as dammit to a matter of life and death. And yet here Anna was, going along with it all, saying 'trust the system' like a good little drone, even though it went against everything she believed in. It was a wonder she wasn't embarrassed, perpetrating this act of fraud.

Zoe tramped up the stairwell, let herself into the flat, shut the door behind her and leaned against it, tired and dejected. The place was oddly quiet. Usually when she got in, the TV or the radio was on, or some music, or at the very least she'd hear Carol moving about, making dinner or getting ready for work. Today there was only a still, unnerving silence.

Poking her head into the kitchen, she found Carol seated at the table, hands clasped on top of a folded newspaper, staring into oblivion. She didn't even turn to look at Zoe.

'Caz? Everything OK?'

'Uh-huh.'

She didn't *sound* OK. Telling herself this was just more of the 'tough love' Carol had been practising since Sunday's bust-up, Zoe crossed over to the sink to get herself a glass of water. As she ran the tap, waiting for it to cool, she saw that Carol still hadn't moved.

'Sure ye're awright?'

'Peachy.'

Zoe had had enough. She turned off the tap and set her glass down on the counter with a thump.

'D'ye know what? Enough. I've had it up tae here wi this . . . ' She gesticulated ineffectually. '*This* . . . whatever this is. If ye've got a problem, fucksake gonnae just out and say it, 'stead of all this passive-aggressive shite?'

Carol tossed the paper across the table. It fell open on one of the inside pages. As Zoe moved towards it, the headline came into focus.

KELVINGROVE KILLER'S SISTER PARTIED WITH LESBIAN LOVER BEFORE PRICE TRIAL!

And below it, a picture of her and Fin leaving the G-Spot.

Oh Jesus. Oh FUCK.

Snatching up the paper, she briefly skimmed the first paragraph her eyes alighted on, written in the usual lurid style so beloved by the gutter press.

> . . . the two women, believed to be in an illicit relationship, were seen leaving an exclusive lesbian bar in the city centre on Friday night. When approached, Ms Callahan's lover became aggressive, making verbal threats and at one point lunging violently at this reporter . . .

As Zoe slowly lowered the paper, Carol's face came into view. She was glowering at Zoe, the hurt in her eyes raw and burning.

'It's . . . it's not—' Zoe began.

'It's not what? Not what I think it is? Go on, then – tell me what it is.'

Silence.

'Who is she?'

'No one. Just someone I know. We're no—'

'Are you having an affair with her?' Carol hurled the question at Zoe like it was a grenade.

'No! We just . . . we've been . . . we've been daein' some work the gether.' The denial sounded feeble and pathetic in Zoe's own ears.

'Work?' Carol's voice dripped incredulity. 'What work?'

Zoe began to arch her shoulders in a shrug of defiance, but she stopped herself. She knew that wasn't going to be enough. Not this time. Carol wasn't going to let this lie.

It was time to come clean.

Standing in the living room, she told Carol everything. She told her about meeting Fin at the self-defence class, about deciding to investigate Ryland herself after the case against him collapsed, about breaking into his house and about the contents of his laptop. Throughout it all, Carol sat hunched forward on the sofa, elbows on her knees, lips resting on her clasped hands. As Zoe fell silent, Carol lifted her head and stared up at her in horrified disbelief.

'God,' she said, 'I wish you *were* just having an affair.'

Zoe tried to laugh, but it died in her throat.

'Are you crazy? Are you actually clinically insane? There was me fretting cos I thought you were obsessing about the trial, staying out late getting wasted to numb the pain or whatever. That would've been bad enough. But this . . . ?' She shook her head, as if trying to convince herself that this wasn't happening. That it was all just a bad dream. 'Have you any idea the fire you're playing with, going up against someone like that? And stalking him? Breaking into his house? Christ, Zoe, you could go to jail for a really long time.'

'I know,' Zoe said feebly. 'But *someone* needs tae do something about it. Someone needs tae take a stand.'

Carol threw back her head and gave a hollow, humourless laugh. 'Jesus, you really picked your moment to become a social justice warrior. Answer me this: why does that someone have to be you?'

Zoe shrugged helplessly. 'Cos I was there.'

Carol scoffed and threw up her hands in disbelief.

'I don't get what ye're so pissed off about,' said Zoe. 'Here's me helping someone who cannae help theirselves. *Work as if you live in the early days of a better nation.* That's what you always say, in't it? Well, how's that no what I'm daein'?'

'For the love of God, Zoe, wake up and live in the real world!' Carol all but yelled. She was on her feet now, burning with a righteous, direct anger that Zoe wasn't used to from her. 'This isn't like one of your movies. You don't get to bring the bad guy to heel yourself and make the world a safer place. You're just a regular woman with regular responsibilities. You've got a job and a student loan to pay off and your share of the rent to pay.'

'This guy gets his rocks off roughing up women. I'da thought that'd mean something to you.'

'Don't.' Carol shot up a warning finger. 'Don't try and play the self-righteous card with me. We both know you'll lose that one.'

'Aye, ye're no kidding,' Zoe muttered, unable to help herself.

Carol stared at Zoe for a long moment before speaking again. 'You're not helping this woman. Don't kid yourself. That's not what any of this is about.'

'Gonnae tell me what it *is* about, then? Seein' as how I obviously don't know my own mind.'

'Victor.'

Zoe was too dumbfounded to even manage a disbelieving *huh?*

'It's about Victor, and about you, and about what he did all those years ago. You obsess over it, you keep . . . ' She trailed off. 'I dunno whether you're doing this as a penance, cos you think you're somehow to blame for what he did, or to redress some cosmic imbalance – like somehow one Callahan doing some good makes up for the bad things the other did.' She looked at Zoe beseechingly. 'But you're deluding yourself. You're choosing to refight the battles of the past because it gives you an excuse to ignore your responsibilities in the here and now.'

Zoe just stared at her, unable to believe what she was hearing. Where the fuck did she get off on bringing Victor into this?

'And . . . and back in the early days, I accepted it. Really I did. You were mourning. I could hardly hold it against you if you weren't interested in finding a vocation, setting anything aside for a rainy day, bringing home a halfway decent wage so I could stop paying nearly all the rent and we could finally think about moving out of this shit-hole. But it's been nearly four years. Four *fucking* years, Zoe, and I don't think you even realise you're doing it. It's become ingrained in you, living in this limbo, always fixating on everything but the stuff that actually matters, like you're the only one who doesn't have to grow up and be an adult.'

Zoe shook her head vehemently. She wasn't going to listen to this. She didn't have to accept it.

'You use him, Zo. You use him as a crutch, to avoid moving on, to get out of taking charge of your own life, whether you know it or not.' She gave a small, sad shrug. 'Victor doesn't need you to atone for him. If you want to honour his memory, honour it by setting your own life in order before you go about interfering in other people's.'

'Oh right, and of course you're completely blameless in all this? You haven't been totally wrapping me in cotton wool, nagging all the time, telling me what tae do, how tae live, who tae *be*? You want me tae start acting like an adult. Well, mibby try *treating* me like one for once in yer life.'

Now it was Carol's turn to stare at Zoe in disbelief. 'Zoe, I never—'

But Zoe wasn't finished. She'd found her voice at last, and now that she'd managed to get a word in edgeways she was determined not to give Carol an opportunity to draw breath.

'Aye ye do. Ye do it all the time. Ye think I don't know what yer little game is? Remake me in yer image, intae yer perfect wee drone who'll tag along tae yer vegan bake-sales and yer talking-shops wi yer dykey friends all bumping yer gums about oppression and the patriarchy but never actually *daein'* anything about it cos ye know it'd mean an end tae yer cosy, safe wee existence. Cos when all said and done, you actually *like* being the victim, don't ye?'

She wasn't even sure what she was arguing anymore. This had moved way beyond the initial dispute and had long ceased to be about anything more than being as hurtful as possible. And Carol didn't say anything. She didn't fight back. She just stood there and took it, wide-eyed and slack-jawed like a landed fish.

'Oh, sorry, should I have prefaced that wi a trigger warning? Well, why don't ye go find a safe space tae crawl intae? Oh aye, that's right: cos in real life there *aren't* any safe spaces. Folk like Jasmine and Jenny Guilfoyle didnae get tae hide behind trigger warnings when they were getting fucking banjaxed, so why the hell should poor little you?'

For about five seconds, the silence was broken only by the sounds of traffic rumbling by outside. Then, without warning, Carol broke down and began to weep. It unnerved and horrified Zoe, the sound hitting her like a knife in the guts. She suddenly realised that, in all the time they'd been together, she'd never once seen Carol cry – and now she was certainly making up for lost time.

'Aw Jesus, I didnae mean . . . '

But that was just it. She *had* meant it. Every word.

Carol wiped her eyes roughly with the back of her hand. 'Is that what you think of me? Christ, Zoe, I don't want to change you. I fell in love with *you*. The way you are. With all your foibles and all mine. I've never wanted you to stop being you. I always knew we were different, that we didn't see eye to eye on everything. And folk said I was making a mistake, that it could never work, and I told them they were wrong – that differences were a virtue rather than a fault, that we made each other more than the sum of our parts. I thought . . . I thought you felt the same.'

Zoe opened her mouth, then stopped herself. She couldn't claim she'd just been lashing out in the heat of the moment. Everything she'd said, every word of it, was an accurate representation of how she felt, expressed in a manner tailored to wound as deeply as possible. And at the time – for, like, fifteen seconds – it had felt so, *so* good. But the cold reality of it was that all that shit was great to listen to, to soak up, to nod her head in vigorous agreement to, while Fin was espousing it in the G-Spot over endless beers and mojitos. But throwing it in the face of someone she loved and watching them crumble – that was another matter entirely.

'I shouldnae have . . . '

She moved towards Carol to comfort her, but Carol held up a hand, stopping her in her tracks.

'No,' she said stiffly. 'No. It's better to have these things out in the open. You're right. Maybe I've been too controlling. Maybe I've been holding you to too high a standard.'

For a moment, Zoe's spirits rose. Maybe it was all going to be OK. Maybe this was something they'd work through. Something that would end up making their relationship stronger.

Fat chance.

'But I think it's safe to say things can't carry on like this,' Carol continued, voice husky from crying, cheeks glistening with tears. 'Things aren't right between us, are they?'

Zoe lowered her eyes and shook her head. 'Nuh.'

'And they haven't been for a while now.'

'Nuh.'

'Maybe . . . ' Carol stopped. She expelled a heavy breath. 'Maybe we'd both benefit from some time apart. It's obvious we've both got issues we need to work out and . . . well, I guess we need time to figure out whether we still want the same things we thought we did.'

'Aye,' Zoe found herself saying. 'Aye, I guess we should do that.'

'Right.' Carol straightened up, her narrow ribcage contracting as she sucked in a deep breath. 'Obviously it makes more sense for me to move out. I've got my mum's place I can go to, whereas . . . '

. . . *whereas all my family's dead.* So practical of Carol. So infuriatingly sensible. But that was always her way. *Identify the problem, then take action to remedy it.*

She moved towards the door. 'I'll pack an overnight bag.'

'Now?'

Zoe hadn't expected it to happen this fast. She'd thought they'd at least sleep on it – a part of her, perhaps, hoping that, in the fresh light of a new day, they'd realise they'd both overreacted and take a rain-check on this course of action.

'Well, there's no point delaying it. This . . . ' Carol gestured vaguely with her hand. 'This – it's toxic, whatever it is. And the more we delay, the worse it's gonna get.'

And Zoe, in her heart of hearts, knew she was right. The grievances she'd expressed might eventually fade; go back to just being minor differences in how they each saw the world. Differences they could both live with. But, sooner or later, those grievances would come back stronger than ever.

Carol let her words hang in the air for a moment, then turned and left the room.

She took less than five minutes to pack. Zoe sat on the sofa, picking at a loose chip of wood on the coffee table, as Carol moved about the bedroom, opening drawers and rifling through the wardrobe, stuffing various items into a large hold-all.

When the taxi came, Zoe found herself insisting on accompanying Carol to the street, lugging her case down the steps for her. Carol kissed her goodbye before she got in – a chaste peck on the cheek – and for a few brief moments Zoe kidded herself on she was just seeing Carol off on her summer holidays and that she'd be back in a week's time with a tan and a truckload of souvenirs. But the fiction faded as Carol pulled the door to behind her and the cab pulled away, farting out a cloud of exhaust smoke behind it. And deep down, Zoe knew this was the end.

22

Consequences

The sensible thing to do under the circumstances would have been to make no sudden, knee-jerk moves but to wait for the dust to settle and a new day to dawn, and to see if things really did look different in the light of morning. But as always, when the chips were down, the self-destructive part of Zoe took charge, doubling down on the same ruinous behaviour that had got her into trouble in the first place. And so, a half-hour later, she showed up at Fin's door, looking for . . . what? Company? A shoulder to cry on? Something more intimate? She didn't know, but she must have been a picture, for the moment Fin opened the door and took in the sight of her, her eyes widened in disbelief.

'Jaysus,' she exclaimed, 'you wake up with a face like that or did someone *do* something to it?'

Fin got them a couple of beers and they settled on the sofa, where Zoe told her everything. She'd been afraid she was going to start blubbing, but when it came down to it there was no great surge of emotion, only a numb emptiness, as if she hadn't eaten for twenty-four hours.

'Sorry,' said Fin, once she'd finished. 'I mean, Stevie Wonder coulda seen it coming, but still. Anyways, you're welcome to doss here as long as ya want. *Mi casa es tu casa* or however it goes. Not that this is *mi casa*, strictly speaking, but who's splitting pubic hairs?'

'It's fine. Carol's already moved out. She's . . . decent that way.'

'Well, look on the bright side. Least now you can leave the toilet seat up without anyone yelling at ya.'

Grateful for the minimal I-told-you-sos, Zoe managed a tight smile.

'How'd it go in court?'

Zoe shook her head. If Fin thought this change of subject would prove a welcome distraction, she was sorely mistaken.

'That bad, eh?'

'Worse.'

'Surprised?'

'Guess not, no.'

Fin shrugged. 'Sorry. Again.'

Zoe shook her head. 'You told me all along how it'd be. He's gonnae walk. He's gonnae fucking walk just like every other smarmy fucking git who's learned how to wear a fancy suit and smile for the cameras and convince everyone he's Mr Fucking Untouchable.'

She was aware they were talking about a different case from the one Fin had opined about when she'd first set out her 'us and them' treatise, but the two had become so intertwined in her head that the distinctions had now all but broken down. Ryland and Price, the politician and the professor – what were they if not two sides of the same coin? They both stood for everything that was wrong with the world and were both going to walk away from their respective crimes free as the wind.

Fin thought about it. 'Well, ya never know. Could still turn out all right. Ain't over till the fat lassie sings.'

It was a hollow attempt at reassurance, but Zoe appreciated the

effort nonetheless. Platitudes weren't normally part of Fin's repertoire: she was obviously making an extra effort.

'Aye, mibby.' She tilted her beer to her lips and slugged back a
mouthful.

Fin picked at the frayed fabric on the sofa's arm. 'I could have
him killed for you, you know.'

She threw it out there as casually as if she was making an obser-
vation about the weather. Initially, Zoe wondered if she'd misheard.
Then she began to laugh weakly, thinking it was a bad-taste joke,
only to stop when she saw Fin's expression remaining resolutely
neutral.

'Could ye? How?'

Fin shrugged. 'Talk to a man who knows a man who . . . well,
you get the picture. These things aren't that tricky to arrange. There's
lotsa folks'd be willing to help out . . . for the right price.'

'And I, what, just give the nod and you get the ball rolling?'

'Say the word and it's yours.'

For all of ten seconds, Zoe genuinely entertained the idea. The
thought of someone putting a bullet in Gavin Price's skull, or
slipping a noose round his neck, appealed to her on some deep,
primal level that went far beyond the sort of *God, I'd love to kill that
guy* sentiments folk casually tossed around every other day. It
sounded so tantalisingly straightforward, and was certainly no less
than he deserved.

And then the reality of what they were actually discussing hit
home and blind panic set in.

'No! *Fuck*, no! Ye cannae. I mean, Jesus, just don't! Seriously,
don't even think about—'

'Shh.' Fin placed a forefinger on Zoe's lips, silencing her. 'Relax.
If you don't want me to . . . ' She withdrew her finger. ' . . . I won't,
OK?' She picked up her bottle and took another swig. 'Worry less,
Bright Eyes. You'll live longer.'

She sat there nonchalantly tapping her foot in time to the music on the stereo. Zoe necked from her own bottle, watching her warily from the corner of her eye. *Who ARE you?* she thought. Was it really possible she'd fallen in with someone who was in a position to pick up the phone and order a man's execution?

Something else occurred to her – something she'd forgotten all about what with the double whammy of Jenny's breakdown on the stand and Armageddon with Carol.

'Ryland showed up in court the day.'

'Oh?' Fin sat up a little straighter.

'Aye, in the public gallery. Only for a minute or two, mind, but I'm pretty sure he didnae just wander in off the street by accident. I followed him to this pub in the East End – the Royal Arms. Know it?'

'Sounds like a UDA-type joint. Not exactly my scene.'

'Or mine. Or his, I'da thought. But he was there all right. I seen him in the back office, talking. You'll never guess who to.'

'His Holiness the Pope.'

'Aye, you're hilarious, so ye are.' She paused, relishing for once being the one in possession of desired knowledge. 'Gordon Tannahill.'

'Aye?'

'That's the second time I seen they two the gether. Funny, that. And here's the thing: I'm ninety-nine-point-nine-nine-nine percent sure he was in that courtroom looking for me. Too much of a coincidence otherwise. Then, straight after, he takes a cab to a dodgy pub and has a confab wi a guy whose stock-in-trade is breaking knee-caps. That's gotta mean something, right?'

Fin frowned as she sipped her beer. 'Maybe.'

'I guess what I'm saying is, should I be worried?'

'Possibly. I dunno. Put it this way: I doubt he's gonna send the Black 'n' Tans round for ya. But all the same, I'd watch my shadow if I was you. Don't wanna take any chances. Might be an idea if you shack up here for a few days after all.'

'Ye think he might try something? I wouldnae wanna bring trouble tae yer door.'

Fin laughed. 'Bitch, please. I've been doing that all by myself since I was a snapper.'

Refusing to let Zoe doss on the couch again, Fin set about making up the bed in one of her AWOL flatmates' rooms. Zoe was glad not to be going home tonight – though it had less to do with the thought that she might be in danger than the thought of returning to an empty flat.

As they stuffed the pillows and laid the sheet, something else occurred to her.

'By the way – Ryland's laptop. It's no still here, is it?'

'Be pretty careless of me if it was. Nah, I took it somewhere secure after you skedaddled on Monday morning.'

'Where?'

Fin tapped the side of her nose and winked. 'Need to know, Bright Eyes, need to know. Worry not – it's safe.'

Zoe stood there watching her as she crammed a pillow into its slip, whistling nonchalantly. She gazed at her muscular arms, thinking she'd feel safe with them around her. Safe and wanted and worthy of another person's love. As Fin leant past her to tuck the sheet in at the corner, on impulse Zoe moved to intercept her and tried to kiss her. It was a clumsy manoeuvre; she misjudged her timing and Fin turned her head away at precisely the wrong moment, but it was a near enough miss that there could be no dressing it up as something other than what they both knew it had been.

Fin took a step back. 'Whoa. Easy, tiger.'

Shit. Dumb move. *Seriously* dumb move.

'Don't think that's a great idea, do you?'

'Oh God. Sorry. Fuck.' The words came tripping out of Zoe's mouth as she fought to hide her embarrassment. 'I thought . . . '

Fin cocked her head to one side, smiling a tad sheepishly. It was the closest Zoe had ever seen to her looking genuinely awkward. 'Look, don't think I'm not flattered 'n' all, but it's gonna have to be a hard "no" from me. Believe me, it's not cos I don't think you're a catch. You are. Betcha anything you're an absolute firecracker in the sack. Thing is, me, I can do the whole "shagging with no consequences" thing. But you . . . ' She shook her head. 'Yeah, we'd have a great time in the here 'n' now, but in the cold light o' morning? Sure you'd only regret it. And I wouldn't want that on my conscience, if I had one.'

Zoe wanted to say no, that she could totally do the 'shagging with no consequences' thing. But she knew the moment had passed, that it was too late to row back and undo all the awkwardness and self-consciousness. Pleading would only make her seem all the more pathetic. And the last thing she wanted was a pity fuck.

Fin finished making the bed, tossed a pillow to her and gave her an amicable pat on the shoulder. 'Get some shut-eye. Don't want ya getting crow's feet and bags under yer eyes.' She paused in the doorway and offered a surprisingly tender smile. 'It'll all work out, y'know. Night.'

Hours later, Zoe lay staring up at the unfamiliar ceiling, listening to the sounds of nocturnal merriment from nearby Byres Road – all these happy people unburdened by her problems, enjoying themselves little more than a stone's throw away.

She knew from experience that, when you've fucked up, the worst thing you can do is lie awake thinking about it, playing the 'woulda-shoulda-coulda' game, but she couldn't help herself. She thought back to what Carol had said – about the business with

Ryland being about her trying to make up for what Victor had done. Maybe she'd had a point. Maybe it *was* about trying to erase his bad deeds by doing some good. And maybe she *was* stuck in a holding pattern because she'd failed to come to terms with his death. The sensible thing, the *right* thing, would have been to accept all of this and promise Carol under pain of death that this was the end of it; that she would become a fine, upstanding citizen who went to her shitty, boring job each day and never allowed the name 'Dominic Ryland' to cross her mind again. But Zoe Callahan had never done the sensible thing before when her back was to the wall, and tonight was not a night for firsts.

She clenched her eyes shut, willing sleep to come and wondering if things could possibly get any worse.

23

Who's the Daddy?

The following morning, Zoe woke to find the flat empty. There was no sign of Fin – just a note taped to the fridge in what Zoe assumed was her barely-legible handwriting:

> *Out all day. Maybe back tonight, maybe tomorrow. Help yourself to food & don't wait up. F.*
>
> *PS. Forgot to mention last night. Picked up a rumour about our man Ryland. Supposedly his true lineage would turn the political class on its head if it got out. Might be worth looking into.*

Zoe thought back to her own initial investigations – to the lack of clarity regarding the identity of Ryland's father and the inconsistent explanations Ryland himself had given. She pondered the meaning of Fin's note. Perhaps Ryland's mother had had an affair – or a one-night stand – with some high-ranking member of government? If a cabinet minister or secretary of state was responsible for knocking up a dinner lady from Bridgeton, they'd want to keep that quiet – which, in turn, potentially explained where the money to put Ryland through Glenavon and Oxford had come from. Zoe could feel a scandal brewing. It was *definitely* worth looking into.

She raided the fridge, then got washed and dressed. She didn't have her toothbrush, so she used Fin's – an act which felt loaded with inappropriate intimacy. Reluctant to put on the same clothes she'd worn yesterday, she rummaged through Fin's things, trying to find something that wouldn't make her look *too* much like she was auditioning for an all-female remake of *Easy Rider*. It was easier said than done, and in the end she decided simply to embrace Fin's fashion sense and the aura of invulnerability that came with it. Shortly afterwards, decked out in combat bottoms and a leather jacket similar to the one Fin normally wore, she set off, swaggering slightly because it seemed to come naturally in these clothes. She locked up with a spare key she found hanging on a nail by the door. When she got outside, Fin's moped was missing from its usual spot. Zoe pictured her roaring off through the back alleys at first light, off on some top-secret mission of her own.

She arrived at the Mitchell Library and booked onto a computer, glad to have something to distract her from both what had gone down with Carol the previous evening and the interminable wait for the verdict in the Gavin Price case. As before, she didn't have much sense of what she was trying to find, but figured she'd know it when she eventually saw it. She started by looking into the political scene during and shortly before Ryland's birth: who the local heavy hitters and been and which ones, if any, had served in government. She knew virtually nothing about the political landscape of the 1970s, apart from lurid stories about power outages, bodies lying unburied and a three-day work week – the latter being something she'd always thought sounded quite appealing. Plus there was the small matter of Mrs Thatcher having arrived on the scene at the tail-end of the decade, the effects of which the country was still experiencing now.

A couple of hours later, she had a list of names and dates and not much else. Few politicians from Scotland, let alone Glasgow, had held positions in any of the various governments that had come and gone throughout the sixties and seventies, and, of the various pictures of jowly men in suits who stared back at her from the computer screen, none appeared to bear so much as a passing physical resemblance to Ryland. This was like looking for an especially small needle in an exceptionally large haystack. Perhaps, if she was more organised in her approach, more knowledgeable about politics, more *something*, she'd have got the 'eureka' moment she so desperately craved. As it was, she was the equivalent of the proverbial monkey throwing shit at the wall in the hope of some of it sticking.

She sighed and closed the browser window, consigning her research to the void. Crap sister, crap girlfriend, crap private eye – there was, it seemed, no end to her uselessness.

She spent the rest of the day alternating between riding aimlessly on the subway and loitering in supermarkets and shopping malls – places where she could at least rely on a respite from the relentless heat. It was boiling in the leather jacket, even in the air-conditioned shops, but she kept it on, partly out of obstinance and partly because she genuinely liked how it made her feel: tough and sexy and totally in command of herself. She understood now why Fin dressed the way she did. When you *looked* like you didn't give a fuck, you started to *feel* like you didn't too.

She remained glued to her phone all afternoon, waiting for a call or a text from Anna saying that the jury had reached a verdict, but nothing came. When she returned to White Street in the late evening, Fin was still AWOL, with nothing to indicate that she'd been back during the course of the day. Zoe fired off a text asking her where she was, though she didn't really expect an answer. She already knew from experience that Fin was more than capable of remaining *incommunicado* till *she* decided it was time to resurface. Finding nothing in the flat that could be made into a meal – unless that meal was to consist exclusively of cornflakes and beer – she headed out to Byres Road in search of sustenance. Then, Lucozade bottle in hand to keep her hydrated, she set off once more, letting her feet dictate her direction of travel.

As she made her way along Clarence Drive, hungry for stimulation and thirsty for company, it occurred to her that she might call on Anna. She and her man lived in a renovated terraced house up near Hyndland Road – one of those very tall, very narrow old buildings that looked like it had been squeezed horizontally and stretched vertically. Nearing the house, she could see the two of them through the living room window, curled up together on the sofa, the light of the TV flickering on their faces. What was on, she wondered? Probably something hifalutin and beyond her comprehension. A documentary on some esoteric subject, or an arthouse movie, preferably one with subtitles. Or without, if it happened to be in Italian or German, the two other languages Anna spoke. It was a matter of some irony to the irredeemably monoglot Zoe that, despite her being the one who'd studied film at uni, her own taste in movies was far less cultured. She watched as Anna tilted her head up towards Daniel and gave him a gentle peck on the lips. It was an incredibly natural-looking gesture, seeming almost unconscious, and it made Zoe's gut ache with yearning. She couldn't bring herself to intrude, not on that perfect picture of domestic bliss. She walked on by, leaving them to their canoodling.

As she continued on up Hyndland Road, past the glowing lights of the trendy Italian wine bar next to the tennis courts, she remembered she'd heard a rumour that Gavin Price was back staying with his folks. They'd lived near here back in the day, just a few houses down from Anna and her parents. Her curiosity was too strong to pass the opportunity up, so she continued up the pavement and crossed over onto Cleveden Road.

Slugging back a mouthful of Lucozade, she gazed up at the fir trees and sprawling sandstone villas that lined either side of the street. It really was like a different world, compared to Dumbarton Road and to her and Carol's cramped little flat. Well, Carol's flat. Zoe supposed she'd have to find somewhere else to live now. She could hardly justify going on squatting there while Carol, whose place it had been originally, shacked up with her mum. Not that she had any idea how she was going to afford a place of her own. She was sure the cleaning firm would cut her loose sooner rather than later, especially if she failed to turn up for work tomorrow – and given that the verdict in Gavin's trial could be called at any moment, there was no way she was going to be putting on her nylon tunic and picking up her bucket and mop. She pictured herself hopping from sofa to sofa, relying on the charity of others, and it was as if all Carol's criticisms the previous night had come home to roost.

As the road began to curve round the gentle rise of the ground, she came to the Price residence, a lush three-storey affair bordered by a meticulously-trimmed hedge and shaded from the street by a couple of tall, leafy oaks. The lights were on, suggesting that someone was home. As darkness slowly encroached, she stood at the foot of the driveway, sipping her Lucozade, daring Gavin to give some sign that he was in there. He didn't, of course, and as the night deepened, she began to wonder just what the hell she was doing there.

'Can I help you?'

Someone else, it seemed, had had the same thought as her: a middle-aged woman standing in the garden of the house next door, peering over her own well-tended hedge with a look that conveyed both unbridled suspicion and deep disapproval. It dawned on Zoe what an utter wackjob she must look, standing there with her bottle of Lucozade, her uncombed hair and her biker jacket. The old curtain-twitcher had probably seen her and thought she was casing the joint. She could hardly blame the woman. People Like Her didn't belong in Places Like This at the best of times, and especially not when they looked like they were gearing up to indulge in a spot of housebreaking – something, it now occurred to her, for which she had form.

She realised the woman was still staring at her in anticipation of an answer. Might as well go for broke.

'I was just passing,' she said. 'I'm looking to buy a property in the area and I quite fancied the look of this one.'

She was quite pleased with that. Folk from this social strata always referred to where they lived as their 'property' – presumably because it denoted ownership, or because 'house' didn't have enough syllables or something.

'It's not on the market,' said the woman stiffly. 'And in any event,' she added, with a barely-disguised smirk, 'I hardly think it'd be in *your* price range.'

Of course – because it was perfectly fine having a suspected rapist for a next-door neighbour, but riffraff like her? Perish the thought!

Without taking her eyes off the woman, Zoe drained her bottle, tossed it into the Prices' garden out of sheer spite, then turned and sloped off down the hill.

She returned to Fin's flat to find both her and her bike still gone. After weighing up her options, she decided to head back to Dumbarton Road. It felt wrong sleeping in someone else's home when they weren't even there, *tu casa* or no. Besides, she wanted her own clothes and her own bed. And she wasn't going to allow herself to be driven out of there by fear of reprisals from Ryland and his dodgy mates. Still, she couldn't help but glance over her shoulder as she fitted her key into the lock, just in case there was someone lurking in the shadows, waiting to pounce.

The answerphone was blinking when she got in. She hit the Play button in passing and made her way through the flat, opening windows and putting on lights. The robotic voice informed her that she had *One. New. Message.*

'Zoe, this is Valerie Shawcross at Sigma Housekeeping. Look, I've been more than lenient with you, but that's four days' work you've missed now, the last three without any explanation. As it stands, if I don't see you tomorrow I'll have no choice but to terminate your service with us. I'd like to remind you of your terms of employment—'

Bla, bla, bla. Zoe pressed Delete, cutting Valerie off midstream. She flopped on the sofa, and for a while just lay there, her mind a vacant shell. She felt anger welling up inside her – at Valerie, at Carol, at Fin for doing a disappearing act, at Gavin Price, at Dominic Ryland, and most of all at herself for being such a colossal fuck-up. In exasperation, she struck out with her foot, kicking the lamp off the table at the end of the sofa. It landed on the floor and smashed into pieces.

She let out an almighty 'FUUUUUUUUUUCK!', yelling as loud as she could, not caring who heard her.

On the floor above her, someone pounded the floorboards with a foot or a walking stick or some other implement designed to convey outrage, and for a moment Zoe thought they were going to come downstairs and have a set-to with her, the prospect of which she positively relished. At least it would give her an outlet for all her pent-up rage. But nothing happened. Silence descended once again, broken only by the hum of traffic on Dumbarton Road.

* * *

Several miles south, in the wood-panelled study of a bungalow on the edge of a wealthy South Lanarkshire village, a man stood lost in thought, the contours of his face illuminated by the lamp on the desk in front of him. At length, he lifted the cordless phone, dialled a number and put it to his ear.

'It's me,' he said, when the call was answered. 'I've thought about the matter we discussed earlier, and . . . well, I've decided to take you up on your offer.'

24

Verdict

The call from Anna came through shortly after eleven the next morning, jolting Zoe into consciousness; she'd finally passed out in the wee hours following another sleepless, sticky night. When she arrived at the High Court, the press were out in force, a heaving mass of folk with cameras and microphones, and she had to fight her way through to the entrance. Either they'd belatedly and collectively decided the Price case was newsworthy after all or they were here for something else entirely. A nice juicy murder, maybe.

Anna was waiting for her in the lobby. Together, they went through security and made their way to court six. The public gallery was already teeming, the stuffy air crackling with anticipation. Gavin's parents were there, of course, occupying seats in the front row. Tony Guilfoyle was present too, standing in a corner on his lonesome, looking two beats away from a heart attack. He failed to respond to Anna's nod – and really, who could blame him? The poor sod had enough on his mind without having to concern himself with the niceties. There was no sign of Jenny.

Gavin was escorted in by his two guards. As he shuffled along to the middle of the bench, Zoe tried to read his expression, but came up with nothing . . . though of course there was no reason to infer anything from that. He had to wait for the verdict like everyone else.

'Just remember,' said Anna, 'whatever the outcome is, he's a diminished figure. He's got no job. His reputation's in tatters. He'll forever be remembered as the boy who watched his girlfriend being gang-raped and did nothing.'

'Right enough, aye,' said Zoe blandly.

She thought Anna was going to say something else, but before the chance presented itself, the door to the jurors' room opened and the fifteen men and women filed in, assuming their seats amid much shuffling and murmuring. For the first time, Zoe noticed that they numbered nine women to six men. That was good, she thought. She supposed women would be more likely to convict someone accused of a crime against one of their own. It tipped the odds in their favour. Or did it? Someone had once told her women judged other women far more harshly than men. Fuck it. She didn't know *what* to think anymore.

The defence and prosecution teams took their places at the table. The judge was led in, and there was much scraping back of chairs and dipping of heads in obeisance. Once everyone was seated, and the rifling of pages and creaking of chairs came to a stop, the clerk of court stood, clipboard in hand, and addressed the jury.

'Members of the jury, will your spokesperson please rise?'

A slight, middle-aged man with jowly cheeks and sad eyes got to his feet.

'Have you reached a verdict in respect of the accused, Gavin James Price?'

'We have.'

On impulse, Zoe reached for Anna's hand. She found it without difficulty: Anna had been in the process of doing the same.

'What is your verdict in respect of the charge on the indictment?'

Zoe tightened her grip on Anna's hand.

'Not guilty.'

'Was your decision unanimous or by majority?'

'By majority.'

'Thank you. You may be seated.'

What struck Zoe afterwards was how quiet everything was. There were no cheers, no howls of outrage, not even an audible release of pent-up breath. The only sound came as Tony Guilfoyle rose from his seat and, with a degree of measured calm that really shouldn't have been possible under the circumstances, left the room. Because of that, it didn't quite seem real. It was as if it hadn't happened yet and they were still all waiting for the verdict. For a few blissful moments, Zoe experienced a strange feeling of weightlessness, as if she was floating high above the courtroom and all its machinations and stupid routines were of no concern to her. But gradually she became aware once again of Anna's grip on her hand, squeezing it so tight her circulation was being cut off, and of the judge telling Gavin he was a free man and could leave at any time. And then the jury was discharged, and everyone was on their feet, and the rod was taken down from the wall and paraded out, and with it went the judge and his dead sheep's wig, and the legal teams were shaking hands and congratulating each other on a jolly good show, what what, and suddenly everyone around Zoe was gathering up their things and making for the exit, and she realised that that really was it.

She emerged blinking into the foyer, half-conscious of Anna's arm looped through hers, guiding her – or perhaps keeping hold of her in case she went ballistic. But Zoe was beyond all that. In her heart of hearts, she'd known this was coming. Really, hearing it read out had only formalised it. And now there was nothing. No resolution, no closure, no justice. Just a great gaping void. In three and a half years of horse-trading, the prosecution and defence agreeing what was admissible evidence and what wasn't, and all the doctors assessing Jenny, determining whether or not she was fit to go on the stand, nothing had been achieved. They might as well not have bothered.

She sensed Anna's pace slowing, and a moment later she saw why. Up ahead, Gavin and his parents were clustered together, talking to his lawyer and Streule. Gavin's father was shaking Streule's hand vigorously, thanking him for getting the fruit of his loins off the hook. There were no cameras in the vicinity. Must've been there for another case after all. On impulse, Zoe made to move towards the gathering – though to do what, she didn't know. Call Price a piece of shit, or beat the living hell out of him . . . She was in no state to think it through.

She felt Anna's grip on her arm tighten. 'Leave it,' she hissed. 'He's not worth it.'

Zoe would have gladly got the hell out of Dodge then and there, but Anna had other ideas. With Guilfoyle having disappeared without a trace, she took it upon herself to step into the breach, taking Quaid and his junior counsel out to lunch at the pub across the road. It was a subdued, melancholic affair, with a lot of picking at food and no one saying very much. Zoe could tell that the junior counsel, a small woman with bird-like features who looked more like a little girl playing dress-up in her daddy's robes than a grown adult, was gutted – though Quaid, for his part, had the air of a man who mentally had already moved on to his next case. She suspected he'd never truly believed they could win.

Quaid and his deputy headed off as soon as it was polite to do so, citing prior work engagements, leaving Zoe and Anna nursing their drinks. Neither spoke. Dust motes danced in the multi-coloured light filtering through a stained-glass window. 'Samba Pa Ti' was playing on the sound system. Seriously, '*Samba Pa Ti*'. It was like someone was deliberately taking the piss.

Hearing the door opening, Zoe glanced over her shoulder to see a little deputation entering: Gavin, his parents, his lawyer and Streule. Trust them to choose the same place for their victory banquet. She turned to find Anna sitting like a drawn bowstring.

'If he comes anywhere near us—'

'He won't.' Anna's tone was adamant. 'He's not that stupid.'

But Zoe wasn't done. 'If he comes anywhere near us, I swear I'll finish what Victor started.'

Anna met her eyes and said nothing. More than likely, she was trying to gauge the idleness of this threat.

When Zoe spoke once more, it was to ask a question which she'd often pondered in her darkest moments but had never, until now, given voice to.

'Why the hell could ye no have just let him get on wi it?'

And to that, Anna had no answer.

25

Gone

As soon as Zoe turned onto Dumbarton Road, she knew something was wrong. Up ahead, outside her flat, three police cars were parked at the kerb, one at such a haphazard angle that the driver would surely have been booked if he worked for anyone else. Traffic had been reduced to one lane, and a policeman was waving cars through a few at a time. A crowd of onlookers had gathered on both pavements, several with their phones out, recording the goings-on for posterity. Zoe wondered if Mad Effie from up the stair had finally made good on her frequent promises to chuck herself out the window.

She quickened her pace. As she neared the building, she saw that the entrance had been cordoned off with tape. A few feet away, a couple of officers were talking to Mr Bakshi, the paunchy owner of A Taste of India. A bolt of sudden fear hit her right in the heart. Before anyone could stop her, she'd darted under the tape and was scrambling up the stairs, taking them four at a time. She reached the first floor and stopped dead. The door to her own flat lay wide open. She knew she hadn't left it like that, even if she *had* gone out in a mad rush. She heard feet hurrying up the steps behind her, then felt a hand on her shoulder, and before she knew it, multiple pairs of hands had grabbed her from behind and she was being manhandled backwards down the stairs. She began to scream, howling at the top of her lungs. But it wasn't in response to being grabbed and treated like a rag-doll.

It was the dark streak of blood she'd seen on the off-white wall just outside the flat.

The official police records, the product of numerous witness statements taken at the scene, tell – more or less – what happened. At between five and ten past twelve, Carol Novák of Flat 1/2, 427 Dumbarton Road was seen approaching her residence from the direction of Partick Station, carrying a large hold-all. One witness stated that she'd been talking on her phone at the time and had been discussing 'going to pick up some stuff'. She entered the building via the ground-floor entrance, a fact confirmed by Sohail Bakshi, proprietor of the A Taste of India takeaway, who at the time was supervising the unloading of a delivery truck. Approximately a minute after Ms Novák entered the building, two men emerged from an unmarked white van that had been parked around five hundred yards further west along the road since the early morning. No consensus could be reached as to when it had first arrived, but Mr Bakshi confirmed it had been there when he arrived at 7 a.m. to fire up his oven. According to eyewitnesses, the two men entered the building via the same door as Ms Novák – though that in itself was no cause for alarm, as it was a communal entrance with no security code, and tradesmen often used it.

Opinions differed as to the precise order of the events which followed, but of the following there was little doubt. At fourteen minutes past ten, the white van reversed without warning and at considerable speed, narrowly avoiding a collision with the departing delivery truck. Concurrently, the two men re-emerged from the building, one with what to Mr Bakshi initially appeared to be a heavy sack slung over his shoulder. On taking a second look, he realised that it was in fact a body – an assertion subsequently backed up by three other witnesses. All four attested that the rear doors of the van had been hauled open, the body was flung inside and the men leapt aboard. The van then performed a chaotic one-eighty-degree turn and took off at full speed, swerving to avoid two pensioners crossing at the traffic lights and haring up Dumbarton Road in an easterly direction.

Considerable disagreement existed over the van's licence plate number and the appearance of the two men. One account stated that the tall, heavyset man was the shaven-headed one, while another insisted it was the small man. A third was unclear as to whether *either* was shaven-headed, or whether the tall one was heavyset or merely of average build. Memory is an imprecise thing, and the mind tends to create detail where none exists to fill in gaps.

The police, upon their arrival, found further evidence in the stairwell to support the theory of abduction: a hold-all containing items of clothing and various other personal effects belonging to Carol Novák, including an Android phone registered in her name and a keychain containing keys for both Flat 1/2, 427 Dumbarton Road and the Pulse nightclub on Argyle Street. Furthermore, a smear of blood was noted on the wall directly outside Flat 1/2. Analysis was ongoing, but the working assumption was that it too would be confirmed as belonging to Carol Novák.

Yorkhill Police Station. Three Christmases ago it had been Zoe's home away from home, and now here she was again, sitting on a hard plastic seat in a poorly lit basement interview room answering questions put to her by a pair of men whose detached professionalism was increasingly coming to feel like disinterest. What were her living arrangements with Carol, how long had they been a couple, in whose name was the flat rented? – as if any of that held any relevance. Then the particulars: how old was she (thirty-four), how tall (five foot ten), and the spelling of her surname (N-O-V-A-K, with an accent on the 'A'; she was Czech on her mum's side). There followed the inevitable question as to why she used her mother's name rather than her father's, and the even more inevitable answer that her father had been a drunken waste of space who frequently took his fists to both of the women in his life, until one day he bit off more than he could chew in a bar-fight with someone who wasn't afraid to hit back. Any distinctive features? Two missing molars (you lot did that to her), a birthmark on her lower back, a peace tattoo on her right hip. What about piercings? A stud in her left nostril, three in her right ear, two in the left, both nipples. And she sometimes wore a signet ring on her right thumb. Any historic injuries? Yes, a fractured left ulna, sustained when her dear old dad threw her down the stairs when she was eight. Next?

They were still going over Carol's particulars when Cauley arrived from London Road. From the get-go, Zoe had insisted on her being summoned, and had refused to listen when the local officers told her Partick didn't fall under her jurisdiction. In the end, they'd caved in, and now here she was, a touch out of breath and looking seriously harangued. Zoe refused to say a word in front of the two Yorkhill cops, and Cauley – after conferring with them for a few brief moments – persuaded them to leave the room.

As the door swung shut behind them, she turned to face Zoe, arms folded.

'Now, you want to tell me just what the hell's going on?'

Zoe nodded towards the door. 'They tell ye what happened?'

'They gave me the gist. Now I want the detail. What is it you think I can do that they can't?'

Zoe took a deep breath. She knew there was no way of putting this without sounding like one of the criminally insane.

'I think Dominic Ryland arranged to have my girlfriend kid-napped.'

It was to Cauley's immense credit that she didn't immediately burst out laughing or dismiss the assertion out of hand. Slowly, she lowered herself into the chair opposite Zoe and laid her folded hands on the table.

'OK, so tell me why you think that.'

The account Zoe gave would perhaps have been more convincing had she not had to leave out certain vital links in the chain for fear of incriminating herself. She explained that it had all started with her involvement with Jasmine; how, after the police closed the case against Ryland, she'd continued with her own investigation. She left Fin's name out of it, and needless to say made no mention of the small matter of breaking into Ryland's house and making off with his laptop, but she did tell Cauley about him showing up at Gavin Price's trial and about his trip to the pub for a *tête-à-tête* with Tannahill.

That name certainly got Cauley's attention. 'What do you know about Gordon Tannahill?' she demanded, sitting up considerably straighter.

'Just that he's an enforcer for Jim Cottrell.'

Cauley's eyes narrowed. Evidently this was another name that meant something to her. 'Who have you been talking to?'

The last thing Zoe intended to do was land Fin in it – not least because, if the police questioned Fin and she talked, it would be curtains for them both.

'Look, I've told ye what I think's going on. You need to drag Ryland in here and question him – just like ye done before.'

'Just like that, aye?'

'Aye.' She responded to Cauley's sarcasm in kind. 'You're polis, aren't ye? Yous can do they kinda things.'

Cauley gave a hollow laugh. 'Believe me, there's a whole lot of things I'd love to drag Dominic Ryland in and do to him. But we don't have that kind of power. We can't lift someone just because we feel like it, especially . . . ' She stopped herself before she went any further.

'What? 'Specially someone as connected as he is?'

'I didn't say that.'

'Didnae have tae. Yous are all the same. One law for the rich and famous and another for the rest of us.'

Cauley's eyes flared angrily. Zoe's words had hit her where it hurt. She got to her feet stiffly, hands gripping the cuffs of her suede jacket. How could she wear that in this heat, Zoe thought. She must be suffocating.

'Look,' Cauley said, 'right now the most important thing is that cool heads prevail. You're upset – understandably so – but I'm asking you to be realistic. We can't just lift people because we feel like it. We need evidence, corroboration, probable cause, and that applies to anyone accused of a crime, whether they're a multimillionaire or a tramp sleeping in a doorway.'

Zoe stared at the floor and said nothing. She wished she could believe it, but practically all her life experiences – and especially the events of the last few days and weeks – told her otherwise.

Cauley ran a hand through her greasy locks. 'I'll pass on what you've told me to the SIO. But while the situation is still developing I'd advise you to do what the folk here tell you to. No running around hurling around accusations you can't back up – and for the love of God don't even think about confronting Ryland yourself.'

'So, what? I'm just supposed to go home and wait?'

Cauley shook her head. 'I doubt you'll be able to go back to your flat anytime soon. My colleagues won't have finished gathering evidence from it yet. And I expect they'll want to monitor it in case the perpetrators come back. Is there anyone you can stay with? Your parents, maybe? Or do you have any siblings?'

Dead, Zoe wanted to say. *They're all dead. Every last one of them.* She was exhausted, utterly worn down by the events of this and the last few days. She desperately wanted someone to take charge. To absolve her of all responsibility. To tell her what to do. And she could think of only one person in her circle of friends who was equipped for that.

'Anna,' she said. 'I want Anna.'

PART THREE

26

Something Awful

Saturday 20 July

Zoe opened her eyes. For a few brief, idyllic moments she lay at peace, her mind blissfully empty. Then, in a vast deluge, it all came flooding back, and she wanted nothing more than to curl up into a ball and die.

When Anna had arrived at the police station the previous day, she'd wasted no time in taking charge, demanding to know what steps were being taken to locate Carol and ensuring that Zoe had a dedicated liaison officer assigned to her immediately. They were still trying to secure an audience with someone in charge when Carol's mother had shown up in a whirlwind of tears and recriminations. Zoe, with enough on her plate already, hadn't even thought to contact her, and she'd therefore found out what had happened the hard way: by ringing Carol's mobile to ask where she'd got to, only to get a gruff-voiced SOCO instead of her daughter. Despite her acute distress, she'd nonetheless been coherent enough to make her feelings about Zoe abundantly clear. As far as she was concerned, Zoe had never been good enough for her daughter, and her misgivings were now well and truly vindicated. She'd left Zoe under no illusions as to her continued presence being either necessary or welcome, and so, some time after 8.30 p.m., Zoe and Anna had left the station and made the unhappy journey back to Anna's house on Clarence Drive.

Zoe spent Saturday morning and much of the afternoon on the living room sofa, Anna barely leaving her side. They didn't say much to one another, partly because there wasn't much *to* say and partly because Anna had quickly got wise to the fact that Zoe was in no state to string a coherent sentence together. At least Daniel was out of the picture – away at some day-long conference in Stirling. He'd offered to cancel, but Anna had shooed him out the door, saying she'd call him if there were any developments. Zoe was privately relieved. She and Daniel never seemed to know what to say to each other at the best of times, but last night the chasm between them had felt like it had magnified tenfold, to the point that being in the same room as him had been physically uncomfortable. She'd always got the feeling that Daniel disapproved of Anna's friendship with her in some unspoken way, and she suspected that he, like Carol's mum, probably now felt he'd called it right all along.

It was cooler in Anna's house than in her own flat, but as the day wore on the heat nonetheless began to steadily build. The police had advised them to keep the windows and doors locked at all times, and bit by bit the house was turning into a greenhouse. It was forecast to be the hottest day of the year, with the mercury hitting thirty, but to Zoe it felt just the same as every other day for the last two and a half weeks: grim, sticky, sweaty and miserable, and now with the added bonus of feeling like she was going to spew at any moment. The air pressure, too, was steadily rising, making her even more restless and on edge. It was bad enough being cooped up at the best of times, but when the thing you wanted to do more than anything in the world was run outside and scream the place down, it was akin to Chinese water torture.

She dearly wished she was back in the flat, waiting for news there. She was sure that was where the kidnappers would contact her if they were going to, but the police weren't having it. She imagined them now, going through the flat, tearing up the floorboards, rifling through her belongings (and Victor's belongings, and Granny's belongings), leaving them in total disarray. It was just like it had been with the press coverage of Victor: once again, her problems had become public property and she was just a powerless bystander, watching as others raked through her life.

The liaison officer had been keeping her briefed as to the progress made by the cops, or lack thereof. They'd picked up the van on CCTV and had succeeded in tracking it for a time as it headed east, only to lose its trail somewhere between Parkhead and Baillieston. Several hours later it was found torched in the woods near the old Gartloch Asylum. It was being combed for forensic evidence, but the early indications apparently weren't promising. For the time being, things were being kept low-key, on the basis that a media blitz would likely be more detrimental to Carol's safety than helpful.

She'd told the police about Ryland, of course, and they'd nodded and taken copious notes, but nothing about their demeanour had persuaded her that they regarded her words as anything other than the ramblings of a madwoman clutching at straws. For the millionth time, she ran over the possibilities as to how this all might play out. Carol had been taken to get at her – that was self-evident. But to what end? Were they planning on hurting her? Demanding a ransom? Or just Zoe's silence? She struggled to imagine how she'd pay them if they did ask for money. She'd probably have to rob a bank or something.

And she'd do it too, if it meant getting Carol back. She no longer remembered the fights, the annoying habits and the ideological differences, only the good times. Like their jaunt to T in the Park last year where it had poured with rain and they'd both ended up with the water up to their ankles inside their wellies but had been too caught up in all the buzz and excitement to notice. Or the time she'd been confined to her bed for three days with food poisoning, and Carol had sat with her throughout, uttering not a word of complaint even though Zoe kept puking all over both of them. Zoe's own religious convictions might best be described as agnostic leaning heavily towards atheistic, but she now found herself mentally bargaining with either God or some other undefinable entity, promising that, if he brought Carol back safe, she'd get a proper job and find a purpose in life and never complain about her lot again.

She came to, finding herself alone on the sofa with the texture of the cushion she'd been lying on imprinted on her cheek. Her phone was trilling at full volume. She was bolt upright at once, snatching it up and pressing it to her ear.

'What?'

'Zo, it's me.'

'Anna? Where are ye?' She looked around, belatedly realising that she was alone.

'I went out to pick up some provisions. I didn't want to wake you – you looked so peaceful.' She paused. 'Zoe, you need to put the TV on.' There was a worryingly frantic tone to her voice.

Zoe fumbled with the remote. 'OK, now what?'

'Turn to the news.'

She channel-cycled until she came to a twenty-four-hour news channel. On the screen was bird's-eye-view footage of a winding urban street populated by leafy evergreens and upmarket villas. The helicopter from which the video was being beamed cast a shadow on the pavement below and on a group of police officers clustered together in the middle of the road. An ambulance could just be made out at the edge of the screen. Zoe thought she recognised the street, though she couldn't place it. Then she noticed the headline emblazoned on the bottom third of the screen:

BREAKING NEWS
KNIFE ATTACK IN GLASGOW WEST END
Ambulance Service: victim pronounced dead at scene

She realised now why the view looked so familiar. It was Cleveden Road, little more than a ten-minute walk from where she now sat. In fact, as she listened, she realised that the low hum outside, which until now she'd only been half-aware of, must be coming from the chopper idling overhead.

She turned up the volume and listened in stunned silence as the newsreader – evidently still having up-to-the-minute information fed into her earpiece – conveyed, in a halting and slightly overawed tone, what was currently known. At around 4 p.m., a man in his early thirties, making his way up Cleveden Road from the direction of Great Western Road, had been set upon by a figure in a ski-mask armed with a knife. His throat had been slashed and the figure had fled, leaving him bleeding on the pavement. A neighbour, who'd witnessed the attack through her kitchen window, had immediately called the emergency services, then rushed out to administer first aid, but by then it was already too late. The wound was catastrophic and the victim had bled out in a matter of seconds. Police were downplaying any suggestion of this being a terror-related incident, but given the murder of that soldier down in England only a few weeks earlier, the footage of which was still etched into Zoe's consciousness, she wasn't sure she bought it.

'You still there?' Anna piped up again.

'Aye. Jesus. Whit can ye say?'

Anna was silent for a moment. 'The police got in touch with me.' Another pause. 'Zoe, it's Gavin Price. Someone's killed Gavin Price.'

* * *

In the time it took Anna to get home, Zoe had tried calling Fin on at least a dozen occasions, each time greeted by nothing but a brief answerphone message delivered with her usual manner: 'I'm off doin' shit. State yer case and I'll call ya back if I give a crap.' It wasn't the first time Zoe had tried to contact her, of course. She'd tried multiple times over the past twenty-four hours – generally during the fleeting moments when she was alone in the toilet, or when Anna briefly left her side to take care of some urgent business or other – but to no avail. It was as if Fin had disappeared off the face of the earth.

I could have him killed for you, you know.

Those words reverberated in her mind as she paced the hallway, waiting for the sound of Anna's dinky wee Mini Hatchback pulling up and the sight of her shimmering form behind the frosted glass door. She went over and over what had happened – trying, in her head, to absolve herself of responsibility. But she couldn't. And, as the door swung open and Anna charged in, clutching her shopping bags and with her eyes out in stalks, Zoe knew there was no point holding back.

'Aw Christ, Anna,' she said, 'I think I done something awful.'

She told Anna everything, giving her a complete account of her activities since the night at the Madeira. Fin, the 'investigation', breaking into Ryland's house, Fin's offer to have Gavin killed – all of it. By the end, Anna was slack-jawed with disbelief, completely incapable of making sense of what she'd heard.

'We have to go to the police,' she said at last. 'They're the only ones that can sort this out.'

Zoe didn't respond. She knew she should stop digging before she made the hole she was in any deeper. She knew the longer she withheld what she knew, the worse it would be for her. But the thought of owning up to her complicity, the thought of taking responsibility like that, made her want to retch.

'We don't know for sure,' she said weakly. 'I mean, she might've no done it. Mibby it was just . . . I dunno, banter.'

'We can't take that chance!' Anna all but shouted. Relenting a little, she squeezed Zoe's hand. 'If you know something about a murder that's been committed and it comes out you kept it to yourself, they'll throw the book at you.'

'They're gonnae throw the book at me anyway, but. I'm fucked if this gets out. I helped her break into a man's house and steal his computer. She said she could have someone killed and I practically gave her the thumbs-up.' She paused to gulp down a breath. 'We wanted tae see Gavin Price sent down for turning a blind eye tae a crime. How'm I any different fae him?'

Her chest seemed to be contracting. She was finding it increasingly difficult to get her breath. As she felt her knees begin to turn to mulch, Anna grabbed her by both shoulders, forcing her to make eye contact.

'Listen to me,' she said. 'You're nothing like Gavin Price. Nothing at all. You're a good, decent person, Zoe, and they'll see that. And maybe you're right. Maybe this Fin has nothing to do with what's happened today. But we can't sit on this.'

Zoe remained silent. Anna's words, however heartfelt, sounded uncomfortably close to the sort of argument gun-nuts always rattled off after there'd been another mass shooting in the States, claiming that it wasn't guns that were the problem, just the lone individual who'd pulled the trigger. And she knew, whatever Anna said, that the police wouldn't see it like that. The walls were closing in around her, suffocating her, threatening to crush her.

'So here's what we'll do,' Anna said at length. 'We're going to find this Fin, and confront her, and see what she has to say for herself. *Then* we'll go to the police. A couple more hours won't hurt.' With her hands on her hips, she put Zoe in mind of a disappointed parent giving an errant child one last chance to redeem itself. 'Whereabouts does she stay?'

They drove down to Fin's place, Zoe chewing her cuticles in the passenger seat. Fin's moped was still missing when they arrived, and, seeing this, Zoe's heart sank. During the drive, she'd briefly allowed herself to believe that they'd find her inside the flat, kicking back with a cold can of beer; that she'd explain that it was all just a misunderstanding and everything would be fine. Well, it *wouldn't* be fine, but she'd at least be able to cross one worry off her inordinately long list.

But there was no answer when they banged on the door, and when they unlocked it using the spare key, they found no sign of life inside. The bedclothes in Fin's room were a tangled mess, but that in no way proved she'd actually slept in it the previous night: Zoe didn't get the impression Fin was someone who diligently made her bed each morning.

'See if you can find any leads,' Anna told her. 'Emergency contact details, a next of kin. There's bound to be something.'

Zoe dutifully set about working her way through the contents of the various cupboards and drawers in the bedroom. However, it quickly became apparent to her that, whoever the room actually belonged to, it certainly wasn't Fin – not unless she'd once been a size four and had a strong penchant for frilly undergarments. Fin's own clothes were there too, strewn all over the floor and tossed over the backs of chairs and other assorted surfaces, but the contents of the various cupboards and drawers clearly belonged to someone else entirely. The same pattern was repeated in the other rooms. Zoe found clothes and other assorted odds and ends belonging to at least three different people – but little, if anything, that was identifiably Fin's.

They headed out into the hallway, where Anna knocked on the door on the opposite side of the corridor. It was opened by a wizened-looking woman in her seventies. She eyed the two of them suspiciously.

'Yes?'

'Sorry to disturb you,' said Anna. 'We're trying to find our friend. She lives in the flat across the hall. Have you seen her about at all today?'

'They're always coming and going from there,' said the woman, in a tone that indicated severe disapproval. 'Students, you know? Up and down they stairs all day and all night, nary a thought for those of us who need our beauty sleep.'

'It's not just students, though,' said Anna. 'Another woman lives there too. A bit older.'

'Short hair,' Zoe added. 'Wears a leather jaiket. Drives a moped. Name's Fin.'

The woman shook her head vehemently. 'I told you, it's students that live there. These flats are all halls of residence, 'cept for mine. Council sold 'em off to the university years ago. I'm the last of the hold-outs.'

'So ye've never seen a girl with spiky hair and a leather jaiket?' said Zoe, wishing to God she had a copy of her and Fin's tabloid appearance to show the old woman.

'Mibby. I dunno.' The woman was reaching the limits of her patience. 'I've no idea who belongs here and who doesn't. Their faces change with the seasons. And do they give me so much as a how-d'you-do when they pass me on the stairs? Do they buggery. So I keep to myself.' She raised a knowing eyebrow. 'Frankly I've got my doubts it's all above board.'

It was obvious the neighbour wasn't going to be of any assistance. Anna left her her number, entreating her to ring it if she happened to see Fin, then she and Zoe headed back down to the street.

Neither of them said a word till they were back inside the car, key in the ignition and air-con running.

'That settles it,' said Anna. 'We have to go to the police.'

Zoe said nothing. The nausea that engulfed her was overwhelming. For all she knew, Fin could simply have been dossing in the flat while its rightful residents were away. Chances were they'd never even heard of her and would come back from their travels in September to find the living room inexplicably awash with empty beer cans and all their bog-roll used up.

'We'll figure out what we're going to say,' Anna went on. 'There are ways of minimising your involvement. And the more info we can give them, the more likely they are to be satisfied.'

'Aye,' Zoe muttered, unconvinced.

'Let's start with what you know about this woman. Everything she told you about herself. Any details about her upbringing, where she came from, stuff like that.'

'Ireland,' said Zoe helplessly. 'She's fae Ireland somewhere.'

'OK, that's a start. You've no idea where?'

'Nuh.' Zoe shook her head forlornly.

Anna was staring at her, her attempts to conceal her incredulity increasingly futile. 'What about her name? Her full name, I mean. Is "Fin" short for something, is it—'

'Her name . . . '

Zoe's stomach turned to lead. As she racked her brains, trying to come up with some relevant detail, she realised that, while she could ream off Fin's opinions on everything from how to ignite the revolution to why Dairylea cheese spread didn't taste as good as it used to, as a person she was more or less a complete enigma. And she'd just remembered something else: herself, standing outside Gavin Price's house the other night, wearing Fin's clothes, looking for all the world like she was plotting a break-in. Or something worse. She'd even been seen by one of the neighbours. Perhaps the same one who'd tried unsuccessfully to give Gavin the kiss of life earlier that day.

She felt the tears welling in her tired, itchy eyes, and she was powerless to stop them.

'Christ, Anna,' she said, 'I dunno her name. I dunno the first thing about her.'

27

Flesh Trade

In the end, Anna took an executive decision, driving them back to Clarence Drive while Zoe sat virtually catatonic in the passenger seat. They needed to regroup, Anna declared with admirable conviction. Regroup and figure out how they were going to play this.

Daniel was home by the time they got back, already in the midst of preparing the evening meal. Soon enough, the dining room table had been laid and they were all sitting down to eat together. Zoe tried her best, for Anna's sake if nothing else, but the food tasted like ash in her mouth, and after a while she excused herself, took herself through to the living room and lay on the sofa, knees drawn up to her chest.

Five minutes later, Anna joined her.

'Hey.' She waved a half-full bottle of Smirnoff and a couple of tumblers and gave Zoe a weak smile. 'I've brought voddy.'

Zoe scooted up, making room for her. Anna poured them each a generous measure and clinked glasses with Zoe.

'Cheers,' said Anna.

'*Sláinte.*'

Zoe drained hers in a single gulp and signalled for a fill-up.

*   *   *

They sat side by side, making their way through the bottle and talking about nothing of any great importance. It was as if they'd come to a silent, mutual understanding that whatever painful decisions had to be made were on hold until tomorrow, and for the time being they were going to act like this was just a regular Saturday night catch-up between old friends. Through the dull haze of exhaustion and alcohol, it occurred to Zoe that she'd seen more of Anna in the last few days than she had at any point in the past year. Nothing quite like a crisis for bringing folk together.

As the night drew in and she became progressively more inebriated, she found herself talking about Carol, recounting to Anna the events that had originally brought them together. How they'd got to talking one night at Pulse – Carol serving the drinks, Zoe buying them – and, over the course of the next several weeks, had ended up seeing more and more of each other as Zoe found herself making a beeline for Carol whenever she was serving, and looking forward to their brief encounters with a relish that, to an outside observer, would have seemed wholly disproportionate to what were ostensibly just cold, cynical business transactions.

Eventually, a couple of months after they'd first met, Carol had invited Zoe back to hers for a nightcap after Pulse's doors had closed, with an invitation to kip on her sofa afterwards if she didn't feel like shelling out for a taxi home. As they'd made their way down to Dumbarton Road together, Carol wheeling her bike, they'd quickly discovered just how little common ground they had – Carol a West End anti-capitalist feminist who considered Simone de Beauvoir's *The Second Sex* her Bible; Zoe a loud, brash party girl from Ruchill who worshipped at the altar of consumer capitalism and whose stance on women's lib could basically be summed up by the refrain of a certain Cyndi Lauper hit from 1983. Not that this had come as much of a surprise: Zoe had worked out that Carol was 'one of them' almost immediately, and had taken a certain perverse delight in revealing that not only did she think the Struggle was irrelevant in the twenty-first century, but that she wasn't – and never had been – registered to vote. Carol had responded by lecturing her about her responsibilities as a citizen and as a woman, and Zoe had quickly written her off as one of those crazy revolutionaries she'd done her best to avoid during her time at uni.

She remembered crashing into Carol's flat, still tipsy from the night's frivolities, and sinking to her knees on the living room floor to peruse the extensive vinyl collection while Carol retreated to the kitchen to make coffee. She'd quickly realised that their musical tastes were as incompatible as their political views, with virtually all Carol's music being from before either of them was even born. Zoe couldn't understand why anyone their age would want to listen to what she thought of as dad music, and she certainly couldn't fathom how you could have an emotional connection to stuff that was already old hat when your parents were still making googly-eyes at one another. 'Hen, yer tunes are shite!' she'd informed Carol, and Carol, returning from the kitchen with a mug in each hand, had informed Zoe that an education was long overdue.

Over the course of that night, Zoe had learned about the origins and credos of groups as wide-ranging as Pink Floyd and Bananarama. She couldn't recall the precise order of events with any clarity, but she remembered Carol putting on a bunch of different records for her enlightenment, and there being dancing, followed by more alcohol and a deep, philosophical conversation on the sofa about why 'Bird on the Wire' was the most important song ever written. Or was it 'Imagine'? Zoe had a feeling Carol had changed her mind more than once during her treatise. And then there had been kissing, and yet more drinking, and then a short, flat-footed stumble through to the bedroom, where there had been mutual undressing, punctuated by more kissing, followed by an ungainly collapse onto the bed, and then a series of sensations Zoe had never experienced before, not in all her various – and varied – dalliances with the men who'd come and gone from her life as fleetingly as summer rain.

She'd known Carol was gay from the off – or at least, it hadn't come as a surprise to discover that she was. With some people, when you found out you'd be like *Whoa, never thought* they *swung that way.* With others, it was more a case of *Oh aye, totally makes sense in hindsight.* But with Carol there'd been none of that. She'd seemed to wear it like a second skin – not in a flashy or ostentatious way, just in the sense of it being part of what made her *her*, as integral as her white-blonde hair or the missing molars you only saw when she *really* smiled. And, while Zoe had never thought of herself as being someone who was interested in women in that way, when she'd woken up the next morning to find herself still in Carol's bed, Carol asleep by her side, it had taken her all of five seconds to make her peace with the new normal.

'See, I got this theory,' she said, as Anna refilled her tumbler. 'When folk ask what it is ye see in someone, what makes ye love 'em, ye come up wi all these fancy explanations after the fact. It's the sparkle in their eye, that snort they do when they laugh, the way they always give up their seat on the bus to an old yin. But I reckon it's all hooey. I reckon ye make up yer mind about someone in like five seconds, and everything else is just making sense o' that first impression.' She gave a sad little smile. 'I reckon I knew she was the one for me right fae that night she first took my order. My brain just needed time tae get the message.'

Anna turned towards her, returning the smile. She was a little tipsy herself, and tending towards maudlin – to regarding every utterance that came out of Zoe's mouth as beautiful and profound. 'See that thing you've just described – that instant connection with another person? I reckon most fold spend their entire lives searching for that and never finding it. But you – you didn't even have to look for it. It just fell into your lap. You've no idea how special that is.' She paused. 'And I know, I just know, if Carol comes back . . . *when* she comes back, the two of you are going to have a long, happy life together and have, like, a million babies together.'

Zoe nodded soberly. 'I'd like to have a kiddo one day,' she admitted. 'Only trouble is I'd make a crap mum.'

'What are you talking about?' said Anna, drunk-affronted. 'You'd be brilliant. Pure. Dead. Brilliant.' She punctuated each word with a thrust of her tumbler in Zoe's direction. 'Way better than I ever would. I mean,' she gave a mischievous grin, 'let's face it, you're kind of a big kid yourself anyway.'

Zoe managed to smile, but truthfully Anna's words had hurt more than they helped. Carol had said pretty much the same, accusing her of being stuck in some sort of state of arrested development. It had stung then and it stung now, however benign Anna's intentions had been. She raised her glass to her lips and said nothing.

The hours ticked by, and it grew steadily darker outside. They lay there, side by side on the sofa, watching the lights of passing cars as they glanced across the ceiling. Towards midnight, Daniel leaned in and told Anna he was going to bed.

'OK,' said Anna, not moving. ''Night.'

Daniel hesitated. 'Will you, uh, will you be . . . ?'

'I think we're just going to kip here,' said Anna, glancing at Zoe for confirmation.

Zoe said nothing.

Daniel dipped his head in understanding, though Zoe couldn't help but note the slight hesitation in his response. She knew only too well what he was thinking: that Anna needed a proper night's sleep herself and was unlikely to get it parked on the sofa.

'All right,' he said after a moment. 'I'll see you upstairs if you have a change of plans. If not, see you in the morning.'

He slipped out, closing the door softly behind him.

Anna settled down again, resting her head in the crook of Zoe's neck. Zoe lay rigid, staring up at the ceiling. Not content with ruining her own relationship and life, she was now allowing herself to infect Anna's as well, generating conflict merely by virtue of her presence. She couldn't allow that contagion to spread. Nor could she allow Anna to compromise herself by participating in any cover-up regarding Fin and her possible role in Gavin Price's murder, which she was sure was what things were leading up to. She resolved then and there to extricate herself from this situation as soon as possible.

She waited till Anna's breathing turned slow and regular; gave her a few minutes more. Then, once she was certain she was asleep, she slid free, putting a cushion under Anna's head in place of her shoulder. She scribbled a note for her – *Please don't look for me. Let me be alone* – and left it on the coffee table. Then, after taking one last, fond look at her best pal, still fast asleep and none the wiser, she crept out into the hallway, slipped the door off the latch and vanished into the night.

For a Friday night, the streets seemed strangely quiet, though that might have had something to do with the fact that someone had had his throat cut within shouting distance just a few hours earlier. As Zoe turned onto Crow Road, the dark expanse of Cross Park came into view, its leafy trees blotting out the grey-purple night sky. At the little gate leading into the park stood a forlorn figure: a woman with long, silky hair, smoking a cigarette and dressed so skimpily that, despite the still-cloying heat, Zoe couldn't help but shiver involuntarily.

It wasn't until she drew parallel on the pavement opposite that Zoe realised she knew her.

'Jasmine?'

Jasmine started like a rearing horse and turned in Zoe's direction.

Recognising her, she relaxed somewhat, resuming her prior hand-on-hip, time-is-money stance, her cigarette held between two fingers just inches from her lips. Zoe crossed over to her.

'What are ye doing out here?'

'What's it look like? Plying my trade. Earning my daily crust. Whichever of the various euphemisms *du jour* you happen to prefer.'

'But out here? I thought ye didnae work the streets.'

'Since my night of unbridled passion with our right honourable friend, it turns out I've slid down the league tables somewhat.'

'Eh?'

Jasmine sighed patiently. 'There's a pecking order to our ancient and noble profession. A hierarchy. At the top, those who've got the looks and the breeding work the "champers and cocktails" end of the flesh industry. The ones who won't look out of place in the Hiltons and the Radissons, who know how to hold a spoon correctly, who answer to "escort" rather than to "whore". Then at the other end you've got your assorted cast-offs: the junkies, the smack-heads, the over-forties. The ones whose looks have started to slide, if they ever had any. Only a select few start at the top, but almost everyone who stays in the game long enough finds themselves at the bottom sooner or later. Thing is, I figured I had at least a few more years before that was me. Funny how life can sneak up on you like that, isn't it?'

Up close, Zoe was able to get a proper look at Jasmine's face. The swelling and bruising had long since gone, but they'd left an array of unsightly bumps and scars that no amount of makeup could hide – and she was wearing a lot of it.

'Ye shouldnae be out here. 'Specially no on yer tod like this. It isnae safe.'

Jasmine drew on her cigarette. 'I'm a working girl, darling. Clue's in the job title. And if I'm not working, I'm bringing home none of that thick, juicy bacon, which means the nice men I work for start to become not-so-nice. Unless, of course,' she went on, 'you're offering to relieve me of my debts.' She gave an ugly smirk. 'But then, I'm not flavour of the month with you anymore, am I? Dropped me like a hottie patottie the second you found yourself a new target for your virtue-signalling.'

That stung, and yet Zoe could hardly argue with it. Now that it came down to it, she had to admit that, in the last couple of weeks, she'd barely given Jasmine and her plight a second thought.

'Mibby,' she began, 'mibby I could—'

Jasmine shook her head. 'Save your breath, toots. The kind of money I owe, the likes of you wouldn't even make a dent in it if you spent every day paying it back till the day you die.'

'Is that how ye ended up daein' this? Owing money?'

'What, I can't just get a sense of fulfilment out of spreading my legs for greasy strangers?' The sardonic smile faded from Jasmine's lips. 'When I was young and stupid, I made a few bad decisions. Several, actually. Ended up severely indebted to a very bad man. He and his associates sat me down and told me there were a few ways I could set about balancing the books. This was the best of a bad bunch.'

Zoe knew a thing or two about bad decisions. She'd made more than her fair share of them of late. But she still couldn't picture herself ever being so desperate as to hawk her body to complete strangers, either on a street corner or within the comparatively more hospitable confines of the Madeira. She wondered what Jasmine's other options had been for her to consider this her best bet.

'Why don't ye just leg it? Hop on a train and go someplace far away. Like back home, wherever that is.'

'I'm from Reading, darling. It might seem like a different world to you, but I'm fairly certain a man with half the criminal enterprise in Glasgow on his balance sheet wouldn't be too taxed by tracking me down there. Took him all of five minutes to find out where *you* lived.'

Zoe felt her stomach turn to lead. 'Pardon?'

Before Jasmine could reply, they were interrupted by a car roaring round the corner and pulling over next to them. A pair of young men were inside: early twenties, Glasgow University Union-type roasters, high as kites and drunk on their own self-importance.

The one in the passenger seat leaned his entire body out the open window. 'All right, laydeeeez!' he exclaimed, in that homogenised West End drawl that always set Zoe's teeth on edge. 'Is it two-for-one tonight?'

'Fuck off, prick,' Zoe snapped, finding her voice in her anger. 'Go choke on some Jägerbombs.'

The driver guffawed and hauled his companion back inside the car by the exposed waistband of his Calvin Kleins. As they drove off, their honking laughter lingering in the air, Zoe turned to Jasmine once again.

'What did you *do*?' she demanded, the words coming out as a strangled hiss.

'He asked me and I told him, all right?' Jasmine's tone was petulant and defensive. 'Jim Cottrell's not a man you say no to when he asks you for something.'

The name sent a fresh bolt of horror coursing through Zoe.

'I gather there was quite a disturbance in our street the other day,' Jasmine went on, her defensiveness having given way to what sounded like bland disinterest. 'Vans speeding off, cops taking statements. How's your girlfriend, by the way?'

Zoe could only stare at her, unable to articulate anything meaningful. 'You . . . you . . . '

'I, I what? Betrayed you? Sold you down the river? Hurts, doesn't it, thinking you've got a friend, only to find she stabs you in the back just as soon as it becomes expedient?' She took a defiant drag on her cigarette. 'Well, nice as it's been to catch up, I'd best be getting on. These cocks aren't going to suck themselves.'

She turned away, giving Zoe the cold shoulder.

Zoe stood there in impotent disbelief. She should by rights have flown at Jasmine for what she'd done, torn her silky hair out at the roots. But she couldn't. She didn't have it in her. Jasmine, Ryland, Tannahill, Cottrell, back to Jasmine again . . . She knew it all joined up somehow, but she hadn't the energy or strength of will to follow the thread. She turned and began to walk away.

'So that's it, then?' Jasmine's mocking voice rang out behind her. 'You're not going to tell me I'm not on my own? You're not going to try and save me?'

But Zoe didn't reply; nor did she look back. She just kept walking.

She reached her flat a little after 1.30. A policeman was standing guard on the pavement just outside the entrance, hands tucked into either side of his stab vest, trying hard not to yawn. Seeing her approaching, he leapt to attention and moved to intercept her.

'What's your business here?'

'I'm going home, all right?' she snarled. 'I live here. This is my fucking house.'

He didn't even try to argue with her. She clomped up the stairs, ripped the police tape off her door, headed straight for the bedroom and flopped face-down on the bed, letting herself go limp, no longer making any conscious effort to carry on living.

28

Wrong Girl

Morning came, and Zoe dragged herself into some semblance of wakefulness. She hadn't actually slept – not in the conventional sense, at any rate. She'd just lain there semi-catatonic for the last several hours, her mind an empty vacuum. Victor, the trial, Carol's abduction, Gavin's murder and her own culpability in pretty much all of these – her brain had run out of capacity to cope with all this trauma, so had done the only thing it could under the circumstances and gone into total shutdown.

Like an automaton, she went about her daily business: rinsing her face at the sink, sticking on the TV, making breakfast. She collected the previous day's mail from the doormat and dumped it on the kitchen table, then took her cornflakes to the sofa and skimmed through the various news channels. No bodies had turned up, but in the early hours of the morning, the Royal Arms in Bridgeton had been firebombed, completely gutting the premises. No one had been in at the time, though the family living on the floor above another pub in Balornock hadn't been so lucky. It too had been set ablaze, and all five – mum, dad and three weans – were in hospital, being treated for burns and smoke inhalation.

She called the police liaison officer for an update, only to be told that there was none. Not that she was all that surprised. She'd read somewhere that, with abduction cases, the first forty-eight hours were critical. Typically, the victim was either rescued, released or killed during that window, which had now all but closed. She contemplated asking whether the cops had made good on her urging to question Ryland, but in the end she didn't bother. She already knew what the answer would be.

She wiped her brow with the back of her arm. She was hot and frustrated and exhausted and miserable. She wandered over to the window and peered out. Heavy clouds were gathering overhead, blotting out the sun and the blue sky that had been a constant, unwelcome presence over the past two weeks. It felt like being smothered under a stifling blanket of grey.

She spent much of the day sloping from sofa to bed to sofa, lying like a limp dishcloth on whichever surface she thought might give her some succour at that particular moment, dozing in fits and starts. Her sleep pattern had been shot to pieces for ages now. She wasn't sleeping properly at night, with the result that she was crashing out at weird times during the day and coming to to find that whole hours had disappeared into the ether. It was disorientating and left her in a state of near-permanent exhaustion, the mere act of continuing to exist sucking up all her energy.

She came round from one such black-out to an almighty hammering inside her skull. She sat up, blinking, trying to orient herself to her whereabouts and the time of day. Her phone said 08:43, but that could be either a.m. or p.m., and at this time of year the fact that it was light until close to midnight didn't help narrow it down. As the sleep gradually left her system, she realised that the source of the pounding wasn't her head but rather the stairwell. Her front door, to be precise.

'Zoe? You in there?'

Anna.

In truth, she was a little surprised it had taken Anna until now to come looking for her. After her abrupt exit the previous night, there hadn't been so much as a concerned text from her, and Zoe had begun to believe she might actually have taken the hint. That, or she'd finally had enough of Zoe's crap and decided to wash her hands of her once and for all.

She got to her feet and stumbled out into the hallway. As she unlocked the door and hefted it open, Anna stumbled in, flushed and breathless.

'I knew you wanted to be left alone,' she gabbled, 'but I'm just off the phone and I knew you'd want to—'

'Spit it out, Anna. What's the craic?'

Anna paused to catch her breath. She stared back at Zoe with wide white eyes.

'They've found her, Zoe. They've found Carol.'

They, it turned out, were a pair of weekend labourers at a scrapyard in the Cumbernauld area. They'd discovered her, naked and lifeless, in the boot of an aged Volvo condemned to a future as dog-food cans and had immediately rung 999. In fact, only the sheer good luck of her arm slipping out of the half-open boot and one of the men being sufficiently on the ball to spot it and raise the alarm had saved her from being crushed inside her rusty tomb by the jaws of the demolition vehicle. Paramedics and the police had arrived in short order, the latter of whom identified her based on the description and photograph circulated to them forty-eight hours previously. The labourers had assumed she was dead, but a cursory examination by the paramedics confirmed that she was in fact very much alive, though she'd clearly been given something to knock her out. She was badly bruised all over and had a broken arm and several cracked ribs, though whether she'd been deliberately assaulted or had sustained the injuries while being bounced around inside the boot was unclear. In any event, the effects of whatever she'd been given had begun to wear off in the back of the ambulance, and by the time they'd reached Monklands Hospital, she'd been conscious, if not exactly coherent.

Zoe and Anna arrived at the hospital a little before ten, the twenty-mile drive having taken longer than expected due to a chunk of the M8 being closed for roadworks. They hurried in and, after presenting themselves at reception, were directed to a recovery ward on the second floor. There, in a side room adjacent to the nurses' station, they found Carol in the middle of giving a statement to a couple of uniformed cops. She was sitting up in bed, her mother by her side, and stopped mid-stream as Zoe came barging in. Her right arm was in a sling, but that wasn't the worst of it. Her whole face was covered with grazes and bruises, and both eyes were swollen almost completely shut, the skin around them a variety of shades of blue and purple. She turned her head towards the doorway, but Zoe had no idea whether she could see her or not. Her mum, on the other hand, definitely could, and the look she gave Zoe could have pickled liver.

Several terse, silent moments passed, then Carol turned back to the officers and resumed her account as if Zoe wasn't even there. Her voice sounded unfamiliar and flat, as if she still wasn't quite with it. They drove her tied up and blindfolded in the back of the van, she said, for getting on for half an hour. Then they pulled over and hauled her out. She couldn't see anything, but from the distant roar of traffic and the smell of the air, she sensed that they were outside the city. They bundled her into the boot of a car and set off again. After a while, the terrain became extremely rough and she was bumped and bounced about until she conked her head on the roof and, presumably, lost consciousness.

When she next came to, she was being carried again. She could hear birdsong, and from the sounds of twigs crackling under her abductors' feet she guessed they were in a wooded area. They seemed to be going uphill, but that was about all she could tell geographically-speaking. They took her indoors, someplace damp and hollow-sounding. A shed, maybe? Then, before she had a chance to orient herself, she was being held upright, the blindfold was whipped off and there was a click and a blinding flash as someone snapped a photo of her. Then the blindfold was put back on and she was tossed onto the floor. She heard muttered voices – three different men, she was reasonably certain – then silence for a while. She lay there for a good fifteen to twenty minutes, not daring to move, breathing in the smell of pinewood. Then she heard a ringtone and a gruff 'Hello?' There was some more muttering, and then all hell broke loose.

'YOU FUCKING IDIOTS!' someone bellowed. 'IT'S THE WRONG FUCKING GIRL!'

There followed an almighty commotion – bumps, yells and other assorted sounds of struggling – and she knew that a fight of some sort was going down. Eventually, one or another of the belligerents got the upper hand, then she heard a door slamming, and footsteps receding outside, and she began to drift again.

From then on, time ceased to be something she was able to quantify. She kept slipping in and out of consciousness, despite her best efforts to keep her mind active and alert. She had no idea how long they kept her there, but she was aware of being moved at least one more time – once again in a car boot . . . And then, the next thing she knew, she was coming to in the back of the ambulance with a paramedic leaning over her to fit an oxygen mask over her face.

As Carol fell silent and lowered her head, her account seemingly having sapped all her strength, Zoe felt herself moving towards her instinctively. She hadn't taken more than a handful of steps when Carol flinched away so violently that the drip came out of her arm.

As the nurse who'd been standing guard in the corner throughout the whole account came scurrying forward to stick it back in place, Carol's mother got to her feet and placed a hand on her daughter's shoulder.

'Your presence is not required here,' she said to Zoe. 'You've heard what you've done. Now you can leave.'

Zoe looked from Carol's mum to the nurse to the two cops, as if one of them might come to her defence. No one said anything. Last of all, she turned to Carol, but Carol steadfastly refused to so much as look at her.

She felt a hand on her arm: Anna's.

'We should go,' Anna said gently. 'Come on.'

Zoe made no further attempt to object. She lowered her eyes, allowing Anna to take her by the arm and lead her out.

They made their way back through the ward in silence, Zoe in a daze, Anna still keeping a hold of her, as if she feared she'd break free and go haring back to Carol for one last try. Zoe's eyes bounced listlessly from sight to sight, taking in various unconnected, irrelevant details: the flickering strip-lighting overhead; the trio of nurses clustered round a computer in the nurses' station, giggling at something one of them had up on the screen; the poster on the wall warning of the dangers of MRSA; the overflowing surgical trolley parked next to a side room . . .

As they stepped out into the corridor, the lift doors up ahead opened and a woman got out. She was tall, with frizzy hair and a somewhat authoritarian demeanour about her. As they passed one another, Zoe was left with the distinct impression that they'd met somewhere before. It wasn't until she and Anna were nearly at the lift that she realised where she knew her from: the victim suite at London Road Police Station.

Dr Marion Chambers, duty Sexual Offence Examiner.

'Oh Jesus.'

Zoe felt her legs turning to putty. She gripped the wall to steady herself, then turned to look back down the corridor. But even as she did, she knew exactly what she'd see: Dr Chambers turning off into Carol's side-room to examine her for signs of sexual trauma. She heard herself babbling something incoherent, then Anna reassuring her, telling her that it was just a precaution because Carol had been unconscious; that they just wanted to rule out—

But Zoe was no longer listening. An image leapt unbidden into her head of a pair of long-bladed surgical scissors lying on top of the unattended trolley back on the ward. She realised she'd registered their presence at the time on some subconscious level, and the carelessness of leaving such a dangerous object unattended. Someone'll get their erse skelped for that, she'd thought.

And then, without really actively thinking about what she was doing, she wrenched herself free of Anna's grasp, did a one-eighty turn and hurried back down the corridor. She felt the cold steel of the scissors in her hand without even having been aware of lifting them. And then she was off, rejecting the lift in favour of the stairs. She sensed Anna tripping down the steps behind her, saying her name over and over, *Zoe Zoe Zoe*, but she paid no heed. There was no room in her mind now for anything other than her goal: finding Ryland and making him pay.

As she reached the ground floor and began to make her way across the concourse towards the exit, her ears seemed to pop and they were once more filled with the normal sounds of a busy hospital. She could hear Anna properly now; hear the words tumbling breathlessly out of her mouth.

'Zoe. Zoe, stop. Don't do this.'

'Why no?' She kept walking. 'Why the fuck shouldn't I? I'm basically a killer by proxy anyway. Might as well go the whole hog, get my own hands dirty.'

'You don't want to do this. Please, let the proper authorities deal with it.'

Zoe ground to a halt and turned to face Anna. 'Seriously? After everything that's happened, *that's* yer line? I've *tried*, Anna. I've tried really fucking hard to do the right thing, and what've I got tae show for it? What've *any* of us?'

She was within touching distance of the doors now. A few more strides and she'd be clear of the place. But Anna had other ideas. She grabbed hold of Zoe's arm, dragging her to a standstill.

Zoe turned to face her again. She was in no mood for this. 'Don't get in my way, Anna.'

Anna held her gaze, eyes glittering with steely resolve. 'I'm not going to let you do this.'

'And I'm no gonnae tell ye twice.'

Anna continued to hold Zoe's gaze and cling to her arm. Zoe gave her a couple of seconds to reconsider, then did something that, a few short hours ago, she'd never have contemplated doing in a month of Sundays. She balled her free hand into a fist, drew back her arm and socked Anna square in the jaw.

The speed with which Anna crumpled took her by surprise. She let go of Zoe, took a couple of tottering steps backwards, then immediately went down, landing arse-first on the floor. Clutching her jaw, she stared up at Zoe with an expression that somehow managed to simultaneously convey pain, confusion, shock and deep, deep disappointment. Zoe recognised these emotions all too well, for she'd spent the last few days heavily immersed in them herself. But there was no time for guilt now. That would have to come later. Right now, she had a fire in her belly and a job to do. She turned towards the doors once more.

And walked straight into Fin.

29

Guardian Angel

The hospital canteen was deserted, a sign at the till informing would-be customers that it was manned from 8 a.m. to 8 p.m. But some considerate soul had left the lights on, and now Zoe and Fin sat facing one another on opposite sides of a table near the window, the Formica surface lying between them like a neutral broker. Anna sat a little way off at another table, silent and wary – like a witness, there to corroborate what was said at some unknown future deposition.

'I got the gist from the news,' said Fin. 'Gotta say, I didn't 'spect 'em to come after us like they did. Figured they'd be less gung-ho about it. To actually snatch a bod in broad daylight, with witnesses and everything – that takes balls, or desperation.'

'Us? They came for you too?'

'Why else d'ya think I scarpered like a scalded cat? Thursday night I got home late and you weren't there. Figured, "Hey, maybe the trial verdict came in and she wants to be alone to drown her sorrows. Or go out celebrating". Then, next morning at first light I'm woken by some creep trying to pick the lock. I look out the window, see a couple o' heavies in the street guarding the door. End up having to climb down the back drainpipe in my skivvies. Been laying low ever since.'

She grinned, trying to elicit a smile from Zoe. Zoe didn't bite.

'You could've called me. Got word to me. Let me know where ye were.'

Fin shook her head. 'Too risky. State I figured you'd be in after they took yer girl, you'da been capable of anything. How was I to know you wouldn't blab everythin' to the authorities, including certain extra-legal affairs of which we both partook?'

It was a fair point, but Zoe wasn't ready to concede it. Not yet.

'But I didn't just jet off into the wide blue yonder,' Fin went on. 'Tempting as it was. I was never that far off, even if you didn't see me. I've been keeping an eye on ya, ready to step in if you got into any bother . . . or decided to do something daft.' She winked cheekily. 'Told ya I'd watch yer back, didn't I?'

Again, Zoe was silent. She pictured Fin prowling behind her like a cat-burglar, keeping to the shadows and loping over back walls as she tailed her throughout the city. Her dark guardian angel.

'Hey.' Fin reached out and slapped her on the arm. 'I risked my neck for you. Everything you've asked for, I've done. Figure the least I'm due is a bit of gratitude.'

'And Gavin Price?' Zoe shot back. 'Did I ask ye to do *that*?'

For a moment, Fin stared at her in incredulity, as if she'd been speaking a foreign language. 'What're you blathering about?'

'What, you're gonnae tell me ye don't know anything about that?'

Fin scoffed. 'Course I know about it. I got eyes 'n' ears, don't I? But if what you're really asking is did I have anything to do with his not-so-untimely demise, then I'm sorry to burst yer bubble, but my grabbers are clean.'

'I seem to remember you saying ye could have him killed for me.'

'And *I* seem to remember *you* begging me not to, and me saying all right then, I wouldn't. You made yer stance on the whole extra-judicial killing thing pretty crystal. Anyway,' she added, a touch ruefully, 'ya gotta know by now not to take everything I say at face value. Don't be thinking I'm some super-connected master crim. I ain't got the means to hire a hitman. Heh, best I could prob'ly've managed would've been paying some ned to key his car.'

'You told me ye did time inside,' said Zoe. She still wasn't quite prepared to take Fin at her word. And yet something about the utter vehemence of her denial told her she was telling the truth.

'Juvie counts, doesn't it?' said Fin a tad defensively. She gave one of her crooked little smiles, trying to coax a similar response out of Zoe.

It wasn't happening. She saw nothing funny or light-hearted about her current situation. Though, having said that, all of a sudden Fin seemed greatly diminished in her eyes. Whereas before Zoe had held her in something approaching apprehensive awe, what with her apparent underworld connections and casual offers to have men assassinated, she now came across as something of a sad fantasist, making up grandiose claims to make herself seem more interesting. When it came down to it, it seemed she was all mouth and no trousers.

'So what was the plan, then?' Fin broke the silence. 'Knock on yer man's door and stick those in his belly?'

Zoe looked down and realised she was still clutching the surgical scissors in her fist. The blades had been digging into her flesh for some time, and she now felt them with considerable acuity.

Fin shook her head. 'You're no killer, Bright Eyes. No reason to become one now.'

Zoe set the scissors down on the table and pushed them away from her. She suddenly felt incredibly sheepish. She still felt guilty as fuck about Carol – about the way she'd treated her, about the danger she'd put her in – but Gavin's murder wasn't her fault, and that had to count for something. It certainly made the guilt that little bit less insurmountable. Though now the dull ache in her knuckles served as a reminder of the blow she'd dealt to Anna – yet another thing she'd have to apologise for. She stole a glance at her pal. Anna was still seated at the table opposite, staring into the middle distance as if none of this had anything to do with her. But you just knew she was listening to every word.

'So what now?' Fin piped up again.

Zoe shook her head. 'Dunno.'

She was at a loss. The drive to actually do violence to Ryland had faded, but one way or the other, he still needed to pay – for Carol, and for all his other myriad crimes. But try as she might, she couldn't see a way. He was too powerful, too well-connected, and the police had made it abundantly clear they didn't want to know.

'Where d'ye reckon I stand?' she said. 'Honestly.'

'You mean is our friend the hoor-basher gonna come after ya again?'

Zoe shrugged an affirmative.

Fin frowned, running her tongue along her gums as she thought about it. 'That's a toughie. It's just possible he might settle for having put the fear o' God into ya. But something tells me he's not gonna stop at having duffed yer girl Friday up and given you a couple o' sleepless nights over it. Still, if he's looking for Cottrell to help him out again, odds are he'll be standing holding his todger awhile yet.'

'How d'you mean?'

'Dunno if ya noticed, but in the last forty-eight hours, fuckin' World War Three broke out. The McGills've gone full Tony Montana. Torching Tannahill's pub in Bridgeton, that one out in Balornock, and I heard Mental Willy McLaren got put in the hospital and all. I dunno what's sparked it off, but it's like they smell blood or some-thing. But if Ryland used Cottrell and Tannahill to come after us, the fact they got their hands full with the McGills prob'ly 'splains why they didn't try again after they realised they'd nabbed the wrong girl. Prob'ly also 'splains why they were sloppy enough to leave her alive to tell the tale.'

The thought of Carol only having survived because her abductors' minds were elsewhere did nothing to make Zoe feel any better.

'Still,' Fin continued, 'if you want my advice, I'd clear out for a while. Go somewhere no one knows ya, least till things die down a bit. Hey!' Her eyes lit up. 'What's say we hit the road, you 'n' me? The sun on our backs, the wind in our hair, the world our oyster. Whaddaya reckon?'

Zoe thought about it. Forty-eight hours ago, she'd probably have taken Fin up on her offer in a heartbeat. But things had changed since then. Taking Carol had made things personal, to the extent that running away was no longer something she was prepared to contemplate. For better or worse, she had to see this through. She'd started this, and it was up to her to end it, even if it meant handing herself over to Ryland and submitting to whatever it was he wanted to do to her.

And somehow, Fin seemed to sense what she was thinking. She gave a wan smile. 'Shame. And you such a natural riding shotgun. But I get it. Always figured you'd have a hard time letting go.' She got to her feet, neck clicking as she stretched. 'I'll be clearing out sooner or later. Reckon I've outstayed my welcome in this fair city. But I'll stick around awhile yet, even if I end up keeping a low profile. Wanna see how this all pans out.' She made to leave, then paused and turned back towards Zoe. 'But if ya change yer mind – y'know, 'bout bidding adieu to this whole sorry lark – the offer's still good.'

She hesitated for a moment, glanced in Anna's direction and gave her a curt nod of acknowledgement. Then, affecting the same swagger that, in Zoe's eyes, had become her trademark, she turned and strode out.

Anna waited until they were alone once more before getting up and making her way over.

'So,' she said, 'that was Fin.'

'That was Fin, aye.'

'What are you planning on doing now?'

Zoe wondered what that meant: what was she going to do now, this very moment, or, more generally, what was she going to do about the almighty clusterfuck she'd gotten herself into? She had a lot to think about, and she wasn't going to be pushed into any sudden decisions. There'd been more than enough of *those* lately. One thing was for sure, though: there was nothing to be achieved now, here, at one in the morning in a hospital canteen on the outskirts of Airdrie.

She looked up at Anna. The skin under her jaw was red and sore. She was going to have a beezer of a bruise twenty-four hours from now. Zoe felt like the heeliest of heels asking for anything after inflicting that on her, but, with nothing with her but the clothes on her back, she knew her present options were extremely limited.

'Can I get a lift home?'

Anna made it blatantly clear she wasn't happy about letting Zoe go home alone, not least because she agreed with Fin's assessment that the danger hadn't passed, but Zoe was adamant: she wanted to sleep in her own bed. There was no sign of their friendly neighbourhood police guard when they pulled up to the kerb. Evidently, with Carol found alive and well-ish, they'd decided their resources were better spent elsewhere. That, or that it wasn't worth sticking around to be abused by Zoe again.

Anna came up to make sure the coast was clear and to check that Zoe had everything she needed. She continued to hover, showing no inclination towards leaving, and eventually Zoe had to as good as order her out. In the end, she did go, promising to be in touch the moment she heard anything about Carol. Zoe stood at the door, listening to her footsteps clomping down the stairwell. A part of her wished she'd apologised for thumping her, but she hadn't been able to think of anything to say that wouldn't have sounded mealy-mouthed and inadequate.

As she heard Anna's car departing, she made her way through to the kitchen. She was parched. She hadn't had a thing to drink or to eat since middayish. She remembered that there was a bottle of Glenfiddich hidden at the back of the glasses cupboard. Carol had been saving it, she recalled, for the day when one of her many job applications bore fruit. Not much point holding out for that now. She found it, poured herself a generous measure and went to check the answerphone for messages. There was only one: a slurring, semi-coherent ramble from an obviously blootered Jasmine.

'I'm sorry,' she drawled, her normally crisp vowels slipping and sliding all over the place as she spat the words out through floppy lips. 'Sorry for being such a minge to you last night. And sorry about your ladyfriend. I didn't know they were gonna grab her 'stead of you.' A pause, accompanied by the sounds of sloshing liquid as she poured herself another measure of whatever she was drinking. 'You're . . . you're all right, you are. A bit head-in-the-clouds, a bit of a spaz, but basically all right. Anyway, heressst'yerhealttthhhh.' This was followed by the sound of what sounded suspiciously like a glass smashing, a muttered 'For fuck's fucking sake!' and then a click as the call ended.

Zoe wandered over to the kitchen table, where she'd left Saturday's mail lying unopened. For want of anything better to do, she began to sort through it. Most of it consisted of circulars and pleas for donations to various charities: Carol had always been a sucker for a picture of a wide-eyed African kiddie or a mangy puppy. There was also a letter from the cleaning firm, informing her of the termination of her contract on the grounds of sustained unexplained absence. It seemed so trivial she almost laughed. She tore it in half and tossed it in the bin.

At the bottom of the pile was a padded jiffy-bag, the words 'ZOE

CALLAHAN' printed in all caps on the front. No address. No postmark. She gave it a squeeze and a shake. Something rectangular, about the size of a small phone, was rattling around loose inside it. She broke the seal and tipped it out onto the table.

At first she thought it was an MP3 player. It had an LCD screen, Play and Pause buttons, and headphone and USB jacks. Which was strange, because she didn't remember ordering an MP3 player – and if she had, she didn't see how it could have got to her without her address on it. As she picked it up to examine it, she realised there was a post-it stuck to the underside. She turned it over. Written on it, in the same hand that had printed her name, were four words:

DO THE RIGHT THING

30

The Asset

Three days earlier

Cauley returned to her desk at London Road Police Station on Friday afternoon, her conversation with Zoe Callahan still churning over in her head. She tried to lay the accusations about Ryland to one side and get on with her duties, but try as she might, she couldn't let go of them. They might not pass the 'smell test' as such, but at the back of Cauley's mind was a nagging sense that they weren't *wholly* unbelievable.

The first time she'd encountered Dominic Michael Ryland had been on a wet Monday morning in September one year earlier. It began with an accusation of sexual coercion from a former aide – one Claire McDade, a shy, softly-spoken woman in her early twenties who alleged that, during an overnight stay in a hotel in Perth, he'd made multiple advances towards her, offering various financial and career incentives to spend the night with him, and, when she continued to refuse, cornered her in the empty bar and tried to forcibly kiss her and push his hand up her skirt. She fled back to Glasgow and went straight to her local police station – London Road, where the case landed on Cauley's desk. She would never forget McDade's tears as she recounted the experience, or Ryland's smug self-assurance as he sat in the interview room the following day, one leg crossed over the other, listening to the accusations levelled against him. Cauley prided herself on not succumbing to knee-jerk responses, but she hated him on sight, and that hatred – and her certainty as to his guilt – only deepened as the interview progressed. There was something utterly loathsome about him that eclipsed the other abusers and misogynists she'd met – and she'd met more than her fair share. The hubris, the sneering contempt for the whole affair, simmering beneath a thin veneer of civility . . . They both knew he was guilty, and yet he clearly saw himself as untouchable.

The following day, she discovered that his self-assurance had been well-placed when Claire McDade abruptly and without explanation retracted her testimony, and Cauley's boss, DI Carlaw, ordered her in no uncertain terms to drop the matter and give Ryland no further grief. She was in no doubt that McDade had been got at, but Carlaw had clearly been leant on too, and that shocked her. She'd long been aware of rumours about a *quid pro quo* arrangement between police top brass and members of the political establishment, but until then she'd never seen it in action in such a transparent way. That was why, when the chance for a second bite at the cherry had presented itself three weeks ago in the shapely form of Jasmine Mooney, she'd leapt into action, ramming the case through the system over the weekend before Carlaw and the other high heid yins got wind of it. She'd caught holy hell for it afterwards, of course, but by then the report had already been with the Procurator Fiscal, leaving it too late for them to try to bury it. Not that it had mattered a jot in the long run: Jasmine, like Claire McDade before her, had withdrawn her accusation, and the chance to see Ryland hoisted by his own petard had evaporated like an escaping fart.

I think Dominic Ryland arranged to have my girlfriend kidnapped.

Cauley scratched the back of her scalp irritably – something she kept telling herself not to do, as it always left flecks of dandruff on her good jacket. Try as she might, she couldn't force herself to look the other way. She lifted her desk phone and dialled.

'Hello, Archives,' said the chirpy-voiced secretary.

'Yeah, hi, this is DS Cauley in CID. I'm following up some discrepancies relating to an old case and need to cross-reference some notes. Can you arrange to have all records pertaining to a Dominic Michael Ryland, that's R-Y-L-A-N-D, delivered to me on the second floor?'

'Okey-doke, no problemo.' She heard the clack of long fingernails on a keyboard. 'Just two ticks and I'll . . . oh. Right. Hold on a sec.'

The line went silent for considerably longer than a sec. When the secretary next spoke, her tone was positively dripping with remorse.

'I'm *afraid* those records require Level Three clearance. That would mean submitting a written application countersigned by a—'

'—countersigned by a DI or higher, yes,' Cauley finished, inwardly seething. 'All right, fine. I'll get back to you.'

She hung up and swore to herself. The odds of Carlaw countersigning such a request were roughly equal to those of Ian Paisley attending High Mass at the Glasgow Metropolitan Cathedral. She pondered this challenge for a moment, tapping her biro against her cheek, then remembered that Paul Vasilico on the Vice Squad still owed her a favour – or was it her who owed *him* a favour? Hopefully he too had lost track. Anyway, he was considerably less loathsome than most of the pit-dwellers she worked with – and, more importantly, despite the fact that she had a good few years on him, was a detective inspector, and therefore in possession of the necessary clearance. Concluding that this was a matter best handled outwith the official channels, she abandoned the desk phone and instead rang Vasilico using her personal mobile.

'Well, well, well, Detective Sergeant Cauley,' he said in his smooth Kelvinsider's purr, 'to what do I owe the pleasure?'

She decided not to beat about the bush. 'Hey, Paul, long time no speak. Listen, I was wondering if you could do something for me.'

'That's what I like about you, Rona. Always straight down to business.'

'Aye, well, some of us've got busy lives. We don't all have the luxury of delegating the grunt-work to our underlings.'

'Darling, you say the *nicest* things. So what can I do ya for?'

She told him, much to his amusement. 'What's this, Rona? You been poking your nose where it doesn't belong again? I *suppose* I could do a spot of fetch-and-carry for you. But it'll cost ya.'

Cauley sighed. She'd known it would be like this. 'How much?'

'Oh, no more than you can afford. A romantic break to Paris, a night of unbridled passion . . . or I *might* be persuaded to settle for a slap-up meal at an eatery of my choosing, to be paid for in its entirety by your good self, service charge included. Don't worry – it won't be anywhere that'll break the bank. I know what you DS's earn.' He chuckled to himself. 'Deal?'

She thought about it for all of two seconds. 'Fine. I'm going to give you a name, OK?'

'Shoot.'

'Dominic Ryland.'

There was silence for several seconds. When Vasilico next spoke, all trace of humour had left his voice. 'Cauley, if I were you, I'd leave that one well alone. That's one can of worms you don't want to open.'

'I'll be the judge of that.'

'I'm serious. You don't want to—'

'*I'll* decide what I do and don't want to do. This is on me, all right?'

'That's just it, though. It's not on you, it's on *me*. *My* name on the release form. *My* arse getting hauled in to account for every mouse-click. It's not like it was when you were still a sprightly young thing, Cauley. Nowadays you don't just waltz into Archives and snatch the relevant ring-binder while the secretary's busy powdering her nose. It's all in cyberspace, all tracked, and they can trace *everything* back to you.' He paused and sighed, and she could picture him pinching the bridge of his long Roman nose, the way he so often did. 'Sorry, Cauley, but even the prospect of dinner with your lovely self isn't enough to make me commit career hari-kari. And by the way, this conversation? Never happened.'

Cauley, by now, was deeply frustrated, not to mention mystified, but it was late and there wasn't much more she could do, what with the administrative side winding down for the night anyway. She headed home to a ready-meal for one and far too much of a bottle of cheap red, Zoe Callahan still playing on her mind. *Cottrell, Tannahill* – she hadn't just plucked those names out of thin air. And if she had credible evidence linking them to Ryland, why the hell wasn't she sharing it?

The following morning, she arrived at the station bright and early, her questions still unresolved. As she made for the stairs, the corpulent, persistently perspiring figure of DI Carlaw came into view, heading her off at the pass. His beetle brows were even more furrowed than usual, and she knew straight away that this wasn't going to end well.

'A word, Cauley,' he growled.

She allowed him to escort her up the stairs to his office, where she found DI Bibby and DCI Oakshott, two other mouth-breathers from CID, waiting. The three musketeers – or, more appropriately, the three stooges. Thick-sliced, prime-cut gammon, all of them – the sort who called you 'darling' and tried to look down your top when you bent over. But they were also powerful, vindictive men, just as liable to pull you up on a disciplinary for giving them lip as to grope your ass in the lift. So she bit her tongue and took a seat as directed and waited for them to say their piece.

'You're to be reassigned,' said Carlaw. 'Effective Monday.'

'An eight-week secondment to Govan,' added Oakshott. 'Drugs Squad. One of their DS's is off with stress, another on mat leave. They need the extra manpower.'

'Or in this case womanpower,' said Bibby, who, unlike everyone else on the planet, thought himself a comedian.

Cauley was at a loss for words. 'Where's this suddenly come from? Why me? Why not someone with drugs experience?'

'A chance to broaden your portfolio,' said Bibby, earning himself approving 'mm's and nods from the other two.

'I've got cases in progress, some at critical junctures. What's to become of them?'

'They'll be reallocated,' said Carlaw. 'You're not so brilliant as to be uniquely capable of seeing them to completion.'

Cauley stared up at the three men in disbelief. None of them had taken a seat, with the result that she had three rotund bellies in her eye-line, each spilling over a severely strained belt. *We're the grown-ups,* their posturing said, *and we're calling the shots.*

Her eyes narrowed. 'This is about Dominic Ryland, isn't it?'

It was as if she'd lit a fuse under Carlaw. 'You were told to let that drop!' he roared.

Bibby and Oakshott both looked shocked, and when he next spoke, he managed to moderate his tone somewhat – she suspected with some difficulty.

'You never listen, do you, Cauley? Never do as you're told. Why d'you have to be a shit-stirrer? What are you trying to prove?'

Cauley folded her arms and stood her ground. 'I've a right to know what's going on here. That's twice now I've had investigations into this man blocked. What's he got on you lot, huh? Why are you moving heaven and earth to protect him?'

'You obstinate—' snarled Carlaw, but before he could say anything more, Oakshott clapped a hand on his shoulder and stepped forward, placing himself between him and Cauley.

'Because the Chief Super says so, that's why. This comes from the highest level. Look.' He folded his arms, cocked his head to one side, adopted a smile of long-standing paternalistic sufferance. 'It's a change of scenery, a chance to broaden your horizons. Look good on the old CV when the next round of promotions takes place. Be a good girl, do your eight weeks and you'll be back pounding streets this side of the river before you know it.'

She looked at them, from Oakshott to Carlaw to Bibby, and saw that there was no getting out of this. And she also saw something else. Beneath all the bluster and machismo and patronising sexism, they were, to a man, spooked by something.

Cauley returned to her desk to discover a post-it on her monitor:

BACK STAIRS, 11. V.

She showed up at the top of the open-air fire escape steps five minutes early to find Vasilico already there, a half-smoked cigarette between his fingers. Wordlessly, he offered her a drag. It took all her willpower to decline.

'I heard what happened,' he said, once they'd waited for a couple of passing uniforms to get out of earshot. 'I want you to know I had nothing to do with it. It was that call you made to Archives wot dun for you. That request for Ryland's files raised so many red flags it was like Joe Stalin himself had seized power. I gather the Chief

Super cut short his jaunt to Mykonos last night and came back to fan the flames personally. That's how serious this is.'

'But *why*?'

Vasilico shook his head. 'It's better for you if you don't know.'

Cauley sighed. 'Come on, Vasilico. We go back a-ways. I'm asking you to be straight with me here. Think of all the favours I've done you.'

For good measure, she even allowed herself to lay a hand on his arm. He flinched slightly – as if, by the very act of contact, she was contaminating him with her status as a *persona non grata* – but didn't pull away. At length, he nodded softly and took a draw on his cigarette for fortification.

'That offer of dinner still on?'

As she recalled it, dinner had been his suggestion rather than her offer, but she chose not to point this out.

'I buy you dinner, you give me the lowdown. The whole low-down, mind you, not the edited highlights.'

Vasilico flicked his now-depleted butt down the steps and nodded.

'Deal.'

The hours dragged by at a glacial pace, even though Cauley was kept busy, tidying up loose ends and setting her affairs in order in preparation for her move to Govan – a move which she was in little doubt would be made permanent at some point before those eight weeks were up. Not that she was in any great way attached to the East End, and she could count the number of colleagues from London Road that she'd actually miss on one hand – and a Mickey Mouse hand at that. No, it was more to do with the fact that she was being forced out so transparently, booted out the back door because she'd been asking awkward questions about one of Chief Superintendent Strickland's golfing buddies. Or something.

At nine o'clock precisely, they were being shown to a table for two at the Amarone Ristorante in the city centre. Cauley bided her time over apéritifs, dinner itself and drinks at the bar, conscious that any attempt to rush Vasilico was likely to result in him closing down altogether. It was only when it was getting on for eleven and the bar was beginning to empty that he finally got down to business.

I'm going to tell you a story (said Vasilico). It's a story about a boy, born into what's officially known as abject squalor. A slum in Brigton, to be precise. Single mother, hard grafter, brings the boy up herself while simultaneously holding down two jobs to make ends meet. One might reasonably anticipate that a child given such an inauspicious start would be doomed to a short life dominated by disappointment and the abuse of various substances. And yet, wonder of wonders, that's not the case. Our boy – for talking's sake, let's call him Sandyman – shows himself to be academically gifted from an early age, racing ahead of his peers, and he bags himself a place at Glenavon College of all places.

Of course, even the brightest spark in the world doesn't get into Glenavon without so much as two brass pennies to his name. Those eye-watering fees won't pay themselves, dontchaknow? Enter the mysterious benefactor. We'll call him JC, though to the best of our knowledge he's never turned water into wine. He *is*, however, a big noise in Glasgow's organised crime scene, and getting noisier – of which one doubts the Good Lord would approve. Anyway, old JC dips in and out of mummy dearest's life at regular intervals throughout Sandyman's childhood. It's less of a relationship than a reciprocal arrangement, and JC is far from exclusive when it comes to his women. But from the get-go he takes a keen interest in the boy, and wouldn't you know it, he only goes and pays the bloody school fees, and sees to it he gets all sorts of extra tuition to make the grade for Oxford when the time comes. While the boy's still sitting his Highers, dear old mum pops her clogs, and yet JC, far from ske-daddling now that he's a free man, only takes an even greater interest in the lad. Now, one doesn't like to jump to conclusions, but picture this: child of uncertain parentage, big question mark under 'father' on the birth certificate, and yet here's this fella whip-ping out the chequebook on account of one of his mistresses' brats. As the Yanks would say, you do the math.

But our friend JC isn't content with merely being a silent bene-factor. No, he wants a return on his investment. A man at the heart of the establishment, to be precise. A tame pet to stalk the corridors of power and advance his interests. So he pushes the boy down the PPE route, has him attend the correct debating societies, moulding him into a facsimile of the political class he loathes so much. And all the while he's whispering in his ear, *Always remember the source of your good fortune. I made you and I can break you.* So the boy goes along with it, and he comes out of the sausage factory a good little soldier – right clothes, right politics, almost the right accent. Lands a job as the Home Secretary's personal gofer. Only trouble is, it's now 1997 and it's no longer quite as fashionable to be a mem-ber of the Conservative and Unionist Party as it once was. And when May the second dawns, he and his fellow lizard people are out on their collective ear.

Now, of course, JC's beginning to realise he's backed the wrong horse, but he's poured too much time and energy into his little project to cut him loose and start over with a child of the glorious New Labour revolution. So he bides his time. He consolidates his power-base at home, taking control of half the city, while Sandyman spends the next decade or so in the political wilderness. A direc-torship here, a consulting role there – these people never truly disappear. But he and JC remain in touch, partly because JC never truly lets go of an asset, and partly because the boy's developed what might be euphemistically termed a dependency, which JC is more than happy to indulge. Cocaine, to be precise. Got a taste for it at uni, like so many of his ilk, and JC just happens to have all the best dealers in his pocket.

As chance would have it, it's this dirty little secret that proves to be Sandyman's undoing. Eighteen months back, less than a year after he's finally managed to get himself elected through a quirk of the system, he's careless enough to be caught with an industrial-size portion in his possession during a routine bust at a little soirée where contraband was reputed to be available. A bust, incidentally, masterminded by yours truly, though I can't say I expected in a month of Sundays to land such a prize specimen. *You're going down, amigo,* I says to him. *You're going down for a long, long time.* And you know what he does? He bursts into tears. Sits there in front of me in the interrogation suite, bawling like a babby. And he tells me everything. Who his supplier is, the nature of their relationship, how far back they go. And it's one of those lightbulb-above-the-head moments. I know I've hit the jackpot.

I leave him to stew in his own juices and come back with Strickland in tow. As you'll recall, he was head of Vice back then. We lay it out to him in black and white. *The choice is simple,* I says. *You spend six years in jail and kiss goodbye to the MSP's salary, the cushy directorships, the luxury pad in Thorntonhall, and probably your good lady wife while you're at it. Not to mention your reputation. Or, you come over to us and inform on your sugar-daddy. Keep us abreast of his latest moves, what he's planning, where he's vulnerable.* He didn't even need time to think about it. I'm not sure whether it was cowardice or a lust for power or both, but from that moment on, we owned him.

So for the next few months, me and Strickland play him like a fiddle. On our orders, he embroils himself in JC's affairs like never before, feeding everything back to us. We run him off the books, of course. More leaks than a sieve, this place. Operation Sandyman, Strickland calls it. On account of . . . well, you get the idea. And it's like all our Christmases have come at once. We've been trying to get a man on the inside for years, to no avail. See, the thing with JC is, we like him where he is because he's a known quantity and, most importantly and in stark contrast to his rivals on the other side of the river, not clinically insane. He's not going to launch the count-down to Armageddon just because someone cut him off at the intersection. But we want to know what he's up to, what he's cook-ing up, and, as far as possible, to contain him. Make sure he stays where we want him and doesn't start getting ideas above his station.

Of course, JC's a clever bastard – keeps his hands clean, makes sure everything's nice and deniable – but Sandyman's intel's all solid stuff, and late last year we get our first breakthrough in the form of the arrest of JC's *numero due*, Francis Brady, Esq. Meanwhile, time passes, and Sandyman's becoming increasingly cocky and self-sure. Sees himself as this big, important double agent – a veritable James sodding Bond. And he gets it into his head he's invulnerable. Reck-ons he can get into all the scrapes he wants and his powerful mates in Vice will come along and bail him out. And he's not far wrong. Last September, Strickland, now ascended to the role of Chief Super, steps in to bury an investigation into an allegation of sexual harass-ment. One of yours, Cauley, if memory serves. Sorry about that, but you know – greater good and all that.

Of course, we knew he was a swine when we brought him into the fold. Figured we could keep him in check. Which we did, as much as was humanly possible. But there's only so much one can do. To be honest, if I could go back and do it all over, I'd have to conclude he's more trouble than he's worth, 'specially now his star's in the ascendancy what with the leadership bid. I'd have burned him long ago but for the damage he'd do to us by going public. A DI and the Chief Super, running a secret agent, who by rights should be occupying a six-by-eight in Barlinnie, *indocumentado*? A Vice Squad within the Vice Quad? Our public image's deep enough in the shitter as it is without fanning the flames.

But anyway, there it is. That, since you so dearly wanted to know, is why your attempt to access his files yesterday afternoon very nearly set off a fresh Cuban Missile Crisis. Sandyman's ours, and as long as that remains the case he's Teflon Charlie. He's Mr Un-Fucking-Touchable.

By the early hours of Saturday morning, Cauley had learned two things about Vasilico that she hadn't previously known. One, that he was circumcised. Two, that he liked having his nipples twisted. She came into possession of this knowledge in the king-size bed in his riverside apartment – a luxuriant piece of prime real-estate that made her own pokey flat in Shawlands look like a hovel. *The things I do for this job.* Not that this was purely a professional matter. On the contrary, it was, on a personal level, quite gratifying to know that a younger man still found her sufficiently attractive to go to bed with her. But she couldn't deny that she was seeking something other than just sexual satisfaction. And, as they lay there in the aftermath of what had been a seriously vigorous bout of lovemaking, the moonlight kissing their still-glistening bodies through the sliding glass door leading out onto the balcony, she found it.

'There's one thing I'm still wondering,' she mused, lazily running a hand down his chest.

'Whazzat?' His reply little more than a murmur, sleep rapidly encroaching on his already drowsy state.

'You and Strickland. How do you keep in touch with the asset?'

'How d'you mean?'

'I mean, I'm guessing you don't just pick up the phone and say, "Fancy meeting for an espresso tomorrow?"'

'No, course not. Far too insecure. The walls have ears.'

'Well then, what's your system?'

'What's it matter?' He turned away from her, throwing an arm over his eyes.

'Tell me.'

She made a fist and rubbed his chest like she would a jakey passed out in a doorway, just forcefully enough for him not to be able to ignore it. He groaned and tried to bat her arm away.

'Tell me.'

She reached beneath the sheet and began to stroke him down there. She wasn't sure he had it in him to go again so soon, but she figured the prospect of further action might loosen his tongue nonetheless. She kept going till he was hard again and moaning away nicely, then abruptly withdrew her hand.

'Tell me.'

He groaned irritably. 'It was something he came up with. Sandyman. If either party needs to see the other urgently . . . '

'Yes?' She ran her finger up the shaft to remind him she was still there.

'The bins at the top of the steps into Central Station. Union Street entrance. It's' – grunt – 'it's on both Strickland and Sandyman's daily commutes. One of them marks the bin on the far right with a black line, the other sees it and knows to come to the meeting-place at eleven-forty-five sharp that night.'

'What meeting-place?' Another little stroke.

'Why do you care?'

'Morbid fascination.' Stroke.

He grimaced and twisted his head to one side. He was having trouble holding it in and remembering at the same time. 'The McLennan Arch, Glasgow Green.' Grunt. 'Sandyman's idea. "Moscow Rules", he called it. Christ, the man's not half up himself. Thinks he's fucking Kim Philby.'

She had what she wanted. She finished him off with a few quick, no-nonsense tugs, wiped her hand on his stomach and lay down next to him. But she didn't sleep. She waited until his breathing grew steady, then got up and stole over to her shoulder-bag, lying on the floor at the foot of the bed. From it, she took out her trusty Sony ICD-BX140 audio recorder, chosen for its impressive capacity and long battery life, and pressed Stop. She crept over to Vasilico's side of the bed, took his lighter and Malboros from the nightstand, slid open the door and stepped out onto the balcony. She leant on the railing, savouring the feeling of the night air on her naked body, gazing out across the Clyde as she smoked her first cigarette in twenty-nine days, nineteen hours and however many minutes it was. And it tasted glorious. She saw the clouds gathering in the east. A storm was coming, and not before time.

Fifteen minutes later, she dressed, gathered her things and, in the grey hour before dawn, slipped from the apartment, the precious cargo in her bag nestled against her hip.

31

The Deal

Zoe listened to the recording from beginning to end. It ran for over three hours in total, and large chunks consisted entirely of irrelevant small talk or the hum of traffic and, during one extended period, sounds corresponding to an act of congress of a distinctly non-political variety. When it finally fell silent, she turned the device over and stared at the words on the post-it.

Do the right thing? She wasn't even sure what that meant anymore. There was a time when it would have meant taking what she knew to the police and letting them deal with it as they saw fit. But she no longer had any faith in them to dispense justice. More to the point, by the looks of it neither had Cauley, and she was one of them, for Christ's sake.

She glanced at her phone and saw that it was a quarter past six. How had the morning crept up on her without her noticing? Normally by this time the sun was already riding high in the sky, engulfing the flat in its unwelcome glow. As she turned towards the window, she saw why. A heavy layer of black cloud had blotted out the sky completely. The street outside, whose lights must have gone off at 4.30 a.m. as scheduled, was as dull and lifeless as the sky above it. She'd almost forgotten what the place looked like when it was overcast.

Identify the problem, then take action to remedy it. She knew what her problem was, or rather her problems: Ryland, Tannahill and Cottrell. And, as the morning wore on, a plan began to form in her mind. It was a dangerous, desperate one, but she could see no alternative. She'd exhausted all other available channels, and she knew this wasn't something she could resolve on her lonesome. And, for her plan to succeed, she was going to need Jasmine's help.

At midday, she crossed the road and hammered on Jasmine's door. Jasmine eventually opened it, looking considerably the worse for wear after last night's bender.

'What d'you want?' she almost snarled.

It took an eternity to get Jasmine to agree to do what Zoe was asking of her, but in the end she yielded. Zoe, after all, had one major trump card up her sleeve. Thanks to the answerphone message last night, she knew that, whatever her outward façade, Jasmine's role in Carol's abduction was eating her up inside. Armed with that knowledge, Zoe made a good pitch, presenting this as Jasmine's responsibility to assuage her guilt, atoning and restoring balance to the Force all at the same time. And in the end, Jasmine agreed, though she did so with incredibly bad grace.

'I'll see what I can do,' she scowled. 'I'll call you if it's a go. But I'm not making any promises.'

Concluding that this was the best she could hope for, Zoe took her leave and headed back across the road, stopping at the ATM to withdraw all the money left in her account – a meagre sum that would have been unlikely to cover the rent, bills and other assorted overheads beyond the next couple of months. Then she went back to the flat and waited.

Mid-afternoon, a couple of police officers came to the door. They repeated a great many of the questions they'd asked Zoe when Carol was first taken, along with a number of fresh ones prompted by her reappearance and her account of what had happened to her. The most pressing of these was, if Carol was the wrong girl, then who was the right one? Knowing that it was in her interests for the police to know as little as possible, for the time being at any rate, Zoe acted glaikit – which, given her current state of mind, wasn't much of a stretch. *What you see is what you get.* Eventually, concluding that there was nothing more they could dredge out of her, they left her to her own devices.

At around three, a call came in from Anna. Zoe let it go to voicemail. It was good news – or, at least, it wasn't *bad* news. Dr Chambers' examination of Carol had uncovered no evidence that she'd been interfered with in any way. She was to be released from hospital later today, Anna said, and would be going home with her mum. Zoe knew she was supposed to feel something – relief that it hadn't been so much worse, despair at having to hear this third-hand. But instead, she felt nothing. It was as if her body knew it couldn't afford to succumb to any form of emotion just now and was storing it all up until the all-important task that lay ahead of her was over and done with.

Throughout the day, clouds continued to gather, growing ever heavier and darker. The air pressure was rising steadily, leaving her feeling as if her head was being squeezed in a vice. She was like a coiled spring, perched on the edge of the sofa, ready to leap into action the moment word came.

Just after four, her mobile rang. She snatched it up.

'It's done,' Jasmine said. 'Be under the M8 bridge at Argyle Street tonight at midnight. This is a one-time offer. Don't be late.'

Before Zoe could even draw breath, Jasmine hung up. As she lowered her phone, she heard a rumble of distant thunder.

Late evening, the clouds burst. It was as if all the rain that hadn't fallen in the past month had been stored up and was now being vomited out by a sky that could hold it in no longer. It came down in torrents, soaking pedestrians still dressed for the heatwave, turning Dumbarton Road into a fast-flowing river.

It was still bucketing down at a quarter to midnight as Zoe stood under the bridge at Argyle Street, wishing the pavement was a little wider so she could avoid getting splashed by every car that swept past. She'd arrived nearly an hour early, determined not to leave anything to chance. She clutched the shoulder strap of her rucksack to make sure it was still there. She'd be royally screwed if it wasn't.

Mind you, odds were she was royally screwed anyway.

She peered out through the curtain of rain pouring down from the bridge above her, trying to catch a glimpse of . . . well, something. When the time came, she wasn't sure how they'd come. On foot? Unlikely, especially not in this deluge. Nah, they'd come by car. But which car? How would she recognise it? She supposed she'd just have to content herself with the knowledge that *they* probably knew what *she* looked like – a less than comforting prospect. Every time a car approached, her gut contracted with the same mix of fear and anticipation. A couple of times, it looked like one was about to pull over and she stiffened in readiness, but each time it cruised on by.

At precisely one minute after midnight, she heard the purr of a car pulling up to the kerb behind her. A shiver ran up her spine. Somehow, she knew this was it. Slowly, she turned to face it. A black Mercedes was parked about a hundred feet away. The same one – she just knew it – that she'd seen at Ryland's house back at the start of her investigation. As she continued to eyeball it, not budging, the driver's window slid down and a hand emerged, beckoning her over.

Swallowing to force down the bile rising in her throat, she slowly approached. As she drew level with the window, she saw that Gordon Tannahill was behind the wheel. He glared up at her with his mean little eyes and jerked a thumb over his shoulder.

'Get in.'

She opened the rear door. Inside, a tall, thin man in a suit sat on the opposite side. He too glowered up at her. But if Zoe still harboured any ambitions about changing her mind, they were quickly wiped out as she sensed a presence looming behind her. The rucksack was torn from her back and she felt a hand on the back of her head, forcing her into the car. She tumbled forwards, narrowly avoiding landing in the thin man's lap. As she righted herself, the man who'd pushed her in – a shaven-headed brick shithouse who'd give any pro wrestler a run for his money – got in after her, rucksack tucked under his arm, blocking any hope of escape.

Wordlessly, Tannahill pulled away from the kerb, re-joining the easterly flow of traffic. The big guy pulled a black slip from his pocket and fitted it over Zoe's head, covering her eyes and nose, leaving only her mouth free. All that was missing were the slow drumbeat and the noose round her neck. Engulfed in darkness, she did her best to remain calm and keep her breathing slow and steady. Was this how it had been for Carol, she wondered, when she was taken? It could have been worse, she supposed. At least they hadn't stuffed her in the boot.

Yet.

They drove for a good hour, periodically stopping at what Zoe assumed were traffic lights. The men didn't exchange so much as a word, and only the fact that she was shit-scared stopped her from saying something to break the silence. She was starting to wonder if they were going to be driving all night when the car slowed and took a sudden right-hand turn. The ground became rough and tussocky, causing her already queasy stomach to do backflips. They slowed to a halt, and she heard the doors opening on either side of her, and she felt the air on her skin again.

She was hauled out, an arm was looped through each of hers on either side, and she was marched at a brisk pace across the uneven terrain, her toes catching every now and then on a stone or clump of weeds. She'd seen any number of films like this, with a pair of hoods hauling some poor schmuck to some desolate stretch of waste-ground in the middle of nowhere. It never ended well for him.

The rough terrain gave way to something smooth and hard – concrete, maybe, or stone – and she knew, from the change in the air and the way their footsteps echoed, that they were now indoors. They walked on for perhaps another hundred yards, then came to an abrupt halt. The blindfold was taken off and she saw that they were in what looked to be some sort of derelict factory. Rickety gangways loomed overhead. Rusted hulks of machinery, whose original purpose she couldn't guess, lay abandoned in the shadows on either side of the walkway ahead of them. Tannahill stood facing her.

'Take off your clothes,' he said.

Zoe's stomach lurched again. She thought of Carol, of Jasmine, of what these men might have in mind for her. The possibilities were limited, and none of them good.

Gingerly, she began to undress. She kicked off her plimsolls, shuffled out of her Capri pants, slipped her tank top over her head.

'Everything,' said Tannahill.

For a moment, Zoe didn't move. Then, with a feeling of resignation, she bent down and shed her underwear, and with it her last sliver of dignity. She stood up as tall and straight as she could manage, hands clenched by her sides, enduring their mocking smiles.

'Give us a twirl, gorgeous.'

Bare feet shuffling on the concrete floor, Zoe performed an awkward three-hundred-and-sixty-degree turn. She was trembling uncontrollably, but she was determined not to let them see she was afraid. She came to a stop and faced Tannahill, glaring at him defiantly. The big guy, meanwhile, was rooting through her ruck-sack, examining each item inside it in turn. He stopped when he came to the voice recorder and held it up, frowning suspiciously at it.

'That's—' Zoe began.

But the big guy seemed satisfied with his examination. At a nod from Tannahill, he tossed it back in the bag.

'OK, that'll do,' growled Tannahill.

He nodded to the pile of clothes on the floor. Zoe didn't need telling twice. She snatched them up and began to dress as quickly as possible. She was still struggling into her Capris when her three chaperones turned their backs on her and set off, heading deeper into the innards of the factory. She crammed her feet back into her shoes and hurried after them. Now that they were confident she wasn't wearing a wire, or whatever it was they'd expected to find, they seemed content to leave her to her own devices – presumably surmising that, having gone to the trouble of getting this far, she was unlikely to turn tail and run now.

Up ahead, around fifty feet above them and accessible via a steep flight of steps leading up to the gangway, was some sort of control room – a small, square appendage with a door and a single window overlooking the factory floor. As Zoe and the three men drew near, the door opened and Jasmine stepped out onto the balcony, looking every inch the gangster's moll in a navy cocktail dress, a cigarette clenched between her fingers. A moment later, another figure emerged behind her – a small, wiry man in a suit/shirt combo, no tie, with a scruffy grey beard and wizened, hollowed-out features. Zoe judged him to be in his early seventies, but she'd seen enough of the Glasgow Effect in action to know that he could easily be twenty years younger than that. He leaned both elbows on the handrail and gazed down at Zoe, screwing up his eyes in a way that suggested he suffered from short-sightedness but was too proud to wear glasses.

'So,' he said, his voice as rough and gravelly as his features, 'this is the wee lassie who's been causin every yin so much trouble.' He looked in Tannahill's direction. 'She clean?'

'Aye, boss,' said Tannahill. 'She had this with her.'

He motioned to the big guy, who stepped forward with Zoe's rucksack. He took out the various items one at a time, holding each up for inspection.

'Phone. Half-eaten stick of Fruit Pastilles. Tampons. House keys. Nine hundred and seventy pounds cash. Sony voice recorder.'

'That's so's ye can tape us for insurance purposes, aye?' said the old man, addressing Zoe.

Tannahill and the other men laughed, but half-heartedly, like they knew it would end badly for them if it turned out they'd misjudged the mood. Zoe couldn't help but notice how on edge they seemed in the presence of this little old man who looked like he'd have trouble swatting a fly. She guessed they had good reason to fear him all the same.

'Um, no,' she stammered, finding her voice. 'That's—'

The old man silenced her with a dismissive wave. 'Gie her the bag.'

Wordlessly, the big guy handed her back her rucksack.

'Come up tae me, wee pet,' said the old man. 'Don't worry' – he gave a rictus smile – 'Ah willnae bite.'

For a moment, Zoe didn't move. Her feet seemed glued to the ground, every neurone screaming at her not to go up there. She reminded herself that she'd come here for a reason and, forcing herself to put one foot in front of the other, climbed the steps.

The old man gestured to the control room. 'Let's mosey on intae my office, shall we?'

Zoe did as she was told. As she passed Jasmine, their eyes met for a brief moment, and Jasmine acknowledged her with a terse, almost imperceptible nod. Zoe saw the fear in her eyes and wondered what price Jasmine would pay – or had already paid – for arranging this.

Inside the control room, a console with various buttons and dials, covered in cobwebs and a heavy coating of dust, sat under the window. In the centre of the room stood an old wooden table and a couple of chairs. The situation had a thrown-together, make-shift feel to it. She doubted this was the gang's base of operations. No way was this man running his criminal empire out of some grotty old factory. She wondered what to make of the fact that they'd brought her here rather than to the heart of the operation, and what it meant for her chances of getting out in one piece.

She heard the door shutting behind her and turned to see the old man drawing a bolt home.

'There. Now we'll no be troubled while we have our wee chat.'

He came over to the table with slow, shuffling steps and slumped into the nearest chair in a manner that suggested staying on his feet for so long had been a serious ordeal for him. He motioned to the other chair. Eyeing him apprehensively, Zoe took a seat. From the inner pocket of his suit jacket, he produced a cigar and a book of matches.

'Ye willnae be offended if Ah smoke, will ye?' His eyes twinkled mockingly.

She shook her head.

'That's guid. Cannae abide they clean living freaks. Sanctimonious pricks, the lotta them. Ah'd offer ye a drink, only they turned the watter off a while back.'

He struck a match, lit the cigar and inhaled deeply. Immediately, he was beset by an almighty coughing fit, causing him to almost double over. Choking and spluttering, he pounded his chest with his fist. Zoe was just trying to work up the courage to ask him if he was all right when the coughing finally subsided. He cleared his throat noisily and spat a mouthful of phlegm onto the floor.

'Right,' he gestured to her with his cigar hand, 'would Ah be right in thinkin ye know who Ah am?'

Zoe nodded.

'Let's hear it, then.'

'You're Jim Cottrell.'

'Got it in one. And who's Jim Cottrell when he's at hame?'

Zoe thought quickly, trying to figure out what he wanted to hear. 'You're in charge of half the organised crime in Glasgow.'

Cottrell grinned broadly, seemingly tickled pink by this description. 'Gie that girl a gold star! Slightly mair than hauf, actually, but let's no split hairs. So' – he slapped his legs decisively – 'now's we're both sittin comfortably and we've dispensed wi the formalities, perhaps ye wouldnae mind tellin me whit aw this is aboot. Ye'll forgive me for rushin ye, but Ah've goat a gie busy calendar.'

'I want to make a deal with you,' said Zoe, trying hard to keep the tremor out of her voice. 'I want you to leave me and the people I care about alone. I don't wanna spend the rest of my life looking over my shoulder wondering when yous're gonnae come for me.'

'Ah see.' Cottrell seemed singularly unimpressed. 'And whit is it ye're proposin tae offer in return fer such an act of benevolence?'

'Information.'

'Information?' Cottrell laughed. 'Wee pet, Ah've goat all the information Ah need. Ah've goat information comin oot ma oxters. There's no a thing happens in my domain wi'oot me gettin tae know aboot it.'

'It's about Dominic Ryland,' said Zoe.

Cottrell paused, cigar close to his lips. He contemplated this for a second, then lowered it slowly. 'Whit aboot him?'

So Zoe began to talk. She told Cottrell everything: Ryland's double-cross, how he was turned by Vasilico and Strickland, how he'd spent the last eighteen months reporting to them about Cottrell's doings, his role in Freddo Brady being taken down. She took the voice recorder out of her bag and played him Vasilico's account in its entirety, ending with the disclosure of Ryland and his handlers' preferred method of contact.

Throughout it all, Cottrell smoked his way through a further two cigars, saying nothing, though he interspersed it with periodic coughing fits and phlegm-hacking. When the recording came to an end three hours later, he reached across the table for the device, pressed Stop and weighed it thoughtfully in his hand.

'Well now,' he said, 'it seems we have a viper in wir nest.'

His voice betrayed no emotion. Either he was unaffected by what he'd heard – which, given the scale of Ryland's betrayal, was unlikely – or he had the poker-face to end all poker-faces.

'So. Ye come tae me and ye say, "Don Corleone, give me justice". That it?'

Zoe felt the wind go out of her sails in the face of his sarcasm.

'I just want this to be the end of it,' she muttered, eyes in her lap.

Cottrell took a draw on his now considerably depleted cigar and blew a smoke-ring, tapping the table with a finger. 'Well, Ah've goat all the info Ah need,' he mused. 'And Ah've goat this.' He pointed to the voice recorder. 'So whit's tae stoap me havin my lads take ye oot the back, tie rocks tae yer feet and drop ye intae the Clyde? That'd tie up aw the loose ends nice and neat, don't ye think?'

Zoe's blood ran cold. 'Someone once told me ye had a code of honour,' she stammered.

Cottrell laughed heartily and hacked some more. 'Code a honour? That's a guid wan. First time a'body's accused me a havin wan a *those*. Some wit been fillin yer heid wi tales aboot a noble gangster wi a hert a gold?' He grinned, showing off two rows of sharp little teeth. 'Sorry tae break it tae ye, but Ah'm no Robin Hood, and these folks ootside aren't ma merry men.'

He fell silent again, leaning back in his chair and puffing away. Zoe watched him, not daring to move an inch or make any sound at all. She'd toyed with the idea of some sort of an insurance policy – making a copy of the recording, for instance, or giving Cottrell just enough info to whet his appetite, then telling him that, if he wanted the rest, he'd have to let her go. But she'd decided against it for one very simple reason: she didn't think he was a man who could be bullshitted. Now, sitting here in the same room as him, she wasn't inclined to revise that assessment.

At length, Cottrell stirred. He took a phone from the inner pocket of his jacket, keyed in a number and put it to his ear. The recipient couldn't have let it ring more than once before picking up.

'Head up tae Central Station,' he said. 'Union Street entrance. Bins at the toap a the steps. Mark the wan oan the right wi a black line. Aye, you heard. Dinnae make me repeat masel. And have someone watchin the McLennan Arch the morra night at quarter tae midnight.'

He hung up, closed the lid of his phone and pocketed it. For several moments, they sat in silence, Zoe listening to the sounds of men's voices – Tannahill's and one of the heavies' – beyond the door.

'I gather you an' ma wee Jasmine are neighbours,' said Cottrell.

'We live across the street fae one another,' said Zoe, caught off guard by this sudden digression into small talk. 'You . . . you know what Ryland did to her?'

'Ah do that, aye.' Cottrell nodded sagely. 'Ah wis hert sick aboot that. S'posed tae be a present tae him, so she was – a way of expressin ma gratitude for all his efforts thus far. Ah knew whit sorta kink the man was intae, a course, but Ah never counted on him markin her face.' He looked at Zoe with something approaching a benevolent smile. 'And you tried tae help her, so's Ah hear. That's real neighbourly compassion right there. But Ah couldnae hae the polis involved. That woulda ruined everyhin we'd been working towards. So Ah had tae show her how the land lay. But you, ye wouldnae let it drop.' He shook his head in a manner that somehow seemed to signify admiration.

'He used you to get at me.'

'Aye. Turned up at oor Mr Tannahill's premises in a flap the ither day, so he did, saying you an' some ither lassie'd broke intae his hoose, made aff wi his laptop an' aw. Got a bit of a complex about you, does Mr Ryland. Says ye were at the polis station when he got took in fer what he done tae Jasmine, then a couple a weeks later ye show up again, ransackin his hoose. He wanted us tae lift the both a yese and make yese talk – find oot whit yer game was. Course, if they fuckheids hadnae bollocksed the whole thing up . . . ' He shot a venomous look in the direction of the door.

Zoe didn't need to ask how that sentence ended. If Tannahill and his goons hadn't messed up, chances were she and Fin would now be swimming with the fishies.

With some difficulty, Cottrell got to his feet. 'But then,' he mused, 'this profession isnae whit it once was. Standards have slipped, know?'

Zoe didn't, but she supposed she should be glad that they had.

Cottrell made his shuffling way over to the window. For a while, he stood there in contemplation, staring out at the ruined factory below.

'Aye, there's change in the wind and nae mistake. They say ye dinnae appreciate whit ye've goat till ye feel it slippin through yer fingers. God help the poor sod who has tae sort this all oot when Ah'm six feet under.'

Another coughing fit took hold, and Zoe understood. *He's dying. He's built this empire and he knows he's going to lose it all.* She watched as he continued to hack away, struggling to breathe through the phlegm and other detritus he was bringing up.

Eventually, the coughing subsided and he turned to her again.

'Ah'm no gonnae kill ye, wee pet. No the now, anyway. Too much fuss an' bother, havin a boady tae dispose of an' aw. Right now, Ah've got bigger fish tae fry than some daft wee lassie who got hersel in too deep.'

Zoe couldn't take her eyes off him. She didn't dare to breathe.

'Aye, you can live, as a token o' my appreciation fer this.' He held up the voice recorder. 'And mair's the point, if ye behave yersel, ye can go on livin for many a year tae come. But mark me: Ah ken yer face. Ah ken where ye live. Ah ken who yer loved ones are 'n' where they live. And if Ah get the slightest whiff o' a double-cross, or that ye've breathed a word a this encounter tae the filth, then we'll be speakin again – imminently.'

He moved over to the door, unbolted and opened it. Leaning out, he snapped his fingers and beckoned. Footsteps pounded up the metal steps, and a moment later Tannahill arrived on the gangway.

'Boss?'

'Ms Callahan is leavin. Be so kind as tae arrange an escort for her.'

Zoe blinked several times, trying hard to keep up with the twists and turns the night was taking. Then, realising the folly of looking a gift horse in the mouth, she scrambled to her feet, rucksack in hand, and stumbled towards the door. As she drew near Tannahill and Cottrell, she spotted Jasmine, standing just outside the control room, cigarette in hand.

'There's one more thing I want.'

'Oh aye?' There was more than a hint of amusement in Cottrell's voice.

'Jasmine. I want you to let her go too. Whatever she owes ye, this can go towards it.' She pulled the wad of notes from her rucksack and offered it to Cottrell.

A chunk of ash fell from Jasmine's cigarette. Tannahill stared in open-mouthed disbelief, his beady little eyes opening wider than

Zoe had thought possible. Cottrell, for his part, met her gaze, his expression giving nothing away. Then, to her surprise, he threw back his head and guffawed.

'Ach, why no? Tonight Ah feel generous.' He pushed her outstretched hand, and the money, back towards her. 'Keep it. Dinnae take this the wrang way, petal, but Ah fancy a grand in the hand is worth a sight mair tae the likes a you than the likes a me.'

Tannahill and his two heavies escorted Zoe and Jasmine back through the factory. No one spoke a word. Zoe didn't look back. She knew better than to risk it. She knew she wouldn't breathe easy until she was far away from this place, and from Cottrell and his mob – and probably not even then. She was conscious of Jasmine walking beside her like an automaton. Like someone who'd long since lost any sense of agency or self-worth and simply took what life threw at her without questioning it.

She expected to be blindfolded and bundled into the Merc again, but to her surprise, as she stepped out into the factory's overgrown grounds and once more felt the night air on her cheeks, Tannahill and the other two came to a stop.

'Well, ladies,' said Tannahill, in a tone that was part-amused and part-bewildered, 'seems tonight's yer lucky night.'

He pulled the heavy metal door to behind him, shutting Zoe and Jasmine out.

Zoe looked this way and that, trying to get her bearings. She could hear the roar of fast-moving traffic not too far off, and as she turned back to look up at the rotting hulk of the building they'd just exited, she realised to her surprise that it was the old Gray Dunn Biscuit Factory, a stone's throw from the M8 motorway and little more than a ten-minute walk from the Clyde Arc. She'd assumed, from all the driving they'd done, that she'd been taken somewhere far beyond the city limits, when in fact they'd barely gone south of the river. Either the traffic had been mental or they'd been driving round in circles for ages.

While they'd been inside, the rain had stopped, and the air was rich with the smell of hot, wet tarmac. She sniffed it gingerly, still not quite ready to believe she'd actually made it out in one piece.

'Smells pretty good, doesn't it?'

She turned to see Jasmine looking across at her. There was something approaching disbelief on the other woman's face as well, mixed in with something else: a sense of relief, of finally being able to breathe after an eternity of holding it in. She had the look of someone who'd just been released from a life sentence – which probably wasn't too far off the mark.

'I . . . he let us go,' said Zoe.

'Seems that way,' agreed Jasmine, a last lingering flutter of doubt in her voice.

'What'll ye do now?'

Jasmine thought about it, then shook her head. 'I honestly have no idea.'

'What about back tae yer folks? Back to Reading?'

'I could go anywhere. It's not an either/or.' She shook her head again, clearly still not quite able to believe it. 'I don't understand why. I mean, after everything I . . . '

Zoe dismissed her concern with a wave. It didn't matter now. None of it did. She rummaged inside her rucksack and once more took out the money she'd withdrawn from the bank. She thrust it towards Jasmine.

'Here. Take it. To get ye on yer feet.'

Jasmine stared at the bundle of notes for a moment without moving. Then, taking it, she counted out £100 and handed the rest back to Zoe.

'You're all right, you are,' she said. 'A bit of a spaz, but you're all right.'

It was as close to a genuine 'thank you' as Zoe had ever heard coming from her, and she chose to take it in that spirit.

Jasmine slipped the money into her cleavage in lieu of her non-existent pockets. Zoe raised an eyebrow. Jasmine, seemingly realising the ridiculousness of what she'd just done, blushed and giggled like a wee girl, shrugged awkwardly, then turned and walked off, heading towards the unknown.

32

Euphemia

Zoe walked the two miles back to her flat. The pubs and clubs were in the process of shutting their doors, and as she tramped up through Finnieston she ducked and weaved to avoid the revellers spilling out into the streets – groups and couples of various ages, backgrounds and genders, all in high spirits, all oblivious to the high stakes being played out on their very doorsteps. She reached her flat just after three and collapsed straight onto the bed. For the first time in ages, she was out like a light within seconds of her head touching the pillow, and she slept like a log.

Late next morning, the rain began again, accompanied by periodic rumbles of thunder. Zoe remained holed up in the flat for the duration of the storm. The forecaster on the evening news proclaimed that the heatwave, the longest prolonged period of hot weather in Scotland in fifteen years, was officially over.

The following morning, Wednesday the twenty-fourth, the whole country was shocked and appalled – or so the newsreaders insisted – to learn that Dominic Ryland, Conservative MSP for Central Scotland and frontrunner in the battle for leadership of the party, was in hospital following a brutal attack in the early hours of the morning. The full picture was still emerging, but it seemed that masked men had broken into his house in Thorntonhall, dragged him from his bed and set about him with baseball bats while his wife screamed the place down. His attackers had fled the scene, leaving behind neither trace nor motive. The pundits, usually so quick to issue pronouncements on any and all matters relating to figures in the world of politics, were uncharacteristically reluctant to speculate. One Maurice Glaspie observed that a man of Ryland's stature, intellect and political ambition was always liable to be a target for those with an axe to grind.

Two days later, it was announced that the severity of the damage to Ryland's spine was such that he was unlikely to regain use of the lower half of his body. The evening news carried a brief statement issued by his campaign manager, Steve Michener, to the tune that he was withdrawing his candidacy from the leadership race and, furthermore, would be standing down as an MSP with immediate effect to focus on his recovery. The party issued a statement of its own, expressing its collective sadness at recent developments but stressing that the party was never about any individual politician and that they had no doubt that whoever became leader in his place would 'honour his longstanding commitment to modernise the party and improve its electoral fortunes'. The rival parties all gave polite but perfunctory messages of condolence.

On Friday, Marcella came round to the flat to pick up the last of Carol's belongings. Zoe, forewarned of her arrival, had everything packed up and ready to go. Marcella didn't step over the threshold or so much as look at her, but, from the curl of her lip, Zoe suspected that she was deriving no small amount of satisfaction from the fact that her reservations about their relationship had belatedly proved to be well-founded. Carol hadn't spoken to her since fight night – preferring, it seemed, to arrange all essential business between them through intermediaries. And this was how they all treated her. The one person who hadn't cut her adrift was Anna, who phoned at least once a day to check if she needed anything and to make sure she was all right. Zoe kept the calls brief and to the point, and so far had succeeded in rebuffing any moves on Anna's part for them to get together. She had a lot on at the moment, she said.

On Sunday, just before midday, there was a knock on the door. Zoe answered it to find Fin on the doorstep, motorcycle helmet tucked under her arm. She greeted Zoe with a shrug and a 'howya?' Zoe opted for a diplomatic grunt rather than the truth.

'Ye wanna come in?' she said, when the silence had become uncomfortable.

Fin shook her head. 'Nah, you're all right. I'm not for stopping long. Certain parties've got a vested interest in getting their hands on me, and me – well, I've got a vested interest in making sure they don't.'

Zoe had a feeling she knew who these certain parties were. The sort who drove about in cars with blue flashing lights.

'Hear a mutual friend of ours had an unfortunate accident the other day.'

'Aye,' Zoe nodded. 'Aye, he did that.'

'Hey.' Fin gave her a rough but affectionate nudge. 'What's with the hangdog expression? It all worked out in the end, didn't it? Managed to keep yer hands clean.' She chuckled. 'Didn't hafta sell yer soul.'

'I guess,' said Zoe.

She was far from convinced by this line of reasoning. In truth, she'd wondered, on various occasions, why Cottrell hadn't just killed Ryland. A last act of mercy bestowed on a wayward son by an injured father, maybe? Or perhaps Cottrell still had some as yet unrevealed purpose in mind for him that could still be accomplished with him merely crippled rather than dead. She'd assumed, when she'd handed over the evidence of his betrayal, that she'd effectively been condemning him to what would no doubt be a particularly nasty death. And she'd accepted that as a necessary means to an end – a deal with the Devil born out of sheer desperation. Ryland had needed to be put out of action, or else she and everyone she cared about would have spent the rest of their lives in constant danger. It had been different with Gavin. However much of a monster he'd been, his death hadn't helped thwart an imminent threat to anyone or made the world a safer place. That, she supposed, explained why the thought of having inspired the murder of one man, however indirectly, had filled her with such churning guilt even as she'd managed to make relative peace with the thought of signing the death warrant of the other.

Uncomfortable silence fell once again. On the floor above, Mad Effie was having another of her episodes, hollering out into the stairwell about how the day of final reckoning was approaching and it was time for all right-thinking folk to arm themselves for the struggle ahead.

Fin stirred. 'Well, like I said, flying visit 'n' all that. Heard on the grapevine that I'm considered a "person of interest" in the Ryland affair. Something about some home videos of me doing a number on his office.'

Zoe suddenly remembered. 'The laptop. Where is it? Have you—'

'It's safe.' Fin flashed her a wink. 'Ya never know. Might come in useful one o' these days. If our friend ever gets notions about running for office again, a well-timed leak might be in order. Way I figure, he knows we've got it, knows we can use it. Should give him something to chew on in his newfound leisure time.'

Zoe eyed Fin's helmet. 'Ye taking off straight away, then?'

'Aye. I might be back, I might not. Depends which way the wind's blowing. But keep an eye out for me, yeah? 'Specially when ya least expect me.'

Zoe could have queried the logic in this statement if she'd been minded to, but it made about as much sense as anything else had over the past four weeks.

'You haven't had second thoughts, then? 'Bout cutting loose.'

Zoe gave a weak, half-hearted shrug and opened her mouth to reply, but Fin beat her to it.

'Figured. You'll never leave this place. Got it written all over ya. It's cool. I get it. Home is where the heart is.'

Zoe lowered her eyes and said nothing. Her reluctance, her lack of willingness to take a leap into the unknown, shamed her, and she imagined that Fin must secretly think her a sorry specimen.

Fin held out her arms. 'Ah, come on. Let's do this for realsies.'

They embraced awkwardly, all arms and elbows. As Zoe made to withdraw, Fin gave her the briefest of pecks on the lips. It was a decidedly chaste kiss, but one of considerably more tenderness than Zoe would have thought her capable. For the brief moment it lasted, she wondered once more what might have been if the dice had been thrown differently, if some other set of circumstances had conspired to bring them together.

They drew apart.

'Catch ya around, Bright Eyes,' said Fin, and turned to go.

'Wait.'

Fin stopped. She hovered, half-turned, looking over her shoulder. 'Yeah?'

'Your name,' said Zoe, feeling decidedly foolish. 'Ye never told me your real name.'

For a moment, Fin hesitated. Then she turned to face Zoe fully with a sheepish shrug.

'It's Euphemia.'

Somewhere, deep within the depths of her, Zoe felt a laugh bubbling up. 'Your name's Euphemia?'

'Aye, all right. Why d'ya think I prefer Fin?'

Then she smiled, and Zoe smiled, and that was that. Fin pointed to her own eye, then to Zoe, and made a clicking sound with her tongue, then turned and jogged off down the stairs.

* * *

That afternoon, Zoe opened all the curtains and windows and embarked on a full-scale clean-up operation. The flat was a tip, and that wouldn't do. Not that it hadn't been a tip already, but the police's seemingly random rearrangement of everything hadn't helped matters. She stripped the bed, hoovered the floor, gathered up all the dirty dishes and washed them in the sink, filled two black bags with rubbish and hauled them down to the bins in the street. She then began to systematically go through Victor and Granny's old things, sorting out what was bin-worthy and what could potentially go to Oxfam. They'd taken up space for long enough. Time to put the past to bed.

On Monday morning, she was standing at the door to the cleaning supervisor's office in Neptune House bright and early before the first shift arrived at 6.30. She'd combed her hair, scrubbed her face and, just to show how serious she was, cleaned and put on her interview suit. Her goal was clear, if humiliating: to grovel before Valerie for her old job back.

Valerie appeared less than bowled over by her pitch. 'You let us down badly, you know,' she informed Zoe gravely. 'A job's not just something you can put aside and pick up again as fancy takes you. I need grafters on my team, not wastrels who think they're above earning an honest day's pay and that the world somehow owes them a living.' She paused, letting her words sink in. 'Because I've got news for you, Ms Callahan – you're not special. There's a million and one other girls just like you.'

'I don't think I'm special,' muttered Zoe, head bowed in contrition.

But Valerie was getting into her stride now. She was enjoying this, knowing she had a captive audience that was in no position to answer back.

'Let me tell you, you're no different from all the other young ladies who dreamed big only to find out the real world doesn't work that way.'

She paused for breath. When she continued, her tone was marginally more conciliatory.

'I need to know that you're committed. That you're serious. I need to be able to rely on you to show up on time, like clockwork, every day. And I need to know that, as long as you're on company time, you'll give me one hundred and ten percent. And if you can't do that, you can turn round right this minute and walk straight back out that door.'

Zoe stared at her hands, folded in her lap. The humiliation wasn't the worst part – it was the complete and utter soul-crushing finality of it all. The knowledge that this was it, this was all she'd ever amount to. Through her own foolhardiness, she'd ended up in a situation where she had to scrabble to get back less than she'd had to begin with. Even so, she knew she deserved a whole lot worse.

'I'm serious,' she said. 'I need this job.' That didn't sound quite committed enough, so for good measure she added, 'I *want* this job.'

Valerie shook her head. 'Don't overdo it. No one *wants* this job.' She regarded Zoe with a look that wasn't unsympathetic. 'I know it's not glamorous. I know it's not what your big, fancy degree prepared you for. But it's living.'

Zoe nodded. *Ain't that the truth.* She was, after all, alive, and she had her health, and a job, if she could prove she was ready to give it her all. All the things that, in the last few weeks, she'd done everything she possibly could to throw away.

Valerie folded her arms, looking Zoe up and down. At length, she gave a curt nod. 'Your uniform's still in your locker. I want to see you on the floor and hard at work in five minutes.'

Zoe didn't need telling twice.

33

Cruel Summer

Over the following week, the weather reverted to that of a typical Glaswegian summer. The skies were grey and cloudy, the barometer remained stubbornly fixed between 18 and 19 Celsius, and the same people who'd spent the last three weeks perspiring in Mediterranean temperatures went back to complaining that they never got any decent weather. 'Taps aff' season was officially over.

On Friday the second of August, the results of the Scottish Conservative and Unionist Party leadership contest were announced. Fergus Leach, depute to outgoing leader Archibald Croft, was crowned the victor with a three-to-one majority over the only other remaining candidate, Esther Vickers – a bepearled spinster whose sole contribution to rethinking party policy had been to propose a plebiscite on dissolving the Scottish Parliament, thereby putting her and her fellow MSPs out of a job. In his valedictory speech, Leach praised his rivals – including the one who 'couldn't be here today due to unfortunate circumstances' – and promised that a renewal of fortunes for the party was just around the corner. Politics had evidently reverted to the status quo.

The police were no further forward in identifying Ryland's attackers or establishing a motive. It remained one of life's great mysteries why anyone would wish to harm such a respected pillar of the community, and columnists the length and breadth of the land pondered The Great Leader That Might Have Been. The investigations into the murder of Gavin Price and the abduction of Carol Novák had, it seemed, reached similarly dead ends.

A week later, Zoe emerged from her afternoon shift at Neptune House to find a familiar figure waiting a little way up the pavement. Rona Cauley was wearing sunglasses and her ubiquitous suede jacket and nursing a cigarette. She had a folded newspaper tucked under one arm. Spotting Zoe, she took a final drag on her ciggy, tossed it aside and made her way over. She greeted Zoe with a nod, then proceeded to stand there, surveying the pedestrians as they hurried by in both directions.

'Soon be autumn,' she observed.

'Aye,' said Zoe.

It was true. There was a breeze in the air today for the first time since she could remember. She eyed Cauley warily, wondering what had brought her here. She somehow doubted this was merely a social call.

Cauley took out her phone and angled the screen in Zoe's direction.

'This woman.'

Zoe affected an expression of neutral disinterest. On the screen was a photo of Fin – a post-arrest mugshot that looked to date back several years, the name 'EUPHEMIA FINLAY' below it. She glowered into the camera, bottom lip protruding sullenly.

'Ever come across her on your travels?'

Zoe shook her head.

'There's evidence that she was involved in a break-in at Dominic Ryland's place on the night of Sunday the fourteenth of July. Further to that, he alleges she was involved in his assault on the twenty-fourth – even though his wife is adamant that both his attackers were male.' She lowered her shades and gave Zoe a hard, probing look. 'You're sure you've never seen this woman?'

Zoe met her gaze without blinking. 'Positive.'

Cauley held Zoe's gaze a moment longer, then pocketed her phone and pushed her shades back up her nose. 'Well, if you *do* come across her, or hear anything you believe to be of relevance to the ongoing investigation into this very serious incident, don't hesitate to come forward.'

'Course.'

Cauley paused for a moment. 'That said – and this is strictly off the record – I for one will not be losing a great deal of sleep over the fact that a serial abuser of women will spend the rest of his days confined to a wheelchair without a functioning cock.'

Zoe didn't trust herself to say anything. She wondered how much Cauley knew about her role in all of this. She must have at least some idea. The way she was acting and the things she was leaving unsaid certainly pointed strongly in that direction. Plus, she was far from stupid.

Cauley stirred, breaking the silence. 'Well, I'd best be heading. A lot of packing still to do.'

'Packing? Ye going somewhere?'

Cauley nodded. 'Jedburgh, to be precise. Know it?'

Zoe shook her head.

'It's a little town in the Borders, about two hours' drive from here. Population roughly four thousand. Fella who wrote "Rule Britannia" hailed from there, which in my book is reason enough to condemn it to the ninth circle of Hell.'

'So what's taking ye there?'

Cauley smiled drily. 'An edict from on high. I'm being transferred. My ah, face . . . no longer fits, see? It's considered mutually beneficial for all parties if I move on to pastures new.' She paused for a moment, then handed Zoe the newspaper. 'Here. I'm done with this.'

Zoe took the newspaper, more out of politeness than because she had any intention of actually reading it.

Cauley took a fresh cigarette from a packet in her pocket and waved it in farewell. 'You look after yourself.'

And with that, she turned and began to head down St Vincent Street – a small, forlorn figure with rounded shoulders and a weary gait, shambling into the distance.

As Zoe watched her go, it occurred to her that Cauley's superiors – and Vasilico in particular – probably wouldn't have had too hard a time putting two and two together and figuring out she was responsible for blowing Ryland's cover, even if they hadn't worked out all the specifics. She realised that, in all likelihood, Cauley had knowingly torpedoed her own career to bring him down.

She looked down at the newspaper in her hand. It had been folded with one of the inside pages facing outwards, in a way that somehow felt deliberate. She unfolded it to see the familiar photo of her and Fin leaving the G-Spot together – a lifetime ago, or so it felt. She checked the date in the top corner. It was an old issue – the same one, in fact, that Carol had confronted her with that night at the flat. She almost laughed. *Well played, indeed.*

Tucking the paper under her own arm, Zoe headed in the opposite direction, past the Mitchell Library and on towards the bridge at Bath Street. Along the way, she passed a newsagent's. On the stand outside, one of the local papers was given pride of place. Its bold, all-caps headline caught her eye:

'WHERE IS JUSTICE FOR MY BOY?' DEMANDS MURDERED GAV'S MUM

Below, and almost as large, was a colour photo depicting a candle-lit vigil. Behind the crowd of half a dozen or so people, Zoe recognised the gateposts of the Price residence on Cleveden Road. At the head of the gathering, each clutching a candle and wearing a painfully earnest expression, were Gavin's parents and a striking dark-haired woman whom she recognised as Charlotte MacConnachie, Gavin's ex-girlfriend. As far as Zoe was aware, she'd dumped him when the Jenny Guilfoyle accusations first came to light. That she was now firmly back in the fold and demanding justice in his name just went to show that the old adage was true: all dead people were saints. Gavin Price truly had come full circle, from rape enabler to wrongly accused would-be victim of a miscarriage of justice to tragic martyr cut down in his prime.

The strains of eighties synth-pop met her ears. It was coming from inside the newsagent's – a bouncy, maddeningly catchy little number that sounded vaguely familiar. As she listened, nodding her head almost instinctually to the beat, she realised it was 'Cruel Summer' by Bananarama, one of the songs Carol had played for her during her 'education' at the flat on Dumbarton Road that night in October nearly four years ago. The girls were singing about hot summer streets and being left on their own. But you're not on your own, she felt like saying. You've got each other. I'm the one that's alone.

In her mind, she was back in the living room, her right hand clasping Carol's left, the other wrapped round her waist, stumbling drunkenly around the living room, trying not to collide with the furniture or with Carol's two left feet, the pair of them laughing at their own ridiculousness as their lips inched closer and closer before locking together. Dear, sweet, right-on Carol, her fiery Amazon queen – the only woman she'd ever properly loved.

She understood now that her attraction to Fin had never really been sexual per se – at least not primarily. Rather, what she'd been drawn to had been Fin's confidence, her boldness, her certainty as to the way the world was and her own place in it. Her firm grasp on her own identity. Fin was someone who knew who she was and she didn't look to anyone else for validation. And, when you were still trying to figure out who you were and what your role in life was, that sort of certitude was more intoxicating than any drug.

Lesbian, bisexual, feminist, socialist, militant-anarcho-anti-capitalist . . . She was surrounded by people who were happy to define themselves – or allow themselves to be defined – by labels like these, all of which came with all sorts of baggage – some of it good, much of it bad. As soon as you said you were an '–ist' or an '–an', you instantly conjured up all sorts of preconceived notions about who you were, how you thought, what you believed. It suggested you were a closed book, a finished story; that you were done, complete. And she knew she wasn't complete – not even close. She didn't know what her beliefs were, if any. Didn't know how she felt about the great matters of state that vexed other people so much. Didn't know who she was, other than that she was Zoe Joan Callahan, thirty-one years, seven months and twenty-three days old, unable to turn back to the past, uncertain where the future led. She was a work in progress, and progress seemed to have irrevocably stalled.

In a newsagent on Gibson Street, a large man in his sixties stood reading the same headline as Zoe while he waited for the shop-keeper to ring up his purchases. As his eyes skimmed the text below the picture, one sentence in particular caught his eye:

> Even now, almost three weeks after the shocking incident, there has been no breakthrough in the investigation and no arrests have been made.

Tony Guilfoyle allowed himself a smile of grim satisfaction. Someone had once told him the hardest thing about having committed a crime was keeping it to yourself. The need to tell somebody, *anybody*, it was said, grew and grew until it became unbearable. That hadn't been his experience at all. He was more than content to live with the knowledge of what he'd done, to carry it with him to the end of his days without breathing a word of it to a soul. Besides, who would he tell? It was just him and Jenny, and neither of them needed anyone else.

'You buying that, pal?'

Guilfoyle stirred and turned to face the shopkeeper. He shook his head. 'No, I don't think so. Not today.'

The shopkeeper smiled. 'Aye, can't say I blame ye. Too depressing. Better off not knowing what's happening in this world.'

Guilfoyle paid for his shopping and made his way back up the hill towards the house on Lynedoch Place, where Jenny would be waiting. As he thought of her, he felt a pang of regret at the way things had played out. His decision to put her through the ordeal of the trial and the very public way in which it had been conducted was, in retrospect, a grievous error on his part. He should have known from the start that it was a bad idea and turned to his ultimate solution much sooner. At the time, however, he'd felt he had to at least try to go through the proper channels before giving up on the institutions in service to which he'd dedicated the better part of his life.

The house had gone on the market the previous Thursday, and already there had been a sizeable interest. The thought of leaving it behind pained him, but there was nothing else for it. Downsizing was essential: Gavin Price's fate hadn't been bought cheaply, but it had been the only way to avoid it being traced back to him. Not that he imagined his former colleagues would be in any great hurry to charge him, or indeed to judge him, if they ever found out the truth.

Still, best to keep such matters to oneself. Some things you didn't talk about. Some things were private, and that was that.

*   *   *

In his high office at the Strathkelvin Police headquarters on Pitt Street, Chief Superintendent Peter Strickland stood at the window and gazed out across the city skyline. Two Tuesdays ago, arriving at Central Station on the 8.47 from Newton Mearns, he'd followed his usual route, picking up his favourite macchiato from the coffee stand before heading for the steps down to Union Street. As he'd passed the bins, he'd clocked the vertical black line slashed on the side of the rightmost one. They'd hit on this method, he and Sandyman, as the most failsafe means of signalling a need to meet. Probably safer than a phone call, *definitely* safer than email. And if you used permanent marker, there was next to no chance of the station staff having cleaned it off before the other party had a chance to see it.

And so, at a quarter to eleven that night, he'd arrived at Glasgow Green and stood under the McLennan Arch, collar turned up against the eddying rain. Sandyman had arrived in short order, an impatient stride in his step, shoulders raised in an irritable shrug. What, he'd demanded, was so important that he'd been dragged out here on a night like this? Strickland had immediately hit back with a similar demand, a refrain on the old 'crossed wires' scenario – *No, YOU called ME.* A brief back-and-forth had established that each thought the other party was responsible for the summons, at which point Strickland had realised the day he'd always dreaded had finally come. Without another word, he'd turned on his heel and departed into the rain, his opposite number's perplexed exclamations resounding impotently behind him.

Strickland ran a hand across his jaw, trying to force his mind back to the present. He should have been preparing for tomorrow's interdisciplinary task force briefing, but try as he might, he'd been unable to put pen to paper, preoccupied by the knowledge that forces beyond his influence were now in play. Since Sandyman had been blown, it had all gone dark, and his heart was full of foreboding for what was to come.

Zoe stood on the Bath Street bridge, gazing down at the roaring vehicles on the M8 below. She followed the path of the southbound traffic as it stretched off into the great unknown, past the Mitchell Library, past Neptune House and the Marriott Hotel, towards the distant hills on the horizon. She thought about following that road and seeing where it led. It would be the easiest thing in the world to do: hop on the first bus heading out of Glasgow, sever all her ties with the place that had brought her nothing but heartache and misery.

But she knew she never would. This was her city. She was born here, was raised here and would, in all likelihood, die here – later, or perhaps, if Cottrell had a change of heart, sooner. As she crossed the bridge and made her way down towards the railway station, she was left with the overwhelming sense that she now had a second shadow, invisible but forever attached to her, inescapable. The world was a cruel and indifferent place, and she was awake to it now, properly awake, with no hope of going back to sleep.

Soon, she joined the throng of pedestrians and became just another anonymous face in the crowd.

Author's Note

As this author recalls with no great fondness, the heatwave of July 2013 did indeed take place, largely corresponding to the timeframe specified in the text, though for narrative purposes some of the exact dates have been adjusted. Aggrieved meteorologists should address their complaints in writing to the usual channels.

My sincerest thanks goes to Alan McCulloch and Lynsey Scobie for plugging the numerous gaps in my knowledge of High Court procedure. All errors, deliberate or otherwise, are mine rather than theirs. Special thanks also to Ashley Lane, logic bomber extraordinaire, for helping me see the wood for the trees on several occasions, and to my trusty band of guinea pigs: Sarah Kelley, Catherine Mackenzie, Daniel Sardella and Caroline Whitson.

Finally, my immense gratitude goes to my editor, David B. Lyons, for once again agreeing to undertake the task of helping me to corral my ramblings into something approaching coherence, and for his advice in all manner of matters relating to the perils and pitfalls of novel-writing and publication.

The Gray Dunn Biscuit Factory was finally demolished in May 2017 to make way for a cash-and-carry.

Continue reading for a sneak preview of *The Shadow Men*, the third instalment in the Anna Scavolini series.

THE SHADOW MEN

**They see everything. They hear everything.
They *know* everything.**

When a young police officer, Derek Sullivan, goes missing, the detective investigating his disappearance turns to criminologist Anna Scavolini – Derek's one-time university lecturer – for help. Consumed by the belief that she failed in her duty of care towards her former student, Anna finds herself drawn increasingly deeper into the investigation.

Meanwhile, Zoe Callahan – once Anna's best friend, now unhappily estranged – becomes preoccupied by unsettling rumours involving her old school. Uncovering a trail of evidence implicating the most powerful men in Scottish society in a scandal stretching back decades, she soon attracts the attention of sinister forces who don't look kindly on those who disturb the past . . .

A missing police officer, a highly coveted list of names, a fatal car crash on a rainswept night – what connects these seemingly unrelated threads? And who are the mysterious Shadow Men, whose very name strikes terror into the hearts of everyone who hears it?

AVAILABLE NOW IN PAPERBACK AND EBOOK

Harbinger

Autumn 2015 roared in on Glasgow with biblical fury. It had been a mild, dry summer with rainfall well below the historical average, but as September arrived, the heavens opened their reserves and spared no effort in making up for lost time. Gale-force winds pummelled the city, the Clyde threatened to burst its banks, and flood warnings were issued for low-lying areas. Mother Nature, it seemed, was determined to inflict a reckoning for sins as yet unatoned for – a reckoning which, judging by the unrelenting ferocity of the assault, would not be complete until blood had been spilled.

On the night of Tuesday the eighth of September, Mother Nature got her wish.

Gil McLaren hadn't wanted to be out tonight. As far as he was concerned, there was no such thing as a good time to be asked to work the 1900–0700 shift, but a night like this one made him crave his warm bed and electric blanket all the more fervently.

The call had come through at 0045: *Road traffic accident on the M8. Driver killed on impact. No other persons in the vehicle. Road Policing shift sergeant required to coordinate at scene.*

As he roared up the dual carriageway, tail-lights of the car in front shimmering on rain-slick tarmac, he took one hand off the wheel and slid it inside his coat, feeling the contours of the hip-flask in his breast pocket. Only the challenge of simultaneously unscrewing the lid and maintaining control of the wheel stopped him from helping himself there and then.

Hopefully, if the locus was as chaotic as he was anticipating, he'd manage to secure a crafty swig once he got there.

Up ahead, the flashing lights of a stationary police car blocked one lane, while a constable in a hi-viz jacket occupied the other – a last defence against any driver who'd ignored the 'ROAD AHEAD CLOSED' sign some way back. McLaren leaned forward, peering past the swishing wipers to get his first glimpse of the scene that awaited him. The unfortunate vehicle, a blue hatchback, had careened off to the right, the metal barrier having done nothing to halt its trajectory. That task had finally been accomplished by the granite pillar supporting the A814 overpass as it crossed over the M8 before curving round and joining the main expressway some two hundred yards further back.

The cop in the hi-viz jacket waved him through. He continued for another fifty yards before coming to a standstill. He steeled himself, his hand once more straying automatically to his breast pocket. Then, suppressing the urge, he pulled on his peaked cap – less a nod to protocol, more a forlorn attempt to keep his head dry – and got out.

There were three other cop cars present; six officers in total milling about in their waterproofs. No sign yet of the Ambulance Service – but they could afford to take their time. As McLaren tramped towards the mangled hatchback, one of the plods – a babyfaced lunk who looked like he probably got carded at off-licence checkouts on a regular basis – approached and fell into eager step with him.

'Looks like a straightforward case of the perils of driving in adverse weather, sir. Consensus is the brakes were to blame.'

'That right, is it?'

'Aye. One of the lads was saying these old Honda Civics are notorious for it. Rainwater gets on the discs and then they don't kick in when you need 'em to.'

'I'll be sure to convey your hypothesis to the Fatal Accident Inquiry.'

The plod grinned eagerly. Either he was thick as mince or McLaren was losing his sarcastic edge in his old age.

They halted in front of the hatchback. There wasn't much left of its front end, and the driver hadn't fared much better. His face – which, judging by the blood splatter, had bounced off the steering wheel upon impact – resembled battered roadkill. And yet, as McLaren gazed at the man's ruined features, it dawned on him that he'd seen them somewhere before. The gears of his mind, impeded by a lack of sleep and a surfeit of something else, cranked slowly as he tried to match the face to a name, and to recall the context in which he'd previously encountered both. As these three disparate elements finally aligned, like pictures on a slot machine, a trickle that wasn't rainwater ran down his back.

He stirred, becoming aware of a hubbub developing behind him. He turned as an unmarked black sedan drew up, waved through by the hi-viz-jacketed officer on traffic control duty. The driver scrambled out, unfurling an umbrella. Holding it aloft, he hurried round to open the rear door. A figure stepped out: short, unimposing, his unassuming presence belying the waves his arrival had created.

'What's the Chief doing at an RTA?' McLaren heard one of the plods asking in an awed whisper.

Peter Strickland, Assistant Chief Constable (West of Scotland), strode across the tarmac towards McLaren, his driver hurrying after him, umbrella shielding him from the rain. The babyfaced PC quickly melted away. All around McLaren, a newfound spirit of industriousness had taken hold, as officers who five minutes ago had been catching flies all suddenly seemed to find tasks which demanded their urgent attention.

Strickland came to a halt facing McLaren. He took in the sight of the totalled hatchback, then gazed at McLaren with his sad, hangdog eyes, and shook his head ruefully.

'My God, this is a rotten business. No way for a man to go.'

'Yes, sir,' McLaren agreed obediently.

Strickland took the umbrella from his minder, dismissing him with a barely perceptible nod, then turned to McLaren with an inviting hand.

'Shall we?'

Mystified, McLaren allowed himself to be led along the road, away from prying ears.

'You look tired, Gil.' Strickland's hand hovered behind the small of McLaren's back, guiding him.

'It's one in the morning, sir.'

Strickland smiled slightly, conceding the point. 'And no time for an old sea-dog to be abroad. This job makes old men of us all sooner or later. It's a youngster's game, perhaps more so now than ever.'

'I cope, sir,' said McLaren, the response mechanical, unfelt.

Strickland slowed to a standstill. The two men met each other's eyes – one small and slight, the other a stocky, ungainly giant. And yet there was no doubting where the balance of power lay.

Strickland sighed. 'I thought we'd turned a corner with you, Gil. You promised me you'd turned over a new leaf.'

'Sir, I don't know what—'

'Please don't embarrass us both by denying it. Every man and his dog knows it's still happening.' The same reproachful look. The same bitter disappointment. 'I can *smell* it on you.'

McLaren was suddenly acutely aware of the hip-flask in his breast pocket, burning a hole in the fabric, scalding his skin. He opened his mouth to – what? Protest his innocence? Come clean and throw himself at Strickland's mercy?

Strickland beat him to it. 'I don't hold it against you, you know.'

His manner was sympathetic, but tinged with a weary disgust which he couldn't quite manage to conceal – like a grown-up child who's come home to discover an elderly, infirm parent lying in their own filth and too incapacitated to do anything about it.

'It's simply who you are,' he continued, his tone philosophical. 'I know it, you know it, so let's not make a song and dance about it. Better to cash one's chips on one's own terms and leave the table with some degree of dignity than to lose everything and be escorted out by the in-house muscle. Better to avoid any unnecessary embarrassment – both to oneself *and* to the house.'

Until now, Strickland's tone had been philosophical – speaking, it seemed, more to himself than to McLaren. Now, his expression intensified, those hangdog eyes suddenly sharp and piercing.

'Do we understand one another?'

McLaren swallowed heavily. Oh, he understood. He understood all too well.

'Yes, sir.'

Strickland smiled. He patted McLaren's arm kindly: the level-headed child telling the embarrassed older man that there's no need to worry – they'll take care of the mess.

'Time to call it a night, I think. You're no good to anyone – not in your present state. Go on – home to your bed. We'll soldier on without you.'

The conversation over, Strickland turned to go. His driver was by his side in an instant, hair plastered to his forehead from exposure to the elements. Taking command of the umbrella once more, he escorted his master back to the sedan, deftly thrusting the rear door open for him while simultaneously shielding him from the downpour. McLaren watched, rainwater running into his eyes from the brim of his hat, as the sedan performed a one-eighty-degree turn and departed the scene, rear lights receding into the distance.

McLaren remained there a little longer, watching the plods hurrying to and fro. Already, it was as if he no longer existed. A bystander at his own incident scene, his presence immaterial to the smooth running of the operation. A relic of the past. An unperson.

He realised it came as something of a relief. It wasn't so much that he was leaving with his dignity intact. That had been expunged long ago, along with his self-esteem, self-respect and belief that what he was doing made any sort of difference, let alone one for the better. But at least it was an end of sorts; a line drawn in the sand, a laying to rest of the ghosts of the past. He took out the hip-flask and, in full view of his colleagues, downed a hearty draught. No one paid him the slightest attention.

He screwed the cap back on, turned and squelched back towards his waiting car.

On a street corner near the city centre, soaked by both the rain and the periodic splashes from vehicles howling past at full speed, a man waits, clutching the strap of the laden rucksack weighing his shoulders down. He's been standing there for over an hour, his windbreaker barely protecting him from the thundering downpour.

The person for whom he is waiting will not come tonight, nor indeed any night. Factors and forces beyond his control have put paid to that, though he doesn't know it yet. It is now 2 a.m. – more than forty-five minutes past the agreed rendezvous time.

And yet still he waits.

1

Vasilico

The figure had been standing at the back of the lecture hall for at least the last ten minutes, leaving Anna wondering what precisely he thought he was doing here. There was something purposeful about his presence; something unapologetic, as if he had a God-given right to be here.

What made it doubly frustrating was that she couldn't see his face. The room was built in the old theatre style, with two columns of benches on an incline running down to the stage where she currently stood. As such, he was standing the equivalent of two or three storeys above her, and every time she looked up at him her eyes caught the full glare of the ceiling-mounted lights pointed at the stage, all but blinding her in the process. All she could tell was that he was male, that he was wearing a suit, and that he was tall and broad-shouldered. Beyond that, he was just a hazy, ill-defined shape. A shadow.

In the pocket of her slacks, her phone hummed: her two-minute warning.

'So,' she addressed her assembled first-years, 'we return to our original question: what *is* criminology? We must be able to define our topic before we can successfully study it. And before we can define criminology, we must first answer another, more fundamental question: what is *crime*?

'It's tempting to think we all have a solid understanding of what constitutes a criminal act – some innate knowledge that we're all somehow imbued with. But in reality, there are multiple variables at play. There are acts which are considered crimes in some jurisdictions but not in others. Some acts *were* criminal in the past but no longer are, and vice versa. Who decides what is a crime and what isn't? Governments? Academics? Broad public sentiment? And how do we approach legislation like the Nuremberg Laws, duly enacted according to the rules of the German constitution but themselves now considered to be crimes against humanity?' She raised her shoulders in an exaggerated shrug. 'I'm not posing these questions because I have definitive answers for you. I'm posing them to give you some idea of the complexity of your chosen topic of study.

'Over the next several weeks, I want you to do your best to clear your minds of what you think you know about crime, about criminals and about their victims. Let go of your assumptions, be willing to embrace new and sometimes challenging ideas. If you were hoping for an easy ride, this is not the class for you. But, if you're willing to park your preconceptions at the door and approach the subject as open-mindedly as possible, you should find the next three months both stimulating and intellectually satisfying.'

Sensing that she was done, and no doubt as aware of the hour as her, the students began to gather their belongings. It took a few minutes for the room to clear. As the last remaining stragglers headed for the exit, the stranger strolled down the steps towards her.

'Dr Anna Scavolini?'

Anna glanced up from jamming her laptop into her shoulder-bag. 'That's right.'

'Oh, super.' The man grinned, flashing twin rows of even teeth. 'And there I was worrying I'd come to the wrong place. An *honour* to make your acquaintance. Detective Chief Inspector Vasilico, Major Investigations Team.'

He was, as she'd already surmised, tall, and in his mid-thirties. He was also impeccably groomed, his suit clearly expensive and cut to measure, hinting at the well-honed muscles that lay beneath it. She eyed his outstretched warrant card with some suspicion. As far as she was concerned, anyone prepared to launch such a transparent charm offensive had to have an ulterior motive.

'What can I do for you, Detective?'

'I was rather hoping you'd consent to sparing a few minutes of your no doubt invaluable time.'

'As long as it really is just a few minutes. I've an appointment I can't be late for.'

'Naturally. Rest assured, I've not the slightest intention of detaining you any longer than *absolutely* necessary.' His extended pause gave immediate lie to this claim. 'Derek Sullivan. What can you tell me about him?'

Anna zipped her bag shut and turned to face him. 'He's one of my postgrad students. Been doing a part-time Masters in Criminology with us for the past year.'

'And presumably you're aware that, in addition to being a part-time student, he's also a serving police constable?'

Anna nodded. 'The department has a partnership with the police – providing opportunities for officers to expand their knowledge-base and develop their analytical skills. Derek's one of four who are with us at the moment. Why? Is he in some sort of trouble?'

'That rather depends. When was the last time you saw him?'

'We had a supervision meeting just over three weeks ago. Since then, we haven't had any contact.'

'And is that normal?'

'More or less. We're scheduled to meet once a month, and he attends group lectures in between, some of which I teach. I don't remember seeing him at any of mine since our last supervision – but then, his attendance has always been . . . ' She hesitated, unable to shake the feeling that she was somehow betraying a confidence. ' . . . *spotty.*' She put one hand on her hip, gazing up at him entreatingly. 'Look, I'm really not sure what I can realistically tell you unless you give me something more to go on.'

Vasilico was silent for a moment, as if considering how much he should say. At length, he exhaled a breath.

'Derek Sullivan was last seen leaving work just over a fortnight ago. He failed to report for duty on Friday the eleventh of September, and since then has made no contact with his colleagues, friends or family.'

The silence that followed was so absolute Anna could hear the creaking of the building's foundations.

'I'm sorry to hear that,' she said eventually, not knowing what else *to* say.

'As you can no doubt appreciate, the more time that passes, the more concerned we grow about his wellbeing. I take it from your somewhat tongue-tied reaction that he hasn't made contact with *you*.'

'No, and I wouldn't expect him to.' Anna shrugged helplessly. 'I really didn't know him all that well. To be honest, I find it hard to believe there's not someone better placed to answer your questions than me.'

Vasilico winced, as if this pained him on a personal level. 'That's just it. I'm not sure there is.'

'You'll have to explain.'

'If I asked you to describe Derek, what would you tell me?'

It was a trickier question to answer than she'd anticipated. 'Quiet, I suppose,' she said after a moment. 'Not especially talkative or outgoing. From what I gather, he kept himself to himself.'

'Then we're on the same page. Over the last few days, I've spoken to more of his squadmates than I've eaten hot dinners, and they all described him in more or less the same terms as you: quiet, preferred his own company, didn't go in for socialising out of hours with the other lads.'

'That's not a crime.'

'No. Does make it markedly harder to build up a picture of his movements, though.'

Anna studied Vasilico's face, taking in the knitted brows, the pensive frown. She still wasn't sure she altogether trusted him, and there was an overbearing slickness about him that set her teeth on edge, but he seemed sincere in his concern for the missing constable, and she found herself wishing she could do something more to help them both.

'Well,' he said, stirring, 'I suppose it always *was* a long shot. I shan't detain you further. I appreciate you taking the time to . . . ' He stopped, frowning for a moment as if he'd lost his train of thought, then smiled knowingly. 'I've just realised.'

'What?'

He wagged a knowing finger at her. 'I know where I know you from.'

'Oh?'

'You're *the* Anna Scavolini. The one who wrote that screed in the *Tribune* about the toxicity of police culture – how we're all a bunch of unreconstructed bully-boys who go around breaking skulls and trampling on folk's constitutional rights. What was that phrase again? "To be the law is not to be above the law"?'

There seemed little point in denying it – not least since she stood by every word. A few months earlier, the *Glasgow Tribune* had invited her to contribute to a package of articles about the changing face of the modern police force – though, as she'd insisted in the piece she subsequently penned, the words 'changing' and 'modern' could scarcely be less appropriate when applied to the Strathkelvin Police Force, the body which served the entire Greater Glasgow area. She'd been forthright in her language, highlighting both the moral conservatism that multiple studies had shown to characterise law enforcement officials in general, and a string of recent scandals that had dogged the Strathkelvin force in particular. The former included accusations of an aggressively macho 'canteen culture' which ostracised and targeted those who failed to fit in; the latter the heavy-handed treatment of protesters at a recent climate change rally, which had left one teenager with a fractured zygoma, as well as the burial of a report on institutional sectarianism within the force, the contents of which had only come to light following a lengthy Freedom of Information battle. She'd ended by calling for – amongst other measures – a root-and-branch overhaul of internal and external complaints procedures, and the establishment of a new supervisory body consisting solely of non-police officers to review all operational policies. *'The Strathkelvin Police Force,'* she'd concluded, *'is the oldest in the world, but it's time they joined the rest of us in the twenty-first century.'*

'Yes, I rather enjoyed that.' Vasilico was still smiling – an arch, self-satisfied smile that left her with an overwhelming urge to wipe it from his face by any available means. 'You'll be pleased to know you made waves at HQ. Wouldn't *believe* how exercised the head honchos were by it. I gather the phrase "set public relations back to the Palaeolithic Age" was uttered.'

'I'm glad it provided you with some amusement,' Anna said, not sure which irritated her more: his implied belittlement of her or his seemingly blasé attitude to the serious charges levelled against the organisation he worked for.

Vasilico raised his hands in a gesture of truce. 'Of course. Forgive me. Rest assured, we treat all accusations of misconduct with the utmost seriousness. Tricky though it may be to believe, the vast majority of us are in fact fine, upstanding individuals.'

'Present company included, naturally.'

Vasilico chuckled. 'Perhaps the problem is one of perspective. *Walk a mile in another man's shoes* and all that. Now don't mistake me,' he added quickly, forestalling whatever objection he'd anticipated her making. 'I understand the need for accountability and due process. But I also understand the practicalities – that, in life-or-death situations, it's not always possible to dot every "i", say "please" and "thank you".'

This time, it was Anna's turn to smile, though hers was considerably more saccharine. 'Or perhaps you're just too close to the action, Detective. Perhaps you lack the necessary distance to see what's screamingly obvious to the rest of us.'

Vasilico threw back his head and laughed – a rich, deep laugh that reverberated in the high rafters. *'Touché.* I suppose I should have known better than to get into a battle of words with someone who bandies them for a living. And now I really *have* exhausted my welcome.' He gestured to the stairs with a grandiose sweep. 'Go! Attend your appointment, and let it not be said that the officers of the Strathkelvin Police Force are guilty of preventing citizens from going about their lawful business.'

Anna turned to go, hiding the involuntary smile that was threatening her lips. As she shouldered her bag, a thought occurred to her. She turned to Vasilico once more.

'If there's any news about Derek Sullivan . . . '

' . . . I assure you, you'll be among the first to hear it.' Vasilico paused, fixing her with an earnest look. 'We'll bring him home safe – just you watch.'

Anna smiled, this time not entirely insincerely. 'Don't make promises you can't keep, Detective,' she said, and headed up the stairs.

.

Printed in Great Britain
by Amazon

32811268R00212